Praise for The Thief

"Filled with memorable characters, The Thief is a tale of hopelessness turned to hope, of high stakes made higher, and ultimate love. What happens when a character at the lowest rung of society crosses paths with the most well-known figure in history? The story of The Thief. I couldn't stop reading."

—Tosca Lee, *New York Times* bestselling author of *Iscariot*

"WOW! LOVE IT!!! I started reading on my way home from a conference and was so engrossed in the book I almost missed the flight! The Thief stole my heart and lifted my spirit. Masterfully told, this story of a Roman centurion and a Jewish girl explores familiar New Testament passages but plumbs new spiritual depths. A powerful message of faith and hope intersecting at the foot of the cross."

—Mesu Andrews, author of *Love in a Broken Vessel*

"You know the feeling you get looking at a mountain sunset, listening to sacred music while James Earl Jones reads the Sermon on the Mount? The Thief captures that emotion in an unforgettable story of desperation and beauty."

—Regina Jennings, author of *Caught in the Middle* and *Sixty Acres and a Bride*

"A compelling story and vivid characters immediately come off the page and into your heart as Stephanie Landsem brings ancient Jerusalem to life in her enthralling second novel, *The Thief*. As you run through the streets with the little thief, Mouse, or dip in the Pool of Siloam with the secretive Nissa, a masterful tale full of adventure, heartbreak, and hope unfolds. A must-read for anyone who loves a good book they simply can't put down."

—Laura Sobiech, author of *Fly a Little Higher*

"To read *The Thief* is to be completely transported to another time and place. Landsem's impeccably researched novel moves at breakneck speed toward a climax that doesn't disappoint."

—Rebecca Kanner, author of *Sinners and the Sea*

"Powerful and moving, Landsem grabs hold of the soul and never lets go. As compelling a portrait of mercy as I have ever read. Don't miss this one!"

—Siri Mitchell, author of *The Messenger*

ALSO BY STEPHANIE LANDSEM

The Living Water Series

The Well

The Thief

The Tomb (coming April 2015)

THE *Thief*

A NOVEL

STEPHANIE LANDSEM

HOWARD BOOKS
A Division of Simon & Schuster, Inc.
New York   Nashville   London   Toronto   Sydney   New Delhi

Howard Books
A Division of Simon & Schuster, Inc.
1230 Avenue of the Americas
New York, NY 10020

All Scripture quotations are from the Revised New Testament of the New American Bible, St. Joseph's edition © 1986 CCD. All rights reserved. Catholic Book Publishing Co., New York, NY.

First Howard Books trade paperback edition February 2014

HOWARD and colophon are trademarks of Simon & Schuster, Inc.

For information about special discounts for bulk purchases, please contact Simon & Schuster Special Sales at 1-866-506-1949 or business@simonandschuster.com.

The Simon & Schuster Speakers Bureau can bring authors to your live event. For more information or to book an event contact the Simon & Schuster Speakers Bureau at 1-866-248-3049 or visit our website at www.simonspeakers.com.

Interior design by Davina Mock-Maniscalco

Manufactured in the United States of America

10 9 8 7 6 5 4 3 2 1

Library of Congress Cataloging-in-Publication Data

Landsem, Stephanie.
 The Thief : a novel / Stephanie Landsem.
 pages cm
 1. Christian fiction. I. Title.
 PS3612.A5493T48 2014
 813'.6—dc23

                                            2013022674

ISBN 978-1-4516-8910-5
ISBN 978-1-4516-8911-2 (ebook)

To Bruce, with all my love

So faith, hope, love remain, these three;
but the greatest of these is love.

I CORINTHIANS 13:13

Part One

The Feast of Tabernacles

Mouse darted through the crowded streets of Jerusalem. His name suited him. Small and drab, he fled from one street corner to the next as though stalked by an unseen predator. Dirt and ash streaked his face, and the tatter of wool covering his head was no less filthy. Both his worn tunic and the cloak over it looked like they had been made for a man twice his size.

Not a head turned as he zigzagged around caravans, street vendors, and plodding donkeys. He was invisible—poor, dirty, worthless. Just another half-grown boy in the lower city whose parents couldn't afford to feed him. If a Greek trader or a Jewish woman noticed him at all, that's what they'd see—just what Mouse wanted them to see.

Mouse skirted the Hippodrome, built by Herod the Great to show off his fastest horses, and moved like a trickle of water past slaves carting oil jars and women haggling over the price of grain. He didn't stop to admire the trinkets laid out under bright awnings. He couldn't be late.

There had been no food in his house for days, and the rent was due. Another week and the landlord would throw them into the street.

Thou shalt not steal, the commandment said.

A familiar voice whispered in his mind, dark and compelling. *You don't have a choice.*

He'd seen the mark on the wall this morning, just across

from the Pool of Siloam. Scraped on the bricks with a chalky stone, the straight line down and one across had made his heart race and his fingers tingle. It meant Dismas would meet him in the usual place when the trumpets blew. After, Mouse would have enough silver to satisfy the landlord and his empty stomach.

Mouse bounded up the Stepped Street toward the temple. The drone of prayers and the odors of incense and burnt animal flesh drifted on the afternoon breeze. The Day of Atonement had brought throngs of pilgrims to Jerusalem to witness the sacrifices of bulls and goats—atonements for the sins of the Chosen People. Soon these tired, hungry pilgrims would swarm the upper market. Easy targets for talented pickpockets.

Three trumpet blasts rang out across the city. The sacrifices complete already? He wasn't even past the temple. He pushed by a pair of loaded donkeys and broke into a run. A stream of pilgrims poured out of the temple gates like a libation, flooding the street. Mouse plunged into the packed crowd. He'd be late if he couldn't get through this river of pious Jews. And Dismas wouldn't wait.

The high priest, Caiaphas, led the procession with a goat beside him—the scapegoat, on which he had laid the sins of Israel. Pilgrims followed wearing sackcloth, their faces and hair covered in ashes. They sang songs, begging for mercy from their sins, as they processed toward the Jaffa Gate to drive the goat out of the city and into the rocky northern desert.

Guilt pressed upon him as firmly as the bodies crowding on every side. His father came from the seed of Abraham, just like the priests and the pilgrims. And Mouse had fasted today, just like the men in sackcloth and ashes. But his father didn't offer sacrifice anymore, and his fast wasn't by choice. *The scapegoat won't atone for my sins.*

Mouse broke through the crowd and skirted the procession, picking up speed as he reached the bridge that stretched over the Tyropoeon Valley. He couldn't afford to worry about sins and the law like the rich priests and Levites. The Day of Atonement would end tonight at the first sight of the evening star. Jews were already hurrying to the market for food to break their daylong fast. And that's where he and Dismas would be, ready for them.

A frisson of anticipation tingled up his arms. He slipped through streets flanked by high walls. Beyond them rose fine homes with cool marble halls, quiet gardens, and rich food, but here the air was thick with dust and the odor of animal dung and unwashed bodies.

A labyrinth of streets crisscrossed the upper city leading to the market that sat just south of Herod's magnificent palace. Mouse turned into an alley hardly wider than a crack and slid into the meeting place—an alcove between the buildings, shadowed and scarcely big enough for two people. His breath sounded loud in the close space.

"You're late." A tall shadow parted from the gloom.

The scent of peppermint oil and cloves tickled Mouse's nose even before Dismas stepped into a dim shaft of light. He wore a tunic and robe like the Jews of the city and spoke Aramaic, but his accent betrayed his Greek heritage. Mouse spoke enough Greek to barter with merchants in the marketplace and understood even more, but Dismas didn't know that. There was much Dismas didn't know about Mouse.

Dismas's face was narrow, with deep grooves curving on each side of his mouth. The afternoon sun picked out glints of gray in his dirt-brown hair and short beard. How old he was, Mouse couldn't guess and didn't ask. Old enough to have a wife and a flock of children, maybe even grandchildren. But instead of a family, he had a slew of fallen women, if his stories could be believed.

"Maybe you couldn't find me?" Dismas's grin showed crooked teeth the color of a stag's horn.

Mouse bristled. He hadn't gotten lost in the upper city for months. "I just followed my nose until my eyes watered."

Dismas let out a bark of laughter. "At least I don't smell like a tannery." He flicked a long finger at Mouse's dirty tunic.

Mouse lifted his shoulder and pressed his nose to it, sniffing. He did smell bad. Maybe he'd overdone it a little. He bounced up and down on the balls of his feet, his chest cramped with tension. It was always like this before they started, but once they reached the market, he would be focused and calm.

Dismas rubbed his beard. "Settle down, Mouse. The gods will smile on us today."

The gods? A knot tightened in Mouse's belly. Maybe Dismas's Greek gods smiled on what they were about to do, but the God of Abraham surely did not. "Let's just go."

Dismas raised his brows. "What's the first rule?"

Mouse huffed out a breath. "You get half."

Dismas's deep-set eyes scanned the street. "And the second, boy?"

"Do whatever you say."

The tall man nodded and shifted past him into the street. Mouse counted to ten, as Dismas had taught him, and followed.

The upper market, stretching before Herod's palace in a chaotic maze of stalls and tents, resounded with clamor and babble. Donkeys brayed, their feet clattering on the stone street. Greek and Aramaic voices rose in heated debate over the price of oil and the quality of wheat. Merchants haggled with loud-voiced women over pyramids of brightly colored fruits and vegetables.

Dismas pushed through the crowds, his head visible above the bent backs of patrons looking for their evening meal. He glanced over his shoulder, caught Mouse's eye, and winked.

Mouse's taut anxiety lifted; his mind cleared.

Dismas stepped in front of a portly Greek woman weighed down with a basket of bread and dried fish. Her arms jingled with gold bangles. Mouse bumped her from behind, spilling the basket.

"Watch where you're going!" She bent to gather the bread.

Mouse mumbled an apology and fumbled to help her, dropping more than he gathered.

"Just let me! You're filthy." She brushed him off and hurried away.

Mouse shoved the gold bangle up his sleeve as he caught up with Dismas at a stall selling gleaming jewelry. A well-dressed Jew haggled with the merchant over a jade-and-ivory necklace.

The Jew shook his head. "I wouldn't pay more than a drachma for that."

"Robbery!" The merchant swept away the necklace.

Dismas eased up to the men. "You judge well, sir." He nodded to the Jew. "I know a shop down the street with better quality at half the price."

The merchant grabbed Dismas by the neck of his tunic. "Mind your own business."

Dismas pushed back, protesting in Greek. Passersby stopped to watch. The scuffle was short, but long enough for Mouse to do his job and melt back into the crowd. Dismas backed off with a bow and an apology.

A coin here, a brooch or bangle there. Mouse pushed the treasures deep into the pocket of his cloak. He pushed his guilt even deeper.

You don't have a choice.

As the setting sun cast a golden glow across the marketplace, Dismas glided past him. "Last one." He jerked his head toward a Pharisee speaking to a burly shopkeeper. His striped tunic was made of fine wool, and its deep-blue tassels lifted in the evening breeze. A fat purse peeked over the folds of his belt.

Mouse shook his head. The crowds were thinning. *Too dangerous.*

But Dismas was already gone. He approached the man with his head down, knocking into him. "Excuse me, Rabbi!" he said in loud Greek as he righted the man, both hands on his shoulders. As the Pharisee shouted about defilement, Mouse sidled by, snagging the purse and slipping it into his pocket with one smooth movement. He'd done it dozens of times.

A thick hand closed hard around his wrist.

"Little thief!" The words rang out in the marketplace and

echoed off the palace walls. The shopkeeper snagged Mouse's other arm in an iron grip.

Mouse wrenched forward, pain shooting through his shoulder. "Dismas!"

But Dismas had disappeared like the last rays of the sun. Mouse struggled, the third rule goading him into panic: If there's trouble, every man for himself.

A ring of angry faces closed in around Mouse. Hooves clattered on stone, and the angry men turned toward the sound. Two Romans on horseback—both centurions—parted the gathering crowd. One of them jumped from his horse. His polished breastplate glinted over a blood-red tunic. A crimson-plumed helmet sat low on his forehead, and curved cheek flaps covered most of his face. "What's going on here?"

Fear weakened Mouse's legs. Dismas had been wrong. No gods smiled on him today.

The crowd loosened. Some of the men faded away; others started explaining.

The Roman pushed the remaining men aside. "It takes two Jews to hold this little thief?" His Aramaic was heavily accented, but good by Roman standards. He pulled off his helmet to reveal a shock of hair the color of fire. Blue eyes narrowed at Mouse. He grabbed Mouse by one arm, like he was holding nothing more than a sparrow, and motioned to the crowd with the other. "Clear out."

Mouse's heart hammered. *I can't let them take me.* He twisted in the centurion's grip. In an instant, both his arms were wrenched behind his back. Pain brought tears to his eyes. He kicked out at the Roman's shins but hit only the hard metal greaves that protected them.

"By Pollux, you're a fighter." The centurion smacked him across the head—a light slap for a soldier, but it made Mouse's ears ring and his eyes water. He blinked hard.

The Pharisee drew himself up. "That worthless boy has my purse."

With one hand, the centurion gripped both Mouse's hands behind his back. He patted the other over Mouse's chest and midsection.

Mouse gasped. Heat surged up his neck and into his face.

The centurion found the deep pocket in Mouse's cloak, and out came the purse. He threw it at the Pharisee. "Take more care with your money, Rabbi." Then he shoved his hand back into the pocket and drew out a gold bangle, a brooch of jade and ivory, a Greek drachma, and two denarii.

He showed them to the other centurion, still seated on his horse. "See that, Cornelius? It was a lucky day for this boy . . . until now." He pocketed the stolen pieces and pulled Mouse sharply toward him. "Now he'll see how Romans deal with thieves."

Mouse's mouth went as dry as dust. Thieves were scourged, that he knew. But he was more than a thief. If he didn't get away—now—they would find out everything. The Romans wouldn't have to scourge him because he'd be stoned by his own people.

Despair and fear rose in his throat, choking him.

As the centurion dragged Mouse toward his horse and his companion, a shadow shifted in a doorway across the street. A heartbeat later, the Roman's horse whinnied and reared. A stone pinged off armor.

"Mouse! Go!" Dismas shouted.

The redheaded soldier reached one hand toward his shying horse, and Mouse saw his only chance. He wrenched, twisted, and ripped his arms from his cloak. He ran, leaving the soldier with nothing but a billowing cloak and a skittish horse.

Mouse sprinted away from the market. He glanced behind. The second soldier whirled his horse toward the shadow with a shout. Dismas ran toward the palace, the mounted Roman pounding after him. The redheaded centurion was gaining ground on Mouse.

Mouse veered into a side street. The centurion's hobnailed

sandals skidded on the smooth paving stones of the square. A shout and a Latin curse echoed down the narrow passageway.

The centurion was fast, but Mouse was faster. He wove through the back alleys. He darted down a side street, then dove into another that looked like a dead end—to someone who didn't know better. A muffled shout sounded behind him. His pursuer was losing ground. After a quick corner, he ducked through the narrow back door of a wineshop, pushed his way through the crowd of drunks, and sprinted out the front door.

Mouse kept running, his heart pounding faster than his bare feet. *Dismas broke the third rule.*

Mouse circled the upper city and slunk back on the north side of the market. Long shadows darkened the streets. The Jaffa Gate and the meeting spot weren't far, but was it safe to go there?

He stopped, holding his breath to hear something other than his own labored gasps. No hobnailed Roman sandals on the street. No pounding horse's hooves or shouts of pursuit. He approached the gate, staying close to the walls.

What if Dismas had been caught? Dismas knew almost nothing about Mouse, other than that he was an excellent thief. He didn't know Mouse's secret—or even his real name—so he couldn't send soldiers after him. Mouse was safe, but Dismas would be scourged. He might die.

A shiver of dread crawled up Mouse's back. He checked the street behind him. Empty. He crept into the cleft between the walls. Empty. He leaned his hot cheek against smooth stone and closed his eyes. Dismas had been caught. *He shouldn't have come back for me.*

At a whisper of wind and a breath of peppermint, Mouse's eyes flew open, and relief poured through his limbs. Dismas had entered the meeting spot like a wisp of smoke.

Mouse released his held breath. "I thought they'd caught you."

Dismas clapped his big hand on Mouse's shoulder, grinning like he'd just won a game of dice, not run through the city for his life. "They'll never catch me. Did you see that Roman dog's face?" Dismas shook with laughter but kept his voice low. "And you! You were fast, Mouse. I'll give you that. You were made to be a thief."

Mouse slumped against the wall. They'd done it. They'd gotten away. Dismas was right; he was good at this. Good enough to escape a Roman centurion.

Dismas reached into his pockets and pulled out an amber necklace, two silver drachmas, a shekel, and a handful of figs.

"Not bad," he said, popping a fig into his mouth. "How'd you do?"

"The centurion took it all." Mouse's shoulders drooped. How would he pay the landlord? Buy food?

Dismas chewed and leaned a shoulder against the wall. "Too bad. That means I don't get my cut."

Mouse studied his dirty feet. That had been the deal they'd made almost a year ago when Dismas had found him picking pockets in the lower city, rarely pinching enough to buy a handful of food. Dismas had offered to teach him to steal more than copper coins. With Dismas's help, Mouse pocketed silver, jewels—plenty, even after Dismas took his cut. But tonight, Mouse hadn't held up his end of the bargain. And Dismas had almost paid the price.

Dismas straightened and popped another fig in his mouth. "Don't worry about it, Mouse. We're partners."

He slapped the rest of the figs into Mouse's right hand, the silver shekel in the other. "Take this. I know your people don't trade in graven images." The shekel was stamped with a sheaf of wheat, the drachma with the face of Athena.

"But—"

"Shut up and take it, Mouse. I won't offer again." Dismas shoved him in the shoulder, but a smile lurked around his mouth.

Mouse closed his fingers around the coin. He chewed on the inside of his lip. "You broke your rule."

Dismas folded his arms over his chest, his smile gone. "Next time, I'll leave you."

Mouse shoved the coin into his pocket and a fig into his mouth.

Dismas elbowed Mouse aside and peered out into the street. He glanced back over his shoulder, his dark eyes serious. "You aren't worth dying for, Mouse. Nobody is." He faded into the shadows of the city.

Next time? Mouse chewed his lip until he tasted blood. Tonight had been close—too close. If he was caught . . . if they found out who he was, what he was . . . he'd have more to fear than a Roman centurion.

No. He was done stealing. Dismas was safe, and Mouse had enough silver to keep the landlord quiet for a month. He would find a job—anything that would bring in the money they needed.

This time, Mouse vowed, he would stop stealing for good.

Chapter 2

NISSA SLIPPED THROUGH the darkest, narrowest street of the lower city. She passed a tumble of buildings that looked like they'd fall down at the first breath of the winter wind. A cart filled with refuse rattled toward the Dung Gate, leaving an eye-watering stench in its wake.

She turned into a winding passageway, checked behind her, and pushed aside rubble of broken pots and shards of stone to expose a low doorway. She ducked inside. The tiny room, hardly more than a hole in the ground, was filthy. The floor was damp with runoff from the street, rainwater or perhaps something worse. Whatever it had been used for—pigeons, by the smell—it had been forgotten long ago.

Moving with speed born of practice, she removed the length of wool covering her head, untied the tight leather thong at the nape of her neck, and shook out her long hair. The rough tunic dropped to the floor and puddled at her feet. She unwound the length of linen wrapped tight around her breasts and breathed a sigh of relief. Her face burned at the thought of the centurion's searching hands, her arms prickling with remembered fear.

If he had discovered her secret, she'd have been dragged before the Sanhedrin and sentenced to death. Stealing was a sin, but a Jewish woman dressing like a man was an abomination to the Lord.

She donned a smaller, but not finer, tunic, tied her belt

around her waist, and laid her own mantle over her hair. She smoothed her hands down her narrow—but definitely female—body.

She was forgetting something.

Her hand went to her face and came away smudged with dirt. If only she could stop at the Pool of Siloam to wash the dirt and the clinging smell of dung from her skin. But it was already late. Cedron would be worried, and they still needed to buy food before the shopkeepers left the lower market. She spit on her hand and wiped away as much dirt and ash as she could. That would have to do. Her brother wouldn't notice anyway.

She rolled her disguise into a ball and buried it under the damp straw. She wouldn't need it again. No more stealing. And this time, she meant it.

Good-bye, Mouse.

Nissa crawled out of the abandoned roost and into the streets of the lower city. She hurried around a corner, down another street, and struggled to push open the gate leading into a scrubby courtyard. Letting out a deep breath, she closed the gate on the noisy street. Safe again, and with money in her belt.

The square courtyard—bordered on three sides by high walls and on the fourth by a wattle-and-daub house—was empty. The fire was out, and only a few sticks of wood lay scattered in the corner. She checked the water jar. Only half full. A distressed bray sounded from the rickety lean-to on the side of the house.

"I know, I know. You're hungry, too." She rounded the corner to find Amit tied to his empty manger, his dry-as-dust water bucket kicked into the corner. The hungry donkey strained against the rope to nuzzle his soft nose into her hand.

She pulled the silver shekel out of her belt. "See, Amit," she whispered, "this will make Gilad happy to see me." Her stomach fluttered at the thought of the handsome young landlord.

Amit put his lips on the coin and snuffed.

"You know why I had to do this, don't you?" She laid her face against his soft, whiskery cheek. *To feed you and Cedron. To keep us safe.*

Amit nibbled on her shoulder.

She pushed him away. "Let's get you something to eat other than my tunic."

The barley jar held just a handful of grain. She let Amit lick the last kernels from her hand, kissed him between his liquid brown eyes, and ducked into the dark doorway of the crumbling one-room house.

Once, her parents' house had been like other Jewish homes. The courtyard had bloomed with flowers and herbs and smelled of freshly baked bread. Her father had kept the mud-and-reed roof in good repair and the doorposts adorned with the mezuzah. Brass lamps, cushions, and striped blankets had brightened the room where they slept and prayed. But now, one cracked lamp and a jumble of sleeping mats filled a shadowed corner. And the only prayers uttered inside were those of her brother, Cedron.

As Nissa's eyes adjusted to the gloom, she saw Cedron on his mat in the center of the room, his prostrate body facing north toward the temple. He sang from the Tehillim, the book of praises that she knew so well. *"I trust in your faithfulness. Grant my heart joy in your help, that I may sing of the Lord, 'How good our God has been to me.'"*

Nissa chewed on her bottom lip and looked around the sparsely furnished room. *There hasn't been any goodness here for a long time.*

Cedron murmured a few more words in Hebrew, the language of prayer, and shifted toward her. "Nissa?"

"Yes." She crouched in front of him. He was older than her by ten years. A man who should have a wife and children but never would. Not that he wasn't handsome. Her brother had been blessed with a high brow and a straight, broad nose. His brown hair and soft beard contrasted against skin the shade of clover honey. But his eyes were sunken, his drooping lids shielding eyes as sightless now as the day he'd been born.

She took his hand in hers. "You forgot to light the lamp." In the dim light, she saw only a flash of a smile, but it warmed her like the sun.

Cedron squeezed her hand. "I was wondering why it was so dark in here."

She picked up the lamp and pulled at the wick. "We're almost out of oil."

"And everything else." He pushed himself to his feet. "Did you find work today?"

Find work? Her chest constricted. Disguising herself as a boy was bad. Stealing with Dismas was worse. But lying to Cedron made her feel like the dirt under her feet. Maybe she should tell him the truth now that she had sworn to stop.

The sinister voice stopped her. *He'd turn away from you. He loves the law even more than he loves you.*

The voice was right. If she told him, he would never forgive her. He loved the God of Abraham more than their father loved gambling, more than their mother loved wine. She'd have to lie like she'd been lying for months. But after tonight, the lying would stop.

"I did some weaving for the oil merchant's wife again today." Her voice quivered. She might be the best pickpocket in Jerusalem, but she was a terrible liar.

Cedron turned his face toward her, his eyes vacant pools in the dim light. "Weaving? You?"

Nissa huffed. "I can weave."

"Of course you can, sister." His hand searched for her shoulder and gave her a little squeeze. "But you can't weave well."

She shoved him, hard. "Well enough to earn this." She brushed the coin Dismas had given her over her brother's fingers.

"A shekel for a day's work?"

Her heart pounded, and her hand trembled. He didn't believe her.

But he smiled and dug a hand into his belt. "Then we are rich!" He poured a stream of coins into her hands: a bronze as, five quadrans, and at least ten copper lepta. Enough to buy barley for Amit and food for several days.

"Cedron!" She counted the money again. With the shekel, it was a small fortune. "Tell the truth. Did you sing again? Did the men at the gate pay you to stop?"

Cedron grinned and shook his head. "No singing. The men of Jerusalem fasted and prayed for forgiveness today. The Lord inspired them to be generous."

Nissa tucked the coins into her belt. "Generous would be a new feeling for most of them." But at least Cedron had begged today instead of sitting at the temple, listening to the rabbis teach and the revolutionaries complain about the Romans. "Does Abba know?"

"About the money? Am I an idiot as well as blind?"

"And Mama?"

He snorted. "Haven't seen her."

Nissa pulled him out the door of the house. She would have to hurry. "Your coins will be enough to get us some flour and oil, maybe some fish to break the fast."

Cedron shuffled beside her. "I'll come with you. We need to spend it all before Abba comes home."

Nissa hooked a basket over her arm and pulled open the creaking door. "Don't worry, we will. And when he comes home—"

"I know. I won't tell him about the silver."

"We won't have it long enough for him to find out." She took Cedron's hand and hurried through the front-gate and out into the street. Gilad would come for the rent tomorrow, and she'd be ready. She'd go to Siloam early and wash. She'd wear her other tunic, the one that almost fit her. She'd offer him warm bread—with honey, if she could get it cheap.

Maybe Gilad will see that a good wife is more than a pretty face.

At twenty years, her parents had given up hope of passing her off to another family. She'd never been pretty, not even close. Her hair was frizzy instead of flowing, her face was pointed, and her eyes, although fringed with thick lashes, were small and almost black. Not only was she plain, her body wasn't made for bearing children. Most men took one look at her tiny stature and narrow hips and shook their heads.

That was before she opened her mouth. She'd heard the reproaches from her would-be suitors to her disappointed father.

Nissa has a sharp tongue.

She's disrespectful.

Your daughter would do well to soften her words if she wants a husband.

Nissa lifted her chin and straightened her shoulders. But not with Gilad. She would be respectful, modest, hardworking. She'd show him she was exactly what he needed in a wife.

They reached the lower market as the dusk crept over the city. The streets were emptying, the merchants starting to pack up their wares. They had just enough time.

Cedron sniffed the air. "How about some figs?" He faced the booth selling dried figs, apricots, and raisins. "I heard the caravan from Damascus come in today."

Nissa left him at the fruit seller and hurried toward the grain merchant. Her mouth watered at thoughts of a good dinner. She filled her basket with barley for Amit, wheat, and oil. Just a few coins left, but enough for some dried fish and a miniscule jar of honey. She turned the corner and ran into a solid chest covered in fine linen. Smooth hands closed over her bare arms.

"Nissa. I've been looking for you."

Gilad. His hands warmed her skin and the scent of sandalwood embraced her. Her heart faltered a beat as she gazed up at his handsome face. Dark hair, dark skin, captivating dark eyes. The same eyes she thought of as she drifted to sleep at night. If only she'd taken the time to wash.

Gilad released her arms and wiped his hands down his pristine tunic. "Your father is behind on his rent."

Good Jewish women didn't speak to men in the street, but everyone in the lower city knew Nissa took care of the household of Noach, including paying the rent. She lowered her chin and glanced up at him like she'd seen other, prettier women do. "Have you asked my father about it?"

"I did, my sweet. But he just lost at dice. Again."

My sweet. Her heart galloped. Maybe there was hope. If he could just see her when she wasn't so filthy. "I don't have it tonight, but if you come to the house tomorrow?"

Gilad stepped closer and ducked his head close to hers. "Your father has used up all his chances with me." His voice flowed like honey. "Have it tomorrow, my dove, or I'll have to ask your father for another form of payment."

Nissa's cheeks heated, and her lips curved into a smile. He didn't mean it, but it was a start. He'd come tomorrow, and she'd be ready. He'd see what a good wife she could be.

Pounding hooves, louder than her heart, pulled her gaze from Gilad's brilliant eyes toward the center of the market. Shoppers and merchants scattered and shouted. A Roman horse rounded the corner and thundered toward them.

She searched the emptying street. *Where is Cedron?*

There he stood, across the marketplace. The horse bore down on him, but his feet remained planted in the dust. He reached out, his hands searching for her as men and women rushed past him. No one paused to help the blind man to safety.

"Cedron!" Nissa looked to Gilad, but he made no move toward Cedron. Nissa dropped her basket and sprinted toward her brother, directly into the path of the charging horse.

The rider saw her and pulled back, shouting as his horse reared. She threw her body on top of Cedron's. They tumbled to the ground as the horse reared again and plunged over them. Nissa covered her head with her hands. Hooves hammered the dirt just a handbreadth from her face. A searing pain sliced through her shoulder. She closed her eyes and clung to Cedron.

The pounding hooves stopped, and dust choked her throat. Cedron stirred beside her. He pushed himself up, his hands searching over her body. "Nissa, are you hurt?"

She kept her eyes closed, biting down on her lip to keep from crying out.

Sandaled feet slapped the ground near her head. Cedron was pulled away from her with a grunt.

"What's the matter with you, Jew? Are you blind?"

A deep voice—Aramaic with a Roman accent.

No, it can't be. A new rush of fear swept through her as rough hands closed over her arms and pulled her to sitting. Pain shot through her shoulder. She gasped and opened her eyes. It was him, the redheaded centurion.

He propped her back against the wall. "Are you hurt? Speak to me, girl!"

He was so close she couldn't take a breath. He knelt beside her, his crested helmet lying in the dust. He'd been this close only hours before; surely he'd recognize her. Fear weakened her limbs. She swayed as the walls and ground tilted. All that kept her from tilting with them was the Roman's rough grip.

He wasn't much older than Cedron, but she'd never seen a face like his. It wasn't Roman; she'd seen many of those. As if his blue eyes and red hair weren't enough to make him stand out amid the dark, bearded men of Jerusalem, his skin was light tan, lighter than roasted almonds. And sprinkled everywhere—on his crooked nose, over high cheekbones and smooth jaw—were freckles, like stars scattered over the night sky.

He must come from the far reaches of the empire, but the insignia on his breastplate and the crimson plume on his helmet bore witness: he was a Roman centurion, and a dangerous one. She knew that from experience. Any minute he could realize who she was.

No flash of recognition crossed his face. "What kind of idiot runs in front of a horse like that?" His voice was a growl, but his hand was gentle as he pushed aside her torn cloak to expose a crescent-shaped slice on her shoulder, oozing blood. "You could have been killed."

The Roman turned on Cedron. "And you! What were you

doing, standing in the road like a—" He stopped abruptly as Cedron raised his sightless eyes. The anger left the Roman's voice. "You'd be dead if not for this girl."

Nissa struggled to stand. A crowd stood all around her, leaning in, watching. She had to get away from this man. A wave of dizziness overwhelmed her.

Gilad shoved through the crowd and groveled to the Roman. "I saw the whole thing. You couldn't avoid them."

The Roman twisted to Gilad, scowling. "This woman needs looking after. Where is her husband?"

Gilad barked out a laugh. "Nissa? A husband? No man here is that brave."

"Or that desperate," a voice from the back called out.

A few men in the crowd snickered.

Nissa's dizziness retreated, but in its place, anger flared. How dare they laugh at her, these men who had watched from safety as Cedron was almost trampled? She glared at the crowd, pulling her small body up. "Brave?" Her voice rose. "Braver than you! You cowardly dogs would have let Cedron die in the street."

The Roman let out a snort.

She turned on him. He was no better than the others. "And you! This is our home, not the Hippodrome. If you hadn't been tearing through the streets—I'm not the idiot. You are!"

Silence fell over the knot of men. Their mouths dropped open, and they all looked to the Roman.

He stared at her.

Nissa slapped her hand over her mouth. *Did I just call a Roman centurion an idiot?*

The centurion raised his amber brows to Gilad. "I see what you mean." To Nissa he said, "Go home, girl, before you get in more trouble."

Nissa let out her breath in a rush. What was wrong with her? She needed to get away from this man, not insult him. She grabbed Cedron's hand and searched the street for her basket.

The centurion frowned at the group of men. "I'm chasing two thieves—a man and a half-grown boy."

Fear burned in Nissa's chest. She pulled at Cedron's hand. *Please, we need to leave. Now.* But Cedron stayed, his face turned to the Roman.

"The older one was tall and dark, maybe Greek. The young one—he's called Mouse—he's a runt, but he's fast."

The men in the crowd murmured and shook their heads.

The Roman reached up to the corner horn of his saddle and swung himself up with one smooth jump. He gathered the reins in one hand. "There's a shekel for whoever turns them in. Get word to me at the barracks—ask for Longinus." He circled his horse toward the upper city. "You," he called down to Nissa. "Little wildcat."

She ducked her head down. *Don't look at him.*

"Put some oil on that wound. And keep your brother off the street." He kicked his mount and galloped back toward the upper city.

Cedron fell into step beside her, his sightless eyes followed the receding thud of hooves on dirt. "He won't find those thieves." He shook his head. "No one here would help a Roman, even for a shekel."

Nissa scooped up her basket, took Cedron's arm, and hurried toward home. Relief warred with worry. The Roman hadn't recognized her, and Cedron was right. No one here would help a Roman. Anyway, he wouldn't catch Mouse because there would be no more Mouse and no more stealing.

What about Dismas? He risked his life for me. She pushed the rising guilt away. She'd miss his quick smile and his jokes, but it was too dangerous. Her days as Mouse were done.

The trumpets sounded from the temple walls, signaling the end of the day. The Jews of the city were praying over their evening meal, but Nissa didn't hope for prayers and the sharing of bread with her parents. If they were lucky, Abba wouldn't come home at all, and Mama would sink into her usual wine-induced sleep. They could eat their food in peace, and Nissa could tend to her aching shoulder.

Cedron stopped her in front of their courtyard gate. "Are you sure you're all right?"

"It's just a scratch." *A scratch that will scar and probably ache for months.*

He tipped his head sideways. "They're home."

She held her breath and listened. Yes, their parents were home, and Abba wasn't happy. She reached into her belt for the shekel. "Maybe you should hold this."

Cedron nodded as she slipped it into his hand. It would be safer with him. He pinched her sleeve to stop her before she stepped forward. "Nissa," he whispered, "remember, don't make him angry."

"I know, I know. Don't worry." She wouldn't this time. No matter what he said, she wouldn't let it get to her. Her wayward tongue had landed her in enough trouble tonight. Nissa pushed at the gate, juggling the barley and oil. Good, the cooking fire was lit. Bread might calm her father.

Mama jumped up as they entered, looking with relief at the wheat in Nissa's basket. With thin, graying hair and deep furrows on her brow and cheeks, she looked more like a grandmother than a mother.

Nissa had heard the lament countless times. Mama had given birth to Nissa late in life, when she and Abba both had been sure their only child would be the one cursed with blindness. They'd rejoiced in the hope of a boy who could care for them in their old age. Instead, the Lord had cursed them again with a plain, clumsy daughter—a daughter who had been a disappointment to them for twenty years.

Her mother snatched the jar of grain and hurried to kneel at the stone quern, pouring out a generous measure to grind but spilling as much on the dirt.

Nissa curled her hands into fists, her nails biting into her palms. *We don't have enough grain to waste, Mama.*

Her father stood with his hands on his hips. His hair, almost completely gray, was bushy and unkempt, as was his beard. His eyes were bloodshot, and his full lips cast in a perpetual frown. "I come home to no food, a wife who can hardly stand up, and no daughter to wash my feet after a day of labor." He pushed past her and lowered his body onto a bench beside the door.

Day of labor? Abba hadn't labored today, unless he counted throwing dice as work. He'd left Amit tied up instead of carrying bundles of kindling to sell in the wood market. Cedron squeezed her arm. She bit down on her lower lip and patted his hand. *Don't worry. I won't make him angrier.*

She poured water into a wide clay bowl and brought it to her father. Kneeling before him, she untied his sandals like a good Jewish daughter.

He set his dirty feet in the water. "And where were you when you should have been preparing bread for us?"

Nissa tensed. What could she say? "I found work for the day. Weaving."

"And did you get paid?" her father jerked, tipping the bowl sideways and sloshing water on the ground.

Nissa lunged to rescue the bowl before it broke. "She . . . she said she'd pay me tomorrow." Her voice wavered like an old woman's.

"Give it to me." Her father held out his hand.

She shook her head. "I don't have it." That was the truth.

His hand snaked behind her neck and closed on her hair. He jerked down until she was forced to look up at him. "You have it. I know you. Now give it to me."

He demanded her money when he'd spent the day gambling his away? "When Elijah returns." As soon as the words were out of her mouth, she wished them back.

Her father's face darkened with anger. "Don't get mouthy with me, girl."

Didn't Abba understand? They needed the money for rent. "But Gilad was looking for you today."

"I curse Gilad and the womb that bore him. He stole enough from me today. I'm the father and the head of this family." He stood, dragging her up by her hair. The bowl pitched to the side and broke against the rocky ground. His other hand dipped into the folds of her belt and came back empty.

"Where is it?"

She shook her head and blinked back tears from the stinging pain in her scalp.

He released her hair and pushed her away. "Why did the Lord curse me? A blind son and a daughter who can do nothing right. You got a job weaving! The woman must be as blind as your brother. Your fingers can neither weave nor spin. And your cooking! No wonder no man wants you."

He grabbed her by the shoulders and shook her so hard her teeth rattled. "Now. Give me what you earned today."

"No." She wrenched away, pain scorching through her injured shoulder. She ran behind her mother—still swaying over the wheat—as if she could help her. "You'll only gamble it away. Like you do with everything we earn. Why don't you go gather wood and sell it, use your own money for the dice!"

He came after her, his fist raised.

But she couldn't stop. Words flew from her mouth. "I won't work so you can throw dice with the pagans and so she"—Nissa tipped her head toward her mother—"can drink up the rest in cheap wine. The neighbors call you *am-ha-arez*, and they are right!"

Her father swung. She saw a burst of stars as his fist connected with her cheek. Pain arced behind her eyes. She fell to the ground with a swallowed cry.

"Stop, Abba!" Cedron stood suddenly, holding out his hand. "Father. I have it. I took it."

Abba was breathing heavily, but he didn't advance on Cedron.

"You are right." Cedron showed the coin to his father. "You are the head of the family. According to the law, it belongs to you."

Her father stalked to Cedron, snatched the coin from his hand without a word, and ducked into the dark house.

Cedron shuffled toward Nissa, his hands out until he touched her bent head. "I'm sorry, Nissa. I had to."

Nissa sniffed and buried her throbbing face in his chest. She would have done the same if Abba had been hitting him. But Abba never hit him. Only her. *I should have given it to Gilad. At least then we'd have the rent paid.*

She'd have to find another way to pay Gilad. The money Cedron brought in from begging wouldn't keep them fed. Her father was right: she couldn't weave or spin, her bread was always burnt, and her lentils were hard and tasteless. No man would marry her; no woman would hire her. She was a failure at everything—everything but stealing.

Chapter 3

LONGINUS URGED FEROX past the Pool of Siloam, up the Stepped Street, and toward the upper city. The evening trumpets sounded as the last groups of merchants and slaves hurried into the darkening streets.

His fingers tightened on the reins. How he wished he could wrap them around the little thief's neck. He was sure he'd seen the boy turning a corner into the lower city. They all looked alike, these Jews. And they weren't about to help him find the two thieves who had made a fool of him today.

His head pounded, and his stomach growled. He was a Roman centurion, by the gods. He'd battled barbarians from the north and been outnumbered by Numidian troops. But he'd lost a little thief in the streets of Jerusalem just as he'd lost the Samaritan who had killed Scipio.

He snapped the reins, and Ferox loped past the temple and over the bridge that crossed the Tyropoeon Valley. The upper city stretched before him in the twilight. Lights glowed in the courtyards of the wealthy priests and merchants; voices and snatches of music drifted on the breeze with the scents of cooking fires and roasting meat.

What he wouldn't give to be stationed back in Gaul, with its quiet villages and peaceful people. Even Rome would be better than this provincial dung heap. After this feast—which one was it again?—he'd go back to Caesarea, where he'd be reminded each day of his failure to get revenge for Scipio.

Longinus had spent months searching for the Samaritan with the scar on his face, the scar Scipio had put there. He'd almost had him—twice. The first time, a girl had gotten the best of him; the second time, a band of lepers.

His hand rested on the sword at his side. Even his father's sword, his most precious possession, hadn't been able to help him against the horde of diseased cripples who had attacked him on the road in Galilee. For months, he'd watched his skin for signs of sores or white flaking, worrying with every itch that he'd contracted the hideous disease that plagued these people.

At least no one saw me terrified by a band of half-human invalids. He'd screamed like a woman as the lepers had closed in around him, smelling of rot and death. Then he'd run like a coward. If his men had seen that, he'd have lost every iota of respect. And a centurion without the respect of his men didn't deserve the insignia on his breastplate.

Now he'd failed again. Longinus had ridden the streets of the upper city first, then the lower, hoping to catch a glimpse of the dirty little thief and his tall partner. Instead, he'd almost killed the blind Jew and his belligerent sister.

The weight on his heart eased, and his lips twitched. He'd never seen a Jewish woman so dirty or who smelled so bad. And she had a mouth as sharp as his dagger. He'd thought all Jewish women were meek as doves, content to hide behind the walls of their courtyards and the folds of their mantles. A woman hadn't scolded him like that since he'd said good-bye to his mother. Looked like at least one of them had some spirit, even if she was as plain as a brick wall and smelled like a stable. Her father would be hard-pressed to find a husband who could keep that wildcat in check.

He slowed Ferox to a walk as they ascended marble steps that led to the deserted agora in front of Herod's palace. The broad square, the upper city's locus for trade and assembly, was empty of all but the hot wind that swept in from the eastern desert.

A massive arched entrance, wide enough for three chariots, led to the palace built by Herod—not the current fool but his father, the one they called Herod the Great. Just past the arch, another set of marble steps led to a vast central platform, where Pilate sometimes appeared to speak to the Jews or pronounce sentence on prisoners.

On each side of the platform stretched identical marble palaces, one named for Herod the Great, the other for Caesar. Even by Roman standards they were magnificent, towering over the upper city. Gardens, groves of sweet eucalyptus, and fountains fringed the polished stone walls.

But Herod Antipas didn't live in his father's magnificent memorial. He stayed in Caesarea, far away from the Jews who disdained him. Pontius Pilate, the legate and provincial governor, resided in the palace during the great feasts, when he marched his cohorts to Jerusalem to display the might of the empire, but even he didn't stay in the city long. The god of these Jews made him nervous. He'd leave Jerusalem as soon as he could.

After two weeks in the city, Longinus well understood Pilate's avoidance of Jerusalem. In the last few days, the population of the city had swelled to ten times its usual number. Pilgrims from Damascus to the Dead Sea filled the streets to bursting. More Jews meant more trouble. It only took one radical to spark dissent, and a conflict could turn into a riot. Suddenly, you had a rebellion on your hands. Everyone knew Pilate needed to avoid any sign of rebellion in Judea.

The Jewish leaders assured Pilate they came together only to worship their god. The one and only God, they said. Longinus shook his head. Surely this god had deserted them long ago, just as Jupiter had deserted him when Scipio lay dying.

Gods. They're all the same. They cared nothing for the people scurrying like ants in the sand, making sacrifices and asking for mercy. He'd learned that the hard way.

He turned Ferox to the north, where his cohort—four hundred eighty men led by six centurions—camped between the three great towers of Phasael, Hippicus, and Mariamme. Three more cohorts made camp at the Antonia Fortress. Rome believed in an extravagant show of force, even against unarmed and untrained Jews.

The eighty men under his command would be eating their meal and getting ready for guard duty or a game of dice. The lucky ones looked forward to an evening furlough.

Longinus's chest tightened in familiar grief. After half a year, he still expected to see Scipio waiting for him in their quarters with a grin and a scheme. Two weeks in Jerusalem and Scipio would have known every tavern in the city and half the women—and he would have dragged Longinus to enjoy both whenever they were off duty. Longinus let out a long breath. His days of wine and women ended when his best friend died in the streets of Caesarea. Not just his best friend but also the best legionary he'd known in his fifteen years in the Roman army. How could he enjoy the pleasures of this life while Scipio languished in the underworld?

As he entered the garrison, smoke drifted from the mess hall, bringing with it the aroma of roasting venison. His hollow stomach rumbled. At least the hunting parties had been successful. Food first, then the bathhouse and a good night's sleep—if he could block out the sound of Silvanus's snores.

Longinus shared his quarters with one man instead of seven like the rest of the legionaries, but he'd take seven reeking recruits over Silvanus any day. If he had to spend another ten years bunking with the head centurion, he just might kill the man in his sleep. His only hope was that Silvanus would be sent on a diplomatic mission somewhere in the empire—Britannia would suit him well. It was as cold and brutal as he was.

Longinus slid off Ferox as a legionary took the reins and led the horse to the stables for his own rubdown and dinner. Longinus started toward the camp kitchens but halted at the shout of a gruff voice. A heavyset legionary approached, a red-plumed helmet under his arm. He was shorter than Longinus but heavily muscled. His cropped black hair and swarthy complexion did little to hide his many battle scars.

Longinus groaned. *Not Silvanus.* Was it too much to hope that Cornelius hadn't told the story of the thieves to the head centurion?

"Longinus. Empty-handed again, eh?"

Curse Cornelius. Longinus grunted and turned back toward the mess tent.

Silvanus clamped a hand on his shoulder. "Come with me to the bathhouse." His smile was closer to a grimace and his invitation more like an order. But Silvanus was his *primus pilus* and must be obeyed. Longinus pushed thoughts of food aside and fell into step beside the head centurion. They left the camp and strode toward the Jaffa Gate, where a slave stood beneath the arched doorway of a modestly appointed building.

"Give me a real Roman bathhouse instead of this falling-down pile of bricks." Silvanus slapped two bronze quadrans in the slave's hand. "But at least we don't have to bathe like these Jews, out in the open." He clouted Longinus on the back. "Although I don't mind seeing the women stepping out of their holy pools. Wet clothes can't hide much, eh?"

Longinus gave the slave his two coins and followed Silvanus into the frigidarium. He wasn't in the mood to trade complaints about the provinces or stories about women. Yes, the bathhouse was primitive, but he'd volunteer for latrine duty before he'd agree with Silvanus.

A gaunt slave helped them out of their armor and tunics and gave them each a pair of wooden sandals. He carefully folded their garments and took a stance in front of their belongings.

"Keep a watchful eye, or you'll feel the sting of my whip," Silvanus growled at the man, who paled and nodded. Silvanus smirked at Longinus. "Can't be too careful with that sword of your father's, eh?"

Longinus grimaced. After only two weeks, the bathhouse slaves were terrified of Silvanus. Their weapons and armor would not only be safe but also cleaned and polished by the time they returned. He passed the slave an extra bronze coin and hoped he'd use it for a good meal.

Longinus followed Silvanus past the cold plunge baths and into the dry heat of the tepidarium. He took a seat on the wooden bench and poured olive oil on his chest and legs.

Silvanus sank down on the bench beside him. "I'm ready to get out of this dump." He grunted at a hovering slave to pour oil on his back.

Longinus poured more warm oil into his hand and slicked it over his shoulders and arms. Going back to Caesarea sounded good, but Silvanus was too satisfied. He knew that look. What odious duty would Silvanus assign him this time? Scouting duty in the desert? Digging ditches? He massaged his aching shoulders. "We'll be gone in ten days."

Silvanus smiled, slow and mean. "Not you."

Longinus's hand didn't stop its circular motion. He kept his face smooth, but his temper flared as hot as the glowing brazier in the corner. Warmth from the hot stone floors seeped through Longinus's wooden sandals and into the soles of his feet. "Are those my orders from Pilate, then? To stay here?"

Silvanus nodded. "You know how superstitious Pilate is. He hates to be around these Jews with their incessant talk of their god. But he needs two centuries here to babysit until Passover. I volunteered yours and Cornelius's."

Passover? The whole winter in Jerusalem? He clenched his teeth. Sweat trickled down his face and stung his eyes. When had this happened? While he was off chasing that little thief? He chose a strigil from a tray and scraped the oil from his arms, then took a deep breath of the moist air. "What are we supposed to do here?"

Silvanus shrugged. "Drill. Harass the Jews. Keep the *pax romana*." He presented his back to the slave for scraping. "Maybe you should try to find the little thief who made such a fool of you today. I told Pilate about that show of Roman strength in the market. He wasn't happy that his favorite centurion failed again. Especially after he sent you after the Samaritan and you came back with nothing to show for it. I told him he never should have promoted a mutt like you, eh?"

Longinus threw the strigil down and plunged into the hot water bath. Silvanus had hated him from the moment he'd received his plumed helmet. He should be used to his insults by now. Longinus couldn't care less about the two thieves roaming the upper market. But the Samaritan . . . that stung. If it hadn't been for the Samaritan, Scipio would be alive. Scipio was the better legionary, better fighter, better leader. He'd know how to stop Silvanus from telling tales to Pilate.

Silvanus stepped into the other hot bath. "Cornelius said the men were taking bets on whether you'd come back empty-handed today like you did after your trip to Capernaum." He turned with a sly smile. "Face it, Longinus. Pilate only promoted you because your father was his friend and saved his life in Britannia. A half-Roman like you shouldn't even be a centurion."

A rush of anger burned through Longinus, hotter than the swirling water. Half-Roman? His mother might have been a barbarian, but his father was a legend. He took a breath and ducked his head under the water.

He came up gasping for breath. "I'll find them."

"Like you found the Samaritan . . . and lost him again?"

Longinus gripped the edge of the bath hard enough to crumble tile. *I'd like to wipe that smile off his face.* "I'll get them," he growled. "You and the men can bet on that."

"Bet on it?" Silvanus pushed his wet hair out of his eyes. "What will you bet, eh?"

Longinus ground his teeth together. He'd forgotten Silvanus's love for a wager. But if that's what it would take to get Silvanus off his back, he'd do it. He had plenty of silver gathering dust in the legion's treasury. His pay had tripled when he became a centurion, and he'd spent little of it since he'd given up wine and women. "Name it. I'll have those thieves caught and scourged before Saturnalia." Whatever Silvanus wagered, he'd lose it.

The skinny slave entered the room, his arms full of well-polished armor and both their swords. Silvanus's beady eyes fell on Longinus's gleaming sword.

A chill crept up Longinus's back. His father's sword, passed on just before he died in the wilds of Britannia. *Not my sword.* But it was too late.

Silvanus smiled like a snake that had cornered its prey. "Your sword, then, if you're so sure you can find the thieves. And just because I like you, I'll give you until I come back at Passover."

That son of a jackal. Longinus wiped the water from his face. *Silvanus has had his eye on my sword for ten years.*

Longinus climbed out of the bath, his skin tingling, and let a waiting slave wrap him in a dry linen sheet. He picked up the sword, its weight familiar in his hand. The lamplight gleamed over the polished blade and the silver hilt set with gold. The sword of his father: primus pilus of the fifth Macedonian legion and best friend to Pontius Pilate. If he lost it, he'd never live it down.

Silvanus climbed out, water and steam streaming off his body. He eyed the sword like a hungry man watching meat roast over the fire.

Longinus couldn't back down now, not without losing face. But he could make sure Silvanus was the one to regret this wager. What would Silvanus do for a chance to own the sword?

"If I don't have the thieves by Passover, my father's sword is yours." Silvanus reached out a hand to the gleaming hilt, but Longinus pulled it back. "But if I win—and I will win"—Longinus stepped closer to Silvanus, his voice hard and cold—"you get me out of this province."

Silvanus's brow furrowed. "Where to? Rome?"

Longinus narrowed his eyes. Rome, with its gladiators and

chariot races? Its crowds and palace intrigues? Or somewhere else? Somewhere peaceful, where he wasn't reminded each day of Scipio's death and his own fears. "To Gaul."

"Gaul?" Silvanus snorted. "There hasn't been a battle in Gaul in fifty years. You'll be stuck talking to diplomats and sending reports."

Longinus tilted the sword, and lamplight glittered along its razor edge. "If you can't do it—if you don't have the pull with Pilate . . ."

Silvanus eyed the sword again. "I can get you to Gaul—with Pilate's help and plenty of silver." He smirked. "But I won't have to."

Longinus turned the sword over in his hands. Gaul, with its quiet villages and deep forests, where he could finish his service in peace. "Then it's a wager."

Silvanus looked at him sideways as the slave dried him. "How do I know you won't pull two beggars off the street and call it done, eh?"

Longinus snorted. *That's what Silvanus would do.* "Cornelius saw them." At least, he saw the tall one and caught a glimpse of the Mouse. "He'll vouch for me."

Silvanus's lips curled into the semblance of a smile. "Your father's sword if you don't find them, a transfer to Gaul if you do?"

Longinus nodded.

Silvanus held out his dripping hand. "Hercle, I won't pass that up."

Longinus clasped the other centurion's thick forearm and squeezed. Passover was almost half a year away, surely enough time to find two worthless thieves. He'd find them, mete out their punishment, and get away from this stinking province that had brought him nothing but failure and death.

Chapter 4

Longinus woke to a rumble in his belly. He'd returned too late last night to get more than a hard crust of bread and the dregs of the venison stew.

On the other side of the room, Silvanus's cot was already empty. At least Longinus wouldn't have to smell him this morning. The two rooms he shared with Silvanus were spacious compared to the tents they called home during a campaign, but still, the sleeping room was just big enough for two cots and a low table holding a lamp. High square windows let in the morning light and a cool breath of air.

Longinus changed into a clean tunic, kirtled it at his waist with a cord belt, and tied on his hobnailed sandals. He fit his armor over his chest. The polished iron bands mounted on a leather frame were expertly crafted to his body. The armor was light and strong and had cost him plenty of silver, but it had saved his life in battle more than once. A ribbon tied under his breastplate indicated his rank as centurion and reminded him of his wager last night.

He buckled his sword onto his belt. The faster he found the little thief and his partner, the sooner he'd get to Gaul. After his father died, his mother had gone back to her people. She'd be glad to see him. He could spend the rest of his service keeping the pax romana there, then retire. He'd get his pension, a piece of land—maybe even some goats and a wife. His spirits lifted for the first time since Scipio's death.

He passed into the second room. On his side sat a chair, a cedar-and-leather chest holding scrolls and tablets, and a neat stack of clean tunics; on Silvanus's side, a jumble of dirty tunics and a few empty amphorae smelling of sour wine. He picked up his *vitis*, a centurion's vine-wood staff, on his way out the door. With any luck, he wouldn't have to look at Silvanus's mess for much longer.

The glow of early dawn edged over the eastern wall of the barracks. Smoke drifted over the camp as legionaries hurried to the cooking fires or stumbled toward the latrines. Longinus would need to check in with his prefect before inspection, but first his hollow stomach demanded food.

Longinus made a quick round of the barracks along the outside walls where the eighty men of his century bunked. Most were sitting on the ground outside their quarters, breaking their fast amid the clatter of brass bowls and wooden spoons. Longinus helped himself to a loaf of hot bread, just pulled from a beehive-shaped oven, and a hunk of cold meat. He crouched next to a group of his men with a grunt and a nod.

Soon, the men would assemble for orders. They'd need a full cohort on duty today at the temple—the Jews would be packed inside like pickled fish, and they'd smell just as bad. Later, he'd find spies—people who knew the city and its people—and track down the little thief and his partner. Next time, they wouldn't get away.

He wiped the grease from his hands and cut toward the middle of camp. The garrison at Herod's palace matched those in every other Roman province, from the misty shores of Britannia to the deserts of Numidia. He walked the Via Praetoria, the main road that bisected the camp, passing the granaries where men stood in line for their rations of wheat and the hospital tent smelling of dysentery. All was in order, every man at his assigned task.

At the center of camp, past a wide assembly square, sat the headquarters, the *principia*, where administrative officials kept the cogs of the empire turning. Longinus approached the heavily guarded doors. Inside, he would find his prefect ready to pass out the day's duties, more legionaries guarding the cohort's shrine to Mars, and—even more precious—the locked casks that held his men's pay and pensions.

A legionary on duty stepped forward. "Silvanus is looking for you."

"Already?" Couldn't he avoid Silvanus for one morning?

The legionary lowered his voice. "It's Marcellus."

Alarm prickled up the back of Longinus's neck. "What now?"

The legionary didn't meet his eyes.

"Tell me."

His words were clipped and quick. "Fell asleep on guard duty."

Longinus pressed his lips together. *Not again.* "Who found him?"

"Silvanus. He took him to the *carcer*."

Next to the principia sat a squat, low building, probably used by Herod the Great to store his more costly wines. Now the cohort used it as the camp's carcer, a lockup for the occasional prisoner awaiting sentencing or the more frequent drunken legionary.

Longinus pivoted and pushed through the door of the carcer, cursing Marcellus under his breath. Some men weren't meant to be legionaries. Marcellus, quick-witted and clever, would have excelled as an innkeeper or merchant—anything that didn't require strength, stamina, or common sense.

Marcellus had fallen asleep on guard last month in Caesarea. Longinus had assigned the young legionary latrine duty for a year and docked him so much pay he wouldn't see a denarius before spring. Silvanus wouldn't be so lenient.

Inside the carcer, narrow stone stairs descended to a dim

lower-level anteroom. Three heavy doors reinforced with iron bars and locks led to three damp, musty cells. Two doors were open, the rooms behind them empty. From the third door, closed and guarded by Cornelius, came shouted curses and the slap of a vitis on flesh. Silvanus.

Maybe he could talk some sense into Silvanus before he got his hands—and his whip—on Marcellus.

Cornelius stepped aside, and Longinus entered the cramped cell, barely big enough for three people. A narrow, barred window let in the weak morning light.

Marcellus lay on the dirt floor, his hands tied, one eye swollen, and blood trickling from his mouth. Silvanus stood over him, his vitis already stained with blood.

Longinus smoothed his face into a mask of indifference. He leaned against the door frame and crossed his arms. "Silvanus."

Silvanus's breath rasped from his throat. He'd removed his helmet and armor, and his tunic was dark with sweat. "About time you showed up. I suppose you want me to go easy on him again?"

Marcellus was one of Longinus's men, but Silvanus didn't care. Longinus shrugged. "If we were in the field, on campaign, I'd execute him myself."

Marcellus flinched.

Longinus kept his voice even. "But we're not on campaign. He deserves a good beating. Looks like you're doing that." He turned to go.

Silvanus threw down his vitis. "A beating? He's not getting off so easy. He needs to be taught a lesson. You're too soft on him—docking his pay, giving him extra duty. A flogging will teach him to be a legionary."

Longinus inclined his head. "Or kill him. Dead legionaries can't serve Rome."

Silvanus kicked Marcellus in the ribs. "If it does, so be it. I've already told the prefect."

Longinus's gut wrenched. He was too late. A flogging was

standard punishment for falling asleep on duty, and if the prefect had already agreed, it would be done. But Marcellus wouldn't survive Silvanus.

Longinus took a deep breath and squared his shoulders. "You're right. He needs to be taught a lesson. And I'm the one who should it."

Silvanus jutted his chin forward. "You'll do it?"

"He's one of mine."

Silvanus's upper lip curled. "You'll go easy on him."

"No." Longinus looked at the young man lying on the floor. He'd be a bloody mess, but he'd have a chance. "I won't."

Silvanus dragged Marcellus up the stairs and out the door. He summoned one of the guards. "Assemble the men." He kicked Marcellus into the open square and looped his bound arms over a wooden pillar. "Move, and I'll run my sword through you." Then, to Longinus, "I'll get the whip."

Longinus bent to check that Marcellus's hands were securely tied. He gripped the young man's shoulder—hard. "Remember you're a Roman, not some cowardly Jew."

Marcellus met his eyes and nodded.

Longinus stepped back, his throat tight. *Hercle, Marcellus. Why did you have to fall asleep?*

The Roman Empire was only as strong as its army, and the army was only as strong as its discipline. He'd been beaten himself when he was a new recruit. Beaten for losing his mess kit, for not moving fast enough, for a spot of rust on his armor, but he'd never been flogged. He'd seen it enough to know that the result depended on the man doing the flogging. Someone just a little too good at his job ended up with a dead legionary.

Silvanus reappeared with a *flagrum*. Longinus took it from him, grasping the short leather handle with damp hands. Jagged sheep bones stained with decades of blood weighted the tips of three long leather thongs.

The legion—those who weren't on leave or on duty—assembled in the open square in silence. There wasn't a man there who hadn't dozed off at least once. The only difference was they hadn't been caught.

Longinus turned his shoulder to Marcellus. The first few would be the worst. Then, if the gods were merciful, he'd pass out from the pain. Silvanus stood close by, breathing hard. Longinus pulled his arm back and let the whip fly. Marcellus jerked when it hit but didn't cry out. *Good. Just twenty-nine more.* When he pulled back the whip, it left three bright red stripes on Marcellus's back.

The second lash drew more blood. By the tenth, Marcellus's tunic was crimson and hung in torn ribbons. Longinus's tunic and arms were speckled with blood that flew from the whip.

Silvanus walked among the first few rows of men. If he caught a legionary looking away, he hit him with his vitis.

Longinus concentrated on counting. He wouldn't do one more than the thirty prescribed lashes, but he had to make each one convincing. Silvanus would know if he was going easy, and so would his men.

At twenty lashes, Marcellus went limp and slumped into the dirt. *At least he's not feeling them anymore.*

At thirty, Longinus threw down the blood-soaked whip. He strode forward, his gut clenched tight. He stepped around the post and pulled out his dagger. After cutting the ropes on Marcellus's limp hands, he pointed to two legionaries in the front line. "Get him to the hospital tent."

Longinus stalked down the Via Praetoria, his breakfast roiling in his gut. Silvanus couldn't fault him. The men respected him.

Marcellus still might die. *I gave him a chance. I did what I could.*

Suffering and death were the way of life for a Roman legionary, but since he'd watched Scipio bleed to death in Caesarea, a specter had haunted his days and nights. Death. An invincible enemy that stalked closer each day. He'd felt the pain of watching young men die in battle, of seeing his friends cut down before him. He'd been surrounded by death for fifteen years, but he'd never feared it. Until now.

He ducked behind an empty tent and retched up the remains of his breakfast. Wiping his sleeve over his mouth, Longinus closed his eyes, trying to blot out the memory of the young legionary's slack face. Marcellus might live; he prayed to the gods he would. But in the end—whether in Judea, Rome, or a quiet farm in Gaul—death would defeat them all.

Chapter 5

NISSA WAS SILENT as she led Cedron through the streets in the early-morning light. She had woken with a knot in her stomach as the blasts of the silver trumpets rang out over the city, announcing the last day of the Feast of Tabernacles, a joyful feast of water and light. But not for her family. Almost two weeks of surviving on Cedron's daily handful of coins had left her stomach empty and Cedron's cheeks hollow.

Humiliation ate at her like a worm at a fig. After her father took the shekel, she'd begged Gilad for more time to pay the rent. He hadn't flirted—and he surely hadn't talked of marriage—but he'd agreed not to throw her family out of their home. "As the Most High is merciful, so am I," he'd announced. "But there is a limit to my mercy." If she didn't have the full rent by tomorrow, the day after Tabernacles, they would be sleeping in the street by nightfall.

The din of clattering hooves and braying donkeys echoed off the stone walls. She took a deep breath, tasting the dust and promise of heat. Where would they be after tomorrow? They had no one to turn to in the city. Her parents had lost their friends when they'd succumbed to gambling and wine. Her father's family was long buried. Her mother's people in Bethany hadn't spoken to them in years.

Cedron persevered in prayer each day. *The Lord is my strength and my shield,*" he sang. "*My heart trusts in him and I am helped.*"

But Nissa knew better.

She guided Cedron past the Pool of Siloam, rounded a corner, and arrived at the doors of the synagogue where Cedron said the morning Shema. It was crowded with pilgrims, already singing songs of thanksgiving. Women and children lined the walls, waiting to hear the word of the Almighty. She had been like that once.

As a child, she had memorized the words of the Tehillim, the songs of praise and thanksgiving. The songs had filled her with joy, and the praise of the Lord had filled her with peace. But no more.

She pushed through the crowd, ignoring grunts of displeasure from shabbily dressed men. When Cedron was positioned near the front, she left him and joined the women. *Why should I praise the one who abandoned me? And what is there to be thankful for?*

She'd been hopeful when the Feast of Tabernacles began. For ten days, the city was filled with pilgrims. At night, they lived in tents in the olive groves and vineyards outside the city. Each morning, the high priest, followed by the people, fetched water from the Pool of Siloam, carrying it in a golden pitcher to the altar of the temple. Surely, with all the feasting and goodwill, she would find work.

She'd walked the streets of the upper city until her feet bled, knocking on doors. She offered to scrub their marble floors, clean their stables, carry water. They took one look at her and shooed her away with words she wouldn't use on her donkey.

Abba watched others at dice. Mama disappeared most days. Nissa and Cedron shared Amit's barley and drank water from the Pool of Siloam to fill the emptiness in their bellies.

Nissa slumped against the wall and surveyed the men in front of her. If she had a husband, life would be better. But it was too late for that. Several men in this very synagogue had come to her father when she was young, shopping for a wife. But none had wanted her.

Beg or whore, her mother had said as her hopes of marriage dwindled. Those were her choices if a man didn't speak for her. Begging didn't bring in enough to keep her and Cedron fed. And selling her body in the brothels of the lower city? Cedron would die of shame, and they would both die of starvation.

It's not my fault. It's because Abba is one of the am-ha-arez. She couldn't remember the last time Abba had prayed the Shema or tithed to the temple. Yes, it was his fault they were despised, but they would starve just the same.

The bleak voice whispered between the murmurs of prayers around her. *There is another way.*

No. She shook her head to dispel the voice. *No more stealing.* The idiot centurion was still looking for Mouse. Perhaps Abba would come to his senses tomorrow when his family had nowhere to lay their heads. Perhaps he'd take Amit outside the city and gather wood to sell at the market, like he'd done before he'd surrendered to the lure of the dice. She'd do it herself, but no one would buy wood from a woman.

When the prayers and songs ended, she found Cedron outside the doors of the synagogue easing toward a loud group of men, their faces flushed with excitement.

A man in a worn robe spoke out. "There is no master but our God. The Romans defile our city. We've been under their rule for long enough."

Another man, a pilgrim from the country, pushed forward. "But the Sadducees, the traitors, they're in bed with the Romans. They'll do whatever it takes to keep their money and power, even support the pagan occupation of our land."

"The Pharisees are no better. We must fight the Romans, not compromise with them!"

A scruffy young man stepped forward. "I've heard there's a man who calls himself the Messiah."

A man as old as Noah grumbled, "Another messiah?"

The youth nodded. "The Sadducees hate him. So do the Pharisees. But the people love him."

The pilgrim spoke up. "Yes, and he performs miracles. Heals the sick. Makes the lame walk. Thousands flocked to hear him in Galilee."

The youth lowered his voice. "He's in the city for the feast. He speaks in the temple almost every day." He glanced to each side. "Perhaps he is the one to overthrow the Romans. If we can get enough men and some weapons—"

"Come on, Cedron." Nissa dragged her brother away from the group. "This can only lead to trouble." No good would come from the Zealots plotting against the Romans. Enough of them had already been crucified.

Cedron turned his sightless eyes to her, his brows raised. "Nissa. Bring me to the temple. I want to hear this man. Perhaps he is all they say. If he can cure the sick, heal the lame . . ."

Nissa's chewed on her lip. How many miracle workers had they seen? How many times had Mama brought Cedron to a man claiming to be a prophet, a healer? Too many to count. Magic men curing lame beggars who were never lame to begin with. So-called prophets full of promises. Frauds. This one would be no different. She guided him toward the street. "We need food more than we need a prophet."

"Perhaps he is the one who will deliver us from the Romans."

How could he think about overthrowing the Romans when they didn't even have bread? "Today is the last day of the festival. There will be plenty of pilgrims coming through the Dung Gate. Maybe you'll get enough to buy barley." They passed through the dyers' district in the southernmost edge of the city.

"The Dung Gate? Nissa, I need to be at the temple. And it's the Sabbath."

Nissa didn't alter their course toward the southern gate. Better that he get a few coins for barley than chase after a charlatan. "Begging isn't considered work; you know that. But don't let the Pharisees see you tying any knots." Her voice held a note of contempt that made Cedron scowl. He should worry less about the law and more about what they would eat tonight. He sighed and nodded, but she could feel his disappointment in the weakening of his grip.

She squeezed his hand. "I promise, Cedron. We'll see the healer together. Tomorrow." Tomorrow, when they had no home.

After she settled Cedron at the Dung Gate, she trudged home. She pushed through the gate into their courtyard. The fire was out, as usual. Would it be too much to ask of Mama to keep it lit?

"Amit, I'm home." Nissa rounded the corner of the house. No soft-nosed donkey brayed in greeting.

"Mama?" She ducked into the dim house. Her mother slept propped in the corner, her dusty cloak askew, her gray-streaked hair unwashed and loose.

Nissa shook her mother's shoulder. She awoke with a snort.

"Where's Abba?"

Her mother rubbed her hands over her face and wet her cracked lips with her tongue.

"How should I know?"

"But Amit isn't here. Is Abba gathering wood?" Perhaps her father really was going to take care of his family.

"On the Sabbath? Ha!" Her mother stood, swaying unsteadily. "He doesn't work any other day of the week. Why would he work on the Sabbath?"

"He took Amit."

Her mother rubbed her hand over her lined face like she was trying to remember something. "He took him to Gilad."

"To Gilad?" Her stomach dropped. But that made no sense. "Even if he gets a good price, it won't be enough to pay what we owe." Better to keep the donkey. Gilad would throw them out either way. What was her father thinking?

Her mother picked up an amphora, shook it, and dropped it back on the ground. "Said some nonsense about winning him back at dice." She snorted. "With your father's luck, Amit will be at the tanner by tomorrow."

The tanner? Not her dear Amit. Pain squeezed her chest like a clenched fist, and she fought to draw a breath. Amit was gone. Her father had doomed them all to the streets. Was this where Cedron's trust in the Lord had brought them?

Her mother slumped back in the corner.

Nissa ran for the lean-to. She threw herself into the pile of straw, rage boiling up in her. By tomorrow, her Amit—the only one who knew her secret—would be slaughtered, his skin used for cheap leather and his body rendered for tallow. She rubbed her burning eyes. And now they had no way to gather wood, no money for food or rent, and no soft-nosed, brown-eyed donkey to listen to her troubles.

Cedron would say, *"The Lord is my strength and my shield; my heart trusts in him and I am helped."* But the Almighty hadn't helped them, not for a long time. And he wasn't about to start now.

The dark voice whispered its refrain. *You don't have a choice.*

She breathed in the smell of donkey and dry straw. The voice was right. There was only one way to save herself and Cedron, and maybe even Amit.

Dangerous, yes, but in one day—one afternoon—she could steal enough for a week's food and rent. She could move with Cedron to a little house of their own, a place where they wouldn't have to put up with her mother's drunken binges or her father's rage. She wouldn't have to dress in rags and eat barley, and she could save Amit.

Trumpets sounded in the distance, announcing the third hour of the day.

She sat up and wiped her runny nose. Today was the last day of the festival. The temple courts would be crowded with rich Pharisees and Sadducees. The same rich men whose wives had insulted her and refused her a decent job. Why shouldn't she steal from them? They deserved it.

She brushed the straw from her hair and stood up. If the Almighty wouldn't help her and Cedron, Mouse would have to. Mouse would take care of them both.

NISSA SLUNK DOWN the dead-end alley to her hidden hole in the wall. Mouse's disguise lay buried under the dirty straw, just as she'd left it and pungent enough to make her eyes water. She changed quickly, winding the linen tightly around her chest. She bound her hair, covered it with the dirty cloth, and rubbed her face with a charred piece of wood and some dirt. Her father's cloak was a good substitute for the one she'd left in the centurion's hands. She didn't care if he missed it.

She'd made the mark on the wall near Siloam, but would Dismas meet her? She'd ignored his marks for almost two weeks; perhaps he'd given up on her.

If he doesn't show up, I'll go by myself. Without Dismas's skill at distraction, stealing would be more dangerous and she wouldn't get as much, but she had to try.

She was breathing hard by the time she reached the meeting place. Sweat trickled down her back and dampened her tunic, but her fingers tingled and calm focus seeped through her. When she was stealing, she thought of nothing else. Not Cedron, not her parents, not even Gilad.

She'd hardly drawn two breaths inside the cramped space when Dismas eased in beside her. Relief rushed through her limbs. She wouldn't have to go alone.

"So. You decided to try again? I must admit I was surprised to see the mark after all this time." Dismas ran a dirty fingernail between the cracks in his yellow teeth.

"I was busy." Nissa pulled her head covering closer around her face.

"You were scared."

She bristled. "Since when have I ever been scared?"

"Since that centurion scared the *skata* out of you last time. You probably had to wash your tunic that night!" He grinned and shoved her.

A smile tugged at Nissa's lips. Dismas was uncouth and crude, but she'd missed him.

He sniffed her shoulder. "You smell like a stable. I told you, Mouse, you'll never get any girls that way. Clean yourself up. When I was your age, I had girls begging to lie with me."

Nissa's cheeks heated. She hadn't missed Dismas's talk of women.

Dismas picked at his fingernails. "Always have something for them. That's the key, Mouse, a pretty bangle, a little perfume. How about we get you a pretty little something today, and you can get yourself a girl?"

She pushed past him. "Let's just go."

"What's your hurry? And why today, on your feast day? There are only Greeks in the marketplace."

She shook her head. "We're not going to the marketplace. We're going to the temple."

"The temple?" His black brows pulled together.

Dismas didn't like taking chances. But he did like taking money.

"It's the last day of Tabernacles. The temple will be packed with pilgrims. There's a man there, a miracle worker with crowds that follow him."

Dismas rubbed his beard. "I'm with you so far. Crowds, money, plenty of distractions. But also Roman troops and your temple guards."

Her heart sped up. That centurion—Longinus—might be there. But she needed silver. "We'll stay away from them. Keep to the center of the crowd."

"They're looking for us. Especially you."

So Dismas had heard of the reward for Mouse and the Greek. "We'll be fast. They won't even know we're there."

Dismas raised a brow and smiled. "Mouse, I'm proud of you.

You've finally grown some *órcheis*, even if you can't seem to grow a beard."

Nissa flushed and looked at her feet.

"Let's go then, my little friend. Don't get too close; they'll be looking for a pair." He sniffed again. "And stay downwind."

Chapter 6

*D*ISMAS LED THE way, gliding through the side streets and around the marketplace. As they reached the bridge linking the upper city to the temple, a river of rejoicing pilgrims swept them along. A song of praise filled the air. *"Give thanks to the Lord of lords, whose mercy endures forever."*

A woman dressed in rough wool and sturdy sandals smiled down at Nissa. "Come on, boy. Sing!"

Nissa moved her lips to the words. *"The stone that the builders rejected has become the cornerstone. This is the day the Lord has made; let us rejoice in it and be glad."* She'd be glad when she had money to pay the rent.

The crowd marched south to the Huldah Gates. Men and women herded children and carried lambs, pigeons, and baskets of wheat. They lined up to enter the temple through the massive double doors.

Beggars lay on the steps below the doors, crying out for mercy. Blind men like Cedron, men with the vacant eyes of infants, grotesquely disfigured men. But it was the women who made Nissa's heart twist in pity. Women who were little more than piles of dirty rags. One clutched a skeletal baby to her withered breasts. *See what trusting in the Lord brought you?*

She cut through the line, weaving amid the packed pilgrims through the Huldah Gates into wide passageways that crisscrossed under the temple mount. The crowds of pilgrims shoved their way up two steep staircases and finally emerged in the Court of the Gentiles.

Nissa blinked at the bright sun reflecting off a sea of polished stone and searched for Dismas.

The immense Court of the Gentiles ran along three outer edges of the temple. Its wide paved squares were open to both Jews and Gentiles, even to beggars and the diseased. Along the east side stretched the Royal Stoa, four rows of towering stone columns—each as big as the trunk of a cedar tree. A carved cedar roof spanned the colonnade, forming three covered walkways wide enough for ten men to walk abreast. In each walkway, stacks of cages held turtledoves and pigeons, lambs bleated in cramped pens, and money changers stood at tables cluttered with scales and weights.

Groups of pilgrims from Babylon, Thrace, and every other province of Rome lined up to buy sacrifices and change their silver for the Hebrew coins they needed to pay the temple tax. The din of animals, shouts of merchants, and clang of silver ascended like a discordant song to heaven.

Yes, it is a good day to steal.

There was Dismas, in the shadowed stone columns of the Stoa, next to a group of brightly dressed Alexandrians. She slipped past warm bodies and eased close to him. He glanced down and winked.

"Do you see soldiers?"

He craned his neck. "On the east side. By the Beautiful Gate."

In the center of the complex stood the temple sanctuary, rising on terraced platforms and guarded by stone balustrades. A tall, ornate entrance, rightly named the Beautiful Gate, glittered at the top of fifteen wide stone steps. Inscriptions carved in both Greek and Latin warned any Gentile against passing on pain of death.

Languages from every corner of the empire swirled around them as Dismas wove through the crowd with the grace of a leopard. Nissa followed, sliding through even the smallest gaps between pilgrims.

Nissa eyed a gaggle of rich women—the wife and daughters of a high priest, perhaps. One ran a hand over her shining black hair, brass and silver bangles tinkling on her wrist.

These preening pigeons haven't gone hungry a day in their lives. Nissa stumbled forward and came down hard on the black-haired woman's delicate sandal.

"Watch yourself, boy!" She bent to rub her scraped toes and glare at Nissa.

"Please, lady, I'm sorry," Nissa mumbled as she tucked three bangles into her tunic.

A jeweled brooch dangled precariously from the older woman's elaborate braid. When she bent her head toward her giggling daughters, Nissa helped herself to the brooch without disturbing a hair on the woman's head.

Nissa shifted through the milling pilgrims, avoiding the entrances to the central courts where the Roman soldiers stood guard. The pagan Romans couldn't pass through the Beautiful Gate or into the Court of the Women beyond it. Farther into the complex rose the Court of the Israelites, for ritually pure men, and then the Court of the Priests, where bulls, lambs, and pigeons were sacrificed on the great altar of unhewn stone.

Nissa sidestepped pilgrims gazing openmouthed at the Holy of Holies, the dwelling place of the Lord, but she averted her gaze from the gold-and-white-stone structure. If she didn't look up, perhaps God wouldn't see what she was doing in his temple. She reached Dismas in the shade of the Royal Stoa.

He bent to whisper in her ear, "Like robbing the blind and deaf," before jerking his head toward the other side of the Stoa and fading into the crowd.

Dismas was right. It was almost too easy. A coin purse peeked from a short, rotund man's belt as he stretched on tiptoes to see over the crowd. Her fingers itched. There could be enough silver in there to feed her and Cedron for weeks. She eased closer. He didn't blink when she bumped against him and lifted it off his protruding belly.

As the weight in her pockets increased, so did her hopes. They could do it. They could find a house—a small one—just big enough for her and Cedron. Away from Abba and Mama. Mouse would take care of them.

Shouts rang out toward the front of the crowd. Was Dismas in trouble? She squirmed through the tangle of bodies. An elbow hit her in the face. Pushing through, she found herself in front of the Beautiful Gate, just a stone's throw from the line of Roman soldiers. She ducked behind a black-garbed Phoenician and peered around him.

A man stood on the stone steps in front of the gate. He wasn't tall, but he looked strong, like a farmer or builder. His clothes were homespun, and his wood-and-reed sandals were worn and cracked. His hair and beard—both the warm brown of roasted grain—framed a face that wasn't lined with age, but neither was it youthful.

Six Pharisees and a scribe stood at the base of the steps, just ten paces from the solitary man. The blue tassels of their coats trailed on the ground. Their gold-and-purple embroidered tunics fluttered in the breeze, and heavy phylacteries hung over their foreheads.

Between the Pharisees and the lone man, two temple guards held a woman. Her body sagged limply. Her head was uncovered, and henna-dyed hair hung to her waist. A long tear marred her fine linen gown, and blood trickled from her mouth.

Nissa glanced sideways as a tall form pushed close to her. Dismas. Her heart sped up. The soldiers weren't far away. It wasn't safe for them to be so near each other. The crowd pressed in from behind, trapping her. It seemed every person in the Court of the Gentiles was gathering to watch the scene before them.

One of the Pharisees stepped forward and pointed at the woman. "Teacher, this woman was caught in the very act of committing adultery." His booming voice carried to the corners of the court.

The Phoenician shifted and blocked her view. Gasps of outrage came from the crowd.

"Stone her!"

"Harlot!"

The Pharisee's voice was lost in the din. Nissa cringed backward, her heart pounding louder than the voices around her. That could be her, caught by the guards, sentenced to death. She must get out, but the crowd packed even more tightly behind her, pushing her to the front.

Panic surged through her, and she glanced at Dismas. He shifted and shook his head. He was right. If she tried to leave now, she would only draw attention to them. She pulled her head covering closer around her face. Soon, they'd drag the poor woman out of the city to stone her. Then, she and Dismas could divide their spoils and disappear.

The rustic man approached the temple guards. He held out his hand to the woman. The guards released her, and she fell to the ground in front of him. The man leaned down and put his hand on her hair.

Was he comforting her? Once the Sanhedrin passed sentence, they didn't change their minds. The woman on the ground before him was as good as dead.

The Pharisee's voice rose. "Have you nothing to say? This woman has broken the Law of Moses. She deserves to die for her sins."

Still, the man didn't speak. A hush spread over the crowd like a soft breeze. The man began to draw in the dust.

Nissa strained to see. He was writing letters, Hebrew letters. But what did they say?

The Pharisees peered at the ground. One drew in a sharp breath. Another's face whitened, and he stumbled backward.

Finally, the one they called teacher stood. "Let the one among you who is without sin be the first to throw a stone at her." He stared at each man in turn.

Nissa held her breath.

The first to falter was the oldest Pharisee. He muttered a word and turned, disappearing through the Beautiful Gate. The loud Pharisee backed away, then left with a sweep of tassels. One by one the others departed until there was only the watching crowd, the woman on the ground, and the strange man.

The teacher spoke to the woman. "Woman, where are they? Has no one condemned you?"

She shook her head but didn't look at him.

Nissa glanced sideways. Every face beside her showed shock; every ear strained to hear his words.

"Neither do I condemn you." The man put his hand under her chin and raised her face to his. "Go and sin no more."

Nissa let out a long breath.

Shouts and exclamations surged through the crowd.

"Who does he think he is?"

"Did you see what he wrote?"

Dismas ducked close to her. "Who is this Jew?" he whispered.

Nissa shook her head. Whoever he was, he'd saved a woman's life after she'd been condemned by the most powerful men in Jerusalem. Who was this man who could defy the power of the Sanhedrin with words written in dust?

"He knew their sins. That must have been what he wrote. He can read souls." Dismas's face was pale, and his eyes were fixed on the man, still crouched in front of the woman. "Stay away from him. If he knew their sins, he'll know ours."

A quiver of fear ran through her. Could Dismas be right? The man had some knowledge about the Pharisees, something that made them flee.

A woman next to them tapped the Phoenician in front of her. "Who is this man?"

He spoke loudly over his shoulder. "His name is Jesus. He's a prophet, from Nazareth."

From Nazareth? Nissa tensed. Could he be the one Cedron spoke of, the one they claimed had cured the lame and restored sight to the blind? Was he a healer or a prophet? Or could he really know a person's sins, like Dismas said?

Nissa edged backward into the crowd. She must put some distance between her and Dismas and get out of sight of these soldiers. If Dismas was right, she should stay away from this Jesus of Nazareth, but the crowd surged forward, taking her with them. The man named Jesus was speaking. Her breath caught as his words reached her.

". . . be with you only a little while longer, and then I will go to the one who sent me. You will look for me but not find me, and where I am you cannot come."

Did he mean he wouldn't be at the temple tomorrow? *Where I am you cannot come.* Cedron would be crushed; all his prayers would be for nothing. Her stomach twisted into a knot. Even if it was just a foolish hope, she'd made a promise to get Cedron to this man.

Nissa glanced at the sky where the sun dipped low. Not long now before the last horns blew and the Sabbath was over. Surely the prophet wouldn't leave before then. If she was fast, she could keep her promise to Cedron—find him and lead him to the man from Nazareth.

First, she'd settle up with Dismas. She found him working his way back through the crowd and pulled him behind the first row of columns in the Stoa. She fished two bangles and the jeweled brooch from her belt. "I have to go. Here's your half."

He shoved the treasure into his belt and grabbed her shoulder. "Mouse. I mean it. Stay away from that prophet." His grip was fierce. "There's something about him. He'll bring trouble to us both. I can feel it."

Why was he so worried about her? Nissa wrenched away.

Greeks could be so superstitious. "I'll make the mark at Siloam next week. Look for it."

Nissa pushed through the crowded portico, heedless of the shouts and complaints that followed her. Dismas's warning sent a chill across her neck. Maybe he was right. Maybe the man could read her soul. She'd have to be careful.

She hastened down the stairs, through the dimly lit subterranean passage, and out into the late-afternoon sun. As she reached the foot of the marble steps and the line of beggars, she paused, digging into her belt for a coin. There, a silver drachma. She ran to the woman with the baby and dropped it into her outstretched hand.

The woman gasped, but Nissa didn't wait to hear her thanks. *The Lord may not have mercy, but I do.* Her feet pounded down the Stepped Street, past the spice merchants and the Pool of Siloam.

"Watch out, boy!" a man juggling a basket of pomegranates snapped.

Boy? She looked down at her tunic and cloak. *How could I have forgotten?* That Galilean had addled her wits.

Veering back toward Siloam, she ducked into her hiding place. She flung off the robe and tunic, pulled off her head covering, and loosened her hair. Dressed in her own clothes, she slipped the rest of the bangles in the folds of her belt and emptied the purse in her hand. She caught her breath in wonder. It was even more than she thought—enough to last them for weeks. She tucked it securely away and flew out of the alley. Sweat trickled down her back by the time she arrived at the Dung Gate.

Cedron wasn't sitting in his usual place at the entrance to the city.

Where did he go? He'd said he'd wait for her. She spun in a circle, searching for his familiar tunic. There, in the shadow of the wall. "Cedron!"

He stopped and turned, his sightless eyes looking past her.

"Wait." She caught up with him, her breath coming in gasps. "Where are you going?"

"I heard about him. The one from Nazareth."

"I know. I was there." Thank the Lord she'd found him in time. Before he was hurt or killed trying to get to the temple. She took his arm. "Hurry, he's leaving soon."

They zigzagged through the streets, faster than she'd ever seen her brother move. Gasping for breath, they emerged into the Court of the Gentiles.

She dragged Cedron to the Beautiful Gate. The crowd was gone. The man from Nazareth was nowhere to be seen, and a hundred feet had erased the words in the dirt.

They couldn't be too late. She must find him. She planted Cedron on the wide stone steps. "Stay here." Running to the crowded Stoa, she caught the sleeve of a passing woman. "Where is he, the one who was here?"

"The teacher? The one called Jesus?"

Nissa nodded; her hand tightened on the soft cloth.

The woman pulled away, her mouth twisting. "Last I saw of him, they were getting ready to stone him. If he has any sense, he's hiding."

They were too late; he had gone to where they could not follow. She plodded through the shaded Stoa, her head bent low. *Abba was right. I'm a failure at everything.* She'd have to tell Cedron that he'd missed the healer . . . possibly forever.

Nissa reached the steps to the Beautiful Gate and sucked in a breath. Cedron sat where she'd left him, but he was no longer alone. The teacher—Jesus—crouched in front of him. She glanced around. No one took any notice of the blind man and the roughly dressed pilgrim. A group of men stood behind them—some young, some old, all Galileans.

One of them, with a shaggy beard and weathered face, motioned to Cedron. "Rabbi, who sinned, this man or his parents, that he was born blind?"

Who sinned? Nissa froze. Did he know? Would he answer, "His sister is the sinner"?

Jesus spoke: "Neither he nor his parents."

Nissa's blood pounded, and her knees weakened.

"He is blind so the works of God might be made visible through him."

The works of God made visible?

Men and women brushed by Nissa, gathering around Cedron and Jesus, pushing her backward. She inched through the bodies, closer to Cedron but not too close to Jesus.

Jesus spat on the ground once, then again, his saliva a dark puddle on the dust. "While I am in the world, I am the light of the world." He stirred the puddle with his finger—the same finger that had made the Pharisees flee—and scooped the gray mud onto each thumb.

What was he doing? Nissa glanced at his followers. Their faces reflected her question.

Jesus laid the palms of his hands on each side of Cedron's bearded face.

Cedron's eyes fluttered closed.

As gently as a mother with her infant, Jesus smoothed his thumbs over Cedron's sunken lids until they were sealed shut with a thick layer of mud.

Cedron sat as motionless as a stone column.

A few people backed away; others shook their heads and shrugged. The Galileans kept their eyes on Cedron.

Jesus stood. "Go now. Wash in the Pool of Siloam."

Nissa scooted closer. The gray clay was packed over Cedron's eyes like mortar on a cracked wall. *What is this supposed to do?* When she raised her head, Jesus and his followers had disappeared into the crowd. She blew out a breath of relief. At least the prophet hadn't exposed her sins.

"Go." An old woman pulled at Cedron's sleeve. "Go wash, as he says."

Wash in Siloam? All the way down in the lower city?

Cedron tipped his head to the side, and his brow creased. "Nissa?"

"I'm here."

"Take me to Siloam." His hand went to his eyes but stopped short of touching the mud already drying on his lids. "Hurry."

She helped him up. *The Pool of Siloam? He's lived beside it his whole life. He washes in it, drinks from it every day. How could this time be any different?*

Chapter 7

LONGINUS SHIFTED RESTLESSLY on Ferox. Just a few minutes into his watch at the temple and he already itched to get out of the packed courtyard. His men lined the eastern wall, and more were stationed at each of the gates. So far, everything was peaceful. He'd make sure it stayed that way until the evening horns blew and the feast was over. There would be no revolution while he was on duty.

He scanned the faces passing below him—young, old, dark-skinned and light-, Jews from every province of Rome. But not the little thief and the tall Greek he'd been seeking for two weeks. Not likely to find them in this crowd, but he watched nonetheless.

At least it was the last day of the feast, and the city would soon empty of pilgrims. He couldn't wait to see the back of Silvanus tomorrow when he and most of the legion returned to Caesarea. Silvanus had put more than a few of his men in the hospital tent with his bad temper and brutal reliance on his vitis.

Thank the gods Marcellus was better today; he'd even managed to make a joke when Longinus had checked on him this morning. The salve that cost Longinus a week's wages and a day's travel to the Dead Sea was probably what had saved Marcellus from infection and a lingering death, the physician told him. Good. It was about time the worthless legionary stopped lounging on a cot and got back to his duties.

Voices rose in the center of the court. Something was happening near the marble steps leading to the gold-covered door. He nudged Ferox into a walk and angled him through the crowd. Disputes in tight quarters were never a good thing. These Jews could get worked up and start a revolt faster than any people he knew.

A group of men clustered at the edge of the crowd. "*Vigilate!*" He raised his vitis, and the men scattered. The rest of the crowd moved aside, giving him a narrow passage to the steps.

A man stood on the second step, his head down. A girl with familiar wild hair and a dirty tunic held his arm and pulled him forward.

"You there! Girl!" Longinus nudged Ferox up a step. Yes, it was the one from the lower city, the little wildcat he'd almost killed and her blind brother. He'd seen plenty of Jewish women bathing in the pools around the city. Why was this one always so filthy? "What's happening here?"

Her face went white under the dirt, and her mouth dropped open. "We were"—she grabbed her brother's arm—"leaving."

An old woman hobbled close to him and pointed at the brother. "Look. He put clay on this man's eyes and told him to wash in the Pool of Siloam."

So that was what was on the blind man's face. "Who did?"

"The teacher, Jesus."

Jesus. He'd been warned about a man of that name. A man causing trouble with the leaders of these bothersome people.

The old woman hurried off, following the girl as she pulled her brother toward the Huldah Gates. A crowd followed in their wake.

Rumors of the man called Jesus claimed he cured the lame and diseased—even lepers—but Longinus had heard that kind of talk before. He'd even witnessed so-called miracle workers. Longinus had yet to see a miracle that couldn't be explained by deceit, trickery, or plain good luck. Still, this Jesus stirred up the crowds. Longinus spurred Ferox toward the gates. He barked commands to his men. "Twenty legionaries with me. The rest of you stay here."

When he'd managed Ferox down the stone steps, a throng of at least a hundred people had gathered behind the blind man and his sister, like guests at a wedding feast. As they trooped down the Stepped Street, women and children came to their doors. Some threw mantles over their heads, grabbed their children's hands, and joined in the procession.

By the time they reached the lower city, the crowd had doubled. Longinus prodded Ferox and cut his way toward the front of the column. Dust dried his throat as he coughed out orders to his men. "Stay here. Be ready if there's trouble."

He'd seen a so-called healer stoned in Caesarea when the man he'd healed had turned out to have never been lame. *This* man—the brother of the little porcupine—was truly blind. He'd seen that himself. What would happen when he washed that ridiculous mud from his eyes and exposed the hoax? Disappointment could turn into anger, and a crowd could turn into a mob.

Just ahead, broad stairs—at least twenty of them—ascended to a wide stone platform the size of a modest palace. He threw his leg over the front of his saddle and jumped to the ground. Pushing the spectators aside with his vitis, he followed the blind man and his sister up the stairs.

The girl—Nissa, they'd called her that night in the street—threw a frightened look over her shoulder, then urged her brother up the last few steps with a hand under his elbow.

Longinus followed, catching his breath as he reached the top. He'd seen Siloam rising above the lower city, but had never climbed the stairs that led to the water. An immense rectangular pool stretched thirty paces long and almost as wide, with stone-paved borders on each side. Marble steps led down into water so clear and sparkling his eyes pricked with tears. He blinked and shaded his eyes.

People eddied around him and clustered at the wide ledges around the pool, pushing and bickering.

"Let me see!"

"I was here first."

The blind man and his sister were pushed backward, toward the low wall that ran around the platform.

"Make way. Move!" Longinus shouldered his way through the crowd. *Let's get this over with so I can get back to my post.* He opened a path with his stick and a gruff shout. "Get out of his way." He jerked a hand to the sister. "Bring him through."

Nissa didn't look hopeful; she looked terrified. The girl was as prickly as a thorn bush, but she protected her brother like a mother lion. And from the look on her face, she knew that her brother was in for a cruel disappointment.

The crowd of people continued to chatter. Children sat at the edge of the pool and dipped their feet. Women scooped water into jars. Some seemed to have forgotten why they had joined the procession to the pool; perhaps some never knew.

Nissa led her brother into the water and splashed in beside him. The water lapped to the middle of his thighs, while she was up to her waist.

The crowd pressed close, their chatter dimming. He turned to a group of old women in heavy mantles. "How long has he been like this?"

"Cedron's been blind since he was born," a woman with no teeth replied.

The blind man scooped water into his cupped hand, held it to the sun, and murmured indistinctly.

"What is he saying?"

"The words of repentance," she said. "*Wash away all my guilt; from my sin cleanse me.*"

Cedron splashed the water on his eyes and scooped another handful, still praying.

"*Wash me, make me whiter than snow,*" the old lady intoned.

Another splash, and another. The chattering crowd quieted. Even the children stopped their play to watch. *These Jews. Do they actually believe this will work?* He'd never seen a more gullible people.

The man Cedron straightened, his hands cupped over his eyes, his face raised to the sun directly overhead. Water lapped against the top step of the pool, and birds called in the distance. He angled to the north, toward the temple that could be seen rising above the dirty stones of the lower city. His eyelids fluttered, then opened.

Longinus held his breath, and his pulse quickened. *What's the matter with me? A blind man can't be cured with mud and water.*

Cedron's gaze didn't falter, but his eyes still stared into the distance as they had in the marketplace, as if he could see only something far away.

Longinus dismissed a twinge of disappointment. Of course a pretender from Galilee couldn't cure a blind man. He turned away; the spectacle was over. Now he could disperse this crowd and get back to his post.

The old woman bent toward the pool, her hand cupping her ear. "What did he say?"

Longinus twisted back to Cedron.

His gaze hadn't changed, but it had sharpened on the white edifice rising above the city. "The temple," he said. "I see the temple."

It can't be. Longinus stepped down into the water. It had to be a trick.

Cedron whirled to the woman beside him. He raised his hand to her face and ran it down her cheek and jaw. "Nissa?"

Her mouth dropped open. Something between a sob and a laugh broke from her.

Cedron threw his arms around his sister and lifted her, twirling her in a circle, splashing water in a shimmering arc around them. "Nissa, I can see you. I can see you!"

People crowded into the water, touching, questioning.

"Who healed you?"

"How do you know him?"

"Where is he now?"

The old woman began to sing. Some men chanted a prayer, while others danced on the side of the pool. Children laughed and joined in the celebration.

Longinus waded deeper into the water. How could this be? He'd seen the man himself less than two weeks ago. He pulled Cedron around to face him, waving his hand in front of his face. "What do you see?"

Cedron's eyes widened, and he stepped backward. "A Roman. And I know your voice. You're the one who almost killed my sister and me."

Longinus swallowed hard. The man could see. His deep-set eyes no longer stared into nothingness. They were alert, glaring straight into his own. Goosebumps rose on his arms and prickled the back of his neck. *No. It isn't possible.*

Who was this Jesus? Was he a god or a magician?

Cedron rounded on Nissa. "Is he here? The one who cured me?" He looked over the crowd.

Nissa's face was flushed, and her breath came fast, as though she'd been running. She shook her head, not taking her eyes from her brother. "No. He disappeared at the temple."

Cedron gripped her shoulders. "Take me to him, Nissa."

Nissa flinched. She rubbed her shoulder where Longinus knew a crescent-shaped wound still pained her. "He's gone."

Cedron ignored his sister and climbed out of the pool. "Come. Before the horns blow."

Nissa swayed and put out a hand as if to keep herself from falling. Longinus reached out and caught her elbow.

She gasped and trembled under his hand like a sapling in a thunderstorm.

Cedron pulled Nissa from Longinus's grip, up and out of the water. They squirmed through the crowd and ran down the stairs, Cedron's head swiveling from side to side.

Longinus followed, catching up to them as they reached the street.

Cedron jerked to a stop and stared at a wealthy woman in a silk mantle the color of a sunset. He reached out a hand to touch the filmy fabric, his eyes wide. She jerked away from him with a glare.

Longinus picked up Ferox's reins. *He's never seen colors. Never seen a woman.* He pulled himself up onto Ferox and spurred him behind Cedron and his sister. Cedron ran from one stall to another, fingering fruit, beads, clay pots. At a weaver's tent, he ran his hands over folded piles of wool dyed in greens, pinks, and reds.

The crowd followed behind, growing larger as they shouted news of the miracle. Longinus gripped the reins and sat up straight. If this mob found Jesus, they would declare him the Messiah or some other Jewish absurdity, and then he'd have a riot on his hands.

He urged Ferox closer to the petite, dirty woman who followed the rejoicing crowds. He needed to find Jesus before the crowd did. Nissa had seen the healer. She would find him again. *Then I can question the man myself.*

When they reached the Huldah Gates, Cedron raised his eyes to the towering Holy of Holies. Nissa stopped beside him, staring like she, too, had never seen it before.

Longinus slid from Ferox's back, landing close to her. "You there."

She jumped and cringed toward her brother. She was so tiny; the top of her head barely reached the center of his breastplate.

"Find the man Jesus, and bring him to me."

Cedron frowned. His eyes—those miraculous eyes—flickered over Longinus. "What does a Roman want with a Jewish healer?"

What indeed? He wanted an explanation. Longinus scowled. "He's a troublemaker. Now"—he looked down at Nissa—"find him and bring him to me."

"I'm not one of your soldiers," Nissa spat out. She snapped her mouth shut.

This woman, as dirty as she was, spoke her mind like the

queen of Egypt. He didn't know whether to be angry or impressed. He stepped closer, towering over her.

Cedron darted in front of Nissa and squared his shoulders as if to protect his sister from a blow. He glared at Longinus. "Leave her alone."

As if a scrawny Jew had a chance against him. He scowled at Nissa. "You can find him, or you and your brother will find yourselves on the wrong side of Rome."

Nissa swallowed, and her face blanched. She rubbed shaky hands down her dirty tunic. "Stay here, Cedron," she croaked.

Longinus watched her dart away and weave through the crowds, her head tipped up, searching the faces of the men she passed. She'd find this man—this Jesus of Nazareth—and he'd get an explanation. Then he'd return to his duties and forget about miracles and the blind man and his prickly sister.

Chapter 8

WHEN SHE WAS well away from the centurion, Nissa slumped against a marble column. Her heart pounded; her mind spun. Cedron could see. What had happened there at Siloam? She had been so sure it was a hoax, a fraud, so ready for another disappointment.

But it was no hoax. The man who had saved the adulterous woman from death had given her brother a new life. How could it be? Was he really the Messiah, like she'd heard the Zealots claim?

Now that centurion, Longinus, wanted her to find Jesus. A troublemaker, he'd said. What would he do to the miracle worker? Nothing good.

This Jesus—whether he was the Messiah or not—was a good man. No Jewish man she knew would challenge the Sanhedrin. And never for a woman's sake . . . a sinful woman. And he'd given Cedron a new life, washed him clean from whatever sin had made him blind and asked nothing in return. How could Nissa hand him over to the Romans? He might even be the savior they'd been waiting for.

But if she didn't do as the centurion said, he could arrest her. And if he found out what she carried in her belt—who she really was—he'd turn her over to the Sanhedrin, and they would get the stoning they had been denied.

No. She couldn't chance it. She must bring Jesus to the

Roman. Then Longinus would leave her and Cedron alone. They could go home, start a new life. Cedron could find work, and she could stop stealing. Perhaps even Mama and Abba could change now that their son was no longer blind. They would be a respectable family again, leave the stigma of the am-ha-arez behind them forever.

She pushed away from the column and moved down the center of the court, searching the crowd for Jesus or one of the other Galileans.

Near the Beautiful Gate, a voice shouted. "That's him!"

Another voice cried out. "He's the one the prophet healed."

A force of ten temple guards, dressed in ceremonial blue tunics and cone-shaped hats, marched through the crowd, pushing Cedron ahead of them. What did they want with Cedron?

Nissa rushed to her brother. "Where are you taking him?" A guard shoved her aside. She followed the wake of the guards to the Stone Court, a covered meeting place on the east end of the Court of the Gentiles.

The Sanhedrin waited on a raised platform inside the Stone Court. Priests wearing white tunics with wide linen belts stood with scribes, doctors of the law, and wealthy Pharisees. Caiaphas, the high priest, sat on an ornate chair in the center of the platform. A violet surplice covered his tunic, the lower half embroidered with pomegranates and tied with gold bells. Onyx shoulder pieces jutted from his neck, engraved with the names of the twelve tribes of Israel. The phylacteries hanging against his forehead and cheeks framed a hooked nose, a patch of gray beard, and narrow eyes.

Nissa's hands shook, and her heart pounded. Who could help him? Her family had no friends among the powerful Jews, no one to speak for them.

The march of hobnailed sandals echoed through the courtyard. An authoritative voice rang out with a distinctive Roman accent. "What is the meaning of this?"

The temple guards snapped to attention as the centurion

marched into the Stone Court, his armor glowing in the setting sun. The crimson plume of his helmet swayed like a red flag, and his sword glinted at his side. At least twenty legionaries followed in close formation. He stopped just half a step from the high priest.

Caiaphas gripped the arms of his chair, his knuckles white beneath heavy gold rings.

Nissa's racing pulse slowed. The Sanhedrin feared the centurion as much as she did. The Roman could order them all flogged, even executed, for no more reason than disrupting the peace.

"We are questioning him." Caiaphas cleared his throat. "It is not Rome's concern."

Longinus looked down his nose at the high priest. "Everything is Rome's concern." He took position next to Cedron, crossed his arms, and spread his feet wide.

Nissa caught her breath. Could this Roman protect Cedron from his own people? He had no reason to help her and her brother, especially not with the way Cedron was scowling at him, but she felt better nonetheless.

Caiaphas swallowed and turned his heavily weighted head to Cedron. "What is your name?"

"I am Cedron ben Noach."

"And are you the one they say used to sit and beg at the temple?"

"Yes."

A well-dressed Pharisee stepped forward. "He's not! He just looks like him."

Nissa stiffened at the insult. They were calling Cedron a liar, accusing him of being part of a hoax. She sneaked a glance at the centurion. His jaw tightened, and his bright blue eyes focused on the Pharisee. He knew it wasn't a lie, but the word of a pagan wouldn't help Cedron.

Cedron straightened his back. "I am he. I've been blind since birth, begging at the temple and the Dung Gate since I was a child." He motioned to one of the doctors of the law. "I've listened to you teach many days outside the temple. Surely you remember me."

The rabbi peered at him with milky eyes. "You might be the one."

Another Pharisee came forth. This one was younger than the rest, with a bright white prayer shawl and curling beard. "I am Nicodemus. Tell us. If you are the man, what happened to make you see?"

Cedron leaned toward Nicodemus. "A man called Jesus made clay and anointed my eyes and told me, 'Go to Siloam and wash.' So I went there and washed and was able to see."

Nissa inched forward. *Good, Cedron. Just tell them what happened. Then we can leave.*

Nicodemus stroked his beard. "Where is this man?"

Nissa glanced toward the centurion. His face was set like stone, but he was listening. Of that she was sure. Both he and the Sanhedrin wanted to find Jesus.

"I don't know."

Good. Now we can go.

Cedron raised his voice so all could hear. "But I shall find him and give him honor."

Nissa tensed. *No, Cedron. This would only lead to trouble.*

Caiaphas pushed himself to standing. "This man worked signs on the Sabbath. He is sinful."

Cedron shook his head. "How can a sinful man do such a miracle? He is a prophet."

Nissa cringed. *Please. Don't make them angry.*

The priests and holy men broke into groups of two and three. The one named Nicodemus argued with a Sadducee. Caiaphas tore at his beard. Longinus edged closer to Cedron, his hand resting on the hilt of his sword.

Finally, Caiaphas's voice rang out, quieting the clamor. "Bring forward the parents."

A knot of temple guards pushed through the crowd, Abba

and Mama at their core. Abba's eyes were red and bleary, his steps shuffling. He wore a robe of good quality, but old and threadbare. His white prayer shawl showed far less wear. Mama's hair stuck up around her face, and her skin was creased with sleep lines. Her clothes, too, showed the family had once been respectable, if not prosperous, but the hem of her tunic was ragged and her mantle was askew, barely covering her stringy gray hair. No bracelets, rings, or brooches adorned her arms or clothes.

"Am-ha-arez," whispered some in the crowd, drawing back.

"Mama? Abba?" Hope rose in Nissa. They could help Cedron. They could tell these men who he was, that he had been blind since he was born, that he shouldn't be on trial.

Abba came forward first. His eyes widened, and his mouth dropped open when he saw Cedron. "What? My son . . ." He stepped forward, but a guard pulled him back.

Mama lurched toward Cedron. "Is it true? You can see?"

Caiaphas stepped in front of them, two guards flanking his sides and blocking them from Cedron. He stared at them for a long moment. Abba shifted uncomfortably, and Mama seemed to shrink. "Are you not Noach, the woodcutter who supplies wood for the temple sacrifices?" Caiaphas looked to his scribe, who nodded.

"Yes," Abba said, his back straightening. "Years ago, I supplied wood for your fires."

"But no longer?"

One of the chief priests, a short round man, leaned toward Caiaphas and whispered in his ear. Caiaphas's full brows pulled down, and he turned to Abba. "They say you no longer make sacrifices at the temple; you ignore the law and don't pray the Shema. They say you are an am-ha-arez. "

Abba shook his head and bowed low before the priest. "No, my lord. I follow the laws of Moses. We observe the Sabbath and the feasts. I recite the Shema and—"

"Of course you do." Caiaphas stepped forward and smiled down on the old man. "Of course you do, Noach."

Nissa curled her hands into fists, her nails biting into her palms. How could Abba pretend they were pious Jews? They hadn't made a sacrifice for years, and the only prayer Abba said was for his dice to be lucky.

The high priest raised his voice and spread his hands toward the gathered holy men. "Unfair rumors, I have no doubt. You and your faithful wife"—he nodded to the old woman—"are God-fearing and law-abiding. You have been treated unfairly. I, myself, will see you are once again welcomed among the wood-cutters of the temple."

Abba bowed almost to the ground. Mama did the same. "Thank you, high priest. Thank you."

Caiaphas smiled like a snake about to strike.

Why were they treating Abba and Mama like friends and Cedron like a leper? Cedron was the one who said the Shema. He was the one who kept the commandments. Abba was the am-ha-arez, gambling away what he should be giving to the temple. Angry words formed on her tongue as she pushed forward.

Cedron caught her eye and shook his head.

Nissa clamped her jaw shut and ground her teeth together. He was right. They wouldn't listen to a woman.

"Now." Caiaphas swept his bejeweled hand toward Cedron. "Is this your son, who they say was born blind?"

Abba froze as if he'd been caught in a snare.

Nicodemus stepped forward. His voice was measured and gentle. "Just answer with the truth."

Abba nodded.

Caiaphas frowned and pushed Nicodemus back from the couple. "How is it then, Noach, woodcutter to the temple, that he can now see?"

Abba swallowed, his mouth worked like it was dry. "We know this is our son, and he was born blind." He glanced at his wife. "We do not know how he sees now, nor do we know who opened his eyes."

Nissa strained forward, pressing her lips together to hold in her angry words. Would her cowardly father throw Cedron to the snarling wolves of the Sanhedrin?

Caiaphas raised his brows as though waiting for more.

Abba wrung his hands and looked from Caiaphas to the gathering of priests, then to the temple guard. Finally, he spun toward his son. "Ask him," he burst out. "He is of age. He can speak for himself."

Caiaphas rounded on Cedron. "Give God the praise. Tell us the truth, ben Noach. We know the man Jesus is a sinner. He could not have healed you."

Nissa tried to catch Cedron's eye. *Please, Cedron. Give them what they want. Let the Galilean fight his own battles.*

But Cedron faced Caiaphas, his back straight, towering over the high priest. The centurion took a step closer to Cedron, as though ready to protect him.

Nissa held her breath. She'd seen this look on her brother's face before. He wouldn't back down now.

"There is one thing I know. I was blind. *Blind.*" He said the word like they didn't understand it. "I told you before, and you did not listen." He spoke to the high priest as though he were a slow-witted child. "He spit on the ground, made clay, and anointed my eyes with it. Why must you hear it again and again? Do you want to become his disciple, too?"

Caiaphas reared back and shook his head. "He made clay and healed on the Sabbath! I don't want to follow him. He breaks the laws of Moses."

Cedron pulled off his head covering and threw it on the ground. He pulled his hands through his hair. "Do you not understand what he did? He made a blind man see!" He pointed to his deep-set brown eyes. "How can you not see where he is from?" Cedron bent toward Caiaphas, his face a breath from the high priest's. "Look at me! It is unheard of for anyone to open the eyes of a person born blind. If this man were not from God, he would not be able to do this. Or are you blind as well?"

A shocked silence fell on the gathered crowd. Nissa's hand

covered her mouth as if she had been the one to speak so fool-ishly. *Cedron, no.*

But he wasn't finished. "We know that God does not listen to sinners, but he listens to those who are devout and do his will. I prayed for my sight, and he gave it to me."

Caiaphas stepped back, his face flushed red. "You are a liar and a blasphemer!" Spittle flew from his mouth. "You were born totally in sin, yet you are trying to teach us. You are not one of us. You—not your parents—are an am-ha-arez, and you are ban-ished from the temple!"

Whispers rippled through the crowd. They drew back from Cedron.

Nissa let out a breath like she'd been punched. Banished from the temple? That meant he could never come here to pray and make sacrifice. No Jew would hire Cedron now that he'd been barred from the temple, not even in the lower city.

A guard pushed Abba forward. His eyes darted from Cedron to the powerful men on the platform. "You are no longer wel-come in my house," he stammered. "You are no longer my son."

Anger blazed through Nissa like flames through a burnt of-fering. Of course Abba would betray his son for a few shekels from the temple treasury. And the notion that her parents would change now that Cedron could see, that they would be a family again? How could she have been so foolish? They were worse off than before. Had she really thought she had seen God's mercy? All he'd given her was a cruel hour of foolish hope.

Cedron turned his gaze on his father, for both the first time and the last. "So be it."

Caiaphas commanded the temple guards. "Throw him out."

The crowd erupted, advancing on Cedron with fists raised.

Longinus roared a command to his men. His legionaries marched forward, pushing the crowd back with Latin shouts and thumps of wooden shields against flesh. A few men stood against the soldiers; most turned and fled through the dust-choked court-yard.

Nissa lunged forward and grasped a fistful of her brother's tunic. She didn't let go as the temple guards closed ranks around Cedron and pulled them both out of the Stone Court and toward the Huldah Gates.

The last thing she heard was Caiaphas's voice shouting over the clamor. "Make sure he never comes back!"

Chapter 9

*T*HE MOCKERY OF a trial had turned into a riot. Longinus sprinted back to where Ferox waited by the columns.

"Throw him out!" Caiaphas bellowed.

Throw him out? These people looked like they were out for blood. Cedron's blood.

Longinus pulled himself into the saddle, shouting commands to his men. "No swords. Just move them out." His orders were to keep this crowd under control, not slaughter them.

His heart beat fast and hard. Bloodshed was the last thing they needed today, just as the legion was getting ready to march back to Caesarea. Pilate wouldn't thank him if this incident turned into an uprising.

He whirled Ferox around and pushed through the crowd, his vitis sweeping through the mob, straining to see the tall Jew and his little sister through the fray. His men followed his lead, pushing at the crowds with their shields. Within minutes, the Court of the Gentiles was under control. The dust settled; the temple guard retreated into the inner courts. His men took up their posts again, their swords, shields, and long spears at the ready but unbloodied.

Longinus pulled Ferox to a stop and drew a long breath. That had been close. Pilate would hear about it, and he wouldn't be pleased. Longinus would do well to report the incident himself before Silvanus's spies did it for him.

The evening horns sounded; it would be dark soon. Where were Cedron and Nissa, and what did it mean that Caiaphas had called him an am-ha-arez? He spurred Ferox through the western gate and around the outside wall of the temple.

What was it about these accursed Jews? A man cured of blindness, and they could do nothing but question and argue. Then, to throw Cedron out of the temple and welcome those cowardly parents like they were honored guests . . .

His hands tightened on the reins. He'd seen much in his fifteen years of service to Caesar—men full of life cut down in battle, friends dying of disease and festering wounds. But he'd never seen a prayer answered by any of the gods—Roman, Greek, or otherwise. And here, in this backward corner of the empire where you couldn't find a decent bathhouse, comes a man who can cure the blind. And those dim-witted Pharisees refused to believe it.

Why do I care? The last thing I need is to get involved with these crazy people. But he had seen a miracle, of that he was sure. And now the man born blind might be in danger. Longinus flicked the reins. *I'll just make sure they're safe.* Then he could get back to his duty and finding the thieves.

As Ferox rounded the corner of the temple, Longinus sighted a cluster of men below the Huldah Gates—temple guards brandishing heavy sticks. One of the priests, short and round with a bright red face, urged them on. And there, darting around the outer edge of the mob, was Nissa. She rained blows on the backs of men twice her size. She pulled at their arms and scratched at their faces. They swatted her away like a mosquito.

Was this what the Sanhedrin called justice? *Not on my watch.* He dug his heals into Ferox's sides. He reached the bottom of the stairs, slid off Ferox, and ran toward the mob, drawing his sword. "Break it up! Out of my way!" He hit the nearest man with the flat side of his blade. The man backed off, but the rest of the mob closed in on the empty space.

Nissa appeared at his side. "Stop them. Please," she choked out.

The short priest stepped in front of him. "This man was breaking our laws, not the laws of Caesar. We'll punish him as we see fit."

The priest was right. Unless it was a crime against Caesar, or an execution, the Jews were free to practice their own form of justice. Longinus didn't have any authority here.

A groan of pain and the slap of flesh hitting stone sounded from within the knot of men.

Nissa screamed her brother's name.

Curse what these fools call justice. Longinus raised his sword, holding the point just at the priest's bulbous nose, and stared into the other man's eyes. He'd killed many men, just like this, but he doubted this priest had ever faced the sharp end of a sword. "Call off your men. Now."

The priest swallowed hard and retreated. "That's enough!" He pulled men away and pushed them apart.

Longinus shoved through to the unmoving man curled on the stones.

"Cedron!" Nissa threw herself down beside him.

Longinus pointed his sword on the pack of men. "If I hear of any harm coming to this man, you'll answer to me, not to Caesar."

The priest scowled and muttered to his men. They backed away and disappeared into the murky streets.

Nissa knelt beside her brother, cradling his head in her hands. She bent close to his mouth to feel his breathing. Her breath hitched, but she didn't cry.

Thank the gods. I don't need a weeping woman on my hands.

"How bad?" He crouched beside the beaten man. Cedron's eye was already swelled shut, his lip split and bleeding. Longinus ran his hand down Cedron's arms and across his ribs, checking for broken bones.

Cedron coughed and winced when Longinus's firm touch reached his knee. It was swollen and twisted outward. He probed it again.

Cedron groaned. "We don't need your help, Roman," he ground out through clenched teeth.

Longinus ignored him. "That knee is bad. The rest will heal."

Nissa's hand, soft and trembling, rested on his bare arm, where muscle bunched below his armor and above his elbow greaves. "Thank you," she whispered.

A jolt of surprise shot through him. If she hadn't been so close, he'd never have believed that a kind word had passed her lips. Pretty lips, too—full and shapely, if a little ragged. Her eyes were fringed by thick black lashes that cast shadows on her dirty cheeks as she dipped her head toward Cedron.

Under all that dirt, she wasn't half bad to look at. Not pretty in the way of the lush Jewish women he'd admired in the market, with their wide-set dark eyes, ample breasts, and generously curved hips. No, this girl was more like a half-bloomed lily, with hardly a curve to show that she was a woman instead of a scrawny boy. Her face—even under all that dirt—was delicate, with high, sharp cheekbones and a firm, pointed chin. Her full lips trembled as she bent over her brother.

Stop looking at her. She's trouble, and so is her irritable brother.

Longinus leaned back on his heels. "What does 'am-ha-arez' mean?"

She caught her lip between her teeth.

"Tell me."

Nissa smoothed her hand over Cedron's brow. "It means one of the Chosen People who doesn't know the law. Who does not say the Shema morning and evening. Mostly—to the priests—one who does not tithe." Her mouth twisted. "But Cedron does all those things. It is our parents who ignore the law."

Their parents . . . who had disowned their son. "And what does it mean to be called that? What will happen to your brother?"

She blinked several times, and her voice shook. "It means he's unclean. He can't go into the temple. No Jews will hire him."

"No better than a Gentile, then?"

She chewed on her lip. "Worse."

He needed to go now. Back to his men and his post. It was time to let these two unfortunates fend for themselves. But how would this girl get her brother anywhere? By the swelling in his knee, Longinus guessed Cedron wasn't going to be walking on his own for days, maybe weeks. He stood and sheathed his sword. *Not my problem.*

Cedron groaned again and began to cough.

Longinus pulled off his helmet and ran a hand through his hair. He couldn't leave them on the street. *By Jupiter, what am I doing?*

He pulled Cedron up to sitting. "Get my horse."

"Me?" Nissa jerked and looked at the big animal calmly waiting at the bottom of the stairs.

"He won't bite you." Ferox was as meek as a calf until he was in battle. "Just lead him over here. To the bottom step."

"No. Just leave us. Cedron wouldn't want me to—"

"What are you going to do?" he almost shouted. By the gods, she was stubborn. "You can't get him home. He can't even walk. Will you carry him on your own back?"

"I'm stronger than I look."

Cedron groaned.

"Listen. He's hurt."

"But—"

"Don't be an idiot. It won't do your brother any good." Longinus stared at her like she was a new recruit refusing orders. "Get the horse. Now."

The girl clamped her mouth shut and stomped to Ferox.

Longinus slid his hand under Cedron's shoulders and lifted. The clop of Ferox's hooves sounded against the stones. As skinny as Cedron looked, he was still a full-grown man and heavy. "Closer. To the steps," he grunted.

Nissa's mouth pinched, but she moved Ferox closer and Longinus hoisted the barely conscious man onto the horse's back.

Cedron slumped forward.

Longinus steadied him with a hand. He spoke over his shoulder to Nissa. "Up you go. You'll need to hold him up. It's a long fall, and he's had enough bruises for today."

Her eyes widened and lips parted. He'd seen that look enough on new recruits. She was afraid. Of course she was. For all her bluster, she was still just a woman. "Come on; it's easy." He patted one of the four corners of the saddle that rose up like horns and made a square seat.

She stretched on tiptoe but was too short to even reach a pommel.

"Put your foot here." He made a cup with one hand.

Nissa looked at him with a frown between her brows, lifted her bare foot, and put it into his hand. It was tiny, hardly bigger than a child's and twice as dirty. He put his other hand on her waist to steady her. "Now, up."

She scrambled and pulled her way into the saddle behind Cedron. Her tunic hiked up past her knees to reveal delicate ankles and firm brown calves. She let out a deep breath and wrapped her arms around her brother.

Longinus admired her courage—as well as bits of the rest of her. He dropped his gaze and gathered Ferox's reins. *No more women. And absolutely no Jewish women.* By spring, he'd be leaving Judea and its women behind.

Now, to get rid of these two before anyone saw him. "Do you have any other family here? An uncle? Cousins?"

Nissa shook her head. "No. No one."

Longinus pulled Ferox into a walk. Men, women, and children stopped and gaped as they left the steps and entered the busy street. Longinus, with his shining breastplate and plumed helmet, and Ferox, carrying the dirty, blood-streaked man and the tiny woman.

He knew no one but legionaries in Jerusalem. "You need to

stay out of sight in case those priests of yours send more men. What about an inn? There's one near the barracks that—"

"No."

This was ridiculous. There had to be somewhere he could get rid of them. "You can't sleep in the street."

Her mouth twisted into a scowl. "Didn't you hear, centurion? We're am-ha-arez. The lowest of the low, save one."

"And who's lower than the am-ha-arez?"

She raised her brows and looked down her nose at him. "A friend of the Romans."

Anger rose in him. As if he wouldn't be laughed out of the barracks if Cornelius saw him with two Jews on his horse? "That knife cuts both ways, woman."

She turned her head away. He'd get no apology from this little brat. So be it. He'd get them to the lower city and be done with them. *They can starve to death for all I care.*

He led Ferox down the Stepped Street, Nissa holding tightly to her brother as they jostled and jerked. The stench of animal and human refuse increased as they descended into the narrow streets between crowded, crumbling houses. At the sight of them, women and children scurried into their courtyards and banged gates behind them. By the time they reached the lower city, Cedron's face had blanched even whiter, and his eyes fluttered closed.

Nissa's arms tightened around her brother. "Turn there." She nodded to a narrow side street just before the marketplace. Nissa glanced around like she hoped no one noticed a Roman and a huge horse in the tiny space. When they reached a path no bigger than a crack between buildings, Nissa bent toward him. "Here. Stop here."

What was this place? There was nothing in the alley but a pile of broken pots and some boards. *I don't care. It's not my duty to take care of every homeless Jew.* Especially an unpleasant little thing like Nissa and her ungrateful brother, even if he did admire her courage.

He helped Cedron slide down and gingerly set him on one

leg, trying not to notice how Cedron was bony and thin where he had thick muscles and a well-fed middle.

Nissa took her brother's arm and put it over her shoulders. Surely she couldn't take him far. She was like a baby bird trying to carry a full-grown rabbit.

She looked up at him. "I'm grateful for your help."

He bristled at her tone. She didn't sound grateful. She sounded like she was dismissing a servant.

Without another word, Longinus jumped on his horse where the saddle was still warm from their bodies. He was done with them, this man who was born blind and his obstinate sister.

I have better things to do than help a couple of ungrateful Jews. His duty was back at the garrison. Keeping the pax romana and finding the thieves so he could get out of this infernal city with its ridiculous people. He turned Ferox back toward the main road, kicked him into a fast walk, and didn't look back.

Chapter 10

NISSA TUCKED HER thin cloak around Cedron. The cramped pigeon coop, smelling of bird droppings and stale straw, offered meager protection from the bite of the morning breeze. Her back ached from sleeping propped against the damp wall, and her empty belly and dry throat begged for food and water.

She'd waited until the last sound of the centurion's horse had faded before she half carried, half hopped Cedron to the door of the little shed where she'd changed so often from Nissa to Mouse. It was the only place she could think of. They were on their own. She stayed there through the long, cold night, hoping the temple guards didn't come looking for them.

Now, as the morning light seeped through the cracks in the walls and the holes in the reed roof, she knelt beside Cedron and examined his injuries. His wrenched knee was swollen to twice its normal size, turning an ugly purple. She probed his other injuries—a knot on his head, bruises and scrapes. He groaned and pulled away. He needed a place to heal, and they both needed food and water.

Yesterday, her brother had been given his sight; the promise of a new life had been in their grasp. Now . . . now they were worse off than ever.

She'd hoped, for an absurd moment, that she could give up her life as Mouse. *Go and sin no more*, Jesus had said to the woman who was guilty of adultery. And Nissa had wanted to say good-bye to Mouse forever.

You don't have a choice, the voice thrummed, stronger than ever.

The silver horns rang out across the city, announcing the call to morning prayer. Nissa wrapped her arms around her cold body. How she had loved the call to prayer when she was a child. The chanting of the Shema had soothed her. She would sit for hours, listening to Cedron recite the songs of the Tehillim, and feel the arms of the Lord embrace her. *Give thanks to the Lord of lords, for he is good. His mercy endures forever.*

Nissa lurched to her feet. That was before she'd found out the truth. She had called on the Lord to protect her, but he had forsaken her. Perhaps a plain, sharp-tongued girl wasn't worthy of his mercy. Even what looked like a blessing had turned into a curse.

Yes, only Mouse could take care of them now. The Almighty—and his priests—had left her with no other option.

She bent almost double to go through the tiny opening and out into the alleyway. She'd find a better place, and soon. But first, food. She put her hand over the warm coins in her belt. There was plenty for today and more where that came from.

NISSA SLIPPED INTO the tiny alley, balancing food and a basket of other treasures in her arms. Cedron would be awake by now and hungry. Voices drifting from the opening of the pigeon roost jerked her to a stop. She leaned down to catch the low murmurs.

". . . believe in the Son of Man?" The voice was familiar. Who had found them in the little hole in the lower city?

"Who is he, that I may believe?" Cedron answered.

"You have seen him, and the one speaking with you is he."

Nissa caught her breath and staggered back against the wall. He was here. Dismas had been right; the man could read souls.

He knew everything, even where they were hiding. Why was he here? Hadn't he caused enough trouble for them? She stepped farther away from the opening. She couldn't go in there. He would know about her—about everything.

There was a shuffle, like Cedron had moved, and a low, pained grunt. "I do believe, Lord." Silence stretched for a long moment.

Nissa's heart thrashed in her chest like a caged bird. What would Jesus do now?

"I came into this world for judgment, so that those who do not see might see, and those who do see might become blind."

Jesus made Cedron see, but who would he make blind? Sinners like her? Thieves? She clutched her purchases close to her chest and scooted out of the alley. She couldn't let him see her. She waited, her breath heaving in her chest. Moments later, he appeared, striding toward the lower market. He passed within arm's reach but took no notice of her, as though she were nothing more than a worthless sparrow. She waited until her heart had slowed and her breathing leveled before ducking into the roost.

Cedron hunched on the damp floor, his mouth moving in prayer. "He was here, Nissa. The one who cured me." He pushed himself up with a grimace. "He is the Messiah!"

Nissa nodded as she spread out a feast of fresh figs, honey cakes, and dried locusts. He might be the Messiah, or he might be trouble. Either way, she didn't want to see him again. She helped Cedron to sit, moving his damaged knee carefully. "You need food and water."

"He cured me for a reason, Nissa. He has a plan for me." Cedron's face glowed like the moon on a clear night.

"Did he tell you that? What is it?" She pulled a new cloak from her basket and wrapped it around Cedron's shoulders. *So far Jesus' plans have caused us nothing but trouble.*

"I don't know." He reached for the water jar. "But I will pray that the Lord reveals it to me." He drank deeply, then looked at the jar in his hands, the basket of food, his new cloak. "Where did you . . . How did you buy these things?"

She knew she'd need an explanation, and she had one ready. At least he'd stopped talking about Jesus. She put a fig in her mouth, hoping to disguise the tremor in her voice. "I didn't get to tell you yesterday. I found work in the upper city."

Cedron turned toward her and winced. "Doing what?"

"At the laundry, near the barracks. The owner is a Roman who travels with the legion. He'll give me as much work as I want." She struggled to swallow the fig in her dry mouth. Would he believe her?

"Washing soldiers' linens?" He scowled.

Of course he would disapprove of her working for Romans, but that's what would keep her secret. Cedron would never visit the pagan baths and laundries that surrounded the barracks.

"It's better than starving." That, at least, wasn't a lie.

Cedron sank down onto the dirty straw. "Just until I get work. Then you can stop. We will put our trust in the Lord."

Nissa nodded, but Cedron was wrong. She couldn't afford to trust in the Lord any more than she could trust in the so-called messiah. Nissa would take care of them from now on. Nissa and Mouse.

BY AFTERNOON, NISSA had found Gilad in the lower market. He lounged against the sun-dappled wall and fingered the silver drachmas she had pulled from her belt. "Greek silver. Where did you get it?"

Nissa scooped them out of his hand. "If you don't want them—"

"No, no." Gilad threw up his hands. "Don't get so prickly, little Nissa. Like the nettles under my sandal strap."

She tucked the coins in her belt. Her fingers tingled where they had come into contact with his. *Forget about him.* Gilad would marry one of the pretty girls who stared at him in the marketplace like he was King David. But that hadn't stopped her from washing in Siloam before she'd come to find him.

Gilad ran a hand over his bearded chin. "I have just the house for you and your brother. You will thank me a thousand times."

Nissa followed him through the lower market and past Siloam, then turned west toward the tanners' district. Vats of urine and dung lined the road, ready to soften leather and whiten the garments of the rich. Her eyes watered, and her throat closed at the stench.

They passed crumbling buildings and alleys full of refuse. Through an open doorway, empty wine jugs and sleeping bodies littered the courtyard of a tavern. Dirty men lounged in the doorway of a building covered with obscene paintings. Cedron would never agree to living near a brothel. She drew closer to Gilad. "We can't live here."

Gilad quickened his pace. "Wait. It gets better."

The houses got smaller and the road narrower. He might make her heart race, but she wasn't going to let Gilad cheat her into renting in this cesspool. "Where is it? Gilad, if you are leading me on a fool's chase, I'll—"

"Just here." Gilad stopped at a high-walled courtyard. "Smell."

She took a careful breath. Yes. The wind from the north brought the scent of roses and incense from the perfumers' district, where costly nards and oils were made for the women of the upper city. It was better than the smell of tanneries, but what was the house like?

Gilad opened a crooked gate hanging on one cracked leather hinge. "You can fix that easily."

She followed him into a tiny courtyard.

It wasn't much, just a square of dirt with a cooking fire in the center. On one side of the courtyard sat a squat house with a flat, reed-thatched roof. A rickety ladder leaned against the wall.

She ducked her head through the low doorway. The single room inside smelled musty, but it was dry and reasonably clean. Fresh straw was strewn on the floor. She walked around the house. There were no chinks between the plaster and the rough-hewn stones. No signs of mildew on the walls. A lean-to with a manger was tacked onto the far side. She could see them living here. She and Cedron and Amit, perhaps a few goats. Hope rose in her, but she set her face in a frown.

She returned to Gilad. "There's no place for a garden."

"This is the city! If you want a garden, go to Bethany."

"It's farther from Siloam."

"You're young and strong."

"But I'll have to walk through that," she waved toward the foul neighborhood they'd passed through.

"For five drachmas, I'll give you one month."

Nissa bit her lip. That was a ridiculous price, and they both knew it. Not many people were willing to live in this section of the city, even with the sweet air. Despite the walled courtyard, they would hear the debauchery of the taverns and brothels late into the night. "Four months."

"Robbery!"

She flashed the coins at him. "And I want Amit back. Today."

"Two months is all I can do. And you can have your scrawny donkey."

She worried her lip again. "Give us until after the Feast of Lights." Surely Cedron would be healed and find some sort of work in two and a half months. Mouse would take care of them until then.

Gilad's handsome brow furrowed.

"This isn't the only falling-down house in the city." She brushed by him and strolled toward the broken gate.

Gilad threw up his hands. "Fine. Just until the Feast of Lights. Then two drachmas a month—on time."

Nissa dropped the coins in his hands.

"You are a thief, little Nissa." Gilad smiled and pocketed the silver.

Her heart skittered, but not because of Gilad's handsome face. *I am a thief, and a good one.* The drachmas were the last of her silver, and they needed much for their new home: wood and oil, lamps and blankets. But there was more where that came from.

This morning, she'd made the mark on the wall next to Siloam. When the horns blew, Mouse would go to work.

Part Two

The Feast of Lights

Chapter 11

N ISSA WAITED FOR Dismas in the usual place, anticipation
buzzing through her limbs.

The Feast of Lights was almost over. Any day now, Gilad
would be back for more rent, and she would be ready for him.
She and Dismas stole just enough to get by—once or twice a
week and never in the same place. Most of the Romans had left
the city after Tabernacles, more than two months ago. She
hadn't seen the bully of a centurion since he'd left them in the
lower city after Cedron's beating. *Good riddance.*

Her hope that Cedron would find work had dwindled as
the weeks went by. His wounds had healed, but his knee still
pained him. As soon as he'd been able to walk, he'd brought
Amit outside the city gates to gather wood. When he hadn't
returned by nightfall, Nissa had gone in search and found him
collapsed at the foot of the Mount of Olives, Amit braying
sadly beside him.

"I just need a few more weeks," he'd said as she helped him
on Amit and led them back home. But she knew better. With his
injured knee, he'd never have the strength to load and carry
wood over the rough terrain outside the city walls.

Now, he left every morning hoping to be hired by a Jew who
didn't know of his disgrace at the temple or a Gentile who didn't
care that he was slow and weak. Most days, he returned discour-
aged and empty-handed, with only the outlandish stories he'd

heard about the Messiah and the coming overthrow of the Romans.

"I hate it that you are working for those Romans dogs," Cedron told Nissa as he ate the bread she set before him each evening.

He'd hate it more if he knew she was stealing from the priests and Levites of the temple.

"If I'd been taught a skill . . ." he went on with a frown. But Abba hadn't thought a blind son worthy of an apprenticeship. Cedron sighed and covered his eyes with his hand.

"Don't worry, Cedron." Nissa leaned her cheek on her brother's shoulder. "You'll find something." And until he did, she would take care of them.

The scent of peppermint and cloves drifted over her as Dismas emerged from the shadows. "Where to today, Mouse?"

Her heart sped, and her fingers itched. "Not the market." They'd been there last week. "To the temple." The Pharisees and priests got rich from taxes and temple sacrifice; they could afford a tithe to her and her brother.

She slipped around Dismas and headed toward the towering edifice across the city. A thrill of excitement shivered up her back. At least one Pharisee would go home with a lighter purse because of her.

They hurried down the streets, passing the marble houses and the fragrant courtyards of the very men they would be stealing from. She rounded the corner, and her heart jumped into her throat. A line of Roman soldiers blocked their path. Men shouted and threw clods of dirt at an ebony-skinned man dragging a heavy wooden beam through the street. Blood dripped from his face and arms, and his legs were scored with wounds.

"Get along!" a centurion shouted and brought a stick down hard on the man's back.

She stumbled backward and pressed close against the wall.

Dismas peered around the corner. He fell back beside her, his face pale. "*Feu*, not Ammon."

"Who is it?"

Dismas shuddered. "A man I know—knew. We used to work together."

Work together? Like she and Dismas worked together? A tremble of fear weakened her knees. "But they don't crucify thieves."

"They do if they're caught stealing with a knife, or at night."

"What do you mean?" Nissa pulled at his sleeve.

Dismas's brows jerked together. "For a Jew your age, you don't know much of your own laws." Dismas tugged at the neck of his tunic like he couldn't breathe. "Listen, Mouse. Don't carry a knife when you steal. Not ever. Not even a little one."

"But I don't."

"And only steal in the daylight, right? Like we do. That way, if you get caught, the worst they can do is a scourging." His mouth twisted as though he felt the lash of the whip. "It's bad enough, believe me. But if you have a knife on you—like that idiot always carried, even though I told him not to? Or you are stealing at night?" He jerked his head toward the soldiers. "Death. And the Romans know how to make a man suffer."

A cold shiver passed over Nissa as Dismas hurried in the opposite direction. She had to run to keep up with him. She'd never seen him look like that—shaken, terrified.

Dismas stopped abruptly and grabbed her by the shoulders. "It is a bad omen, Mouse. Very bad. Let's forget this. I never should have gotten you started stealing with me. Go home. Work in the fields, in the mines, anything. If you ended up like Ammon or . . ." He swallowed hard.

Nissa looked into his worried eyes. "Or what?"

He shook his head.

"Tell me." What was it that made Dismas quake like an old woman?

He dropped his gaze to the ground. "Mouse, I've been a thief all my life, but I wasn't always old." His hands on her shoulders gentled. "I had a family in Tyre. A beautiful wife and a daughter. So long ago, it was like another lifetime."

Dismas with a family? Dread thickened her throat.

"I wanted to give them everything. Beautiful things—jewels and gold and clothes." He closed his eyes, and pain crossed his face. "My wife begged me to stop stealing, but I didn't listen."

Nissa swallowed hard. "What happened?" But she didn't want to know.

Dismas slumped against the wall. "I got greedy. I thought . . . I thought I was invincible. I stole from a man, a ruthless man. He didn't catch me, but he found out who I was. When I got home . . ." His voice cracked. "My wife and daughter were dead. Beaten, their throats cut . . . their hands severed from their bodies."

Nissa clenched her hands behind her back. That's why he was so careful.

"I left Tyre and never went back." He ran his palm over his face, looking older than ever.

Another of Dismas's rules chimed in her head. *Don't get greedy.* And now she knew why. Dismas, who loved women, had lost the two he loved the most. "But you're still stealing?"

He grimaced. "Mouse, I have nothing more to lose." He pushed away from the wall. "But you do. Go home; do something else. Anything but this."

She should listen to Dismas. *You've tried everything*, the voice whispered. *You can't do anything else.*

Dismas fumbled through his pockets and came out with a silver drachma. "Here, this will help for a while. Until you—"

She pushed his hand away. A drachma wouldn't last long. Not with the rent due and Cedron no closer to finding work that he could do with no skill and little strength.

No. She had to steal, and she needed Dismas to do it. She wouldn't get caught, and neither would he. They'd be careful.

Nissa shook her head. "Don't worry. Look—" She showed him her empty hands. "No knife. And it's still daylight."

He looked uncertain.

She tried again. "What about those women you talk about? Will they still love you when you come to them empty-handed?" It was unfair, but she knew it would work. Women were his weakness. She pushed the picture of his wife and daughter from her mind. That was a long time ago. He couldn't help them now, but he could help her.

Nissa veered past him and continued toward the temple. When she glanced over her shoulder, he was following her, but he started at every sound and stayed close to the walls.

By the time they reached the Royal Stoa, Dismas still looked grim but led her to the money changers working at their tables. A Pharisee, his tassels long and full, argued with one of the money changers. His purse was open in his hand.

Nissa nodded to Dismas. He sidled alongside the two men, pulled a handful of lepta from his pocket, and bumped into the table. The chime of copper hitting the stone floor turned the head of the Pharisee and the money changer.

Nissa darted forward. As the Pharisee bent to retrieve the worthless lepta and the money changer leaned over to watch Dismas, she dipped a sure, quick hand into the open purse.

As she melted back into the crowd, her gaze fell on a sight that made her fingers tingle. The rotund little priest—the one named Thaddeus who had set the guards on Cedron—entered the Court of the Gentiles, surrounded by a dozen or more pious Jews. His hands, clasped in front of his belly, sparkled with gold and gems.

How she'd love to lighten his fingers.

Guilt fluttered within her. These were God's chosen servants, weren't they? To steal from them would be like stealing from the Almighty.

Remember what they did to Cedron, the grim voice reminded her.

Yes. Their harsh words, the way they had turned her weak parents against them, the men attacking Cedron and beating him. These priests and Pharisees were the guilty ones.

She caught Dismas's eye and nodded toward the jewels.

Dismas moved in behind her. "No, Mouse. Too dangerous."

She swallowed a protest. Dismas was right to be careful. This time. *I'll get a chance, and when I do, I'll get revenge for Cedron.*

By the time the last trumpets rang out into the dusky sky, Nissa and Dismas were divvying up their spoils in a doorway behind the Hippodrome. His worried expression was replaced with a satisfied smile. "You did well, Mouse. You might be the best pickpocket in the city."

Her chest swelled with pride. Abba had been wrong. She was good at something. Even after giving Dismas his cut, she had plenty for a month of rent and more. Gilad would be pleased.

Dismas tucked his own coins in his belt. "How about we go have a jug of wine? I know a place by the north wall. Good wine. Better women. We'll go to the bathhouse on the way so you can wash some dirt off. You proved yourself a man tonight, might as well celebrate with a woman."

The thought of a pagan bathhouse—with Dismas—made her face burn under the dirt and ash. She shook her head. "Not this time."

Dismas's face creased in disappointment. "All right, Mouse. Scurry on home." His yellowed teeth flashed again as he punched her shoulder. "If you change your mind, take my advice. Women like men who smell good."

He disappeared into the gathering gloom.

Nissa hurried toward the lower city. Dismas might bury his memories with wine and women, but she wanted only to wash in the clean waters of Siloam. Tonight, the waters of Siloam would cleanse her, and tomorrow, she'd give alms to the beggars at the temple. Surely that would make up for her sin and lighten the guilt that pressed heavily on her shoulders.

LONGINUS SCANNED THE camp, shading his eyes from the late-afternoon sun. Twenty legionaries worked in the practice yard, sparring halfheartedly with wooden swords. The rest of his century seemed to be lounging outside their tents or playing dice. The stables reeked, and the cooking tent looked like it had been ransacked by a horde of angry Picts.

He scowled at Cornelius. "Keeping the men busy, I see."

Cornelius smirked. "You were gone longer than three weeks."

Longinus cursed under his breath. He could almost hear Silvanus's triumphant laugh all the way from Caesarea. He'd underestimated the wily jackal. No sooner had the legion left Jerusalem than Longinus had been assigned to escort a caravan of supplies to Damascus. He'd had to leave Cornelius in command just when he was beginning to make some progress finding the thieves.

The assignment that should have taken three weeks had kept him at the edge of the empire for almost two months thanks to dust storms, incompetent officials, and unrest among the nomadic chieftains of the desert. Now he was months behind in finding the thieves, and the camp was a disgrace. Leaving Cornelius in command of both centuries was like leaving a drunk in charge of a wineshop.

"Any word of the two thieves—the Mouse and the Greek—while I was gone?"

Cornelius shrugged. "Crucified a thief today."

"Greek?"

"Nah. Egyptian. Got caught a week ago sneaking into one of the houses in the upper city. He pulled a knife. Pilate sent authorization from Caesarea."

At least Cornelius was doing something. Longinus started down the Via Praetoria. Might as well see how bad the rest of the camp looked. "What about the Jew from Nazareth? Is he in the city?"

"No one's seen him, but there have been plenty of stories." Cornelius fell into step beside Longinus.

"What kind of stories?"

Cornelius snorted. "These Jews will believe anything. Curing lepers, feeding five thousand men with a loaf of bread. You know how they are."

Yes, he did know how these Jews were. Rumors of Jesus had blown through the province like dust devils, even all the way to Damascus. Two months ago, Longinus would have scoffed, but he'd seen the blind man healed at Siloam. There was no denying that Jesus had some kind of power.

Cornelius passed by a jumble of empty wine amphorae like he couldn't see them. "Some of the priests say he's in hiding; others say he's in Bethany. Who cares? As long as he's not here."

This wasn't the news Longinus wanted to hear. He had questions for the enigmatic Nazarene. Still, Passover was months away. He might yet see him. "What else? Any trouble brewing in the city?"

"Just the usual—wells are low, crops in danger, they can't pay their taxes. They complain about everything."

They reached the Praetorian gate at the edge of camp. Longinus stared out into the upper market full of people buying and selling. The wet season should have started weeks ago, but no rain had fallen on Jerusalem. Grass was brown on the hillsides, and crops withered in the fields. Drought wouldn't help keep the peace. Hungry people, overtaxed and worried about their harvest, were more likely to rise up against their oppressors. And revolution was exactly what he didn't need.

"You've had a long trip." Cornelius jerked his head toward the city. "How about heading to the lower city brothels with me for a little entertainment?"

Longinus clamped his teeth together. The city on the edge of revolt, and the legionaries were visiting brothels? Cornelius might be Silvanus's favorite, but Longinus still outranked him and it was time he remembered it. "You've had enough entertainment while I've been gone, Cornelius. Guard duty tonight. And tomorrow, be ready at dawn."

"Dawn?" Cornelius sounded like a spoiled child.

This sorry excuse for a centurion wasn't just indolent and

soft; he was pathetic. "Yes. Dawn. A thirty-mile march, full kit. Tell the men."

Cornelius scowled and marched back to the barracks, grumbling under his breath.

The trumpets blew, signaling the end of the day. Longinus needed to think, and he couldn't do it in this pigsty of a camp. He strode through the gate and out into the city. How would he find the thieves now that the trail was cold? He could start asking questions again, but with his Roman clothes and foreign face, he wouldn't get far. These Jews would curse their own mothers before they'd help him.

Longinus kept one hand on his knife as he loped down the streets toward the lower market. Night crept into the city. First backstreets and alleys turned murky; then the haze of twilight stole down the Stepped Street and over the squares and courtyards.

His heartbeat quickened. He wasn't afraid, just cautious. Jerusalem in the night wasn't any safer than other cities he'd been in—Alexandria, Tiberias, even Caesarea had turned out to be deadly. Death could strike when you least expected it; he'd learned that from Scipio.

A dry wind swept through the city, bringing the scent of cooking fires and burning lamp oil. Every tall Greek and roughly dressed man who might be from Galilee caught his eye. He saw the small thief in every half-grown boy. He passed by rickety houses and rowdy taverns full of men. As he approached Siloam, his thoughts returned to the miracle. What had happened to the blind man and his sister? Did they live in the lower city where he'd left them? He wouldn't mind seeing Cedron's little scrap of a sister. She might be rude and stubborn, but she had the courage of a lion.

It had been nearly a year since he'd felt the soft touch of a woman. Where a Roman legion went, a battalion of women followed—wives, mistresses, prostitutes—hard to tell them apart sometimes. They were part of a soldier's life, and a welcome one.

But in the months since Scipio died, he'd had no stomach for carousing with the legionaries. Still, he missed the feel of a woman's soft hair and smooth skin, the sound of her sweet voice.

Nissa's voice was more like a crow than a dove, and her skin was covered with dirt. Not to mention he was a Roman and she, a Jew. A difficult, prickly Jew. A smile twitched at his lips. He didn't envy the Jew who took Nissa as a wife. She wouldn't be docile, but neither would she be dull.

Longinus reached the steps to the Pool of Siloam. It would be deserted by now. Women were at home, serving the evening meal to their men. The water would feel good on his aching feet. He climbed the stairs leading to the wide, flat esplanade that stretched into the darkness. The sounds of the street faded. The inky black water reflected a sprinkling of stars and the thin crescent moon.

He stepped down into the cool water. A welcome chill rushed through him, but a splash across the pool made him tense and step back onto dry stone. He wasn't alone. His hand went to his sword. A willowy form rose from the water at the other end of the pool, hardly visible in the black night except for a clinging white tunic.

A ghost rising from the water? Or a water sprite? The figure turned, and in the wan light of the moon, he discerned slight curves. Just a woman. But what was a woman doing out by herself at night?

Her hand rubbed her shoulder as if to massage away an ache.

Recognition sparked through him. It was Nissa. *So she does bathe. What is she trying to do, get herself killed?*

She bent to scoop up a bundle of clothes. He retreated toward the staircase, careful that his sandals made no sound. He tiptoed down the steps to the street and scooted around the corner of the wall, out of sight.

What if another man had seen her coming out of the water like that? Yes, women bathed in Siloam. But not alone. And not at night, with the moon shining on their hair and turning their skin to alabaster. The little idiot could have gotten herself killed—or worse. If any woman in Jerusalem needed a husband to protect her, it was this reckless girl. What was her brother thinking? The hand of death knew no restraint; it would cut a young woman down with no remorse.

He leaned against the wall and listened for the soft patter of her steps. When the slim form flashed past him, he waited, then fell into step ten paces behind her.

She glanced over her shoulder. Her pace increased.

He sped up. He'd just make sure she got home safely.

She followed the streets toward the tanners' district, where the stench permeated the night air. Houses and shops gave way to brothels and taverns. Shouts and raucous laughter came from the doorways. A drunk man stumbled out of a doorway and retched in the street.

Longinus pulled his dagger. *This is no place for a respectable woman.* He sped up, closing the gap between them.

Nissa darted around a corner.

He broke into a run. What was the little idiot doing now? He clattered around the corner and pulled up sharply.

Nissa stood in the middle of the narrow street, her bundle clutched to her chest. Wet hair clung to her pale cheeks, and she trembled like a cornered rabbit. "Why are you following me?"

He walked toward her slowly. She wasn't quite so prickly now. "Why are you out alone? And in this part of town?" He jerked his head toward the brothel on the corner. "Are you trying to get yourself killed?"

She stepped backward, her hands tightening on the clothes in her arms. "Answer my question; don't ask three of me, centurion." She spit out the last word like it was poison. "And I can take care of myself."

Irritation rose in his chest. He didn't deserve her ire. "My name is Longinus, and believe me, you can't." He checked behind him, tucking his dagger back in his belt. "I'll make sure you get home safely."

She snorted. "I'm safe with a Roman soldier?"

What an ungrateful little minx. He covered the ground between them with two long strides. His hand closed over her wrist, and he jerked her toward him.

She pulled back. He held tight.

Her breath hitched in her throat as she glared up at him. "Let me go."

"You can take care of yourself, can you?" He snaked a hand behind her and caught a fistful of wet hair at the nape of her neck.

She struggled.

He held her wrist and her hair firmly enough to prove she was caught like a rabbit in a snare. "What will you do now?"

"I'll scream."

"And these men will rush to help you?" He glanced at the nearest doorway, a brothel. "They're more likely to join in the fun."

The last woman he'd held like this had been the Samaritan girl. She'd been terrified but ready to fight, just like Nissa. He'd been so angry, intent on avenging Scipio's death. But it wasn't the girl he had wanted, just the man she was with—the Samaritan with the scar. And this time he wasn't angry.

Nissa was stronger than she looked, but she didn't stand a chance against a man. He bent close, whispering in her ear. "You're a brave one"—*by Pollux, she has more mettle than some of my men*—"but courage won't save you against a man's strength. Believe me."

She slumped forward, all the fight leaving her. *Good. She has some sense.* He loosened his hold.

The moment his grip relaxed, she wrenched backward and kicked, her hard-soled sandals connecting with his bare shin and shooting pain up his leg. She spit out words no Jewish woman should know.

Longinus dropped her hand and let out a yelp. The wildcat was a quick thinker, and she knew how to curse in Greek. She turned to run, but he extended his hand and stopped her mid-stride. "You're smarter than you look, little one."

"You're not," she shot back.

He couldn't help it. He threw his head back and laughed. This little Jew was full of surprises.

She stared at him, her eyes as bright as the stars above them. "Let me go now that you've had your laugh."

Laugh? When was the last time he'd laughed? He was enjoying himself for the first time in months. *Flirting with a Jewish spinster? What was I thinking?* He took a deep breath and tightened his hold on her wrist. "I'll see you home."

She stamped toward the north like an angry child, pulling him along.

His grip didn't falter, but he had to lengthen his stride to stay close to her. The air sweetened as they reached the perfumers' district, but the silence between them was as sour as bad wine. *It wouldn't kill her to be civil.* "Is your brother healed?"

She didn't slow or even turn her head.

Perhaps he wasn't. "Did his injuries fester?" That could happen too easily; he'd seen it a hundred times.

She wrenched her arm away, and this time he let her go.

"Is it his eyes? Can he still see?"

She frowned. "Of course." She started forward again and turned down an alleyway. He barely heard her mumble, "Not that it's helped him at all."

"What do you mean?"

She frowned at him like he was a child asking too many questions. "His knee . . . and the priests . . ." She shook her head. "He spends his time talking about Jesus and complaining about the—" She snapped her mouth shut.

Complaining about the Romans. No surprise there.

Nissa had stopped in front of a crooked door clinging to a crumbling wall. "Here. I'm home. Now will you go away?"

By Jupiter, she is difficult. She stared up at him like he was her enemy.

You are *her enemy.*

He had questions and needed answers, but like the rest of the Jews, Nissa wasn't going to give them to him. An idea flickered like the twinkle of the stars in the night sky. If Cedron needed a job, he could give him one. Clearly, they needed money, and he had plenty gathering dust in the principia treasury.

Tomorrow, he'd find Cedron at home, and then he'd lay out his plan. Nissa wouldn't like it, but she wouldn't have a choice. He tipped his head and gave her a wink. "Good night, pretty Nissa. Don't go out alone. You never know who might find you."

Her mouth dropped open and her eyes widened, but for once, no sharp words followed.

He almost smiled as he turned away. For the first time since he'd met her, Nissa was speechless.

Chapter 12

NISSA PLOPPED DOWN on the three-legged stool and almost fell over. She picked it up, flipped it over, and snorted. One leg was shorter than the rest. Cedron wasn't any better at carpentry than at finding work.

She settled more carefully on the stool and leaned her back against the warm wall of the house. Amit lifted his head from his manger of barley and snuffled. Bones no longer poked through his withers, and his belly had grown fat. Onions sprouted through the black earth in the southern corner of the courtyard. A rose vine climbed the wall near the gate, some of its blooms already starting to unfold thanks to the water she brought every day from Siloam. If the rains came soon, she'd almost have a real garden, like when she was young and her family had prospered.

Satisfaction seeped through her like the warming rays of the winter sun. *This is how it should be.* The house was swept clean, the sleeping mats rolled neatly in the corner. A jar of water sat in the shade next to containers of wheat, oil, and honey. Red lentils flavored with garlic and cumin simmered over the fire. She'd added too much salt, but Cedron wouldn't complain.

Unbidden and unwanted, a song from the Tehillim came to her. *The Lord is my strength and my shield; my heart trusts in him . . .* She closed her eyes and shuttered the unwelcome prayer. Trusting in the Lord had given her nothing but bruises from Abba and an empty stomach.

When she was little more than a child, Abba had come home irate at the temple priests who had refused to buy his wood. "It's your fault!" he'd shouted at Cedron, advancing on the blind youth. "You are impure, full of sin, they say. They won't buy from me."

Nissa had thrown herself between her father and unsuspecting brother. "Don't touch him!"

And so Abba had turned his anger on her.

His hand came out of nowhere, slapping her across the face, pain stinging through her cheek. Cedron tried to help, but Abba pushed him aside. "I'll teach you to speak against your father, you worthless girl."

"Mama!" She called out for help, but Mama had stumbled into the dark house, her hands over her ears.

Abba pulled her up by the neck of her tunic. Tears welled in her eyes. She implored the Lord with the words she knew like her own heartbeat. "*Forsake me not, O Lord. My God, be not far from me.*"

Abba's anger rained down on her. "Curse the day you were born. We'd be better off without you." His words hammered as brutally as his fists.

Still, she called to the Lord. But the Almighty didn't hear her, or he wasn't listening.

It was the first time her father had beaten her, but not the last. Each time, she begged for the Lord's help. She knew the stories. He'd saved Daniel from the jaws of the lions, Isaac from his father's knife. "*Forsake me not, O Lord. My God, be not far from me!*" she cried. Why did he ignore her pleas?

When she was old enough to fight back, she did—with words as sharp as daggers. She didn't care that they made Abba hit her harder.

Now, Cedron still sang of the Lord's mercy, but the only words from the Tehillim she believed were those of David: "*My God, my God, why have you abandoned me?*" The Lord had yet to answer.

Nissa breathed deep, turning her face to the warmth of the

sun and pushing the cold memories away. She was no longer that weak girl. Abba couldn't hurt her anymore.

The voice spoke, as smooth as honey. *You trusted in yourself. See now how blessed you are?*

They were blessed, thanks to her.

The clatter of hooves and carts echoed from the street. Birds called from the walls and rooftops. The scent of roses perfumed the air, vying with the tang of straw and dung in Amit's stall. Just a little rest, that's all she needed. She'd lain awake through most of last night, listening to her brother snore, her nerves humming from the encounter with the centurion.

That centurion. Longinus.

The thought quickened her pulse. She'd rather face a dozen drunks and cutthroats than see his foreign face again. He hadn't hurt her, but when he'd grabbed her, she'd been sure he knew—sure he'd found out her secret and was taking her away. Instead, the idiot had been trying to teach her a lesson. As if she needed a lesson in how strong he was.

Good night, pretty Nissa, he'd said. Her cheeks burned. No one called her pretty. Why did it have to come from some infernal Roman? And why was he back in Jerusalem?

She let her head loll back against the wall. She'd been up with the dawn, hurrying to the temple to give alms to the beggars. Perhaps the Lord would smile on them now that she'd atoned for her sins. Perhaps Cedron would find work today.

A shadow blocked the sun. Had she slept that long? She jerked awake, upsetting the stool. A strong hand closed around her shoulder. Another caught her around the waist as the stool lurched from under her. As if she'd brought forth the vision from her dreams, she opened her eyes to see red hair lit from the sun like a burning torch.

"Let me go!" she sputtered and scrambled to get her feet under her, pushing his hands away. She stumbled backward, but the wall of the house was firm behind her, the wall of his chest just inches in front of her. She was trapped.

"Easy, little Nissa." He raised his empty hands.

This morning he wore his shining breastplate with the crest and ribbons over a red tunic and a leather belt. She caught the glint of a knife hilt and the sword at his side.

"Don't 'easy' me. I'm not your horse, centurion." She slid around him and backed into the courtyard. "What are you doing here?" And when would he leave?

"This must be the hospitality you people speak of with such pride?"

This Roman was accusing *her* of rudeness? "You expect hospitality after attacking me?"

He ran a hand over his hair, raising it into fiery red spikes. "Attacking? If I was trying, I could have killed you before you opened your eyes."

She backed toward the fire.

His eyes followed her. He tipped his head to the side with a quick smile. "Maybe I should have stolen a kiss instead." His teeth were only a bit crooked, and a dimple marked the side of his freckled cheek. He suddenly looked not like a soldier but like a man. A handsome man. *But not as handsome as Gilad.*

She glared at him as a flush burned over her cheeks. "I'm not sure which would be worse."

He laughed like he had last night. It was deep and rumbly, like the sound of a far-off rainstorm.

He shouldn't even be here.

"I'm not here to ravage you, Nissa. Although you were a tempting sight with your mouth open, snoring louder than your donkey."

She pressed her lips together. *I don't snore.*

Longinus's bright blue eyes took in the donkey, the garden, and the house in one sweep. He ducked his head into the doorway. He turned to her, the smile and the dimple gone. "I'm looking for your brother."

"He's out." Nissa fumbled to right the toppled stool. "And he won't offer you the kiss of peace when he comes home." Perhaps now he'd leave.

Instead, he picked up the three-legged stool and brought it closer to the fire, settling carefully on it and leaning over to warm his hands. "So he's looking for work?"

Nissa nodded. What was she supposed to do with a Roman soldier in her courtyard? Offer him water like a Jewish visitor? Food? *Don't talk to him. Maybe he'll just go away.*

Longinus glanced at the water jar. "It is a dry day, and dusty."

Nissa sighed and went to the water jar. She scooped up a cool cupful and brought it to him, looking down at his feet while he drank. Even his toes were freckled.

"Thank you." He handed her the cup, and his hands brushed over hers. "I haven't had such good water since I drank from the springs of Gaul."

Gaul. A land she'd heard of over the sea, past Rome, a land so distant it seemed like it couldn't be real. "Gaul? You've been there?" She bit down on her lip. *Don't talk to him.*

He raised his brows at her. "I have."

She shrugged and crouched next to the fire, turning the cup over in her hands. She'd never met anyone who had traveled farther than Damascus.

He held his hands over the flames. They were huge and covered with nicks and scars. "My father was stationed there. My mother was born there."

So that was why he looked so different. His mother had married the enemy. "I thought soldiers couldn't marry?"

He picked up a stick and poked the fire. "They can't, not really. But many do. The wives aren't considered Roman citizens. They can't inherit if something happens to their husbands. And something usually does." His mouth hardened like he was remembering something painful.

"Did that happen to your mother?" *Not that I care.* But she did like the sound of his voice, the way he spoke the Aramaic words so carefully.

"Yes. My father dragged her from one camp to another. Through Gaul, back to Rome, then to the frontier in Britannia." He raised his eyes to hers. They were bluer than the sky above. "So cold, Britannia. Your winter is probably the warmest it ever got there. And wet. I hated it." He shivered.

Britannia. She tried out the word silently. It even sounded cold.

Longinus stared into the flames. "But Gaul . . . the sky is blue, and the grass sparkles in the morning like . . ." He searched for a word. "Like emeralds."

He stirred the fire again. The coals broke into an upward shower of sparks, twisting into the air and disappearing into ash. "There are meadows full of flowers that stretch for miles. And forests so deep and thick." He stared at the glowing coals. "So peaceful. Like you are the only person in the world."

He reached for another stick of wood and put it on the fire.

Peaceful? Flowers and forests? Romans only thought of battles and pillage and destruction. She stood up and crossed her arms over her chest. *I wish he'd go back to Gaul if he likes it so much.* "How do you know our language?"

His brows came down. "I don't like not knowing what the people around me are saying."

He spoke it well, but she wasn't about to tell him that. He was her enemy, in more ways than one, even if his words sounded more like a poet's than a soldier's.

The gate creaked, and Nissa jumped.

Cedron hobbled in, his face creasing in worry when he saw the centurion.

Nissa backed away. Cedron would make him go now.

Longinus stood, and the stool fell over again. "Cedron." He nodded. "You look better than the last time I saw you."

Cedron approached Longinus. "What are you doing here? And with my sister?"

Longinus glanced at Nissa, and the corner of his mouth twitched. "Your sister's virtue is safe with me."

Nissa's face flamed like the cooking fire. How dare he mock her?

Cedron stepped back. "I recognize you, centurion, and I thank you for helping me," he said, glancing at Nissa. "Us. That day." He motioned to the gate. "But you must leave."

Longinus glanced at Nissa, his brows raised, but he ignored Cedron's rudeness. "I've been gone, to the Decapolis. It's the first chance I've had to find you. I'm glad you recovered."

Nissa poured water into a cup and brought it to Cedron.

He drank deeply, his eyes never leaving the centurion. "You're posted here in Jerusalem again?"

"Just until Passover."

"Why? Is there trouble here?" Cedron paced to the door of the little house, then turned back to Longinus and crossed his arms.

Nissa swallowed. Cedron was digging for information on the legions. Information for his Zealot friends.

"No. Unless you count thieves breaking your commandments as trouble."

Thieves? Nissa fumbled with the water jar, almost dropping it. Both men stopped talking and watched her. She hurried to the corner of the house and set the jar on the ground. She knelt, her back to the men, and poured a measure of wheat on the grinding stone. Making bread would hide the tremors in her hands. She just hoped the centurion wouldn't stay long enough to eat it.

"The thieves you were looking for when you ran me down?"

"The same. A little one and a tall Greek."

Cedron drained his cup and paced back to the fire. "There are always thieves in the marketplace. Why do you care? You're here to keep us under Rome's thumb, not to protect us from our own people."

Longinus grunted. "You're right. It's not my problem. But I have my reasons."

Cedron nodded. "They break our commandments. I wish you success in finding them." Cedron looked pointedly at the door.

Longinus didn't move from his place by the fire. "Nissa told me you aren't finding work."

Nissa added water and a sprinkle of salt to the flour and kneaded it, then glanced behind her to see Cedron pacing again.

"We're getting by. Nissa has work."

Longinus's gaze went to Nissa, to the stash of grain and oil, the honey and the new clothes. His brows flickered.

Worry tightened Nissa's shoulders. Longinus was far less naive than Cedron. Would he know the food and clothes she bought were worth more than one woman could earn in two months? Nissa carried the rounds of dough to the fire and pressed one against the flat cooking rock, watching Longinus out of the corner of her eye.

Longinus went on. "I've been asking questions in the marketplace. Someone must know something about the thieves, but they aren't talking to me."

"No, with that Roman sword at your side, they won't."

"That's where I need you."

Nissa froze. What did he mean?

"Me?" Cedron stopped his pacing directly across the fire from Longinus.

"To ask questions. To listen. And to use your new eyes to find the thieves."

Nissa jerked her hand from the fire and stuck her burnt thumb in her mouth. Her chest tightened, and she couldn't draw a breath. Cedron, her own brother, searching the city for her and Dismas? She had to stop this.

Cedron ran a hand over his beard, his brows drawn together. "Why should I help you?"

"They break your commandments. They steal from your people. Isn't that reason enough?"

Cedron didn't answer.

"I'll pay you enough to move out of this section of the city."

He motioned to Nissa. "It's dangerous for your sister to walk past the taverns and brothels to get water."

Cedron turned his eyes on Nissa, his brow furrowed.

She threw another round of bread on the stone. He couldn't be considering this ridiculous idea, could he? "I'm fine, Cedron. You don't want to work for the Romans. You can't—"

"And you can?"

"You'd be a traitor to your own people—"

"I wouldn't be a traitor. They are thieves; they break the commandments." He rubbed his beard. "You've been praying I find work. We both have. Perhaps this is what the Lord is asking me to do." He sat down and stared into the fire.

The Lord wanted Cedron to hunt down his own sister? *This can't be happening.*

Longinus rubbed his hands together. "I'll give you five denarii for each of them."

Ten denarii? For her and Dismas?

"A lot for pickpockets."

"Believe me, I have good reason to want them caught."

Nissa rescued another burnt round of bread from the fire. *Please, no.* She dumped the charred bread in Cedron's lap and retreated to the corner of the courtyard. How could she get enough silver to live on if Cedron himself was searching for Mouse?

Longinus accepted the bread Cedron offered him. He looked at Nissa, a smile lurking on his lips. "Thank you, little Nissa." To Cedron, he said. "You are fortunate to have such a good cook taking care of you. Don't make her walk past that scum twice a day." He jerked his head toward the brothels.

Cedron frowned. He prayed over his bread, broke it, and stuffed a portion in his mouth. He chewed thoughtfully, his brow still furrowed and his eyes on the fire.

Would he really say yes to the Roman? Her brother, who hated the occupation of the land, who spent his time with the Zealots, dreaming of revolt? No. He'd never agree to it.

When they had both finished their bread, Cedron stood. "I'll do it."

Nissa's stomach buckled, and a chill swept over her skin. *No, Cedron. Please don't.* She bit her lip before her words came out.

"I'll start with my friends the beggars. They hear everything."

Longinus strode around the fire and clapped Cedron on the shoulder. "Good. Between the two of us, we'll hunt them down by winter's end."

At least now he would leave and Nissa could speak plainly to Cedron. She could beg him not to work for the Roman. There had to be a way to change his mind.

But Longinus lingered at the fire, staring into the flames. He picked up the stick, gripping it so tightly that his knuckles whitened. "Have you heard word of the man who healed you?"

Cedron raised his brows in surprise. "Jesus of Nazareth?"

Longinus grunted.

Cedron's voice turned suspicious. "Why do you ask?"

Hope flickered in Nissa. Perhaps she wouldn't have to change Cedron's mind. If his new Roman friend wanted to turn Jesus over to the Sanhedrin, Cedron would throw him out of the courtyard and never speak to him again.

"I want to ask him some questions."

Cedron answered carefully. "I've heard much of him these past months. Healing the sick, walking on water. Even bringing a child back from the dead."

Longinus jerked his head up and turned his intense blue gaze on Cedron. "Do you believe it, what you hear?"

Cedron motioned to his own eyes. "I believe every word."

Nissa leaned forward.

Longinus poked at the flames, raising a shower of sparks. "Can you get me to him?"

Cedron's eyes narrowed at the Roman. "There are many who hate him and would like to see him dead."

"Dead? What has he done to them?"

"What he says—what he proclaims—is blasphemy. He

speaks to the poor, the powerless, and he mocks the rich and powerful. He isn't the Messiah the Pharisees are looking for."

"And what of you? Do you believe he is this Messiah?

Cedron was silent for a long moment. He nodded. "And because I believe in him, I am cursed by the priests."

Longinus stood. "I give you my word—as a Roman and as a man. If you bring me to him, I won't harm him."

Cedron looked into the flames, his mouth pulled down.

No, Cedron. Don't even consider it.

"Another ten denarii if you get me to him. I just want to talk."

Cedron ran a hand over his beard. "I'll see what I can do."

Nissa's hope disappeared like smoke from the cooking fire. What else would Cedron agree to do for the Roman? His laundry?

Longinus rose and walked to the gate. "When you have news, tell the guard at the entrance to the garrison. He'll find me." Longinus looked over Cedron's shoulder to where Nissa stood, her back against the house, and raised his amber brows.

She turned away so fast she bumped the water jar, and it tipped, spilling at her feet.

"Good-bye, Nissa." The Roman's deep voice drifted through the gate as he left.

I hope that's the last I see of him. She didn't like his questions, or his dimple, or the way his eyes crinkled when he smiled. And he wouldn't smile if he knew she was the Mouse.

As the gate creaked shut, she rushed to her brother. "Cedron. Don't do this."

Cedron wrapped his gentle hands around hers. "Listen, Nissa. I'll find the thieves, and you can stop working at the laundry. And as for Jesus, I won't bring that Roman anywhere near him."

Find the thieves? *He can't.* "You can't work for a Roman. What will the priests say?"

"What more can they do to me?" Cedron squeezed her fingers and smiled like a boy who'd swiped the honey jar. "And I'm not working for the Roman; I'm working against him. If he trusts me, I can get information from him about the legions. Information the Zealots need."

"The Zealots? Why are you—"

"Don't you see, Nissa?" His voice rose, a note of excitement in it she'd never heard before. "This is why Jesus healed me. To be his eyes in Jerusalem, to be ready."

"Ready for what?" What could Cedron be talking about?

"For revolution, Nissa. That's what the Zealots say. They say that Jesus is the Messiah, that he'll come back to Jerusalem. And when he does, we'll be ready to throw the Romans out of our land."

A cold chill swept over Nissa. Revolution? From that paltry band of Zealots who complained at the synagogue? And now Cedron wanted to use Longinus to plot an uprising? It sounded more like a way to get himself crucified.

He smiled. "God is good, Nissa. His mercy never ceases."

God is good? When Cedron was given his sight, she'd hoped for a new life. Instead, he'd been given a job that would end with her being stoned or him being crucified. That was God's mercy?

Cedron grabbed his cloak and headed across the courtyard. "I'm going to start asking some questions about the thieves. If I can gain that centurion's confidence, I'll have much to tell the Zealots this Sabbath." The gate banged shut behind him.

Nissa covered her face with her shaking hands. Her brother, the only one who hadn't abandoned her, was searching the city for Mouse. What if he discovered her secret? He'd never forgive her, and then she really would be alone.

Nissa ran to the shed where Amit stood peacefully chewing and leaned against his warm fur. "What will I do, Amit?" A soft, gentle voice whispered to her, *Stop stealing; trust in the Lord, as Cedron does.*

But how could she stop? They needed to pay the rent and

buy food. If Cedron didn't find the thieves, he wouldn't be getting any silver. And he wasn't going to find the thieves.

She raised her head from the donkey's soft flank. She'd tried everything else. She didn't have a choice. But she'd have to be even more careful now. She'd follow Dismas's rules and not get caught—not by the aggravating Roman and not by her own brother.

Chapter 13

$\mathcal{L}$ONGINUS FINISHED THE morning inspection of camp and called out the duty assignments. "Julius, take fifty men. Latrine duty and kitchen. Optus, take your fifty to drill. Sergio, pilum practice."

The rest were on their way out of camp with Cornelius for a march around the walls.

The legionaries were soft, slow, and lazy. Saturnalia had just concluded, the feast of the god of the harvest—a thinly veiled excuse for drinking and eating too much. Every centurion knew to work the men hard after Saturnalia, even in the cold, dry days these Jews called the rainy season.

Longinus strode down the Via Praetoria toward the principia. He had spent most of Saturnalia asking questions about the thieves and getting nowhere. Whoever they were, the two thieves were careful. There had been no sightings at the temple, and the upper market had been quieter than usual. He'd put off his report to Pilate long enough. It would have to be done today.

Before he entered the camp headquarters, Marcellus intercepted him. "Centurion."

The young legionary looked good. He had healed well while Longinus was in Damascus. When he'd returned, Longinus had appointed him *optio ad carcerem*, a position that brought him more pay and no sentry duty. As the officer in charge of the carcer, Marcellus had little to do but keep watch on the occasional drunk legionary or criminal awaiting trial, which meant he was usually shadowing Longinus, waiting for orders. He'd even picked up a little Aramaic. Before long, he would speak the language of this foul province better than Longinus.

Marcellus pointed toward the gate. "There's a Jew waiting for you."

Longinus found Cedron leaning against a column. In the two weeks since he'd hired him, he'd heard from Cedron every few days. So far, Cedron had discovered nothing about the thieves or about Jesus. Maybe he'd hired the wrong man for the job.

"Centurion." Cedron straightened as Longinus approached. Legionaries drilled near the gate, their wooden swords clashing against shields and battle cries ringing through the morning air.

"Any news?"

"Not of the thieves." He glanced at the legionaries and lowered his voice. "But I do have news of Jesus."

Longinus prodded Cedron away from the gate. They passed the open agora and Herod's empty palace. "What of him?"

"I have a name. Joseph of Arimathea. A Pharisee."

"Don't Pharisees hate Jesus?"

Cedron shook his head. "Not all of them. They say this man is a secret follower. When Jesus is in the city with his disciples, he stays at his house."

A tremble of anticipation surprised Longinus. He could see him today. "Is he there now?"

Cedron didn't meet his eyes. "I heard some people saw him in the temple."

Longinus pulse sped up. "Where does he live, this Joseph?"

Cedron turned quickly toward the market. "I'll take you to him."

Longinus followed behind the limping man. This was too easy. *Cedron has no love for me.* Why wasn't he worried about leading a Roman to his messiah? Did he need the money so desperately, or was there another reason the Jew was helping him?

The noise of the market faded as the courtyard walls and palaces of rich Jews and Greeks closed in around them. A servant hurried by, his gaze following the Jewish man and the Roman centurion walking together.

Cedron waited for Longinus to come beside him. "When will the rest of the legion return to Jerusalem?"

Longinus glanced sideways at Cedron, his suspicions growing. The Jew wasn't making idle conversation. Was he trying to dig up information? What had Nissa said about her brother? That he complained about the Romans instead of finding work. He grunted.

Cedron spoke again. "There are rumors that Pilate won't come for Passover."

Only a fool would believe that rumor. A fool or a wishful band of rebels.

Cedron paused in front of a tall, ornate gate. "This is where I heard he would be."

Longinus ran a hand through his hair and shifted. *This is a waste of my time.* How much of a fool did Cedron think he was? Cedron probably knew exactly where Jesus was, and it wasn't behind this courtyard wall.

"Let's get this over with." And when Jesus wasn't there, he'd show Cedron what happened to Jews who wasted his time. Then he'd find another way to track down the thieves and Jesus.

Cedron pushed open the gate, revealing a lush courtyard. Fig trees cast cool shade, and flowering bushes scented the air. A fountain burbled in the center. He entered, and Longinus stepped behind him.

A servant hurried out of the house and approached Cedron.

"We are looking for Jesus of Nazareth," Cedron said. The servant held out a hand for them to wait, then darted away with another look over his shoulder. "Joseph may not even speak to us," Cedron said in a low voice. "Most Jews would not welcome a visit from an am-ha-arez and a Roman at any time of day."

A man emerged from the house. His brown hair and full

beard were streaked with gray. He wore a tunic of deep-blue linen and sturdy leather sandals.

This had to be Joseph, the Pharisee. Despite the wealth of his house, he wore little gold, just a wide signet ring on his first finger. He approached Cedron carefully, peering around him to see Longinus. "I'm sorry. Jesus is not here."

Before Longinus could step from behind Cedron, a movement shifted his gaze. A tall, black-haired man—with a scar that stretched from his temple to the corner of his mouth—stepped from the shadows. Longinus's breath caught, and his hand went to his sword.

The man he'd scoured the countryside for last year—the man who had killed Scipio—was right in front of him.

Metal scraped against the scabbard as he pulled his sword free, pushed Cedron to the side, and bore down on the man he'd sworn to kill long before he came to Jerusalem. The Samaritan.

He lunged forward and set the point of his sword over the Samaritan's heart. "You."

Cedron cried out, reaching for Longinus's sword arm. Longinus used his free arm to push Cedron to the ground, as easy as stopping a child. He planted one foot on Cedron's bad knee and glanced at the old man, who hadn't moved. "And you. Stay put. I'll kill you if I have to."

Cedron groaned. "You gave me your word, Roman."

Longinus pushed the blade point more firmly against the Samaritan's chest. "I promised I wouldn't hurt Jesus. This man isn't even a Jew." Why wasn't he running? Or putting up a fight? He was staring death in the face and didn't even look afraid.

Kill him now. Ask questions later.

Joseph spoke slowly and carefully. "He is a follower of Jesus, the man you seek."

"I don't care. I lit the fire on my friend's funeral pyre. I vowed to get revenge for his death." *Why am I explaining myself to these people?*

The Samaritan stood silently, peacefully. Only the twitter

of the birds in the fig trees and the buzz of the bees among the flowers disturbed the silence. Longinus gripped the hilt of his sword more tightly. He would kill him. Just not yet.

"Tell me your name."

The tall man took a deep breath. Longinus could feel the pressure on the tip of his sword increase. "My name when you knew me was Shem. Jesus calls me Stephen."

"You aren't afraid to die?"

Stephen bowed his head. "I'm ready to do God's will."

The fight went out of Longinus's veins. His sword wavered. He'd seen begging, even grown men groveling with his sword at their neck. But never acceptance, never peace. Irritation rose in him—at this man who didn't have the sense to be afraid and at his own hesitation. If Scipio were here, this Samaritan would be bleeding out in the dust at this moment.

Cedron struggled again under his foot. "You'll get no more help from me, Roman."

Longinus grimaced. *No great loss.* "You brought me here. His blood is on your hands as much as my own."

Longinus spoke to the Pharisee. "Is Jesus in the city?"

Joseph shook his head. "No. He left this morning, for Galilee."

So close yet again. The gods must be working against him. He'd never see the man if he killed one of his followers. He could kill the Samaritan now, or he could wait. Consider his options. The am-ha-arez, the Pharisee, and the Samaritan watched him, waiting.

"You—" Longinus pointed his sword at Joseph. "Tie his hands."

When the Samaritan was bound, he lifted his foot from Cedron.

"Where are you taking him?" Cedron asked, pushing himself up from the ground.

Longinus took a deep breath and looked at the man in front of him. The man he'd dreamed of killing for almost a year. The man who should be dead on the ground right now. "To his crucifixion."

LONGINUS SUNK HIS spear point deep into the straw-stuffed dummy tied to the post and pictured Stephen's face. The Samaritan—the man who had been sitting in the camp carcer since yesterday—was a murderer and deserved to die.

Cornelius approached him from one side. The younger centurion wasn't stronger, but he was fast. Longinus advanced, slashing with the wooden practice sword that weighed twice as much as his father's blade.

Cornelius advanced, his practice sword moving like lightning, forcing Longinus to step back once. Then again. *What's the matter with me?* Cornelius was good but not that good. *Have I forgotten how to fight?* He let out a yell and bore down on the legionary, driving him backward.

Cornelius stumbled and fell. Longinus kicked Cornelius's shield aside and pinned him to the ground with one foot. He raised his sword and let out a shout of victory.

He'd won the round, but it had been close. Too close. He pulled off his helmet and wiped the sweat out of his eyes, then threw the practice sword to the next legionary in line and trudged to the water jar.

He dipped a gourd in the water and took a long drink. He dumped another dip of water over his head. He needed to keep his men strong, ready to fight. And he needed to be the same.

He passed the gourd to Cornelius. "Pilum practice for your men." Throwing blunted wooden spears at one another would be good for them. "Then the vaulting horse in full armor." The men needed toughening, and so did he. He was a legionary, by Jupiter. It was time to do what he should have done the moment he saw Stephen.

Longinus entered the carcer and descended the narrow steps. Marcellus stood guard outside the last door. He chose a long iron key from the ring on his belt and turned the heavy pins of the lock. Pushing the door open, he moved aside for Longinus to enter.

Stephen leaned in the corner. He'd had no food or water. His eyes were bloodshot, and his lips were cracked and dry. He straightened and Longinus tensed for an attack, but Stephen's face was untroubled, as peaceful as a child's. Was this the same arrogant youth he had faced in the forum of Caesarea? But it was; he hadn't denied his crime.

"Marcellus, bring me that bench."

Marcellus dragged a bench through the door and left them.

Longinus pulled out his sword and sat. He laid the bare sword across his lap, the razor edges glinting in the weak sun that trickled through the high, barred window. "Are you ready to die?" he asked.

The Samaritan looked at him directly, his gaze clear and steady. "I've been ready for a long time." Did this inscrutable youth have more courage than a Roman centurion? *He faces my sword without a qualm, while I ran like a coward from a band of unarmed lepers.* Shame burned in his chest and turned to anger.

He'll know fear when I crucify him. But first, Longinus had questions. "Tell me, you escaped me twice in Galilee. Why come here, to Jerusalem? Why didn't you stay in the country where you were safe?"

"He told me to come here. To wait for him."

"Who did?"

"Jesus." Stephen said. "He said I would die here, in Jerusalem."

"So he is a prophet." Longinus watched Stephen for any sign of fear. "And don't you care?"

Stephen licked his cracked lips. "If that is his will for me, then I will do it. Before I met him, in Capernaum, I wasn't even alive. I didn't know faith or love. Now I know both. I've seen miracles—impossible things—with my own eyes."

This man was talking nonsense, but perhaps he could explain what had happened at the Pool of Siloam. Longinus leaned forward. "How does he heal? What type of magic does he have?"

Stephen shook his head. "Not magic. Power."

Power to raise an army? "What kind of power? Where does he get it?"

"From the Lord."

The Lord. *I don't want to hear anything more about the god of the Jews.* "But who is he?"

"Some say he is a prophet. Some say he is the Messiah, or John the Baptist come back to life. Even his followers don't agree."

Longinus rubbed his hand through his hair. Leave it to the Jews to disagree, even about their own messiah. "What—Who do you say he is?"

Stephen's dark eyes burned with a fire, an intensity Longinus had seen before—when he sent his men into battle. "He is the son of God. The Messiah. The Taheb. The one we've been awaiting for thousands of years."

"The son of a god?" Like Apollo?

"The son of *the* God."

"And what is he here to do?" Overthrow Rome? *That isn't going to happen.*

At this, Stephen's gaze faltered. "Heal his people. Bring us peace."

Peace? That made no sense. Jesus was a Jew. Everyone knew the Jews awaited a savior who would defeat their enemies and give them back the land they swore had been promised to them by God. They talked, sang, and prayed about it constantly. Peace was the opposite of revolution.

Stephen seemed to read his thoughts. "He doesn't do what anyone expects. But this I know: he will change our world."

Longinus grimaced. This was too much. "The world is the Roman Empire."

"He will change Rome as well."

Tiny bumps rose on Longinus's arms. *Change Rome?*

Stephen paced to the high window and looked up at the sliver of blue sky. "I don't understand it, either. But he told me to come here and to be ready."

"Ready for what?" Another failed uprising? Not while he was in charge.

Stephen turned to Longinus, his face again set in peace and acceptance. "Ready to die for him."

Longinus jerked to his feet and sheathed his sword. He didn't want to hear anything more about Jesus or this one god. "You will die, but at my command. For Scipio, the man you killed."

Longinus pounded on the closed door. "Marcellus!"

The lock rattled, and the legionary pulled open the door.

Longinus stepped out of the dim cell. "Get him some food and water. It will be his last."

Marcellus pounded up the stairs.

Longinus braced himself against the cold, damp wall outside the cell. His chest rose and fell like he'd been sprinting in full armor. If he crucified this man, he'd lose Cedron as his spy—his only spy. He might as well hand his father's sword to Silvanus and forget about the quiet forests of Gaul. But if he didn't crucify the Samaritan, he'd be a traitor to Rome and his dead friend. And if Silvanus found out, he'd be a dead man, or at least wish he were.

Heavy footfalls pounded down the stairs. Longinus straightened his back and crossed his arms. Marcellus ducked into the cell with a round of bread and a gourd of watered wine. After a few moments of muffled talk, he reappeared and took up his post outside the door.

Longinus breathed deeply. He'd send a message to Pilate today, and Marcellus would carry out the order by the end of the week. Longinus wouldn't even have to watch.

Marcellus eyed him, his face wary. "Any luck finding the thieves, centurion?"

"The thieves?" Longinus turned on him. "What do you know about that?"

Marcellus's brows went up. "Everyone knows about the wager, even Pilate."

Longinus ground his teeth together. Of course everyone knew. Legionaries gossiped more than old women.

Marcellus looked at the ground. "The men are taking bets. It's two to one you'll lose your sword."

Longinus rubbed his temple where a pain had started behind his eye. Two to one? His chances wouldn't even be that good after he crucified Stephen. "Who are you betting on?"

Marcellus looked up like he was surprised by the question. "On you, of course."

Longinus's gaze dropped to the scars on Marcellus's arms and neck. So Marcellus put his faith in him—not to mention his silver—even after he'd given him those scars? "You might want to change your bet. My only spy won't point me in the direction of the nearest latrine after I crucify this man."

Marcellus's brow furrowed in thought. "You'll lose your father's sword."

Longinus grunted.

"And Silvanus will win."

Longinus started for the steps, but Marcellus's next words stopped him.

"No one knows the Samaritan is here."

Longinus froze. What did Marcellus mean by that?

Marcellus lowered his voice. "I could keep it quiet. Keep him here. His friend would have a good reason to find the thieves for you. The Samaritan for the thieves. A good exchange."

"Set him free? After he killed Scipio?" Longinus shook his head. He couldn't. But Marcellus had a point. Cedron would have to help him, or Stephen's blood would be on his hands. And he might still have a chance to question Jesus, find out if he really was a threat to Rome. *And perhaps solve the riddle of Stephen's unflinching peace.*

The weight on his chest eased. It could work. He clapped Marcellus on the shoulder. "Keep it quiet. Don't let anyone see him." He hurried up the stairs and out into the bright sun. He'd talk to Cedron, give him another chance to find the thieves and save Stephen. And if Nissa's brother really was spying for the Zealots, it wouldn't hurt to keep a close eye on him.

It wasn't a perfect plan, but it would work for now.

Chapter 14

ARE YOU WORKING today, Nissa?" Cedron hobbled across the courtyard to the fire, where Nissa ate her breakfast of charred bread drizzled with honey.

Nissa shook her head and swallowed. "They don't need me today." The laundry didn't need her today or any day, but she had much to do. Another cleansing bath at Siloam, and later, Gilad would come for the rent. Her stomach did a little flip. This time she was going to look her best.

"Are you going to the city gate?" More than two months had passed since Cedron had been cured. Two months, and she was still stealing. But if Cedron could get work today, just enough to buy food, she could wait another week before making the mark for Dismas. Now that Longinus was looking for her, she'd need to be more careful.

Cedron pulled his cloak around his shoulders. "Later. This morning, I need to go to the synagogue."

Nissa snorted. "To meet with the Zealots, you mean." Since the Roman had made Cedron his dangerous offer two weeks ago, her brother had spent less time looking for work and more time lingering at the synagogue where the Zealots called for war against Rome. She ripped another bite from her bread, talking around it as she chewed. "Besides, I thought they didn't speak to am-ha-arez?"

"We believe in the same end."

The bread stuck in Nissa's throat. "What? Revolution? Do they think with a few rusty swords they can overthrow the Roman Empire?" Cedron was getting in over his head. The talk in Jerusalem was all about Jesus. The Zealots wanted him to be their messiah; the Pharisees and Sadducees wanted him dead.

Cedron crouched close to her and put his arm around her shoulder. "Jesus gave me my sight so I could get his people ready. That's what I'm doing." He pulled her close to his side. "It won't be long now, and we'll be free of the Romans. Then I'll be able to take care of you."

"And until then?"

"Trust in the Lord. Trust in the Messiah. He called me to this."

Nissa let out a long breath. Jesus had given Cedron his sight, and for that she was grateful. But it was Jesus' fault that Cedron was banished from the temple, that he couldn't find work, that he was called an am-ha-arez. And now, that he'd rather plan revolution than help her with the rent.

Cedron flashed her a smile and a wink. "You better hurry if you're going to get ready for Gilad."

She coughed and almost choked. "Gilad?"

Cedron let out a laugh. "Don't pretend with me, little sister. I can see you blushing. All the women talk about his handsome face."

She shrugged.

Cedron batted his lashes at her, and a smile tickled the corner of her mouth.

"Just don't get your hopes set on him. I'm not sure I'd welcome an offer of marriage from that strutting rooster."

An offer of marriage? Not likely. Nissa turned to her brother and assumed her most innocent expression, looking into his brown eyes. "Cedron. I'm sorry, but I don't think Gilad thinks of you that way."

Cedron snorted and pushed her away. "Just be careful, Nissa. I don't trust him."

He doesn't even know I'm alive, other than to pay the rent on time. But, maybe, if Cedron thought it possible . . . "Don't worry. And you be careful, too."

Cedron pushed open the gate and looked over his shoulder. "*The Lord is my strength and my shield.*"

She shoved the last of the bread in her mouth and dismissed the lump of worry in her chest as Cedron pulled the broken gate shut behind him. At least Cedron wasn't out looking for the thieves. After the centurion's betrayal yesterday with the Samaritan, Cedron wouldn't even speak his name. That was a relief.

She licked the last of the honey off her sticky fingers and gave the pot of lentils over the fire a stir before grabbing the water jar. She'd get to Siloam before the drunks woke up and made her journey through the tanneries and brothels a lesson in profanities.

When Nissa arrived at Siloam, women stood in clusters on the broad ledges around the pool, gossiping and smiling. Children splashed on the top steps, the water just covering their ankles, their squeals of laughter echoing off the stone walls and columns.

After Nissa filled her jar, she slipped off her cloak and waded into the cold water. Cedron's words seemed to echo in the talk and laughter around her. "*Wash away all my guilt, from my sin cleanse me . . .*" Whatever sin made Cedron blind had been forgiven. But for her, the water would only wash away dirt and dust.

A group of girls, most younger than her, bathed just a few steps away. She'd seen them here before. A few sat on the edge of the pool, braiding one another's hair. Two more, so alike they must be sisters, splashed nearby.

One smiled at Nissa.

Nissa dunked her head under the cold water and came up gasping for breath.

The girl moved closer. "Cold today, isn't it?"

Nissa nodded and climbed the steps quickly, wringing out her sopping hair. She glanced back at the girl, who watched her with a surprised face. Nissa fumbled her cloak and water jar into her arms and hurried to the steps, her tunic dripping. *I should have been more polite.*

She pounded down the stairs, her sandals echoing on the hard stone. *She's probably a good Jewish girl. She wouldn't want to be friends with a thief and a liar.*

She braved the street of drunkards and brothels and reached her courtyard out of breath and freezing cold. After throwing some wood on the fire, she changed into her new tunic of soft green wool with delicate embroidery on the neckline and hem. It fit better than anything she'd ever owned and made her feel soft and feminine, like the girls Gilad watched in the marketplace.

She wrapped a striped belt of deep blue and white linen around her waist and buckled on her new leather sandals.

It would be nice to have someone braid my hair, like Mama used to do. Before Mama had found more happiness in her wine amphora. The girl at the pool had looked like someone she could talk to, even confide in. Someone who wasn't her brother or a donkey.

She'd had friends when she was younger, friends in the lower city where her parents lived. But one by one, they'd married. Watching them cuddle their babies while suitors rejected her rent her heart. Her friends' pity hardened it to stone.

Then Dismas had found her stealing copper coins and figs in the lower city market. He'd taken her on as an apprentice, and her life had changed. He'd taught her how to distract a shopkeeper, how to slip her hand into a purse, how to disappear in a crowd. They worked together, and they were good at what they did. She brought food home to Cedron and kept a roof over their heads.

Dismas admired her. Cedron loved her. They were enough,

even if she had to hide her true self from both of them. She didn't need friends.

She opened the cedar cask in the corner of the house and took out an ivory comb, a tiny amphora of perfumed oil, and an alabaster pot. She combed out her hair, anointed it with the oil that cost more than she should have spent, and twined it into a long braid. Wrapping it in a coil, she pinned it with a shining brass brooch, then dipped beeswax balm from the tiny pot and smoothed it over her lips.

Pretty Nissa, Longinus had called her. She frowned. *I couldn't care less what that centurion thinks.* But, maybe today, Gilad would think she was pretty.

Finally, she removed two silver coins from the cask. Only a handful of brass was left, but the thought didn't make her chest tighten as it had when they lived with Mama and Abba. There was more money where that came from. She and Cedron had a decent house, new clothes, good food.

All thanks to Mouse.

She tucked the coins in her belt. They should keep Gilad happy until the end of Shevat.

The gate creaked open. Gilad was right on time. She smoothed her hands over her hips and hurried out the door, a smile on her lips. But it wasn't the handsome rent collector stepping into the courtyard. It was the last man Nissa wanted to see.

"What are you doing here?"

The centurion was without his armor and helmet. Just a bright white tunic cinched with a studded leather belt. It was kirtled higher than the Jews wore their tunics, showing freckled knees and a glimpse of muscled thighs. His cloak lay across his shoulders but was thrown back to reveal his sword.

Longinus raised an eyebrow and inspected her from the top of her head to her new leather sandals. "Such a warm welcome, Nissa. Tell, now, did you dress up just for me?"

"For you?" she sputtered. "Don't flatter yourself."

He raised an eyebrow. "You were waiting for someone, that much is clear. When a girl looks as pretty as you, it's for a man."

Her mouth dropped open. Again he called her pretty. Why did he do that? They both knew it was a lie.

He stepped closer. "And your mouth is far prettier when it is closed."

She snapped it shut and clenched her teeth. Was he mocking her? She stamped to the fire and bent to stir it. "Cedron is not here. And even if he was, he wouldn't talk to you."

Longinus ran a hand over his face and frowned. "I've got some questions for him."

"He won't answer them."

Longinus turned to her, and his eyes narrowed. "We had a deal, your brother and I."

"That was before you arrested the Samaritan." She folded her arms over her chest. He needed to leave now, before Gilad came.

"That man killed my friend. It had nothing to do with Cedron."

He had friends? Somehow she'd pictured him alone. Like her. Nissa crossed the courtyard and motioned to the gate. "Cedron should have known not to trust a Roman."

Longinus's eyes narrowed, and his jaw went tight. He moved toward her, his eyes fixed on her face.

She pressed her shoulders against the wall, the tiny thorns of the climbing rose pricking her back. He was so much bigger than her, even bigger than Abba. She raised her chin. *He can't think I'm afraid.*

He stopped, close enough that she could smell the lye that had bleached his tunic white. Nissa's heart pounded, and her legs trembled.

His voice rose. "Tell him I need to talk to him if he wants Stephen freed."

Her temper flared, just as it had so many times when Abba

had loomed over her like this. "I'm not your messenger; tell him yourself."

He expelled a breath like a charging bull. She flinched and closed her eyes, but the expected blow didn't come. She snuck a peek.

His brow furrowed, but not in anger. She stood her ground, her heart pounding in her ears, her chest rising and falling with quickened breath.

He stared at her for a moment, then lifted a hand and reached behind her to the vine that climbed the wall. He snapped off a pink rosebud and tucked it behind her ear, his callused fingers brushing like a hummingbird against her cheek. "I might be a Roman, but I don't hit women."

She glared up at him, her cheeks burning and her mouth as dry as dust.

"Don't worry, I'll find Cedron myself." His mouth eased into a smile, but his eyes looked sad. He pushed through the gate, pulling the sagging door shut behind him.

Nissa pressed her hands to her cheeks. *He is dangerous.* That's why her heart was pounding and her body felt like the burning bush on Mount Horeb. He was looking for the thieves, and he'd never give up.

The gate creaked open. She straightened and caught her breath, her hand going to the rose behind her ear. Was he back?

Gilad sauntered into the courtyard like King David entering his palace.

He wore a royal-blue tunic embroidered with gold and a coat of deep-brown wool. Not a strand of his jet-black hair or perfectly trimmed beard was out of place. His ebony eyes landed on Nissa.

She swallowed and croaked a greeting. "Shalom."

Gilad's glance flicked over her smooth hair, the linen tunic, before resting on the rose. "Nissa. I find you well. A flower in your hair, pink in your cheeks. I've never seen you looking better."

He noticed. Isn't that what she wanted? He stepped closer, close enough to reach out and touch her. Was this the moment she'd been waiting for? Had he finally realized what a good wife she would be? Her pulse fluttered like a tambourine at a wedding feast.

Gilad's mouth twisted. "And that Roman who just left had a smile on his face."

Longinus? What did he have to do with anything?

"I'd wager you have Roman coins in your belt."

Nissa sucked in a breath. Roman coins?

Gilad's ebony eyes narrowed. "Romans seem not to care if their women are flat-chested and sharp-tongued. At least you'll be able to pay me the rent."

"Gilad." Nissa's face flamed as his words turned her hopes to ash. "No. I'm not—it's not—"

Gilad's smile was more like a sneer. "Don't be ashamed, Nissa. Your brother is an am-ha-arez; your parents have thrown you out. What else are you supposed to do? I'm just surprised you are able to make any money at all." He looked around, assessing the jars of food, the bright linen drying in the sun, the manger full of barley. "Beauty clearly doesn't matter to a Roman dog."

How could he think that of her? She'd dreamed of marriage to him since she was a child, and now he thought she was selling her body to a Roman? "Gilad. It's not like that."

He held up a hand. "Say what you will, but I'm guessing your brother doesn't know how you are keeping him in wheat and oil."

Nissa took a step back, shaking her head. He was wrong, so wrong. But how could she explain the food, the new clothes, the rent money? Gilad knew exactly how much everything cost.

"I didn't think so." He advanced on her. "I have nothing against whores, Nissa. But if you're doing business in my house, your rent just doubled. You aren't beautiful, but that doesn't seem to matter. I know centurions pay well."

Doubled? "Gilad, I—You can't—"

"Do you want me to tell your brother about your little business?"

She swallowed hard. Cedron wouldn't believe him. But he would start asking questions. Questions about where she got the money. And once Cedron started asking questions, he wouldn't rest until he got answers.

Hot tears burned in her eyes. *No, I won't cry. Not because of him.* She dug the two silver pieces from her belt and slapped them into Gilad's open hand, wishing she could slap the smirk off his face.

He looked at the coins. "I'll be back next month. And I'll expect six drachmas, two more for this month and four for next." He looked over her hair and tunic, his gaze lingering on her chest. "You better hope that centurion doesn't get bored with you."

Indignation flared in her breast. She stepped up then, her hand flying toward his face, but Gilad was ready. He caught her wrist in an iron grip and stopped her before the palm of her hand met his cheek. He twisted her wrist until she cried out. His fist caught her across her temple, sending her stumbling back against the courtyard wall, blinded by a bolt of pain.

She threw her arms over her head, waiting for more blows. When they didn't come, she risked a look.

Gilad wiped his palm down his tunic. "Have the money by the beginning of Shevat, or I'll have a talk with Cedron." He turned and walked through the gate, leaving it swinging open behind him.

She rubbed her stinging cheek. The pink rose fluttered to the ground, its petals scattering in the dust. Which hurt worse, that Gilad thought she was selling her body to the men of Jerusalem or that he wanted to profit from her humiliation? He might be handsome and rich, but he was a pig.

Longinus was strong—much stronger than Gilad—but he didn't hit women. If only she had someone like him to turn to.

Cedron would never forgive her if he found out she was a thief. Dismas could never know she was a woman. No, she had to keep Gilad from talking . . . and the only way was to pay him.

She crouched next to the fire, wrapping her arms around her knees. Mouse would just have to take more silver. She would find a rich priest or one of the Pharisees. They always had plenty of money. Mouse would be careful—more careful than ever.

She'd make the mark on the wall of Siloam today.

Chapter 15

LONGINUS STALKED PAST the brothels and taverns of the tanners' district. He still needed to find Cedron, and Nissa hadn't been any help, except to demonstrate just how much she and her brother hated him. A pang in his chest surprised him. *Get over it, centurion. A Roman isn't anyone's friend.*

As he turned toward Siloam, he passed the peacock of a Jew he'd met the night he almost killed Nissa. He looked just as pompous as he had months ago, but what was he doing in this part of town?

He wound his way through the maze of narrow streets. At least now he had a small idea of why Nissa looked at him as though he might bite. He shouldn't have raised his voice. But how could he have known that under that porcupine skin, Nissa was afraid? Not of his sword or his position. She probably feared all men, except perhaps Cedron. He'd known enough women to guess why. He'd like to get her father in a dark alley sometime. No wonder she wasn't married, when she used her sharp tongue like a dagger to protect herself. No one else seemed to be stepping up to protect the girl.

Guilt stung him. Who was he to be so self-righteous? No, he didn't hit women, but he and Scipio had harassed many a maiden in Caesarea and every other city where they'd been stationed. They hadn't harmed them, not really. He didn't have to force his women. Even before he'd made centurion, he'd never had a shortage of women willing to be with him. Sometimes for brass coins, more often for a few cups of wine and some sweet words.

Longinus clenched his jaw at the memory of his last night with Scipio. As usual, they'd had too much to drink and had been teasing a woman in the forum. It had been his fault. He should have just let it go. But the wine and weeks of taking insults from the Jews had readied him for a fight. Stephen pulled a dagger, and Scipio had bled to death in the deserted forum while Longinus had begged every god he knew to save his friend. Before that night, he hadn't known real fear. Now he did. Death would come for him as well, and he would be just as powerless against it.

Would he have protected Nissa if he saw her harassed by Roman legionaries, or would he have joined in the fun? He rubbed at his temple. Stephen had stepped forward to protect a woman he didn't even know. *Does he deserve to die on a cross for that?* He pushed the thought away. It wasn't his job to decide punishment, just to carry out the orders.

Longinus reached the east gate of the city and searched the crowd for Cedron's lanky figure. He wasn't with the men waiting to be hired to work in the vineyards, or with the ones waiting to labor in the fields for a day's wage. Would he be at the Dung Gate with the other men desperate for work?

He walked north along the abyss of the Tyropoeon Valley, the flowing water shallow from the winter's drought. Since Scipio's death, he'd stayed away from taverns and women. Both held little appeal, only memories and bitter regret. But he'd seen plenty of Cedron's runt of a sister.

Nissa looked better than when he'd first met her, much better. Curiosity flickered through him as he relived his failed visit. When he'd looked in the house for Cedron, he'd seen generous stores of grain and oil, wine, and even honey and almonds. Nissa's clothes were finer than they'd been two months ago, and when he'd stood close to her, she'd smelled of costly myrrh and sandalwood. And she'd filled out some, too. He hadn't been too angry to notice that she looked more like a woman and less like a scrawny boy.

If Cedron hadn't found work over these past months, where were they getting the money for food and fragrance? Cedron had said Nissa was working for a laundry near the barracks, but washing tunics didn't pay that well. His footsteps slowed as he reached the bridge to the temple. Something wasn't right.

He stopped, unsure of what direction to take. West, where his thoughts were roaming? Or south, to the Dung Gate, where he hoped to find Cedron?

The Passover was less than two months away. He needed to make his bargain with Cedron: Stephen for the thieves, or his sword would go to Silvanus, along with his chance to get back to Gaul. But the question of Nissa was nagging at him like a mosquito. How was she paying for her finery?

He set out to the west, toward the barracks and the businesses that sprang up around every Roman garrison. Negotiating with Cedron could wait. Right now, he had some questions to ask at the laundry houses.

THE SUN WAS at its zenith by the time Longinus left the upper city and trudged toward the Dung Gate. He almost hoped Nissa's brother wouldn't be looking for work with the pagans and am-ha-arez of the city. His stomach twisted, and his feet fell heavily on the street.

Should he tell Cedron not one of the launderers knew of a tiny woman named Nissa? Would Cedron realize how Nissa bought their wheat and oil? Or the costly perfume he had smelled in her hair? There could be only one answer.

If she were his sister, he'd want to know. He'd be angry— mostly at himself for leaving her with so little choice. If she were his sister, he'd make sure she never had to resort to that life again. He'd find her a husband and get her safely married, even if she wasn't a virgin. But these Jews, they were different from Romans, and very different from Roman legionaries. These men expected to marry virgins; women kept themselves pure. What if Cedron threw Nissa out of their house? She'd already been cast off by her mother and father; she'd have no one. He'd seen women like that in every city he'd visited. It wasn't a pretty life.

He pictured her with the sorry excuse of a man he'd seen heading toward her house. Was that pompous Jew one of her customers? Were his own men? He'd known plenty of whores, but those were other women. Not the scrap of a girl who defended her brother like a mother lion. His hand strayed to the hilt of his sword. He'd like to run it through every man who ever touched her. And Nissa—he'd like to shake some sense into her.

I could give her silver . . . but she wouldn't take it. Between her pride and her brother's hatred of the Romans, an offer of help from him would be firmly—fiercely—rejected. She hated him; she'd made that clear enough. *So why am I thinking about her?*

A cluster of Jewish men, their voices raised in debate, blocked the narrow street. They fell into silence and glared as he shoved past them. Nissa wasn't his concern. He had more to worry about than a Jewish woman turned prostitute. He must find the thieves and deal with Stephen—not to mention track down a miracle worker who just might start a revolution. And then to get out of this hateful province. *Talk to Cedron; then forget her.*

He caught sight of a familiar striped tunic in the shade of the Dung Gate. Foul-smelling men scattered as he pushed through the crowd that waited for work. And the worst work it was: carting the dead carcasses from the tanners and unloading them in the wasteland of Gehenna, the dump outside the city gates.

Cedron saw him coming and turned his back. It was midday, and from the look of his clean tunic, he'd had no work.

Longinus pulled him around. "Cedron. Talk to me."

Cedron jerked away. "I trusted you." He moved toward the gate as a man with a cart full of refuse rumbled up.

Longinus snorted. "Trust had nothing to do with it."

Cedron's mouth tightened into a firm line.

"Two men!" The cart master called out.

Cedron pushed forward, but the man pointed to two burly men behind him. "You and you." Cedron's bony shoulders slumped.

Longinus looked over the dozens of men who waited for work. With his lack of skills, his lack of muscle, and the stigma of the am-ha-arez, Cedron would starve before he got work. But Nissa wouldn't allow that.

It was risky to keep Stephen in the carcer. If Silvanus found out that he'd had the Samaritan in his grasp, winning the bet would be the least of Longinus's worries. But, with Marcellus's help, he could keep Stephen a secret. If Cedron found the thieves, he could save the Samaritan, and Longinus would pay him enough to support Nissa for a long time. *Yes, Cedron can solve two of my problems.* But first, he had to get this stubborn Jew to hear him.

He clamped his hand around Cedron's arm and dragged him away from the Dung Gate.

Cedron struggled and cried out, but no one came to his aid against a Roman and he was no match for Longinus's iron grip and battle-hardened muscle. Longinus dragged Cedron around a corner and into a deserted alley. He pinned the protesting Jew against a crumbling wall with one hand on his chest. "Stephen's blood will be on your hands if he's crucified."

Cedron's breath rasped in this throat. "How do you figure that? And why should I care about a Samaritan?"

Longinus leaned in close. "A Samaritan who was sent to Jerusalem by your so-called messiah. Who believes in him just as you do."

Cedron stopped struggling, and understanding widened his eyes.

"You knew Jesus wasn't in the city. But you brought me to Joseph's and handed over one of Jesus's followers to me. You're lucky I haven't killed him yet."

Cedron shook his head wildly. "I didn't know—"

"You betrayed one of your own, Cedron," Longinus growled. "If you want to save Stephen, listen to me now."

Chapter 16

NISSA TRUDGED UP the street, averting her gaze from a barely clothed woman in the courtyard of the brothel.

The water jar was heavy, and her bag knocked against her leg, stuffed with a handful of figs, some dried fish, and two honey cakes for their evening meal. She reached the gate, leaning on it with her hip and juggling the water jar, but something was wrong. The gate hung straight and true. The broken hinge was repaired, and the door swung open with just a touch of her finger. She stepped into the courtyard and almost dropped the jar, her heart leaping into her throat.

Longinus bent over a makeshift worktable, a mallet in his hand and three iron nails clamped between his lips. His tunic was tied around his waist, exposing a broad chest and wide shoulders.

"What . . . ?" Her mouth went dry. She'd seen plenty of naked chests—men working on the temple or hauling loads in the wood market. Just not in her courtyard. And none so scarred and . . . freckled.

He glanced up, surveying her from the top of her coiled hair to the toes peeping out from under her tunic. His teeth clamped tighter around the nails. "Who did that to you?"

Her hand flew to her eye. The swelling was down, but a faint bruise remained where Gilad had hit her days before. "I fell."

His stared at her for a long moment, his mouth pressed on

the nails until his lips paled, then turned back to the three-legged stool upended in front of him.

Nissa settled the water jar in a shady corner and dumped her bag beside it. If she didn't know better, Longinus looked angry. At her. But she'd done nothing to anger him, at least not yet. And what was he doing in her courtyard?

"We don't need your help." The words sprung from her lips before she could think, and she instantly regretted them.

He pounded a nail with two sharp blows.

Nissa bit her lip, feeling like a rude child. She scooped a ladle of water from the jar and brought it to him. He took it carefully, shifting away so that not even her tunic brushed his arm as he drank and passed the ladle back without a word of thanks.

She stared at him as he hammered the last nails into the stool. This man who had just days ago called her pretty was acting like she was a leper.

"There." Longinus flipped the stool over and set it on the ground. It didn't even wobble. He lined the mallet and the nails in a neat row, avoiding her eyes. A muscle tightened in his jaw.

"Thank you." She'd take his teasing before this cold silence. "I have some figs . . . or a honey cake . . . I can—"

"Have you been walking alone at night again, Nissa?" His voice was abrupt and harsh, his accent heavier, as if he had forgotten how to speak her language.

Nissa backed away a step. "Yes. I mean, no. Not lately."

"It's dangerous." He glanced over her shoulder toward the brothels and taverns. "Out there. For a girl like you." He stepped forward. "You should know how to protect yourself. In case . . ." His bright blue eyes met hers, his brows lowered.

In case what? Why was he looking at her like that? And acting like she was in some kind of danger? He was more of a threat to her than anyone she passed in the street.

He advanced on her, so fast she didn't have time to move away. His hand snaked out and grabbed her wrist. "Let me show you something that works better than a kick in the shins."

She pulled back, but he held tight. "What do you—"

"If you're going to . . . walk at night, you need to know how to defend yourself. If a man, stronger than you—"

"I'm strong."

He scowled. "Don't be ridiculous, Nissa. All men, except perhaps a cripple, are stronger than you." He jerked her closer to him and snagged her other wrist in a vice-like grip. "What if a man grabs you like this?"

She pulled again, but his hand tightened. His skin was warm from the sun and smooth. She couldn't break his hold.

"Do this." He lifted her arms. "Lift up, then down, fast. You should be able to break one hand free."

His blue eyes looked into hers, pale and grim. "Do it."

She did as he said. Although his grip stayed tight, she was able to wrench one wrist free of his hold.

"Good." Longinus nodded. "Now, step back and jerk me toward you with the hand I'm still holding. I won't be expecting it, so you'll get some momentum. Then, with the heel of this hand"—he took her free hand in his and turned it upward—"thrust up, right into my face."

She stared at him. What was he doing? Teaching her to hit a man?

"Go on. Do it." His voice was a growl, and his hard eyes stared into hers. His broad chest was close enough for her to smell sweat and sandalwood.

She swallowed. Maybe he would leave if she did what he said. Then her heart would stop pounding in her ears. She moved fast, jerking back just as he'd told her and bringing her hand up to his face with all the power of her undersized body.

He threw up his arm, blocking her just in time. She would have broken his nose. His brows went up. A burst of warmth flowed through her. Was that a flicker of admiration she'd caught in his eyes?

He grunted. "Good." He looked down, dropped her hands, and stepped back like he'd just realized how close they were. "Remember that." He turned his back, pulling the neck of his tunic up and over his chest and thrusting his arms through the sleeves. He adjusted his belt and checked his sword.

"Tell Cedron to report to me at the barracks." He stepped across the courtyard like he couldn't get away from her fast enough, but turned to look at her again, as though he had something more to say.

She crossed her arms over her chest. Why did the look he gave her seem to go right through her, like a nail into olive wood?

He rubbed a hand over the back of his neck and scowled. "Be careful, Nissa." He pushed through the newly hung gate and was gone without another word.

"Be careful"? No dimpled smile? No "good-bye, pretty Nissa"? He'd repaired the gate and the stool, given her a fighting lesson like one of his soldiers, and left? Disappointment clamored over disbelief. Why should she care what this incomprehensible man did?

She'd never understand him. *And I don't want to.*

She stepped back and swung her arm back, imagining Gilad's face. She cocked her wrist and brought it up, just as he had shown her. Yes, she could do it if she had to. She could stop a man in his tracks, at least long enough to get away. She probably would never have to use it, but it was good to know.

LONGINUS CLATTERED DOWN the stone steps of the carcer. He'd avoided the man called Stephen for a week, but perhaps the Samaritan could take his thoughts off Nissa for a few moments.

Going to her house had been a mistake. Repairing her gate and teaching her to fight off a man had done little to ease his worries about the scrap of a girl with the mouse-brown hair and sharp wit. *What else could I do? I'm not her brother.* And he hadn't felt brotherly when she'd been close enough to kiss.

Where is that blasted Marcellus? He should be standing guard outside Stephen's cell. Instead, the heavy door stood unguarded and agape.

His hand went to his sword. Could that cursed Samaritan have overpowered Marcellus and escaped? Stephen had escaped him twice before. He should have known he'd try again.

He pulled his sword and pushed the door fully open, but Marcellus didn't lie dead or injured on the floor of the damp cell. His officer in charge of the carcer started guiltily from the bench, upsetting a game board balanced on his knees. Ivory and onyx game pieces scattered on the dirt floor.

Stephen held an onyx piece in his hand, frozen in the act of making a move.

Marcellus scrambled up. "We were just—"

"I can see what you were doing." Longinus jerked his head at the red-faced legionary and sheathed his sword. "Get back to your post." He'd deal with Marcellus later.

Stephen bent and scooped up the game pieces that lay in the dust. He laid the game board, a piece of carved ebony, on the bench. He set the wooden dice box on top of it, along with three dice.

Longinus towered over him. "What are you playing at?"

"I believe Marcellus called it *tabulah*."

Longinus snorted. "You know what I mean. You could have escaped. Why didn't you?"

"I won't try to escape." Stephen sorted the black game pieces from the white. He set the black in front of Longinus.

"Why not?"

Stephen looked at him for a long time. "Jesus asked me to come here. He told me to wait for him, here, in Jerusalem. If this"—he gestured to the four walls that enclosed them—"is what he wants for me, I won't run from him again."

There was that peace again, as though the Samaritan were taunting him. Longinus couldn't kill Stephen yet. He might as well get some answers to the questions that had plagued him since Cedron's miracle—that is if the smug Samaritan really knew anything. He picked up the dice box and shook it. The ivory dice rattled. "So you really think this man Jesus is the Messiah? The one the Jews are waiting for?"

"I know it."

"How?"

"He said so. When I was in Samaria."

Longinus's hand stopped midshake. "When I was looking for you all over Galilee, you were hiding out in some little hole in Samaria? Where?"

Stephen set the white pieces on his own side of the board, his brows pulled down in thought.

Longinus gave the dice another shake. Of course Stephen wouldn't tell him where he'd been hiding. Why should he? Stephen had no reason to trust him.

"In Sychar. I have grandparents there."

"Aren't you worried I'll go there? Arrest them for harboring a fugitive?"

Stephen tipped his head and stared at Longinus. "You haven't killed me yet. I don't think my grandparents are in danger."

Longinus huffed out a breath. Of course he wouldn't hunt down a senile old man and his wife. He threw the dice onto the board. Two, two, and five.

He placed three black chips in their places on the board, scooped up the dice, and passed them to Stephen. "What about the girl?" Surely Stephen hoped some day to go back to the beautiful girl he'd been protecting on the road in Galilee. "Maybe I'll go find her."

The dice ceased to rattle as Stephen's hand stilled, his lips pressed in a thin line.

Longinus's eyes narrowed. He was right. The girl meant something to the enigmatic Samaritan. *At least I'm not the only one with woman trouble.*

Stephen shook the dice box once more. "You won't." He tipped the dice out on the board.

Longinus cursed. Two sixes and a four. Stephen had that

right. As much as the girl had made him look a fool, she wasn't worth a trip to Samaria.

Stephen placed three more chips on the board, the whites already well in front of the blacks. "He told a woman, the girl's mother, he was the Messiah—the Taheb, as the Samaritans say. The one we've been awaiting for a thousand years."

Longinus scooped up the dice. "He's not the first Jew to pretend to be the Messiah; even I know that. The Pharisees hate him, the people follow him, even some of the Romans fear him."

Stephen nodded.

Longinus didn't even look at the dice that tumbled over the board. "It's ridiculous. Who is he? A poor man with nothing to his name. Why would a god send a messiah like that? Why not as a Roman? Even as Caesar?"

"I don't know. But you've seen what he can do."

The arrogant youth admitted he didn't know something? A miracle. "That doesn't mean he's your messiah, the son of a god."

"*The* God."

Longinus ignored the correction and moved his black pieces forward.

For the hundredth time, Longinus recalled the look on Cedron's face when he first opened his eyes. And what he'd heard since. Even if only half of it was true, this man was someone to watch. Healings, casting out demons, even—and this he wished he had seen—walking on water. "But that's another thing." Longinus leaned toward his prisoner. "If he's your messiah, why isn't he here in Jerusalem? Why isn't he gathering an army?"

Stephen's brows drew down as he gathered the dice. "He doesn't do what anyone expects. The people—not the Pharisees but the poor Jews in the countryside, the ones burdened with taxes from both the temple and the Romans—they are ready to revolt. They are begging for a leader who will promise them revenge on their enemies, triumph over Rome."

Longinus stiffened. "They won't triumph over Rome."

Stephen threw the dice. Three sixes. "Our God is mighty.

If he wanted to wipe Rome off the face of the earth, he could do it."

Longinus snorted. Nothing was more powerful than Rome. "And you believe this man Jesus is from that god? The god of all the old stories—the one that brought down the walls of Jericho?"

"Yes. Jesus could raise an army as quickly as you can assemble your cohort." Stephen moved his pieces forward, knocking two of Longinus's from the board.

Longinus frowned at the dice. The Samaritan had luck on his side; he'd need a miracle to win now. "And yet he hides in Galilee, of all places. He doesn't even come to Jerusalem. And he teaches only twelve men."

"For a Roman, you know a great deal about this carpenter."

"I know enough to wonder what he's about. If he is the son of this one god, as you say, why doesn't he cure every blind man and cripple? Every leper and pathetic beggar out there at the temple?"

"He could."

"But he doesn't. Does that mean he can't or he won't?" Longinus dumped the dice on the board. "If he can but won't, he is a cruel messiah." There, a good throw. A six, five, and three. He moved his chip forward and added two back to the board. Let the Samaritan beat that.

"He cures all who ask him."

Longinus frowned. "You speak in riddles, just like your so-called messiah."

Stephen nodded, and a smile flickered over his face. "I know. I doubted him—called him a fraud, and worse. But the things he said to me . . . the things I saw . . ." He took the dice from Longinus's hand and shook them out onto the board.

Neither man looked at them.

"What did you see?"

"Miracles. Healings." Stephen's eyes burned with the fire of a Zealot. "Mercy."

Longinus shook his head and blew out a breath of disbelief.

"Mercy?" *Mercy doesn't overthrow empires.* "And what does he want from you in exchange for this mercy?" Everyone wanted something. Gold. Loyalty. Power.

Stephen's face settled again into that vision of peace. "Everything."

A shiver passed over Longinus, and his hand tightened on the wooden box of dice. Everything? He'd given everything to Rome, and look where he'd ended up: in a backward province, his best friend dead. He'd given everything and gotten nothing in return but failure and fear. What would he give to find the peace this man had?

He slammed the box on the game board. *I'm no gullible Jew.* He'd make sure this Galilean wasn't a threat to Rome; then he'd win the bet and put these crazy Jews—and their god—far behind him. He'd get out of this province and find his own peace.

Chapter 17

NISSA PULLED HER voluminous cloak around her shoulders and darted through the crowded streets. Instead of the tingle of anticipation she usually had before stealing, her insides churned like a skin full of curdled goat's milk.

For the past month, Cedron had searched for the thieves, asking every merchant in the city, every beggar at the city gates and outside the temple for information on Mouse and the Greek. He had found nothing because Mouse and Dismas had been careful, very careful. They stole just enough to get by, and Mouse's alms to the beggars bought their silence. But tomorrow was the beginning of Shevat, the eleventh month, and Nissa didn't have enough money to pay Gilad.

If Cedron found the thieves before Passover, Longinus would release Stephen. If he didn't, Stephen would be crucified. Even worse, Longinus had doubled the reward for Mouse and Dismas. Now, every Jew and half the Gentiles of the city were watching for them. If they kept stealing, they would surely be caught.

This would be Mouse's last time. It had to be. She needed a big purse, enough to last them through the winter. When spring came, she would think of something. She'd have to.

Dismas won't like it. "Don't get greedy," he'll say.

But she wasn't greedy. She was desperate. Her supply of coins was gone. They needed wheat, oil, and food for Amit. The price of grain had increased tenfold, and if they didn't get rain, it would go even higher. She owed money to the woodcutter and the oil merchant.

The bruise from Gilad had healed, but his threat lingered. If she didn't pay him, he'd have a talk with Cedron. Tell him what he thought she was doing for money. Which was worse, for Cedron to know she was a thief or think she was a prostitute?

She and Dismas would go to the temple and find a rich man with a big purse. Then, she'd atone with alms and wash in Siloam. She broke into a quick run, through the marketplace, down one winding street, then another. Her pace slowed as she approached the meeting place.

Dismas wasn't alone. She stopped and slid into the shallow depression of a closed doorway. His tall figure lounged against the wall like always, but a short man fidgeted beside him. Dismas's low laugh drifted along the alley.

She ducked her head out, and his glance caught her.

He pushed off from the wall. "There you are, Mouse. We were about to leave without you."

The new man turned to her. He was short, only a little taller than her. But his shoulders were wide, and his neck was thick. His face was covered in a coarse black beard, and bushy brows nearly met above close-set eyes.

"So this is your little Mouse?" His voice was like the dull rasp of a saw through a wooden plank. "I hope you are as good as he says."

Nissa looked at Dismas. *What is going on?*

Dismas threw an arm over her shoulder. His scent of mint and cloves soothed her nerves. "This is Gestas. We'll work together. Same as always. You just watch us, and when you get your chance, do your job. We'll split everything three ways."

Three ways? That would be more than she made partnering with Dismas. But could they trust him? Nissa eyed the new man and didn't like what she saw. His eyes looked cold and flat, like those of a snake. She took a step back, the nape of her neck prickling.

"Don't worry, little Mouse. With Gestas here, we can get more, faster. We'll be in and out before those rich dogs even know what they're missing. Trust me."

She shook her head. "Dismas, I don't think—"

Gestas crowded into her. "Don't think, boy. Just do what we say." He poked her in the chest with a hand that looked strong enough to crush a walnut. "I've been stealing since before you were pissing standing up."

Nissa swallowed hard. She needed to tell Dismas about Longinus. If he knew the risk, maybe he'd change his mind about their new partner.

"Dismas." She turned her back on the new man. "The Roman, he's looking for us. I think we should—"

Gestas grabbed her arm and threw her to the ground. "Shut up and do as you're told, boy."

Dismas, quick as a mountain cat, wrapped his hand around Gestas's throat and pushed him up against the wall. "Keep your hands off Mouse or the deal is off."

Gestas stared at the taller man. "So. That's how it is. I forgot you're a Greek."

Dismas's face twisted at his meaning, and he tightened his grip. "Leave him alone."

Gestas coughed and jerked away from Dismas. "My apologies. Just keep your little friend quiet. I—we—make the decisions." He gave Mouse a hard look. "He does what he's told."

Nissa's throat closed as though she were the one choking. A tremor of fear ran up her spine. *I could stop right now. I could find another way.*

The hopeless voice countered, *You don't have another way.*

Dismas pulled her up. He brushed a hand over her cloak. "You all right?"

Nissa nodded and folded her arms over her chest.

He leaned close and whispered, "I owe him money, Mouse. He's going to stick to me until he gets paid. He's got the manners of an ass, but he's good. There will be plenty of silver for us all."

Nissa didn't answer. Dismas wasn't going to change his mind. She chewed on her lip, considering her options. This man reminded her of the men who staggered around the taverns and brothels. But she needed enough silver to pay Gilad and she needed it today.

Gestas eyed her more closely. "Your little friend is safe with me. I don't like boys anyhow." He jerked a hand to Dismas. "Follow me. Today we go to the temple. Their god can do without their gold."

Dismas nodded. "Fine. The temple. But careful, or those soldiers will be after all of us." He winked at Nissa. "Stay close to me."

Nissa brushed herself off. If Dismas was right—if they could get more without being caught—then she would do it. One last time.

They passed over the bridge and around the temple mount, entering from the south through the Huldah Gates. They walked through the underground corridors and climbed the stairs that brought them to the Court of the Gentiles.

A line of Roman soldiers guarded the north side, their spears at the ready and their eyes scanning the crowd. She sidled behind a heavyset Jew with a bleating lamb in his arms. No redhaired centurion. At least not yet. A horn sounded the call to afternoon prayer.

Dismas moved closer to her. "Don't get greedy. Remember, pigs get fat; hogs get slaughtered."

She wasn't greedy. Gilad was, and she needed to keep him quiet.

Dismas grunted and whispered to her, "I'm going to the other side."

He melted into the crowd, but she didn't follow. Gestas was her best chance at stealing enough today to satisfy Gilad. Gestas moved through the crowds toward the column-lined portico on the southern side of the temple.

She edged toward the portico where money changers and

merchants were at work. Gestas slid close to her and nodded at a plump priest exchanging money at a nearby table. His purse full of silver glinted in the dim light.

Nissa's heart sped up. It was Thaddeus, the priest who had ordered Cedron beaten for his testimony. A ripple of righteousness surged through her. He deserved to be deprived of his silver. Dismas had stopped her last time she'd seen Thaddeus, but today the little priest would pay for what he'd done to Cedron.

Instead of moving toward the money changer, causing a distraction so Nissa could dip a hand into the purse, Gestas disappeared behind one of the stone pillars.

What was he doing? Nissa crept in the direction he'd gone. A hand closed around her arm, and a squeak escaped her lips.

Gestas pulled her close and whispered in her ear. "Steal just one coin from his purse, and let him see you. Then run."

Her eyes flew to his face. *Let him see me?* She shook her head. "That's not how Dismas and I—"

His strong fingers dug into her arm. "We're doing it my way this time. Do you want a fat purse or not, little Mouse? Because I can get you enough to live like a king."

She swallowed and nodded. Yes. Enough for months.

The grip on her arm tightened. "Then shut up and do what I say." He leaned in close, and she smelled his fetid breath. "Take a coin. Run to the stairs. The ones that lead down to the lower levels. Make sure he follows you." Gestas slunk away toward the courtyard.

What was he planning? Her heart pounded, and her mouth went dry. *Just do what he says, and get it over with.* She edged closer to the Pharisee whose attention was on the money changer.

Thaddeus shook his head, his heavy phylacteries swaying. "Your scales are surely wrong. That's pure Phoenician silver."

She slipped her hand into his purse and came out with a brass sesterce. Instead of hiding it away, she hesitated, letting the sun glint off its polished surface.

He jerked toward her. "What? Give me that, boy!"

His meaty hand shot toward her, but Nissa dodged it and darted toward the well of steps that led into the bowels of the temple. A crash behind her and a quick look showed he was following, pushing his way through the crowd, tucking his fat purse back into his belt.

She paused at the top of the stairs.

He came into sight, roaring at her.

Where is Gestas? She scurried down the smooth stone steps.

The underground corridor was empty. A few oil lamps cast dim light along the walls.

She heard steps clatter behind her, and the shouts of the priest echoed through the empty hallway. She reached the passage that led to the Huldah Gates. More corridors split off on each side.

A voice hissed nearby. "Mouse." A hand came out of the gloom and caught her tunic. Gestas pulled her down a side hallway. Where did it lead? And what was he doing? Heavy sandals slapped behind her.

"He's following me." Her voice sounded loud in the corridor. Her breath caught in her chest.

The corridor ended in a dimly lit alcove. She looked frantically for a door, a window. There was nothing but smooth walls and flickering torches. They were trapped, and she could hear the priest wheezing close behind.

Gestas backed toward the darkest corner, his dingy clothes blending into the gloom. Only his obsidian eyes glittered in the dark.

Thaddeus rounded the corner. When he saw her and the dead end, his steps slowed. His breath rasped in his heaving chest. "Little thief." He pulled a dagger from his belt. "I'll give you a scar to remind you never to steal from me again."

Nissa backed into the corner. The priest came at her, his knife outstretched.

She tensed, sure she'd feel the slash of the blade, but Gestas leaped out, a curved blade glinting in his hand. The priest didn't have time to turn, didn't even cry out. He crumpled to his knees before Nissa, blood pouring from a wide gash across his neck like a bull sacrificed on the stone altar.

Gestas shoved him over on his back. A gurgle sounded from the priest's open mouth. He held out a hand to her, his eyes wild and terrified. Nissa pressed her back against the cold stone wall. His hand dropped and his body went limp, his terrified eyes staring into the distance.

Gestas pulled the purse from the dead man's belt. A low sound of triumph broke from him as he weighed it in his hand. He pried the dagger from the still man's hand and wrenched a heavy signet ring from his finger. An emerald as large as a grape glinted as he tucked it in his belt.

Gestas turned and flashed a pointy-toothed smile. "Nice work, Mouse. Come on." He darted down the winding corridor without a glance behind him.

Nissa's feet were planted like pillars, unable to move, as she stared at the man before her. He was dead. She might not have slit his throat, but she might as well have. She was not just a thief anymore. She was a murderer.

Dismas rounded the corner. His eyes widened at the sight of the dead priest's body.

"Mouse, get out of here." He pulled her through the corridor and dragged her out of the temple into the golden light of late afternoon. She stumbled as he pushed her into the shadow of the Hippodrome.

She crumpled to the ground. All she could see was the blood pouring out of the priest. Bile rose in her throat. She retched and coughed. She scooted into the shadows, closing her eyes and leaning her forehead on the cool wall.

Dismas stood over her, shielding her from view. "Mouse. We need to get farther from the temple. When they find the body . . ."

He was right, but she couldn't move.

Dismas pulled her up, his arm clamping around her waist. As he straightened beside her, he stared at her like he'd never seen her before. His eyes searched her face, then traveled down to her dirty bare feet. His grip gentled, and he leaned her against his side. "Come on. We need to move fast."

They stumbled along the side streets, Dismas supporting her like a cripple. Nissa's feet weighed as heavy as stones, the burden of her crime increasing with every step. She had killed a member of the Sanhedrin in the temple of the Lord. Cedron could never know. He would despise her. Longinus would want to find them now more than ever. It wouldn't be long before every soldier and all the temple guards were scouring the city for them.

After what seemed like hours, they reached the meeting place. Gestas was there with an amphora of wine tucked under his arm. "Nice work, little Mouse."

Dismas released Nissa and advanced on Gestas. He grabbed the little man by his tunic and slammed him against the wall. "This wasn't our bargain."

Gestas's face twisted. He tried to pull away, but Dismas's hands closed around his throat.

"What were you thinking? They'll be looking for us all over the city."

Gestas choked in a breath. "Find a place . . . hole up for a few days . . . here." He struggled to pull the heavy purse from his belt.

Dismas released him and jerked the purse from his hands. He ran his fingers through the coins, his lips moving as he counted, then pulled out a handful and pressed them into Nissa's damp, shaking hands.

She looked at the coins—blood money—and let them fall to the ground.

Dismas scooped them up. "You'll need this, Mouse. Take it."

She shook her head and slid down the wall. She wrapped her hands around her knees and tucked her head down, wishing she could disappear.

Gestas's voice floated above her. "He'll be fine. Stay out of sight for a few weeks; that should be enough time for things to quiet down. Then look for the mark on the wall."

In the silence he left behind, Nissa's ragged breathing filled her ears. Would she ever close her eyes again without seeing the priest—the one she'd hated—dying in front of her? *Murderer. Murderer.* Her heart pounded out the words.

A warm hand squeezed her shoulder. "Mouse. Let me help you get home."

She looked up. Dismas's face was pale, his mouth grim. Was he angry with her? He had every reason to be. He'd warned her to stay with him, but she'd been greedy.

"No." She shook her head. "Leave me here."

He pushed the money at her. "Take the money, Mouse, and never come back."

She knocked his hand away.

Dismas knelt before her, his hands on her trembling shoulders. "I'm sorry, Mouse. I shouldn't have done this to you. All of it—it's my fault. I taught you to do this; I brought Gestas when I knew he was trouble . . ."

Nissa shook her head. It wasn't Dismas's fault. It was her own.

Dismas tucked the coins in her belt. "Good-bye, Mouse. But take these. You'll need them. When you feel better, you'll thank me. It's all I can do for you now." With another look of remorse, he backed away and was gone.

Revulsion rose in her throat. Would she ever feel better? Would she ever not think with horror on what had just happened? The Lord had forsaken her, and with good reason. She wasn't just worthless; she was a killer. A murderer. Abba had been right. It would have been better if she had never been born.

Chapter 18

THE POUND OF marching feet and the dim shouts from the training ground faded as Longinus moved down the carcer stairs. Marcellus lounged outside the cell. He jumped to attention as Longinus pushed through the door. Not even locked. Golden rays of late-afternoon sun filtered through the tiny window of the cell, lighting the parchment Stephen studied.

A month in the carcer seemed to have been small hardship for his prisoner. Stephen appeared more comfortable each time Longinus visited. A chest of rolled parchments, blankets, a new cloak. He'd even caught Marcellus bringing in fresh figs one afternoon.

Longinus rubbed his forehead, massaging the ripple of pain between his eyes. "Another question for you, Samaritan."

Stephen set the parchment aside and turned his attention to Longinus.

Longinus sat on the bench and set his helmet on the floor. Perhaps this question would rattle the peaceful Samaritan. "If I crucify you tomorrow—I know, I know—" He held up his hand as Stephen's mouth opened. "If it is *Jesus's will* that you are crucified tomorrow, how would your death help your messiah?"

Stephen didn't look afraid of the threat or riled by Longinus's tone. "I will die when Jesus wills it and for a reason. The reason might even be you."

"Me? I'm no Jew." And he didn't need a messiah.

"Neither am I. That doesn't seem to matter to Jesus."

"But I believe in Jupiter and Mars. In the gods of Rome, not this absurd god of yours."

Stephen raised a skeptical brow. "When is the last time you prayed to the gods of Rome?"

Longinus blinked. When had it been? There was a shrine to Mars in the principia, out of sight of the Jews, but he hadn't prayed or left an offering to the god of war since long before he came to Jerusalem. If Pilate knew that, he'd be furious.

Stephen leaned forward. "And when, centurion, have your gods ever answered you?"

They hadn't. They hadn't answered when his father was dying in the damp wilds of Britannia. And they hadn't answered when Scipio had lain dying on the street in Caesarea.

He pressed his fingers against his eyes. As usual, Stephen's answers failed to satisfy him. It was as though the Samaritan were trying to drive him mad. He should have crucified him a month ago instead of listening to his inane nonsense. The more he heard from his prisoner, the more questions he had. Questions that woke him in the night, nagging like a headache.

Perhaps this one would stump his know-it-all prisoner. "So which is he, this messiah of yours?" He held out his index finger. "A fraud and a liar? A man who is duping his disciples and making a mockery of your laws? If he is, then he's a dangerous radical who needs to be stopped, either by your own people or by mine."

Stephen didn't answer.

Longinus brought out his thumb. "Or . . ." He stopped, his mouth suddenly dry.

Stephen's eyes locked on his.

Longinus swallowed. Ridiculous as it sounded, it was the only other possibility. A possibility that was, in fact, absurd. "Or this Jesus, this man from Galilee, really is the son of your god, the one God. He has power over life and death, and he has a reason to be here that we don't understand—that *no one* understands."

"Yet." Stephen finished.

Longinus stared at the floor as their words seemed to echo from the stone walls. The son of God? He couldn't be. But a fraud? He couldn't be that, either. Longinus had seen Jesus' power at the Pool of Siloam.

He needed to meet this man in the flesh, to form his own opinion and not rely on hearsay and stories. But if Jesus was smart, he wouldn't come back to Jerusalem. Too many powerful people here hated him.

And what about the man in front of Longinus? The man who had killed Scipio in the dark forum? He'd like to wipe that peaceful smile off Stephen's face. He'd love to see the infuriating man quake in fear, but nailing him to a cross? His stomach curled in revulsion. *Cedron better find those thieves before Passover.*

The door groaned open, and Marcellus ducked into the gloomy room, two bowls of stew and a round of bread balanced in one arm. "Cornelius was just outside looking for you."

Longinus straightened. Not that spy for Silvanus. What did he want now? "Did you tell him where I was?"

"No. I told him you were . . . in the latrine."

Longinus stared at his optio.

Marcellus shrugged. "I couldn't think of anything else."

"What did he want?"

Marcellus stood aside, holding the door open for him. "Something at the temple. The Sanhedrin is convening. They want you there."

He snagged his helmet from the floor and fitted it over his head. "For the love of Jupiter, Marcellus, stay alert. Cornelius might come back."

Longinus took the stairs two at a time, emerging from the cool underground cells into the bright heat of the camp. He swung up on Ferox and spurred him toward the temple. *Curse these Jews.* Instead of winning the bet and getting back to Gaul, he asked questions about a mysterious Jew he'd never met. Instead of doing his duty, he worried about a sprite of a Jewish girl selling her body in the brothels of the lower city.

Now trouble at the temple again. And with Passover closing in.

Ferox's iron-shod feet rang out in the Court of the Gentiles. Longinus guided him to the Stone Court, where Cedron had been tried and rejected and where the Sanhedrin waited to speak to him. He slid from Ferox and pushed his way through the crowd.

The Stone Court was packed with the priests, Pharisees, and scribes of the Sanhedrin, as well as at least a hundred Jewish men and women—all talking at once.

He tucked his helmet under his arm and pushed forward, parting the sea of rich robes and elaborate headdresses. He stopped in front of Caiaphas. The high priest's robes were so stiff with gold they barely moved. Caiaphas backed a few steps away, as if Longinus's very breath would defile him.

The voices quieted as Caiaphas raised his arms. "Finally."

Longinus bristled. Rome had conquered this land, yet they treated him like a tardy servant. He stood straighter, towering over the Jew. "Why do you call on Rome?"

"One of our priests was killed this afternoon in the temple."

A murder in the temple? That explained the outraged voices and angry faces. What worried these purity-obsessed Jews more, the death of a man or the defilement of their temple? "What happened?"

"Just as the afternoon prayers were being sung, Thaddeus chased a thief into the lower tunnels, a deserted area at that time of day. The thief killed him and stole his purse."

"Why do you call on me? Did you find the murderer already?" The Jews had their own courts of law. A murder was Rome's business only when they wanted the criminal executed. They would convict the murderer, Pilate would give his consent, and Longinus's men would carry out the sentence.

"Not yet."

Longinus turned to go. "Don't bother me until you have him."

Caiaphas raised a heavily embroidered arm. "I've been told that you seek the temple thieves. The Mouse and the Greek."

He stopped. The little thief and his Greek partner? "You think they killed him?" That didn't sound like the thieves he'd been searching for since the harvest feast.

"The money changer saw one of them. A boy, small and quick. Others say they saw a tall Greek with him. A boy that size couldn't have killed Thaddeus alone. They must have worked together. We demand they be found and executed."

It *did* sound like the Mouse and the Greek. And they'd been seen at the temple before.

Caiaphas continued. "They'll have his signet ring, a large emerald."

Longinus snorted. If they were smart, they'd throw the ring in the nearest well. But in his experience, criminals made stupid mistakes, and that's what got them caught.

He strode toward the gate. "I'll find them."

Jumping on Ferox, he pounded through the Court of the Gentiles, Jews scattering in front of him like dry leaves.

He had less than two months to find the temple thieves, now the temple murderers. If Pilate came back to this growing mess just in time for Passover, he'd be cleaning latrines in Judea for the rest of his military career.

Chapter 19

Nissa curled into the farthest corner of Amit's stall, her arms wrapped around her drawn-up knees, her head burrowed in her cloak. The morning horns sounded the call to prayer. Even if she did call on the Lord now, if she could form words to ask for his protection, it was too late. He wouldn't forgive this sin; it was too big, too much.

She'd changed from her disguise, stumbled home, and hid in the corner of the lean-to. Through the evening, every step sounding outside their gate had paralyzed her with fear, and every voice made her heart jump, sure as she was that the temple guards were coming for her.

Cedron had found her as darkness fell. She'd claimed illness, her stomach knotting in guilt as he knelt beside her, concern on his brow. "I'll be better tomorrow." But she wasn't better; she'd never be better.

Amit nuzzled her hair, his fuzzy lips nipping at her cheek. Her lips were cracked and dry and her throat swollen from unshed tears.

Cedron stirred in the courtyard, calling her name. She answered back. Whatever she said must have satisfied him because she heard the gate close behind him. Amit nuzzled her more urgently. His water trough was empty, and he hadn't been fed.

"I know. I'm sorry, Amit."

She picked up the water jar and left the safety of the courtyard, wrapping her head covering tight around her hair. She shuffled down the dusty street. Cedron wouldn't be back until afternoon, she knew. He'd be looking for the thieves. A shiver ran down her back, even as the sun heated the stones around her. Now Cedron had even more reason to find Mouse. But he wouldn't because Mouse would never steal again.

She climbed the steps up to the shimmering water. She wouldn't bathe today. No amount of water, no matter how pristine, would wash away her guilt. No almsgiving would atone for her sin.

At the edges of the pool, the clusters of women talked of the priest killed by a dark-haired Greek and a boy-thief—and in the holy temple. The reward for them was a king's treasure.

Nissa's hands shook as she dipped her jar into the water. Surely someone would point to her. They would say, "She did it," and she couldn't deny it. She held her breath and raised her eyes, but no one was looking at her. No one knew the boy-thief was a woman—a desperate woman who only wanted to take enough to pay the rent.

With her jar full and heavy, she hurried down the steps. She avoided looking at the wall where she and Dismas made the subtle mark to signal each other. *Never again.*

She turned into the deserted streets of the tannery district. The silver coins Dismas had given her weighed heavy in her belt. She'd use them, but that was all. She'd starve on the streets or beg at the temple before she'd steal another brass coin. Somehow she and Cedron would find a way.

A shadow darkened the cobbled stones in front of her. She veered around it, not even raising her head, but a hard hand clamped over her arm. She glanced up, the glare of the morning sun in her eyes. The hand bit into her arm and pulled her into a shadowed doorway. The face she saw took her breath away.

She struggled. "Let go. Leave me alone."

Gestas flashed his pointy teeth in a feral smile. "So it is you, little Mouse. I thought so.

She gasped and tried to jerk free, her heart hammering in her ears.

"I was worried about you yesterday, and so I followed you home. Something . . ." He tapped his nose. "Something wasn't right. I saw Mouse go into that little hideout, but I saw someone else come out, now, didn't I?"

She juggled the jar but lost her grip. It tumbled to the ground and broke, cold water spilling over her feet. "I don't know what you're talking about. Let me go." But there was nowhere to go. Her back pressed against the solid door. She looked over his shoulder. Was there no one to help her? She pulled in a breath to scream for help.

Gestas lunged forward and caught her chin in his hand. He wrenched her face up and to the side until pain shot through her jaw. Squeezing her neck in his other hand, he lifted her until only her toes touched the ground. "That might work on Dismas; he's not the smartest Greek in Jerusalem. But don't lie to me, *Nissa*."

She pulled in short, quick gasps of air as he squeezed her throat. Her vision began to blur. Would he kill her, right there in the street?

"Yes. I know about you. I have to admit, I'm impressed. A girl-thief, and a good one." He tightened his grip. "Now, will you agree we won't waste time pretending you aren't the Mouse?"

Her lungs burned. She nodded tightly as her vision darkened.

His released her, and she slumped against the wall, gasping for air.

Gestas stayed close, his hands braced on either side of her like a cage.

She gulped air until her vision cleared, then glared up at him. "Just leave me alone. I promise I won't tell about the priest."

His hooded eyes swept over her. "Oh, I know you won't tell." He smirked. "Of course you won't tell. And now—now that I know your secret, *Nissa*—I think you'll do even more for me."

She pressed against the door, wrapping her arms over her chest. Anger seeped through her limbs, replacing the weakness.

Gestas's low voice sounded like the snarl of a jackal. "Don't worry about your virginity just yet. I'm not that desperate." His gaze traveled down her body. "It was too much, wasn't it? The blood? The smell of death? If I was a betting man— and I am—I'd say you promised yourself you'd never pick another pocket."

She pressed her lips together. What was Gestas getting at?

"You can tell me. Someone's going to have to break it to Dismas."

She might as well. He'd find out when she didn't show up in the meeting place. She swallowed and croaked, "Never again."

He flashed his pointy teeth at her. "That is where you are wrong, my dear girl. But you'll work for me now, not our dim-witted Dismas."

Nissa's hands closed into fists. *I'll never work for him. I don't care what he does to me.*

"And another thing," Gestas went on like it was decided, "Dismas has a soft heart. He gave you too much. An apprentice should work for nothing, and that's what you are from now on. I'm your master."

She gritted her teeth and straightened her back. Her knees still shook, but her voice was stronger. "I won't steal for you."

Gestas glanced behind him toward the still-empty street. He pulled the dagger—the dead priest's dagger—from his belt.

Nissa's mouth went dry, but courage swelled within her. She wouldn't work for this dog. "Go ahead. I don't care what you do to me." She choked out the words. "No more stealing. No more killing."

Gestas's snake eyes hardened. "No killing? Well, that will be up to you, Nissa."

Her heart hammered in her chest. What did he mean?

"I asked around last night about Nissa and her brother, the am-ha-arez who was once blind. Cedron is his name, isn't that right?" He tested the point of the dagger on his finger. "It would be a shame for him to lose his eyes, or even his life, after he just regained his sight."

Her legs weakened again. Not Cedron. She was the guilty one.

Gestas ran his finger slowly down the gleaming blade.

Nissa's throat tightened. *Gestas wouldn't hurt Cedron.* She thought of the priest dying in a pool of blood. *Yes, he would.* Fear shot through Nissa like a lightning bolt. She had to get away, warn Cedron. She pushed at Gestas, her hands scraping at his face like the talons of a hawk.

Gestas was faster. He caught one hand and twisted her around, slamming her face into the wooden door with a hollow thud. His body—hot and smelling of sour sweat and cheap wine—pressed against her back. The cold blade of his dagger bit into her neck.

"Nissa"—his voice was soft in her ear, like a caress—"your brother will be safe and live a long life . . . if you do exactly what I say."

A bubble of panic rose in her chest. Do what he says? Work for Gestas? Steal and kill again, with no payment? She struggled against his heavy body. Hot pain sliced under her jaw. A trickle of warmth ran down her neck.

"Nissa," Gestas purred, "you don't have a choice."

His words chilled the blood pounding in her veins. How many times had she heard them? But now the dark voice in her ear was all too real. She squeezed her eyes shut.

"What's your answer, little Mouse?" Gestas ground his body into hers, his breath hot on her neck.

There was only one answer. "Don't hurt Cedron."

The pressure against her lightened. "Say it. 'You are my master.'"

She gritted her teeth. The knife at her neck pressed deeper.

"Say it, Nissa."

"You are my master."

He released his hold on her.

She fell to the ground and huddled against the wall, as far from Gestas as she could get.

Gestas towered over her. "We'll wait a few weeks, until they stop looking for us. But when I make the mark on the wall, meet me in the usual place."

He crouched down beside her and pressed the knife against her cheek. "And don't go running to Dismas. If I find out you've told him about our little arrangement, I'll make a surprise visit to your brother."

When she caught her breath and looked up, he was gone.

Nissa curled more tightly against the wall. How long would she have to steal for Gestas—the rest of her life? But she couldn't let Cedron suffer for her sins. She was caught, like a mouse in the talons of a hawk.

She squeezed her eyes shut, wishing she could disappear into the darkness. Gestas was right; she didn't have a choice. Not anymore.

THE TAP OF hobnailed sandals on stone had barely disturbed her shattered thoughts when Nissa felt strong, warm hands on her shoulders.

"Nissa?"

What was Longinus doing here? How long had she been huddled in the doorway? Her heart sped up, and she buried her face in her drawn-up knees.

He crouched next to her, his voice tinged with alarm. "What happened?" He pulled her arms from her knees and lifted her chin. His eyes searched her face, then dropped to the neck of her tunic. His hand flew to the hilt of his sword. "Who did this to you?"

Her blunted mind was unable to form a word. She slumped against the wall.

Longinus shook her gently. "Nissa. Who hurt you?"

She lowered her head. "I can't." It was a choked sound, like that of a wounded animal.

Longinus stared at her for a long minute. He muttered a curse and rubbed his hand over his face. He kicked the shards of the water jar away and curved one arm around her shoulders, the other under her legs.

She struggled, but not before he'd lifted her into his arms. His mouth was set in a firm line, like he had something to say but wasn't saying it, and his blue eyes seemed sad. No helmet covered his fiery hair, and no cold metal armor separated her from his broad chest. She opened her mouth to protest but gave up when the street around her tilted and spun. She closed her eyes. Longinus wouldn't hurt her. At least not while she kept her secret.

He tightened his grip, pulling her closer until her cheek lay against his soft tunic, smelling of lye and sandalwood. His steps were sure and strong, his chest firm, and the beat of his heart even and comforting on her cheek.

Is this what it feels like to have someone take care of you? To be safe?

His stride lulled her; his warmth seeped into her shaking limbs. For this moment, she wasn't alone and abandoned. She was cared for, protected. She let out a long breath, one that she'd held for what seemed like eternity. Her body relaxed and curved into his chest. *If only this moment—this solace—could last forever.*

Too soon, the sun brightened behind her eyelids, and the aroma of roses told her she was home. Longinus shouldered open the gate and brought her inside. The fire smoldered, a few coals glowing dully under the cooking pot. Longinus set her on the bench near the fire.

As he stepped away, the bite of the cold wind replaced the warmth of his arms and snatched away the illusion of safety. The moment of peace was replaced by despair. Nissa buried her head in her hands.

A clay cup nudged her hands. Water. Tepid from the flask he carried at his side. She drank it. She raised her eyes from the almost-dead coals to his feet, spread wide, like he was planted in her courtyard. Then his sword hanging at his side. Her gaze stopped at his crossed arms. She couldn't bear to look into his piercing eyes.

He would ask questions now, demand answers. What could she tell him?

Her mind was as empty as the cup in her hands. She had no lies left to give.

Chapter 20

LONGINUS PULLED A breath deep into his tight chest and let it out slowly.

He'd carve the man's heart out. Squeeze his neck between his own hands and watch his face turn blue. Rip his arms from his body, slice him open from navel to throat. And not just the man who had cut her today. Every man who had laid a hand on her.

Something had happened when he'd held Nissa close and carried her through the streets. A moment when she'd stopped fighting him. She'd softened, her body curving against him. She'd nestled into his shoulder like a child, her soft breath brushing over him, and he'd felt something open inside him as solid and real as a key opening a lock.

Was that what it felt like to be needed? To be trusted?

For a moment, he'd been more than a soldier, more than a centurion. But the moment had ended when he'd put Nissa down beside the fire, and now he felt as bereft and weak as a lost lamb. And he didn't know what to do next.

Blood soaked the neck of Nissa's tunic. A spike of straw clung to her hair, and her clothes were stained and smelled like she'd been sleeping with the donkey. She cowered next to the glowing remains of the cooking fire, her arms wrapped around her chest, her eyes closed like she was waiting for a blow.

This was his fault—as much his fault as the men who visited

the brothels. He'd known for weeks what Nissa was doing. He'd told himself to forget her. He, who knew better than most what she endured at the hands of men.

She probably thought he was just like the man who had hurt her. Was he any better? While he'd searched for the thieves and played tabulah with Stephen, she'd been selling herself to the scum of Jerusalem, maybe even his own men. His stomach lurched, threatening to bring up his breakfast. He should have stopped her.

He ducked though the low doorway of the house and scooped a jar of oil from the cluster of amphora in the corner. Nissa hadn't moved when he reentered the courtyard. He knelt beside her and eased his hand under her chin.

Her eyes flew open. As dim as the coals at her feet, they met his for an instant before her thick lashes fluttered closed again.

The slice ran from the middle of her neck to her sharp collarbone—not deep, but it needed attention. He swiped his thumb over the lip of the jar and smoothed oil over the gash.

She jerked away from him. "I can do it."

He clenched his jaw tight. Why did she have to fight him on everything? He clamped a hand on her shoulder and pulled her toward him. She flinched, and he remembered the crescent-shaped scar. A scar he'd given her.

He lightened his grip and gentled his voice. "You can't even see it. Let me. I've done this before." He'd dressed many wounds after battles. He'd seen lesser wounds fester, turn into fevers, and take the lives of men with ten times her strength. But the knife wound would be the least of Nissa's worries if she went back to the brothel. And she wasn't going back, that much he knew.

He corked the oil jar and rocked back on his heels. Where was Cedron? And how thick was the Jew that he didn't know what his own sister was doing for him? He knew the man was naive, but how could Cedron believe that Nissa was supporting them on what she could earn at a Roman laundry?

Nissa leaned away from him, shrinking into a ball like she wanted to disappear.

His heart squeezed tight in his chest. He couldn't leave her like this. He could give her money. Surely she would listen to reason after what happened today.

But since when had Nissa listened to reason? Especially from him. And Cedron would never accept charity from him. An impossible idea sparked in his mind. There was a way to keep her safe.

Don't even think about it.

He put a hand on her shoulder and pulled her to face him. "I know what you've been doing, Nissa."

Her eyes flew open, and her body jerked like he'd stabbed her. Her face paled, and she struggled to rise. He put both hands on her shoulders. "Please, Nissa. I can help you."

Confusion wrinkled her brow, but she wrenched away from him and stumbled to her feet. "Help me?" Her voice cracked, and she backed away, just a step from the smoking ashes of the fire pit. Her chest rose and fell with rapid breaths, like she was being chased.

Longinus stood slowly, holding out his hand, palm up. "You were lucky, Nissa. Next time you might not be." His eyes searched her panicked face. Surely she could see he was right. "Promise me you won't go back there."

Her brows came together. "Go where?"

He pressed his lips together. She didn't want to admit it, even to him. But he wasn't worthy to judge her. "You've never worked at the laundry, Nissa. I checked."

Her face whitened.

"I know why you live here, how you've been getting by." He swept a hand over the courtyard, the store of food, her clothes. "I know you've been working in the brothel."

NISSA'S MOUTH FELL open, and heat rushed through her like flames through straw. The brothel? A choked laugh rose up her throat, bursting from her mouth in a hysterical chortle.

His brow wrinkled, and he blinked in confusion.

She covered her mouth with her hands. For a terrifying moment, she'd thought he knew her secret. But no, he didn't know anything. He thought she'd been selling her body to the men of Jerusalem. The laughter dried up in her throat, replaced by a shame she didn't own but couldn't deny.

He thinks I'm a prostitute.

Anger sparked within her. He was as bad as Gilad, as bad as Gestas. They all wanted something. What would he want to keep his silence? She had nothing left to give.

He ran a hand over his red hair. "Listen, Nissa. I won't tell Cedron." He stretched out a hand to her. "Nissa, I have plenty of money."

The spark of anger grew to a flame. She stepped back, away from him. He didn't want money, but he wanted something. First Gilad, then Gestas, and now this centurion. "You are no better than the rest of them. You come here with your sword and—and—your . . . blue eyes. And you think you can—"

"Nissa. I can take care of you. No one will know about—"

Nissa jerked away, the movement sending a shard of pain through the gash on her neck. "Take care of me?" She knew just how he wanted to take care of her. And she'd thought he was different. "Until when? Until you tire of me?"

Longinus froze, his brows pulling together as color crept into his face. He shook his head. "No, Nissa. You don't understand—"

She advanced on him. "Oh, I understand well enough. I may be plain, but I know how men think." She pulled herself up to her full height, her chin jutting forward.

Longinus reached toward her. "Listen to me, Nissa."

She slapped his hand away. "Don't touch me."

He ignored her, both hands landing on her shoulders. "I'm giving you a choice. You don't have to—"

"A choice?" She shrugged off his hands. "You think I have a choice?" Between Gilad, Gestas, and this centurion, she had no choice at all. She launched herself at him. Her fists battered at his chest, his freckled arms. "I don't have a choice."

Longinus didn't flinch, didn't protect himself.

She hit higher, her feeble blows landing on his shoulders. "I either keep—" She caught herself. *Stealing, under the thumb of Gestas and blackmailed by Gilad.* "Or become your mistress." She hit higher, blows buffeting his face.

He ducked his head to avoid her flying hands. "Nissa, not my mistress."

Not his mistress? What else could she be? She pounded on his chest. It wasn't fair. He was too strong. They were all stronger than her.

"Nissa, stop. I'm not asking you to be my mistress." He caught her flying hands in his. "I'm asking you to be my wife."

She jerked back. *His wife? The wife of a Roman centurion?* Looking up into his eyes, she saw something in them . . . Was it hope? Or surprise at what he'd just said? The answer to all her problems stood in front of her, red hair in wild spikes, blue eyes guarded. Waiting. Cedron called him their enemy, but was he? What kind of man was willing to marry a woman like her? A woman he thought was a prostitute?

"Why would you want to marry me?"

He looked away, then dropped her hands and stepped back. "I know I'm older than you, but when I've finished my service . . ."

She folded her arms over her chest. He hadn't answered her question.

". . . I'll have land. Just ten more years." His gaze went to the smoking fire pit, her sandals, everywhere but her face.

She chewed on her lip and watched him until he finally looked at her.

"I can take care of you, Nissa. You never have to go back there." He swallowed like he had a lump of dry bread in his throat.

He was right. He could take care of her. Marriage. Safety for her and Cedron. Gilad would have no claim against her. Gestas wouldn't threaten her again, not as the wife of a Roman centurion. And with a centurion's pay, they'd never want for food or shelter. Cedron would object—of course he would—but her father wouldn't. A few pieces of silver would buy his blessing.

Take it. Say yes. The dark voice spoke so strongly she almost jumped.

She couldn't think. Not with those blue eyes staring at her, not with the voice in her head clamoring to be heard.

Amit brayed from the lean-to.

Nissa stumbled to the corner of the house and scooped up a cracked water jar. "I need water . . . I need to think." She rushed toward the gate.

Longinus stopped her with a hand on her elbow. "I'll wait."

Her throat closed, and she nodded, then slipped through the gate and into the busy midday street. She ran, the jar bumping against her side, all the way back to Siloam. She staggered up the steps, set the jar on the platform, and waded in.

Marry a Roman? The centurion who had grabbed her in the marketplace, who hunted her still? She ducked under. Cold silence enveloped her as the water closed over her head. *He's the answer to all my problems.* No more stealing. No more fear.

She would be a good wife to him. He'd never have to know what she had been. She'd keep her secret. She'd marry the man who had saved her and Cedron. The man who was undaunted by her temper or sharp tongue. The man strong enough to protect her, but who'd never lifted a hand against her. A good man.

She came up, gasping for air.

Nissa waded out of the pool and filled her jar. Could she lie to him forever? Have his children, grow old with him, and keep this lie wedged between them? She was already a thief and a murderer. If she married this good man, this man who wanted to help her, could she live with herself?

She dragged her feet down the steps and up the street. She stopped at the doorway where Gestas had threatened her and kicked at the broken shards of pottery on the ground. She was broken. Worthless.

Why would Longinus want her? He couldn't even answer that question.

She plodded past the brothels, past the taverns. When she'd watched the priest die in front of her, she'd thought she'd plumbed the depths of disgrace. She'd thought she could go no lower. But she could. If she agreed to marry Longinus, she'd be so deep in the darkness that she'd never see light again.

She reached her home and paused outside the gate. Could she sink that low? She pushed the gate open.

Longinus sat on the stool in front of the fire, now stoked and crackling. His elbows rested on his knees, his head cradled in his hands. He jumped to his feet as she entered. His bearing, always so sure, was full of uncertainty.

Nissa set the water jar beside the house. Longinus didn't speak, and she was glad. Whatever he said, it wouldn't change her mind, but it might make what she had to say harder.

She bit down on her lip hard enough to taste blood. She had to make him leave and never come back. He deserved nothing less, and so much more than her.

She stood before him, her eyes on his freckled feet. "Get out."

He sucked in a breath like he'd been hit.

She looked up at his stricken face and spit out the words, fast and cruel. "I could never marry you."

His face showed confusion. "You'd rather keep working there?" He motioned in the direction of the brothels.

She swallowed hard. If that's what it took to get him to leave. It was better than the truth. "Yes." She looked him in the eye. He had to believe her. "I'd rather be a whore than your wife." She almost choked on the words.

His jaw hardened, and his body tensed. His throat worked convulsively.

She dropped her gaze to his feet, unable to witness the pain in his face. She was just what her Abba had always called her: worthless. She deserved his hatred, his contempt, and nothing more.

He walked stiffly across the courtyard, his back as straight as a spear, and wrenched open the gate. He didn't turn, but his last words cut like a knife to her heart. "I just wanted to help you, Nissa."

He shut the gate with a soft thud and was gone, the tap of his sandals fading into the noise of the street.

Nissa sank to the ground, burying her face in her knees. *No one can help me now.*

LONGINUS BARGED THROUGH the streets, scarcely seeing the mid-morning crowds scatter before him, barely feeling shoulders slap against him when a merchant or pilgrim failed to get out of his way fast enough. He saw only Nissa's face, her look of loathing, like he was a leper. A fierce ache twisted through his gut.

What had he been thinking, asking her to marry him? He'd been as surprised as she to hear those words come from his mouth. But while he'd waited for her to come back from Siloam, he'd almost convinced himself that it would work. She was a handful, but she'd never be dull. They could go to Gaul together, raise a family. And he had *some* kind of feelings for her. By Jupiter, he'd wasted the past month trying not to think about her! Wasted effort for a woman who would rather sell her body than marry him.

I'm pathetic, an idiot. Thank the gods she said no.

Longinus cursed through the lower city, past the Pool of Siloam, and up the Stepped Street. *Remember who you are—and who your father was.* His allegiance was to Caesar. Not to Nissa. Not to a Samaritan scholar or a Jewish healer. It was time to win the wager with Silvanus and to get out of this dung heap of a city and far away from Nissa.

Part Three

The Passover

Chapter 21

LONGINUS CAUGHT UP with Marcellus as the young legionary left the carcer. "Who's guarding the Samaritan?" he said in Aramaic. They had to be careful. Silvanus had eyes and ears all over camp.

"Petras. Don't worry, we can trust him." Marcellus answered him in the same language but more fluently, no doubt from the hours he'd spent playing tabulah with his prisoner. He stopped walking and surveyed Longinus from the top of his unkempt hair to the hem of his dingy tunic. "You look terrible."

Longinus grunted and ran a hand over his stubbled chin. As winter had warmed into spring, he had driven his men hard and himself harder, falling into bed each night aching with exhaustion. He'd lost weight, lost sleep, and lost more than a few practice bouts to Cornelius, but throbbing joints and aching muscles were nothing compared to the pain in his chest. He felt as though someone had cut out his heart with a dull sword.

He'd done his duty. Kept his men miserable with extra training and drills, sent reports to Caesarea, and ensured that not a whisper of revolution drifted through the city without his knowledge. He'd looked for the thieves with every spare moment. Even rounded up and questioned the beggars at the temple.

He had found nothing but dead ends—with the thieves, with Stephen, and with his search for the Jewish troublemaker. And no matter how hard he drove himself, he couldn't expel thoughts of Nissa. He looked for her every time he rode through the city, both hoping and dreading that he might catch a glimpse of her small form.

Longinus eyed the gate where Cornelius stood guard. Next week, Pilate and the rest of the legion would return for the Passover. His back was against the wall. "We can't keep Stephen much longer."

Marcellus crossed his arms over his chest and narrowed his eyes. "You can't crucify him."

"What else can I do? If I let him go and Silvanus finds out, he'll tell Pilate. You know what they'll do to me."

"What about Cedron?"

"Cedron." Longinus snorted. He'd kept a careful eye on Nissa's worthless brother. The man spent more time with his bunch of would-be revolutionaries than he did asking questions about the thieves. As if the ragtag bunch of Zealots were any threat to Rome. "He couldn't find a wolf in a sheepfold."

Marcellus let out a long breath. "Release him, today, before it's too late."

"It's already too late."

"I've kept it quiet. No one will talk."

Longinus ground his teeth together. A year ago, he'd relished the thought of crucifying Stephen. Three months ago, when he'd found him at the Pharisee's house, he would have tied the crossbeam on himself. But now? Marcellus was right. He couldn't order him crucified, not for defending a woman. And the bargain with Cedron had failed miserably, just like everything else he'd done in Jerusalem.

He left Marcellus outside the latrine and went to the stable for Ferox. It was time to report to the Sanhedrin, as he had each week for the past two months. He'd rather muck out the stable with his own mess kit.

He rode slowly to the temple, entered the Court of the Gentiles, and dismounted. He shouldered his way past the money-changing booths and the merchants selling lambs and pigeons. His breath caught as a slight woman in a soft green tunic and nut-brown hair darted in front of him. She turned, but her lips weren't soft and full and her eyes were green instead of inky black. He growled under his breath and pushed past her.

Don't think of her.

But he did. Every day. Every hour. And on some days, it seemed like every minute. Each time, his stomach twisted in sick knots. Since he'd carried her in his arms, felt her small body lean against his in what only could have been trust, he'd felt a connection with her, as strong as if they were bound together. He'd break it if he could; he just didn't know how.

What was she doing now? How many filthy men had she entertained since his outrageous proposal weeks ago? More than once, he'd found himself riding Ferox through the squalid streets outside the brothels, loathing both her choice and his inability to forget her.

His hands tightened on his vitis, and he pushed a slow-moving pilgrim aside. He was a Roman—a centurion, by the gods. Women lined up to be with him. She was plain, poor, worthless. He had offered her all he had, and she'd thrown it in his face.

Face it, centurion. She'd rather be a whore than marry you. Forget her.

He reached the entrance to the Stone Court, where the Sanhedrin convened, but instead of a dour assembly of priests and Pharisees, he entered into chaos.

Men and women jammed the enclosure, their voices buzzing, hands gesturing wildly. Some were city dwellers, but many were dressed in the rough garments of farmers and shepherds. The linen-clad priests and Pharisees huddled near the front, their faces creased with worry.

What had riled them this time? The drought again? Or maybe their constant harping against the taxes levied by Caesar? Longinus elbowed his way into the shade of a wide column and caught the eye of a well-dressed, portly Jew. "What are they talking about?"

The man licked his lips nervously. "A man in Bethany named Lazarus. They say he was raised from the dead."

Longinus took off his helmet. Perhaps he'd misunderstood the man's Aramaic. "Raised from the dead? Who says it?"

The man gestured to a group that looked like farmers. "Men from Bethany. They say they saw it themselves. The Galilean raised a man from the dead."

Longinus strode to the men from Bethany and grabbed one by the shoulder, pulling him around. "What Galilean? Jesus?"

The man cringed, his eyes flicking from Longinus's face to the vitis in his hand, but he nodded. "We saw him come out of the tomb four days after his death."

A shiver raised bumps on Longinus's arms and down his back. Jesus raised a man from the dead? After four days? Longinus edged along the shadowed portico, moving closer to the men gathered at the front.

One of the priests was speaking, his back to Longinus. "What are we to do? The ignorant country rabble thinks this man is the Messiah. They believe in his trickery. If he comes here, if they declare him the Messiah, there will be chaos, and the Romans will destroy us."

Caiaphas stepped onto the raised platform at the front of the court. His voice dropped as the other priests huddled around him. "We cannot let this happen. It is better one man should die for the people than the whole nation perish."

Longinus pressed his back against the cold column. One man should die for the nation? What were they planning?

The first priest nodded. "Caiaphas is right. If we let him go on like this, the Romans will think we are revolting."

Caiaphas motioned to a scribe. "Send out an order to the people. If anyone sees the Galilean, they are to report it to the temple guard, and we will deal with him ourselves."

Longinus pushed his way back to Ferox. Arrest Jesus? And

then what? Did they think they could sentence him to death? Who did these Jews think they were? He'd decide whether this Jesus was a threat, not these pompous priests.

He wove through the columns and back toward the Court of the Gentiles. He was done coming at the command of the San-hedrin. *I'll talk to Pilate.* But he'd keep the story of Lazarus to himself. Pilate was a superstitious man; there was no telling what he might do if he heard Jesus had raised the dead.

He swung into the saddle. One thing he knew. Jesus must stay out of the city, at least until Passover was over. He circled Ferox toward the gates and spurred him forward. He'd send word to Jesus, a warning not to come into the city. It must come from someone Jesus would trust. And he knew just the man for the job.

LONGINUS CLATTERED DOWN the steps of the carcer and pushed open the cell door. Marcellus sat on one side of a tiny table; Stephen leaned over the other.

"You've won again." Marcellus placed the last ivory piece on the tabulah board. They both looked up at him as the door creaked.

"Marcellus. Leave us."

The legionary jumped up and left the room.

Longinus pushed the door shut behind Marcellus and re-garded his prisoner. "You need to go. Warn Jesus the Sanhe-drin has put out a call to find him and bring him in. Tell him . . ." He blew out his breath. "Tell him not to come to Jerusalem."

Stephen's face creased in surprise. "You're releasing me? What about you?"

"What about me?"

Stephen raised his brows. "You want to talk to him; don't deny it. You've been after me about him for months."

Longinus scowled. "I just want to keep the peace." But Stephen was right. He wanted to meet the man. Now more than ever. But it was too dangerous with the Sanhedrin calling for his death. "Keep him out of the city. He won't be killed by your people, and he won't be any threat to mine." Longinus gathered Stephen's cloak and shoved it at him. "Tell him that. If he has any sense, he'll stay out of the city."

Longinus took a deep breath and eyed his prisoner. Time to say good-bye to the man he had vowed to kill. If the gods were on his side, no one would know about the Samaritan who had spent the last months in the carcer.

He opened the door. *Where is that blasted Marcellus?* Once again, not guarding the door.

The clatter of sandals on the stairs, and Marcellus rushed in, breathless. "Riders coming through the gate. They'll be here in moments." He shut the door behind him.

Alarm quickened Longinus's pulse. "Riders? Who?"

Marcellus's eyes slid to Stephen. "Silvanus and six men. He's got a prisoner; he'll be coming here."

Longinus ground his teeth. It was too late. There was only one door out of the carcer, and Silvanus would be at it before they could get Stephen past him. When Silvanus saw Stephen, he'd know he was the man Longinus had been looking for in Galilee, the one he'd twice lost. The scar would be all the proof Silvanus needed, and there would be a crucifixion by first light tomorrow.

Marcellus pushed them back into the cell and shut the door behind him. He unbuckled his Roman sandals and tossed them to Stephen. "Put those on."

Longinus watched Marcellus unclasp his cloak and pull off his helmet. What was his optio doing?

Marcellus shoved his cloak and helmet at Stephen.

Stephen waited, his eyes on Longinus, his hands full of Roman gear.

Longinus turned to Marcellus. "You're sure about this?"

Marcellus put a hand at the keys on his belt and nodded. "I'm the optio ad carcerem. My word is law here."

Stephen buckled the sandals and fitted the helmet over his head. It covered most of his face and all of his scar. It would do—as long as no one got too close. Silvanus's unmistakable growl and the smack of a vitis on flesh sounded from outside the window. Longinus raised his brows to his optio. What now?

"Don't worry, I'll slow Silvanus down. You get Stephen out the gate." Marcellus opened the door and rushed up the stairs.

Longinus took a deep breath and counted to ten. He heard Silvanus bark at Marcellus. They didn't have much time. He motioned Stephen out the door, shut it behind them, and marched up the stairs at a brisk pace.

They marched out of the building, heads high and eyes on the Praetorian gate. Silvanus, his back to them, stood just ten paces away with several legionaries and a bound prisoner. Marcellus talked fast and loud. Silvanus answered in a growl, but Longinus didn't stop to listen. He glanced sideways at Stephen and increased their pace. No shouts stopped them as they strode toward the gate. Another few steps and they were in the agora, surrounded by Jews who didn't give them a second glance.

Longinus let out his held breath and turned to the man he'd sworn to crucify. He had no love for the man. If anything, he'd be glad never to see his face again. But he couldn't kill him, not anymore.

So this is what it feels like to be a traitor to Rome. Surely Scipio wouldn't have done this, nor his father. *Then why does it feel like the only thing I've done right since I came to this cursed city?*

Stephen reached up to remove his helmet.

Longinus stopped him with a raised hand. "Keep it on until you get back to Joseph's." Cornelius could be watching them right now. "Then get out of the city. Find Jesus, and make sure he knows not to come here for Passover."

Stephen frowned. "I'll tell him. But he'll do what he came to do, no matter the cost."

Then the Samaritan did something that left Longinus speechless. Stephen embraced him and kissed him on the cheek, as Jews do with their friends and brothers. The kiss of peace, they called it.

"Shalom, my friend," Stephen said, "and be ready. The revolution is coming." He turned away and disappeared into the crowded marketplace.

Longinus stared after him. That irritating Samaritan couldn't leave without one last riddle. Peace, he'd said. And revolution. *How could there be both?*

Chapter 22

LONGINUS SWEPT PAST the legionaries assembled in the open courtyard. Armor was polished to a shine, tunics were clean, even their mess kits were sparkling. Silvanus would have nothing to complain about when he inspected the camp.

He'd managed to avoid Silvanus yesterday after Stephen made it out of the camp, but now it was time to face the senior centurion. He stopped in front of the principia, where Silvanus leaned against the wall, one cheek bulging with his morning bread and a cup of wine in his hand. Cornelius smirked beside him.

Silvanus waved his free hand toward the carcer. "Heard you had a prisoner," he said around the mouthful. "A Samaritan."

Longinus tensed and glanced at Cornelius. Keeping a secret for a day in the camp was hard; for months, impossible. "Had."

Silvanus tore another piece of bread from the loaf in his hand and stuffed it in his mouth. "Where is he?"

Longinus's palms grew damp. "He was the wrong man."

Silvanus straightened, took a long drink from his cup, and dumped the dregs at his feet. His eyes narrowed. "The wrong man? You sure?"

Longinus shrugged and turned to the courtyard. "I was there. It wasn't the same man."

Silvanus scratched under his armor. "You kept him long enough. What? Three months?"

Longinus's hands tightened on his stick. Cornelius was a better spy than he'd suspected. "He was a troublemaker." Longinus tapped his vitis on the ground. "I taught him a lesson."

Silvanus straightened and put on his helmet. "Too bad I missed that, eh?" He strode toward the assembled men.

Longinus fell into step beside Silvanus. *Yes, too bad.* "Who did you bring in yesterday?"

Silvanus stopped in front of the first column of legionaries. "A thief and a murderer, goes by Barabbas. He's been attacking travelers, killed a family of Jews on their way to Jerusalem. Some think he's a messiah. These Jews." He smacked a legionary across the shins with his vitis. "Wake up!"

Longinus moved to the next column. He'd heard of a band of brigands under the leadership of Barabbas, but they were in Galilee. "Why did you bring him here?"

Silvanus joined him, his roaming gaze examining each legionary. "Pilate wants him crucified."

Something smelled wrong about this. "Why Jerusalem? Caesarea is closer."

Silvanus mouth curled. "Pilate's been warned." He glanced sideways at Longinus. "By Caesar. One more hint of revolution here will be the end of him. He'll be sent back to Rome, and not to his palace on the Palatine, either."

Longinus let out a breath. So Pilate wanted to show the Jews who was in charge with a crucifixion. *Thank the gods that I don't have Stephen in the carcer and that Jesus won't be here.*

Silvanus slapped him on his armor-clad shoulder. "We'll teach these Jews a lesson, show them who their master is, eh?"

Longinus grunted. As if six thousand men marching into the city next week wouldn't show the Jews who their master was.

Silvanus's gaze dropped to the sword at Longinus's side. "I see you're taking good care of my sword."

Longinus's hand strayed to his side, and he silently cursed the day he'd agreed to that doomed wager. "It's not yours, centurion, and never will be."

"You're no closer to finding those thieves than you were last winter. Admit it, they're too smart for a half-Roman." Silvanus smacked his vitis across the nearest legionary's back. "Mark my words, centurion." He sneered the last word. "It will be mine after Passover, and Pilate will send you back to the ranks where you belong."

Longinus clenched his jaw as Silvanus strutted toward the principia. He wouldn't let Silvanus get under his skin this time. He dismissed the men, sending half to drill and the rest to dig trenches, and headed down the Via Praetoria. Silvanus's threat rankled. He had less than a week until Pilate returned, less than two before Passover.

"Petras," he barked at a legionary standing guard. "Find the Jew Cedron. And bring him here." He couldn't wait for the thieves to show themselves. He would have to make them come to him. And Cedron would help him. The Jew owed him that much for setting Stephen free.

By midmorning, Petras returned with an irate Cedron in tow. Longinus's heart twisted at the sight of Nissa's brother. Had Cedron discovered Nissa's secret? *Not my concern.* Only the thieves were his concern now. "I have a job for you."

Cedron raised his brows. "And I suppose you expect me to do your bidding because you—"

Longinus smacked his vitis against his hand. "I expect you to help me, or I'll show you just how unpleasant it is to be on my wrong side." He stepped close enough to see the sweat shining on Cedron's broad forehead. *Good. He should be scared.*

"Pilate will be entering the city next week, the day after the Sabbath. He'll want every available legionary at the gate"—he nodded toward the Jaffa Gate—"ready to greet him." There was nothing legates liked better than a parade. If Pilate couldn't have a triumphal entry into Rome, he'd settle for a spectacle in Jerusalem.

Cedron crossed his arms over his chest. "What do you want of me?"

"Make sure everyone knows this: no legionaries patrolling the upper market."

Cedron gave him a long look. "You're setting a trap."

Longinus nodded. The thieves had been careful, but surely they'd take this golden opportunity. "Tell the beggars, tell the merchants, tell your friends the Zealots for all I care. Just make sure that word gets to the thieves."

"And where will you be?" Cedron asked.

Longinus hand dropped to the hilt of his sword, the sword his father had given him and that he intended to take with him to Gaul. "I'll be waiting for them."

NISSA SCRAPED THE last pinch of barley into her palm and held it under Amit's whiskery nose. Amit licked it from her hand and looked for more. "I'm sorry, Amit." She ran her hand over the prominent lines of his ribs.

Jews throughout the city were preparing for Passover, just a week away, but she had nothing left. She'd paid Gilad all the silver, and he'd be coming for more. No pile of wood sat next to the dead fire. The chest that once held her expensive scent and ivory comb was empty. The corner of the house, once a hoard of wine and food, now held only a jumble of empty pottery, and nothing but a dusting of flour remained in the grain jar. Cedron hardly noticed their dire circumstances. He spent more time with his Zealot friends and less looking for work. "It won't be long now until the revolution," he told her when he rushed in to eat a hurried meal or change his clothes.

Gestas was a cruel master. Each week, he'd made the mark on the wall, and each week, she'd stolen for him. Keeping the secret from Dismas was the hard part. He was more careful than ever and watched over Mouse like a mother hen. More than once he told her to go home, to find another way. *If only I could.* After they stole and Dismas left to visit his latest woman, Gestas would demand her portion of their spoils. Sometimes he let her keep a few bronze lepta; most often he took it all and left her with only threats.

Amit nosed at his dry water trough.

Nissa let out a long breath. Today she'd say good-bye to Amit. He ate their barley and didn't bring in any coins to earn his keep. She'd been foolish not to sell him months ago. She'd fetch water, then bring him to the market. Perhaps she could get a few brass coins, and Amit could go to a home that could afford to feed him. She swallowed the threat of tears. *He's better off with someone else.*

She hoisted the water jar and let herself out of the courtyard. Her gaze remained on her worn sandals as she trudged the dirty street, but instead of turning toward the Pool of Siloam, her feet led her the opposite way, toward Herod's palace and the barracks of the Roman legion.

Today the rest of the legion would arrive from Caesarea, marching through the Jaffa Gate. Everyone knew the soldiers would assemble with their weapons and armor gleaming to welcome back their legate. Longinus would be there, too. Watching over his men like a red-plumed hawk. Just a glimpse of him before the parade, that's all she wanted.

She reached the upper market, swerved around a line of camels, and slipped into the cool shadows of the palace wall. She wrapped her arms around the water jar and edged forward until she could see past the towers and into the triangular space where the Romans soldiers practiced with their swords and spears.

Longinus was easy to spot. His polished armor glinted in the sunlight, and the crimson plume on his helmet waved like a flag. The muscles of his arms flexed as he advanced on two soldiers with a wooden sword and a shield as tall as her.

He shouted, knocked one legionary to the ground, and pinned the other with his sword. They'd both be dead if this had been a real fight. His deep voice rumbled as he threw down the shield and helped the prone legionary to stand.

Longinus pulled off his helmet, his face set in a grimace. His hand rubbed at his forehead as though it pained him.

Nissa ducked back into the shadow of the arch. How many times had she come here since that day, hoping to see a smile curving his mouth or the dimple flash on his cheek? But each time, she saw his face set in lines of sorrow, his brow lowered in worry.

Her chest constricted, and she struggled to draw a breath as she remembered the look of raw pain in Longinus's eyes when she'd rejected him. Since that day, she'd awoken every morning wishing she were a different person. Some days, she wished she wouldn't wake up at all.

What if she wasn't Mouse? What if she could have said yes when he offered to save her from her sins? She'd be married by now. Married to a man who spoke of deep forests and emerald meadows, a man who laughed at her sharp words and told her she was pretty, a man who was strong but didn't have to prove it.

If she could, she'd run through this arch, begging his forgiveness, begging for another chance. But she couldn't do that. She could never do that.

If he knew her secret, he would hate her, and he'd be right to hate her. He wouldn't turn those blue eyes on her. She'd never see that dimple or hear his rumbly laugh. No. She'd see Longinus the centurion, the man who nailed murderers to a cross to die a slow, excruciating death.

Marriage between a Jewish girl and a Roman soldier was bad enough, although she knew it happened. But a soldier and a thief? A centurion and a murderer?

Never.

Impossible.

She pushed away from the cool stone wall and threaded a path around the merchants and the shops of the upper market. Soon the barracks and Longinus were far behind her.

She hurried back down the Stepped Street, dodging and weaving through the crowds. By the time she reached Siloam she was panting, the water jar clutched to her chest. As she leaned against the wall, the morning sun glinted off the stone. Her heart thrashed in her chest like a wild animal caught in a trap.

The mark was on the wall.

Gestas had been to Siloam, and he'd sent her a message she couldn't miss. A straight line down and one across, the shape of a Roman cross. The mark that could bring death to her if she heeded it, or to her brother if she didn't.

She trudged up the stairs to the sparkling waters of Siloam, where her brother's eyes had been opened. The miracle had seemed like the turning point. Her hope had been kindled for a life without fear, a life without sin. But in the months since, she'd sunk lower than ever. She had no money, no food, and lived in fear for her life and her brother's.

She knelt next to the pool and leaned out over the water. Her reflection looked back at her. A plain woman, yes. Not much to look at. But her heart held the same desires as any other. Safety, security, like what she'd felt when Longinus had carried her in his arms. A home and children to love. She had none of those now and never would.

You don't have a choice, the dark voice chanted, so sure, so strong.

The waves lapped at the sides of the pool, and in them she could almost hear another voice. A smaller, quieter voice. *The Lord is my strength and my shield; my heart trusts in him.* Weak, like a tiny spark searching for a breath of air and a dry speck of straw to catch hold.

She plunged her hands into the water, shattering her reflection and scattering her thoughts. She scooped up the cold, clear water and drank, the water trickling down her tight throat.

No. She couldn't turn to her God, not anymore. But she wouldn't let Gestas be her master, either. She had a plan, one she'd been thinking on for weeks. Gestas carried a dagger, the one he'd stolen from the priest. If she could find a way to get him caught, perhaps even killed, he wouldn't be a threat to her or Cedron anymore. The bitter taste of guilt filled her mouth. King David had betrayed Uriah. Delilah delivered Samson to his enemies—and God had punished them.

But this is different. Gestas brought this on himself.

Nissa was the best thief in Jerusalem. She would lead him to capture, just as she'd led the priest to his death. She filled her jar and hurried down the steps. Today, she would steal. And today, she would find a way to betray Gestas.

Chapter 23

LONGINUS WALKED EVERY step of the camp for the final time. The barracks, the cooking area, the hospital tent—all in perfect order. The standard was raised; the tents were clean. Sentries stood at attention on the walls and at the gates. He stepped into the latrine. The wood floors were scrubbed clean with sand, and the long benches on either side of the room, each with five round holes, were spotless. The trenches beneath had been flushed with water. He sniffed. Not as bad as they usually smelled.

As Longinus left the latrine, Silvanus thundered into the practice square on his horse. He pulled up next to Longinus with a scowl. "I'm riding out to meet Pilate."

Longinus kept his face a calm mask. *You mean riding out to tell lies about me.* By the time they marched into Jerusalem, Silvanus would have filled Pilate's ears with rumors and complaints.

Silvanus eyed Longinus. "He'll expect to see you and the rest of the cohort saluting him when he comes through the gate."

Longinus nodded. He wouldn't be there to meet Pilate at the Jaffa Gate, but Silvanus didn't need to know that.

"And I hope this camp looks better than it does now. It's a pigsty." Silvanus kicked his horse viciously and galloped through the gate.

Longinus turned back to eye the camp. The provincial governor would have no complaints about the barracks, but Longinus would have some explaining to do when Pilate found out he had gone against orders. Taking twenty men into the upper market instead of dancing attendance at the Jaffa Gate could earn him a reprimand, but if he had the temple murderers to show for his efforts, he'd be forgiven.

There would be a great feast tonight at the palace. After Pilate had finished his wine and congratulated him on finding the temple murderers, Longinus would present his petition to be transferred out of Jerusalem. Gaul, if he could get there, but anywhere would do. As long as it was soon. Even the cold of Britannia would be a relief after this infernal city. Away from these Jews and away from Nissa. Silvanus would support him; he'd have no other choice after the thieves were locked in the carcer.

If he got the chance, he'd talk to Pilate about Jesus and apprise him of the Sanhedrin's plans. He'd lost his chance to see Jesus himself—to ask about these baffling miracles and to decide whether he was a threat to Rome or just another false messiah— but at least he'd thwarted the scheme of those self-righteous priests.

Longinus mounted Ferox and signaled his men to march out the Praetorian gate and toward the upper market. Longinus guided Ferox into the marketplace but reined him immediately to a halt. Something was wrong. Instead of the usual crowds buying and selling after the Sabbath, the agora was almost deserted. Where was everyone?

Marcellus hurried across the empty square toward Longinus and his men, dragging Cedron by one arm.

"What is it?" Had he discovered Nissa's secret? Or did he have word of the thieves?

Marcellus pushed Cedron toward him. "Tell him."

Cedron sealed his mouth in a thin line.

Marcellus shook him. "You owe him your life and Stephen's."

Cedron grimaced. "He's coming. He's entering Jerusalem through the Sheep's Gate."

"What? Who?"

Cedron's brow furrowed. "Jesus."

Longinus frowned as a breath of worry brushed over him. Jesus? "He can't. The priests, the temple guards, they want to arrest him." Hadn't Stephen told Jesus to stay out of the city?

Cedron shook his head. "It's too late. There's a crowd with him. Pilgrims coming for the feast. They started gathering in Bethany, where he raised Lazarus. Hundreds, probably thousands by the time they enter into Jerusalem. They are calling him the Messiah."

Longinus shot a look at Marcellus. His optio shook his head. This was bad news. Jerusalem—even on a good day—was like a pile of dry straw, ready to burst into flame at the first spark of trouble. The Sanhedrin out for blood, a man hailed as the Messiah, and six thousand Roman troops marching into the city was more than a spark. "Who knows about this?"

Cedron crossed his arms. "Every Jew in the city is heading toward the Sheep's Gate to see him."

A niggling pain started behind Longinus's eyes. This could get ugly very fast. "You've got to stop him."

Cedron shook his head, and his face hardened. "I wouldn't, even if I could. This is just what we need. The time for revolution is now, and this man—Jesus—is going to lead it." Cedron jerked his shoulder free of Marcellus's grip and hobbled away without a backward glance.

Longinus ground his teeth in frustration. He could—he should—send word to Silvanus. But the senior centurion's way of keeping the pax romana wouldn't do Jesus any good. He'd no doubt throw the Jewish healer into the carcer, fabricate some charges, and crucify him with Barabbas. No, Longinus would disarm the situation himself.

Longinus turned to Marcellus. "We'll go to the Sheep's Gate."

"What about the thieves?"

Longinus turned Ferox and signaled to his men to follow. Pilate and his six thousand men would appear on the western horizon at any moment, and Jesus would arrive from the east with his crowd of believers. Longinus was caught in the middle with twenty men. "We'll get them, but right now, we need to stop a revolution."

NISSA FOLLOWED DISMAS and Gestas around the temple and skirted the high, cold walls of the Antonia Fortress. Anxiety spiraled through her. One look at Gestas when they met in the upper city had been enough to harden her resolve. She must find a way to get rid of him for good.

She'd hardly seen Cedron for days. When she did, he muttered about revolution. After she made sure Gestas was no longer a threat to him, she'd confess about Mouse. Better he find out the truth from her than a lie from Gilad. Yes, with Gestas gone, she'd be free.

Dismas waited for her to catch up to him. "I have a bad feeling about this, Mouse," he whispered. "We should all go home."

"Shut up," Gestas hissed, coming between them. He grabbed Nissa by the arm. "Tell him, Mouse." He glared down at her.

Nissa swallowed, her throat dry. "Don't worry," she squeaked.

Dismas turned on Gestas. "I don't like this. Something will go wrong today. I can feel it."

"Don't be such a woman! Look at these crowds." He gestured to the men, women, and children packing the streets. Pilgrims coming in for the feast like herds of sheep. "And we aren't even close to the Sheep's Gate yet. I heard thousands follow this man. They won't even notice we're here. We'll steal a few purses and get out."

"But the temple guards and the Romans—"

"Didn't I just explain all that to you, you dense Greek?" Gestas said. "Pilate is returning today. And he's coming in the Jaffa Gate, on the other side of the city. The Romans will be there, every one of them. This will be like stealing from the blind."

Dismas planted his feet and crossed his arms. "I still think

Mouse shouldn't be here. I told you before. They're looking for him."

Nissa's hopes sunk like a stone. No Romans patrolling the streets? How could she hope to get rid of Gestas? And why was Dismas suddenly so worried about her? Did he know something she didn't?

Gestas squared his shoulders and glared up at Dismas. "Mouse is the best we've got." He narrowed his eyes at Nissa, and his hand dropped to his belt where the hilt of the dagger glinted. "You aren't turning into a girl on us, are you, *Mouse?*"

Turning into a girl. As if she needed reminding of his threat.

She'd find some way to get him caught. If not by a Roman, then by a strong pilgrim or a temple guard. With that dagger he carried, he wouldn't go without a fight. She'd just have to hope it was a fight he wouldn't win. She shook her head and looked up at Dismas. "It will work, Dismas. It's a perfect plan." She tried to make her voice easy. "Think of the wine and women you'll have tonight." She felt sick at the words. Dismas didn't deserve her lies.

Dismas's shoulders relaxed, but his voice was unsure. "You really think it's a good plan? Even with the Romans after us?"

No, but she didn't have a choice. "Yes. Gestas is right. They're all on the other side of the city. It's our best chance until after Passover."

Dismas's brow was still folded, but he moved closer to the street. "All right, Mouse. But stay close to me." He bent his head toward her ear and whispered, too low for Gestas to hear, "And after, meet me at our old spot, near the tower."

She dipped her chin in a quick nod. He looked so serious. What did he want to talk to her about? If she had any luck at all, when this day was over, Gestas would be gone, and she'd tell Dismas good-bye. A pang of remorse stung her. She'd miss him. But she was so weary of secrets, and if he knew who she really was, he would reject her anyway.

Gestas's smile glinted at her. "Good work," he mouthed.

Nissa dropped behind Dismas, watching his faded blue tunic weave ahead of her toward the Sheep's Pools, two immense, shallow pools on the east side of the city—both bigger than Siloam. The marketplace around the pools was deserted except for pens of mournful-sounding lambs. When Passover arrived, they would be washed in the pools and brought to the temple for sacrifice.

She had to get Gestas alone. Dismas's weakness was his love of women, but Gestas's love was for silver. Somehow, she'd find a way to use that against him.

The crowds thickened, and excited voices buzzed as they neared the Sheep's Gate. Women stood on tiptoe, craning their necks to see over the heads of the crowds. Children were hoisted onto their father's shoulders. Men tore palm branches from trees and passed them to the onlookers. Nissa surveyed the crowd and, for once, was disappointed to see no red-plumed helmets, no armor-clad soldiers. Gestas was right. This was a perfect place to steal.

"He's coming!" someone shouted.

As the crowd surged toward the gate, Nissa spotted three guards—hired muscle for a rich man—pushed close around a well-dressed merchant. They weren't Roman soldiers, but they had weapons and could manage Gestas. All she had to do was get them to chase him . . . without getting caught herself. She sidled close to Gestas, keeping her eye on Dismas, who was still ten paces ahead. "I need money for rent."

Gestas looked at her sideways. "You'll get what I give you."

Anger rose in her chest. *Pigs get fat; hogs get slaughtered.* "I'll make you a deal. I'll find someone, like last time. Someone with a fat purse. It should be easy enough in these crowds. I'll lead him to you, just like we did before with the priest."

Gestas stopped and turned to her, his eyes narrowed. "I thought you said no more killing."

Nissa bit at her lip. There could be no more killing, at least not of the innocent. She'd have to be very careful. "Do what you want. Just give me half."

Gestas's hand dropped to the knife at his belt, and he licked his lips. "Where?"

Nissa kept the rich merchant and the guards in sight. How far could she lead them without getting caught? "The wood market by the Sheep's Pools." It wasn't far from where they stood. When she was a child, she'd spent many hours there with her father. She knew the streets around it as well as any in Jerusalem. The east side of the market was surrounded by high walls and dead-end alleys. "Wait for me behind the pillars on the temple side." If she was fast, she could get out, but Gestas would be trapped.

Gestas looked doubtful and jerked his head toward Dismas. "What about him?"

Nissa shook her head. No. Dismas couldn't be a part of this. He'd try to stop her. "If you want to split the purse with him . . ." She shrugged.

Gestas grimaced. "I'll be waiting for you. Alone. Now go do your job, Mouse."

Chapter 24

LONGINUS, ASTRIDE FEROX, led twenty legionaries at double pace through the city streets toward the Sheep's Gate. His tunic was damp under his armor, and a bead of sweat trickled down his neck.

Anticipation coursed through his veins despite the weight of his worry. He was going to see Jesus, the man he'd heard so much about. He'd finally get some answers to his questions and see if the rumors were true.

They passed under the shadow of the temple wall, then turned north to follow the road past the Sheep's Pools. He turned the corner around the deserted wood market and into the street leading east to the Sheep's Gate.

He yanked Ferox to a halt. *By the gods, where did these people come from?*

Thousands of people filled the streets, waving palm branches and shouting. Well-dressed merchants and landowners pressed close to peasants and farmers. Shepherds and laborers rubbed shoulders with pilgrims in traveling cloaks, all of them gazing toward the east.

"You there!" He brought Ferox alongside a group of men stripping branches from a spindly palm. From their clothes, they looked like Greeks. "What's happening here?"

"It's the Messiah." Yes, definitely Greek Jews in town for the Passover.

"Jesus of Nazareth?"

"Yes. He brought a man back to life in Bethany! A man dead for four days!"

The Greeks passed branches into the frenzied crowd. Longinus looked for a pathway through the mob. He needed to see this man they called the Messiah. "Marcellus, Petras. Stay here. Keep an eye on the crowds. Watch for any disturbances. I'll move up."

He nudged Ferox toward the gate, pushing through the river of people like a fish swimming upstream. Where was Jesus, and how would he know him when he saw him? His hands were damp on the reins. Would he even get a chance to warn him about the Sanhedrin, to question him and decide if he really was a threat?

A man's deep bellow caught his ear. "Stop him! My money!"

People jostled and shouted, one pointing one direction, another pushing through the crowd in the opposite way. But Longinus, seated on Ferox, caught the flash of the familiar dirty tunic on an undersized figure. The Mouse. Of course the thieves would be here, where the people were packed like olives in a jar. He should have known.

A merchant bellowed again and gave chase, along with what looked like three armed guards.

He craned his neck toward the gate. No sign of Jesus yet. From his vantage point, he could see the Mouse pause and glance back, like he was waiting for someone. The guards were close, but Longinus was closer. *Finally, the gods smile upon me.* He could catch the Mouse who had eluded him all winter. He'd win the bet and get back in time to intercept Jesus.

He heeled Ferox's sides. "Get out of the way!" People shoved and shouted but were packed too tightly to move aside. He signaled to Petras, "Take ten men around to the Sheep's Pool; then circle back."

He pulled his sword as he threw a leg over the saddle and jumped off Ferox. "Move!" He charged through the crowd.

"Marcellus!" He pointed toward the gate as he passed his optio. "Watch for him."

The crowds thinned as he moved into the side street. He stopped, listening for footsteps or shouts. Which way?

A bellow sounded from the direction of the wood market. It had to be the merchant and his guards. But why was the boy leading them away from the crowds? He sprinted toward the market.

A short, thick man careened around the corner toward him. Too old to be the Mouse, too short to be the Greek. Longinus let him pass. This time, he wouldn't let anything distract him from capturing the thieves. The wood market was just ahead. He crept through the winding side streets. The noise of the crowds dulled, but a muffled thud caught his ear as he passed a courtyard gate. A covey of pigeons fluttered upward from behind the wall. Whatever—or whoever—had disturbed them was in the courtyard. Trapped.

He moved swiftly to the gate and silently pushed it open, scanning the courtyard. The walls were high, the door to the house barred. The courtyard was empty but for a bank of well-tended rosebushes.

He tightened his grip on his sword and advanced on the bushes. A stone pinged off his armor, another off the wall on his left.

He whirled toward the open gate. There, with a flash of blue striped tunic, the tall Greek darted away. Longinus glanced back at the bushes. The boy might be in them, but the tall Greek was only twenty paces away. Longinus put on a burst of speed. He'd catch him before he rounded the corner ahead.

The Greek was five steps from the corner, and Longinus was one step behind, when Petras and five legionaries appeared at the junction. The man was trapped and surrounded in seconds. He struggled, but a quick strike to his head left him dazed and limp.

Longinus pushed him toward his men. "Get him to the carcer. I'm going back for the Mouse."

He ran back to the courtyard where the gate swung open. Rose petals lay scattered on the dust, a scrap of dirty wool hung from the thorns. The boy had been here, all right, but he was gone. Longinus slammed his palm against the stone wall. The Greek had saved him again. He sheathed his sword and sprinted back toward the gate.

Marcellus held Ferox's bridle. Where the crowds had been standing, there were now only trampled palm branches and clouds of dust. Ferox sidestepped and snorted as Longinus pulled himself up. He turned toward the city where the last stragglers were heading. "Where is Jesus?"

Marcellus shook his head. "He passed by. I followed him, but he disappeared when they got to the temple."

Longinus bit back a curse. Not even a glimpse. The pilgrims who had entered the city with Jesus had disappeared like chaff in the wind. When he got his hands on that Greek, he'd make him pay. And the other little thief as well.

Longinus signaled his men to march back to camp. At least he had something to show for today. He had the Greek, and by the gods, he'd talk. By the time Longinus was done with him, he'd know everything he needed to find the Mouse. And when he got the little runt, he'd have some leverage with Pilate and could warn him not to fall for the schemes of the Sanhedrin. Then, he'd get out of Judea.

NISSA WAITED IN the tiny alcove by the upper market. Her body shook like an earthquake. Her eyes burned with unshed tears. What had happened to Dismas? He'd saved her. Again.

And this time, maybe he didn't get away.

Gestas should have been caught, not him. She'd led the men to the wood market, but Gestas hadn't been waiting. She'd barely escaped herself. She'd climbed a wall, scraping and pushing herself up in desperate panic, and fallen into a deserted courtyard.

But just when she'd thought she was safe, Longinus had

opened the gate. When he'd come toward her hiding place, her heart crawled into her throat, cutting off her breath. Then, out of nowhere, a stone from a sling, and he'd run, giving her a moment to dash out the gate and disappear into the maze of streets.

The horns blew the call to evening prayer. Dismas wasn't coming. If she hadn't convinced him to continue, he'd be in a crowded wineshop right now, drinking cheap wine and flirting, not thrown in a Roman jail, awaiting . . .

She pressed her cheek against the cold stone. Crucifixion. The whole city believed Mouse and the Greek had killed Thaddeus. No one would believe Dismas when he said it wasn't him. And Gestas wouldn't step up to take the blame. But she could. She could save Dismas.

No. They wouldn't believe you. Be grateful that you escaped with your life.

Was the voice right again? Was there nothing she could do? She waited until dark, then crept home through the half-empty streets, not even stopping to change out of her disguise. It didn't matter now.

She pushed open the gate. The courtyard was empty, the fire long dead and cold. Cedron was with the Zealots, getting ready for the revolution he was sure had arrived with Jesus.

Jesus. She wrapped her arms around her shivering shoulders. What would he think of a woman like her? His words to the woman caught in adultery echoed in her mind from what seemed like years ago.

Go and sin no more.

If only she'd listened to those words, listened to Dismas when he'd told her to go home, listened to Cedron when he'd told her to trust in the Lord. Now she had no one to turn to. Not Longinus, who had offered to marry her. Not Dismas, her only friend.

Now she must tell Cedron, and then he would hate her.

She dragged her feet to Amit's empty stall and collapsed into the filthy straw. She'd tell him where the money had come from all these months. She'd tell him about the priest.

If he threw her out in the street, she deserved it. And if he did the worst—turned her in to the Sanhedrin, to Longinus—well, she deserved that, too. She didn't deserve mercy from Cedron or anyone else.

At the creak of the courtyard gate, she drew farther into the shadows, wishing she could disappear.

"Nissa?"

She didn't answer, a lump like a stone lodged in her throat.

Cedron's uneven steps shuffled closer. "Nissa, what are you doing in there?"

She buried her face deeper into her dirty cloak. Gentle hands pulled at her.

"Nissa, what is it? Why are you dressed like—"

He stopped as she raised her face to his. Her stomach twisted into knots. Now she would lose him, too. "Cedron." She choked on a breath of air.

His eyes widened and went from her wild hair, her dirty face, down to the men's tunic and the heavy cloak.

She ran her tongue over her dry mouth. "Cedron. Remember when Abba lost all the rent money at dice. The first time?"

Cedron didn't answer. He pulled her head covering off, his brow creased at her tied-back hair.

"And Mama, she disappeared for days. We didn't know if she was coming back."

He didn't look at her. His hands closed tight around the coarse fabric.

She had to get it out. "And when she did, she was drunk and slept for a whole day. Do you remember, Cedron?"

She waited, but Cedron didn't answer. He balled the head covering between his fists.

Her heart sped up. "We didn't have any food, and Gilad was going to throw us out of the house." Surely he would understand. He had to.

Cedron stared at the scrap of fabric in his hands. "Longinus caught one of the thieves today."

She bit down on her lip. "I didn't know what else to do, Cedron. I—"

"They're looking for the other one. The Mouse." He picked up the hem of her tunic, feeling the rough wool with his fingers. "They say he's quick, the Mouse." His voice was hard, like soil without rain. "And short, like a boy."

She didn't answer.

Cedron ducked his head like he couldn't stand to look at her. "The Greek and the Mouse." He rubbed his hands over his face. "The temple thieves . . . the temple murderers. . ." He raised his eyes to her.

The first time he had looked at her with those eyes had been at the Pool of Siloam. If only she could go back to that time. She swallowed a sob. "I tried to stop. When you got your sight, I wanted to. But the priests—and Mama and Abba . . ." She reached for his hands. If only she'd had his faith. Trusted in the Lord, like he'd said.

He stood and turned his back to her. "The job at the laundry?"

She bent double, hiding her face in the dirty straw.

"They killed a man, Nissa." His voice was flat, his back a rigid line. "You killed a man."

"I didn't mean to," she whispered. "I didn't know he was going to kill him."

She felt his shadow looming over her and ducked her head. Abba had hit her so many times for spilling water, for burning food. This time, she deserved it.

But no blow came.

Cedron walked to the courtyard. He kicked a jar that had once held their store of grain. "I should have known, should have seen it." He expelled a deep breath. "The man, the one they caught—he killed the priest?"

Nissa shook her head. "No. Not him. He's a good man."

"A good man?" Cedron turned to her, his face a grimace of disbelief. "A good thief?"

"Yes." Dismas was good, in his way.

Cedron didn't look convinced. "Then who killed the priest?"

She told him about Gestas. "It was him. We didn't know what he was going to do. We didn't even know he carried a knife." A shiver passed over her. But she had helped. "Then he found out about me—who I was and where I lived. He said if I told anyone, he'd . . . cut out your eyes, maybe kill you." He had to believe her.

Cedron scrubbed his hands over his face. "Longinus said he's keeping him . . . trying to find out about the Mouse, before they . . ."

Nissa's stomach twisted. *Before they crucify him.*

Cedron stiffened. "Does Dismas know where you live? Your name?"

"No. He didn't want to know, in case . . ."

Cedron's shoulders relaxed. "Thank God for that, at least."

She chewed on her lip and tasted blood. *Thank God? Thank Dismas.* "Dismas is a good man. He steals, yes. But he isn't a murderer. He only got caught because he was giving me a chance to run. We have to help him." He'd broken his third rule again. *If there's trouble, every man for himself.* This time it would cost him his life.

Cedron was silent for a long time. "No, Nissa. He taught you to steal. Got you in this mess." He spit out the word. "We can't help him."

Leave Dismas to be killed? "He's innocent, Cedron."

He crossed his arms over his chest and frowned at her, looking very much like Abba. "Of that crime, perhaps. But guilty of others. And what of the other man, Gestas? He got away?"

"Yes."

"The Sanhedrin wants two thieves. And neither they nor Longinus will rest until they have them."

"What do you mean?"

Cedron ran a hand through his hair and paced the length of the courtyard. "They want two thieves. We'll give them Dismas and Gestas."

Turn Gestas in? "But Gestas knows me. He'll send them after me." She'd hoped he'd die with her secret today.

Cedron covered the few steps back to her. "You'll have to leave Jerusalem."

"Leave Jerusalem?"

He didn't look her in the eyes, but nodded.

"And go where?"

"You can go to Mama's family in Bethany."

Go to strangers? "We don't even know them. They won't—"

Cedron's jaw hardened. "They'll have to. They'll have no choice when you show up."

"But you'll go with me, won't you?" He couldn't send her away. Not alone.

He crossed his arms. "I can't leave now."

Leave the city without Cedron? And desert Dismas after he had saved her life? "No. I can't." Her voice rose at the thought of Dismas hanging on a cross. "And what about Dismas? He was good to me."

"Good to you? Look at what he's done!" Cedron stepped toward her and raised his hand.

Nissa flinched and covered her head with one arm, sure she'd feel the hammer of his fist.

But Cedron didn't hit her. A choked cry came from her brother, and warm arms wrapped around her. She buried her face in Cedron's chest, and he let out a long breath. "Nissa. I'm sorry. I've been blind." He leaned back and looked into her eyes. He was her brother again and nothing at all like Abba. "But now it's my turn to take care of you. And you must do exactly as I tell you."

Cedron released her and limped toward the gate.

"What are you going to do?" she asked, as he pushed through the door.

He didn't turn around, and his voice was weary. "I'm going to set a trap."

Nissa sunk to her knees. Her choices pounded through her head like the slam of the closing gate.

Obey Cedron, escape to Bethany, and let Dismas die for her.

Or turn herself in to Longinus, save Dismas, and be stoned by her own people.

The insistent voice was, for once, silent. This time, she had a choice. And no matter what she chose, someone would die for her sins.

Chapter 25

Longinus lashed the whip one more time against the thief's blood-soaked back.

Dismas's tied hands clawed uselessly at the air. His breath sounded in tortured gasps through the room. "I'm a thief," he gasped for the tenth time, "but no murderer."

The sour taste of bile rose in Longinus's throat. The blood of a criminal had never bothered him before, especially not that of a murderer, but something about this was wrong.

"And your partner?" he demanded. "The small one? What is his name, and where is he?"

"Just Mouse. That's what I call him," the Greek choked out—the same story he'd clung to for the past two days. "I don't know where he lives."

Longinus threw down the whip and flicked his hand at Marcellus, who stood stiffly next to the prisoner, his face pale. "Untie him. We're not getting anywhere with this."

Marcellus hurried to the prisoner and loosed his wrists from the iron spike that jutted from the wall of the cell.

Dismas collapsed on the dirt.

Longinus rubbed his forehead. The Greek was tough, he'd give him that. He wasn't begging like so many prisoners did. But something about this chafed at him. Most criminals, especially Greeks, were ready to admit their guilt at the first sight of his whip. This man hadn't.

The Sanhedrin and Pilate wanted both the thieves, and they wanted them now, before the day of preparation for the Passover. Silvanus was gloating, sure the sword would be his. According to Marcellus, most of the men were, too. It was time to admit the Greek wasn't going to give up his partner. Longinus had four days to find the Mouse.

But he also had to find Jesus.

Jesus had yet to be turned in to the Sanhedrin. Jerusalem was like dry tinder, and Jesus, with his incendiary views, could be the flame that started a revolt. But would he? Was Cedron right? Was Jesus here to start a revolution? The Jesus that Stephen had spoken of didn't seem to fit with Cedron's claims.

Pilate knew the danger. When Longinus had reported the capture of the Greek, he'd broached the subject of the Jewish healer. "We need to find this man before his own people do."

"Worry about your thieves," Pilate had cut him off. "I'll worry about the Jews."

Longinus stomped up the carcer steps and out into the dry heat of an unusually warm and dusty spring day. A legionary hurried toward him. "A man waits for you at the gate. A Jew. He says he has information you want—about the other thief."

Longinus brushed past him and jogged to the gate. Cedron stood stiffly, his head swiveling to the right and left, his mouth pulled down in a frown. The familiar ache in Longinus's chest sharpened into desperation. If he could only get out of this city and forget Nissa. Maybe then he'd get some peace.

"Cedron. What do you want?"

Cedron stepped closer. "I can get you the other thief."

"The boy?"

Cedron's mouth bent down. "The one who killed the temple priest."

"I need the one called the Mouse. Are you sure it's him?"

Cedron's eyes flicked to the side. "I can get you the man with the dead priest's dagger and the emerald ring."

The Jew shifted restlessly from one foot to another. It

wouldn't be the first time Cedron had lied to him. "Why are you helping me?"

Cedron crossed his arms like he had something to hide. "For the silver."

I'd be a fool to believe that. But it was the only lead he had, and with the Sanhedrin and Pilate breathing down his neck, he'd have to follow it.

"When?"

"You'll have him before Passover."

Longinus stepped close, his face a handbreadth from Cedron's. "How can I find him? What is his name?"

Cedron jerked back. "I'll let you know when and how. Just wait for word from me."

Longinus watched him hobble into the marketplace. Something smelled rotten. Still, he'd be ready when Cedron sent word . . . and hope the Jew brought him the right man.

NISSA FINISHED WRAPPING the linen band around her chest, slipped the tunic over her head, and tied the rope belt around her waist. Her face was covered in dirt and ash, and the men's head covering hid her hair.

Her heart pounded and her palms were wet, but not with the excitement of stealing. Not this time. No, fear chilled her to her bones. She looked at the sun as she ducked out of the house and into the courtyard. Not much time.

Cedron stared at her like he didn't know her. "I still don't like it."

"We've been over this. I have to be there."

"It's too dangerous."

Nissa huffed out a sharp breath. Cedron didn't know Gestas. "He won't go alone. He'll suspect a trap unless I'm with him."

Cedron frowned into the fire, but he didn't order her back into the house.

Nissa poked at the smoldering embers with a stick. Dismas

had been imprisoned four days. She hadn't eaten and couldn't sleep without seeing his face, wondering if he was alive. This morning she had made the mark on the wall. Would Gestas take the bait, or was it still too soon?

Gestas might smell a trap, or he might think a foray into the upper market too dangerous with so many Roman troops in the city. Nissa was counting on Gestas's greed to push him to go with her today.

Cedron walked to the gate and turned back to her. "I'll make sure Longinus is waiting. Just get him to the silver merchant, like we planned. Then get out of there before they see you." Cedron's eyes were worried. They'd been over this a dozen times.

She wrapped her arms around her chest. "I know what to do."

"Then you'll go to Bethany."

She chewed on her lip, her choices gnawing in her belly. *Cedron says this is the only way. Start over in Bethany.* She owed it to him, after all the lies, the disgrace. But she owed Dismas, too. Who should she choose, her brother or the man who had saved her life?

GESTAS SIDLED UP to Nissa at the meeting place. "I thought you would be cowering in a corner at home after Dismas got grabbed."

Nissa's legs shook like a tree in a thunderstorm, but she answered him with a scowl. "I need the money. And the crowds won't be here forever."

"Ah . . ." His eyes gleamed in the dim light of the alley. "And what makes you think I'll help you?"

"We're safer together. And we can get more. Even you know that."

His mouth twisted. "Safer? You managed to get a centurion and three armed men to chase you. I was lucky to get away. Our friend Dismas wasn't so smart; he went back for you."

Nissa's chest tightened. *I brought the soldiers straight to him.*

Gestas poked a finger into her chest. The emerald signet ring gleamed dully. "I get to split it up."

She didn't care about the money, not this time. But he couldn't know that. She balled her hands into fists and glared at him. "I need enough for rent."

"Don't worry, little Nissa. I'll be fair."

"Fine. You split it. But let's make it worth our while."

Gestas smirked. "You're tougher than I thought, little girl. We'll do well together."

We won't do anything together after this. She fell behind him as they darted through the shadowy streets.

Gestas blended into the throng around him. Nissa had described him to Cedron, who'd passed it along to Longinus. All she had to do was get him to the silver merchant's booth in the upper market.

Tomorrow was the preparation day, but the market already rumbled like the clamor of an approaching storm. Lambs bleated, and donkeys brayed. Women argued with merchants; slaves labored under bundles of wine and wheat. Hot bodies reeked with the odors of sweat and sweet perfume.

Gestas's sharp eyes shifted to her.

"Follow me," she mouthed and headed toward the south end of the square where merchants sold silver, onyx, and ivory. Not far from the silver booth, a grizzled dealer sold pigeons for sacrifice. She eased behind a stack of willow cages, the birds cooing and shifting beside her, and scanned the crowd.

There he was. Even without his red plume and breastplate, she recognized Longinus. Perhaps it was the lock of hair that strayed from his head cover, or the freckled feet under the long tunic. More likely, it was the way he stood, alert and still, like a soldier awaiting battle.

When Gestas appeared beside her, the pigeons fluttered and squawked. His eyes went to the silver jewelry laid out like gifts on the table. He didn't seem to notice the men milling next to the booth weren't looking at the wares in front of them.

The sounds of trumpets echoed from the temple across the city. Her heart thrashed like the captured birds. It was time. But her quaking limbs didn't still, and her mind didn't focus, like when she was ready to steal. A cold chill swept over her, and her pulse pounded in her temples like hammers.

As if from far away, she heard Gestas's voice. "Let's go, Mouse." He moved toward the silver booth.

Cedron's orders were to run, to betray Gestas and abandon Dismas. Dismas's words echoed in her mind—*No one is worth dying for.* Nissa froze like a Greek statue in the middle of the marketplace.

Chapter 26

Longinus stood still and attentive, searching every face and form in the teeming marketplace. The fourth trumpet had blown, and he didn't see what he was looking for.

The rough wool tunic was hot and scratchy, and the cloth tied over his head flapped in the late-afternoon breeze. His sword, hidden under his cloak, was a welcome weight against his side. Dressing like a Jew had been Marcellus's idea and a good one. No one looked twice at them in the crowded marketplace.

He stood motionless, his eyes scanning the faces around him. Cedron said the thief would be here when the horn blew. If this worked—and Cedron had promised it would—he'd win that cursed bet.

Close to the pigeon seller's stall, he saw Marcellus jerk to attention. Longinus followed the legionary's gaze. At the silver table, a man in a brown cloak and black head covering. Short, just as Cedron had described, but thick and powerful. He moved closer. He'd been right to be suspicious of Cedron. This wasn't the Mouse he'd caught in the marketplace and glimpsed at the Sheep's Gate. But there—the glint of emerald—the signet ring stolen off the dead priest. *Imbecile*. This man wasn't the Mouse, but he could be the killer.

Longinus signaled to his men. They closed around the man. Too late, the thief saw them. He tried to run, but Marcellus blocked him. The thief pulled a dagger from his belt. The blade flashed as Marcellus knocked it from his hand with one blow. The men had him surrounded before he could finish a curse.

They had him. Longinus pushed closer to the struggling man. He was old, but still strong enough to fight the three men that held him. Had this cretin killed the priest with the help of the Greek, or was the Mouse somehow involved? Frustration rose in Longinus's chest. He didn't have time to untangle this knot of questions.

A familiar tattered head covering caught the corner of Longinus's eye. He pivoted and scanned the marketplace. There, next to the cages of squawking pigeons, stood the Mouse. The boy he'd caught so long ago. Which one was the true murderer? The man with the emerald ring or the boy he remembered?

No time to decide—he'd take them both and ask questions later. The boy was fast, he knew. Longinus pulled his sword and charged ahead. *This time the little rodent won't get away.* But the runt of a thief didn't run. He didn't even move. Longinus swept his armored forearm across the boy's face, knocking him to his knees. The boy cowered on the ground. Blood smeared his dirt-covered face. The fire in Longinus's blood cooled as he stood over the prone figure. This worthless wretch was the Mouse?

Longinus yanked him up by one arm, shouting orders at his men. "We'll take them both to the carcer." While his legionaries subdued the heavier man, Longinus barked at the crowd pressing in from all sides. "Clear out. Go about your business."

He'd make sure they were punished, placate the Sanhedrin, and appease Pilate. Perhaps there would be four crosses on Golgotha tomorrow.

Longinus gripped the Mouse's arm and dragged him behind the men marching toward the carcer. The runt didn't look like much, but he'd escaped twice. He wouldn't get a third chance. But the boy didn't struggle or even make a sound. He'd spent months searching for this sorry excuse of a thief? *What a waste of my time.* Longinus's grip on the boy's shoulder tightened as his anger rose.

A sharp flinch and gasp from the Mouse stopped Longinus just before they reached the carcer. He squeezed the bony shoulder again. Again the boy flinched. His hand went to his shoulder in a familiar gesture that twisted Longinus's heart.

What in the name of Jupiter? He pushed the boy up against the wall.

The Mouse ducked his head, cowering in the shadow. The wind teased at the dirty head covering, revealing a curl of brown hair and a bit of smooth skin. Longinus's gut wrenched.

"What's your name, boy?"

The Mouse didn't answer but shrank deeper into his cloak.

Longinus narrowed his eyes at the slim form, the small hand. *This is no boy.* He pushed aside the neck of the too-big tunic to expose a delicate collarbone with a thin line of scar, as though from a sharp blade.

No. It can't be. I'm going mad. His mind—his stupid heart—was playing tricks on him. He was seeing Nissa in everyone he passed, even this worthless thief. His fist closed around the tunic and ripped it aside. His breath stuck in his throat. A crescent-shaped scar. He dropped his hands to his sides, and his heart seemed to stop beating.

Nissa.

Nissa whimpered and turned toward the wall, her hands raised over her head as though to ward off a coming blow.

Longinus stared at her. She hadn't been selling her body in the brothel. She was a thief and a murderer. He towered over her, blood pumping through his veins like fire. His hands clenched, yearning to lash out. The Mouse. All this time, he'd ached for her. And she'd made a fool of him.

He slammed his fist against the wall above her head.

She jumped and covered her mouth with a shaking hand.

"You are the Mouse. A thief . . . a murderer? I helped you. I asked you . . ." His voice broke.

She shook her head, her mouth working like a fish gasping on the beach.

He turned his back to her, his heart pounding like he was riding into battle. It all made sense now. The money, her fear. Of course she wouldn't marry him; she was too busy making a fool of him. He never thought he'd wish she were a prostitute, but anything would be better than this betrayal.

He rubbed his hand over his face. What could he do now? He had three thieves. Had they all killed the priest? There was only one way to find out. He took a breath. He'd find out the truth and deliver the punishment. She deserved it.

Nissa hadn't moved. *She'd better not.* She wouldn't get any mercy from him. Not anymore. He pushed her through the carcer door and down the steps. "Get in there." He shoved her into the cell where Dismas slumped in the corner, his tunic in shreds and covered in blood. Marcellus and two legionaries stood in the opposite corner, guarding the other thief.

Nissa crawled to Dismas with a choked cry.

Longinus nodded to the other legionaries. "Stand guard upstairs. Marcellus, you stay with me."

Marcellus retreated a few paces but kept his sword at the ready, his eyes shifting over the three thieves.

The short, thick one started forward. "I'm innocent. Why am I here? I didn't do—"

"Silence." Longinus closed his hand over the man's throat and pushed him against the wall. He yanked the signet ring from the thief's stubby fingers. "I know where this came from. And the dagger."

"I bought them from a—" His words ended in a strangled choke.

Longinus signaled to Marcellus.

Marcellus dug his elbow into the man's thick neck and spoke in Aramaic. "Stay here, and stay quiet."

Longinus turned to the other two. Nissa cowered in the corner, her hands over her face. Dismas crouched beside her. "Not the boy. Let him go." He raised pleading eyes to Longinus.

Longinus stepped closer. What was happening here? The

Greek thought Nissa was a boy? *Is this some kind of trick?* He strode to the corner and pulled Nissa to standing. He ripped off her head covering, reached behind her head, and loosed her hair with a jerk. "She's no boy."

Dismas let out a breath and leaned toward her. "So it's true."

"You knew?" she croaked.

"Suspected."

"When?" It was a tiny sound.

Dismas shook his head. "After the priest, when I told you to stop. I wasn't sure, but—"

"Fool!" Gestas spit out.

Dismas turned to Longinus. "I beg you. Let her go."

Longinus's mouth curled in disgust. Was there more he didn't know about Nissa? "What is she to you?"

"No." Dismas shook his head. "Not that."

A twinge of relief eased the pain in his chest. At least she wasn't sleeping with the old Greek. But it all made sense, now that he had them in front of him. "You lured the priest into the trap"—he pointed at Nissa, then turned to the one with the ring and the dagger—"and you killed him." The tall Greek was innocent, as he'd been claiming for days.

The Greek clutched his shoulders with hands caked in dried blood. "Please, let her go," he choked. The man who hadn't broken under the whip, who hadn't pleaded for his life, was pleading for this worthless girl, begging for mercy, not for himself but for another? Longinus wouldn't believe it if he hadn't seen it himself. But it didn't matter; he couldn't let her go. Longinus staggered to the door. He'd turn her over to the Sanhedrin. They could stone her for all he cared.

The room was silent. Nissa sank down the wall, her face in her hands. Dismas stood over her like a sentry, his face etched in pain. Ringing voices and the clatter of sandals and armor sounded outside the window. Longinus swung around. *I don't need more witnesses to this mess.* "Marcellus."

The legionary snapped to attention.

"Find out who that is, and send them away."

Marcellus hurried out. Gestas's eyes followed him, and he shifted toward the open door.

Longinus pulled his sword and pointed it at Gestas. "Don't even think about it."

He rubbed his throbbing temple. *What can I do?* Could he see her die at the hands of the Jews? But what choice did he have? The Jews were clamoring for the murders. If only he'd stayed in Caesarea. Then he wouldn't feel this ridiculous urge to protect the woman on the floor. If he had never met her, he would send her to the Sanhedrin, where her punishment would be swift and deadly. But he had met her. He'd dreamed of kissing those lips and imagined a life with her. He groaned out loud. And all the while, she'd known she could never marry the man who hunted her. *What a fool I've been.*

Marcellus clattered down the stairs and pushed open the door. "It's Cornelius. He heard you'd captured the thieves."

Longinus tensed. "What did you tell him?"

Marcellus shook his head. "Nothing." He looked at Nissa. "But Silvanus is on his way."

Longinus let out a long breath. He didn't have much time. He paced the length of the cell and then back to stand over Nissa's huddled form. She'd be better off with the Sanhedrin than Silvanus. At least they would kill her quickly. His heart ached as though a knife lodged in his chest.

Nissa raised her eyes to his. "Please, Longinus—"

"Not a word," Longinus spit out. Her voice—the sound of his name from her lips—scraped on his battered heart like a dull blade. He was done listening to her lies. He turned to Marcellus. "Keep her quiet. I don't want to hear another sound from her, or I swear I'll kill her myself."

Marcellus sheathed his sword and wrapped one arm around Nissa, his hand clamping over her mouth. She struggled against him. He looked at Longinus in question.

"I mean it," Longinus answered his look. "Not a word."

Dismas raised an imploring hand. "Centurion. I beg you. Let her go."

"How can I?" Longinus yelled into his face. "How can I let her go?" *Even if I wanted to, I can't.* "The Sanhedrin and Pilate want the temple murderers. Now, before Passover. And they know I have them. If I let her go, I'll be executed for treason."

The tall Greek glanced at Gestas. "Then give them the temple murderers." He bowed his head. "Give them Gestas and me."

NISSA TRIED TO swallow, but she could hardly breathe. The soldier's hand was tight against her mouth, and a hard fist of fear lodged in her throat. Since the moment that Gestas had been caught in the marketplace, she'd been plunged into a nightmare. Now she was like a trapped animal. She couldn't speak, couldn't think, couldn't even move.

And Dismas was trying to save her again.

Longinus stepped back from Dismas. "You'll be crucified."

Dismas's eyes stayed locked on Longinus's face. "I killed the man in the temple. Gestas and I. Gestas waited in the corridor; I led him down."

No, Dismas. I did it. I'm not worth dying for. The words clamored unsaid in her mind.

Dismas straightened until he looked almost like the man Nissa remembered.

Longinus shook his head. "You didn't do it; Nissa did. I won't crucify an innocent man."

Dismas took a deep breath. "I'm not innocent. I brought her into this. I made her what she is." He glanced at Gestas. "Let her go. You'll have your murderers, and the Sanhedrin will be satisfied."

Longinus turned on Nissa, his brows drawn down into a terrifying frown. His voice was gruff. "You'd die for this worthless girl? Why?"

Dismas looked at Nissa. "Maybe I think she's worth dying for."

Longinus shoved his sword back in his belt with a narrow-eyed look at Nissa. "Believe me, she's not. She's made a fool of you and me. She's lied to everyone. Quit trying to protect her. She's not worth it."

Longinus's words struck Nissa like arrows, but he was right. She wasn't worth saving.

Dismas stepped closer to her. "Let the girl go." A muscle twitched in his jaw, but he didn't break Longinus's gaze.

Longinus's mouth twisted.

Nissa squirmed in the legionary's grip, reaching out to Longinus. *Don't do this. Don't let him do this for me.*

Longinus stared at her, his jaw tight and his eyes hard. He jerked his head at Marcellus. "Get her out of here. Without being seen. Then come back. I'm going to need you to take these men to the Sanhedrin."

Nissa strained against Marcellus, twisting wildly. He tightened his grip.

Gestas backed toward the door. "I didn't do it. I'm not part of—"

Longinus swept out a strong arm, throwing Gestas against the wall. "We know your part."

He moved to Nissa, bending over her. "Go back to Cedron, Nissa. I'll keep your secret, and we'll both have the blood of an innocent man on our hands."

"Go, Nissa." Dismas stepped back from her. "Go, and live."

Marcellus dragged Nissa from the room and half carried her up the steep stairs. *What have I done?* She'd betrayed everyone she loved, and now an innocent man would die for her. She struggled in Marcellus's grip. If she could just get back to Longinus, if he'd let her explain. She could free Dismas. *I don't care what the Sanhedrin does to me.* She wouldn't hide in Bethany and let Dismas die for her. *I have to stop this; I have to make it right. It can't be too late.*

Marcellus peeled his hand from her mouth and clamped her

close to his side, glancing at the lines of soldiers marching through camp. "Walk. And by the gods, don't make a sound."

"Please," she said in a choked whisper. "Let me go back. I have to stop them."

Marcellus's words in her ear were quick and fierce. "He's confessed. It's over. Both of them will be crucified in the morning."

Nissa pulled back, her voice pleading. "I'll go to the Sanhedrin, tell them it was me. I'll go to Pilate—"

Marcellus's grip tightened, his face just a breath from hers. There was something there—sympathy? But also hard resolve. "And what would happen to Longinus? Do you know what Pilate does to traitors? Do you want to see him killed for you as well?" Marcellus pulled her close, shielding her from the soldiers, and marched her through the square. He shoved her through the side gate of the fortress.

Nissa turned and clutched at his tunic. "Please, help me." She didn't deserve to go free. Longinus was risking everything for her. Even after she'd lied to him and rejected him. And Dismas was giving up his life for her when she'd been the one who had led the soldiers to him. *There has to be a way to stop this.*

Marcellus pulled away. "Go, woman. And thank that god of yours that the Greek paid your ransom with his own life." He turned and marched back toward the carcer.

She stumbled and fell to the rough pavement in a heap of misery, lying in the street like a worthless pile of rags.

Chapter 27

Nissa pulled herself up and forced her feet to walk the streets of the upper city. Was it too late? Was there really nothing she could do? Her parents had betrayed her, the Almighty had turned his face away, but Dismas had been faithful. Three times he'd saved her, and she had left him to die. There had to be a way to undo her wrong.

The Sanhedrin wouldn't listen to her, a woman. And not to Cedron, one of the am-ha-arez. She raised her eyes to the east, where the slanted rays of the afternoon sun gleamed on the white-and-gold temple. Who had power over the Sanhedrin, the most powerful men in the city?

Her breath caught, and hope flickered in her chest. There was one man—one man who had defied them. Who had taken a woman caught in the very act of adultery—guilty beyond a doubt—and saved her from death.

He knew their sins. When Jesus faced the Sanhedrin, Dismas had said, *He can read souls.* If he was right, Jesus would surely know Dismas was innocent and save him from death. She just had to find him, to beg him for help.

Cedron had been talking about Jesus since he entered the city; surely he would know where to find him. If she ran—not like a mouse but like a gazelle—to find Jesus, she might have time before Longinus brought Dismas to Pilate.

She sprinted through the upper city. Her feet pounded over

the Tyropoeon Valley bridge and down the Stepped Street, weaving past laden donkeys and careening around pilgrims.

The trumpets had blasted the call to evening prayer when Nissa burst through the gate and into the courtyard.

Cedron rushed toward her. "Nissa, where have you—"

"There's no time," Nissa gasped. Her heart pounded in her ears, and her lungs burned. "I must find Jesus."

"We have to get you out of the city." Cedron pulled Nissa's old cloak from her shoulders and shoved her green tunic and sandals into her arms. "Change. Quickly."

She shook her head but kicked off her men's sandals. Where could she start? It would all take too much time to explain, and she hadn't the breath to speak. And would Cedron even listen to her?

She ducked through the door and tore the old tunic over her head. She struggled into the green linen and wrapped her belt around her waist. She hurried out again, tying it as she walked.

Cedron handed her a full water skin. "Get to Bethany tonight, before they close the gates."

She shoved it back at him. "No, Cedron. I need Jesus."

She pulled him out the gate, telling him what had happened, how Dismas had offered himself for her and Longinus had agreed.

Cedron planted his feet and held her still. "Longinus knows? And he released you?"

She nodded. "But I won't leave Dismas." She grabbed both her brother's hands. "Please, Cedron. Help me find Jesus. I know he can save Dismas."

Cedron's brows came down. "No, Nissa. I forbid it. You're in enough trouble."

She dropped his hands. *He forbids it?* Now he sounded like Abba, just when she needed him the most. "He'll die, Cedron. And it will be my fault and yours." It wasn't fair, but she had to make him listen.

"My fault?"

Nissa waved a hand over the courtyard. "You ate the food I

brought home. You didn't ask how I paid the rent. It was Dismas who kept us fed and clothed while you sat at the synagogue with the Zealots." She held her breath. *Please, Cedron.*

He clamped his mouth closed and gazed at her in silence. He turned toward the north, pulling the gate shut behind them. "I think he's with his disciples, at Joseph's house."

She pulled him into a run, north through the perfumers' district. They could be past the Dung Gate and to the upper city in minutes.

Cedron fell behind, his limp growing more pronounced as they reached the ascent to the upper city. Nissa slowed and waited for him. *Hurry, hurry, Cedron.*

He labored next to her up the incline, through the widening streets, and past the sprawling homes and courtyards of the wealthy of Jerusalem. Cedron turned down a side street. "It's not much farther." He stopped in front of a sturdy gate where flowering fig trees arched over stone walls. "Here. I think this is where they are staying. But, Nissa—"

There was no time for talk. Nissa pushed through the gate and into a spacious courtyard.

A servant jumped from his seat at the doorway and hurried toward them.

Nissa rushed forward. "Is Jesus here? His friends? Tell me, quick, where is he?"

The servant's brows lowered. "Who are you, girl?"

Cedron entered the courtyard more slowly. "Please. I know Joseph. We're looking for Jesus."

The servant frowned but turned and led the way into the house.

Nissa followed at his heels, coming into a dim room strewn with rich furnishings. Two women sat close together near a flickering lamp, their shoulders rounded and their backs bent as though in mourning.

"This girl"—the servant eyed Nissa—"is looking for your son."

Nissa stepped closer. One woman was small, just like her, but old enough to be her mother. Her hair was covered in soft blue wool, and her white hands lay open in her lap. The other woman was beautiful. Long, dark hair framed a face that was almost impossible to look away from. Nissa's hand went to her dirty face and wild hair.

Cedron came from behind her. He didn't spare a glance for the beautiful woman but knelt in front of the older one. "I am Cedron. We're looking for Jesus. Do you know where he is?"

Her child-sized hands fluttered like white doves. "They've gone to the garden to pray."

Nissa's heart sped up. "What garden? Where?" She bit her lip, forcing herself to remain calm.

"Gethsemane. On the Mount of Olives."

All the way across the city?

Cedron raised his palm, stopping Nissa before she could speak. He addressed the older woman. "When did they leave?"

The woman looked from Cedron to Nissa. She bowed her head and was silent. Cedron turned to the other woman. "What is it? What happened?"

The beautiful woman looked unsure. "They said . . . just that they were going to pray, but Mary believes Jesus' time has come."

"His time?" Cedron's brow creased. "What do you mean? The time of revolution?"

Pounding feet interrupted any reply, and the gate in the courtyard burst open. A man dressed in the robes of the Pharisees appeared in the open doorway, panting. His face was covered in beads of sweat. "Mary. Where is Jesus? I must—" He bent over, coughs wracking his body.

Cedron went to the man. "Joseph, what is it? What happened?"

The man caught his breath and straightened. "Judas. He's going to hand Jesus over to the Sanhedrin."

Cedron grabbed him by the shoulders. "He can't. We're not ready."

Not ready? Nissa turned to her brother. Not ready for what?

"He is. I was just there. They're sending temple guards to arrest Jesus right now. Where is he?"

The beautiful woman answered, "He's at Gethsemane."

Joseph wheezed. "I thought they were coming here. I don't know—" A deep cough doubled him over. "I don't know if I can make it to them."

Cedron grabbed Nissa's shoulders. "You have to get to Jesus. You're the only one who can make it in time. Tell him, 'Not yet.' We don't have the weapons or nearly enough men."

Irritation rose in her. She should have known the Zealots were planning something and that Cedron was involved. But far too many Romans filled the city. It would be a bloodbath, and of Jewish blood. They waited for her answer—the Pharisee, the beautiful woman, and the quiet, older one. But Cedron was right; he'd never make it to Jesus in time, and neither would the Pharisee. And if Jesus was arrested, her hope for Dismas would be in vain. "I'll find him before Judas does."

Cedron nodded. "And I'll warn the Zealots. Make sure they don't do anything until we're ready."

Nissa darted into the courtyard and through the open gate. She broke into a run, heading across the upper-city streets she knew so well. If she reached Gethsemane in time, she could warn Jesus, save him from whatever the Sanhedrin—and the Zealots—had planned. Then he would have to help Dismas.

Chapter 28

*L*ONGINUS UNBUCKLED HIS sword and threw it on the floor of his room. He'd saved it and his reputation with the men. He'd be back to Gaul within months, but he felt no triumph.

He struggled out of his armor and sat heavily on the cot, his elbows on his knees and his forehead resting on his clasped hands. Tomorrow he'd crucify an innocent man to save a woman who had betrayed him. He'd give his sword and everything he owned to change what he knew about Nissa.

How could he not have known? He'd seen the Mouse—Nissa—twice, even caught her once. She was a liar, a thief, a murderer.

Cornelius had barely glanced at Gestas and Dismas in the carcer before assuring Silvanus that they were the thieves from the marketplace. The Sanhedrin had condemned them in moments. Tomorrow at dawn, they would go to Pilate for sentencing and then to Golgotha with the murderer Silvanus had brought from Galilee. Three crosses and more fodder for death's unquenchable appetite.

His body felt heavy, like he'd never be able to rise again. Yes, he would go back to Gaul, but then what? Whether in Jerusalem or Gaul, he'd spend the rest of his days alone, waiting for his own end. He'd felt the terror of death in Caesarea as Scipio's blood had pooled on the stones, in Britannia as the light in his father's eyes had dimmed. He knew death would return for him.

His success with the thieves would earn him Pilate's grati-
tude, but with only a day before the feast, it seemed that Jesus
wouldn't need Longinus's protection after all. Longinus wouldn't
meet the man who had performed miracles, and he'd never get
the answers to his questions.

Marching feet stopped outside his door. "Longinus."

What did Marcellus want at this time of night? "Enter."

His optio ducked his head into the barrack. His voice held a
note of urgency. "It's about Jesus."

"What is it?"

"The Sanhedrin. They've sent guards to arrest him."

Longinus jumped up. So they'd found him. "What are the
charges?"

"Blasphemy. They are gathering witnesses."

Blasphemy. Just as Stephen had said. A death sentence according to their law. "Why tonight, right before their feast day?
That makes no sense." He walked to the door. "Where is he?"

Marcellus moved aside to let him leave. "A sentry at the
temple, he heard they were going to the Mount of Olives. There's
a garden there where he goes to pray. One of his disciples—Judas
is his name—is going to turn Jesus in to them."

Longinus rubbed a hand over his face. "When did they
leave?"

"The priests were gathering the temple guard and—"

He brushed past Marcellus, not waiting to hear the rest. "I'm
going to stop this." The man had healed the blind, cured lepers.
He deserved a warning that his own disciple was about to betray
him. And those pompous Jews had no right to arrest a man on
trumped-up charges.

Longinus sprinted down the Via Praetoria and through the
Praetorian gate. No time to saddle Ferox. The Mount of Olives
wasn't far, and the temple guards weren't known for moving fast.
Not like the Romans. He could get there before them.

He sprinted through the temple gates and veered through
the portico, deserted now that the money changers and animal

sellers had gone home. He pounded across the Court of the Gentiles and reached the gate leading out the east wall of the city.

Only as he left the city did realize why he felt so light, why his feet seemed to fly along the stones. He clutched at his belt. He'd left his sword in the barracks, along with his armor and helmet. He should go back for it.

No. He increased his pace. He'd be too late. Already the temple guard might be in front of him. He wouldn't need it anyway if he got there in time. A cool wind smelling of dry earth pulled at his hair as he crossed the shadowed Kidron Valley, stumbling over the rough ground.

He was barely winded when the Mount of Olives rose before him, dark and silent except for where the moonlight turned the leaves of the olive trees to silver and the wind rustled through the twisted branches.

He started the climb, his breath even and strong. Halfway up the mountain was a garden carved into the hillside. The glow of the moon threw fantastic shadows from the gnarled trunks of olive trees, and the heady scent of terebinth eddied through the darkness.

This had to be the one. Gethsemane.

He skirted the open area where an ancient olive press stood guard, the chirp of insects and the rustle of the leaves the only sounds. It would have been a beautiful garden, but the winter's lack of rain had left the bushes stunted and the ground rustling with dead leaves instead of lush green grass. The skeletons of dried bushes and naked fig trees shivered in the wind. This had to be the place, but where were Jesus and his disciples?

A noise like a low groan sounded from what looked like the oldest part of the garden, where the tree trunks were thicker than two men and heavy branches blocked the moonlight. Tangles of twisting roots clawed at his sandals as he stepped into the gloom.

Another moan, like a man in pain, slowed him. Was he too late? Had they found Jesus and beaten him, left him to die? He moved farther into the shadows and around an ancient tree. Before him, a patch of moonlight illuminated a man—a man lying on the ground, his head resting on his hands, his body hunched as though in agony.

Longinus froze and scanned the murky shadows. Had this man been struck down? His hand went to the empty place where his sword usually hung. Could this be Jesus, the man he'd been searching for all these months? Longinus eased closer, still under the cover of spreading branches.

The man lifted his head. His hair was matted, sweat slicked his skin, and his mouth twisted in a grimace of misery. Dark droplets of blood trickled down his face.

"Abba," the man called out, his eyes closed, "take this cup from me." His hand clamped over his heart like it was being ripped from him.

What did that mean? Was he speaking to his god?

Even as he watched the man agonize in prayer, anxiety rose in him. There wasn't much time. The temple guards could be searching the garden for Jesus. He must warn him that one of his friends was coming to betray him. He pushed aside a low hanging branch and moved to enter the clearing.

As he stepped forward, agony hit him like a battering ram. The blood in his veins flowed cold as a suffocating weight pushed down on him, stealing his breath. Fear clutched at his heart, a terror he knew well.

Death. Its grip was merciless, its power invincible. He had never felt it this close, this excruciating. Longinus staggered and leaned against the twisted trunk, trying to bear up under the sudden and unexpected onslaught.

Jesus raised his gaze to the sky; his face was twisted in torment. Indescribable groaning came from his mouth, too deep for words but the meaning was clear: loneliness, betrayal, agony.

The sound cut into Longinus more deeply than any blade. The air in the garden pressed down like a mountain falling on him, pushing the breath from his chest. The fragrance of roses and terebinth soured to the smell of rot and decay. The chirps of insects warped to a scraping chant that grated against his ears.

Death walked in this garden, and he was helpless against it.

Longinus fell to his knees. An abyss of despair opened before him, begging him to drown in it. He'd thought there was no pain deeper than watching his friend die, no torment greater than Nissa's betrayal. This was an ocean compared to those drops.

As his vision dimmed and the hand of death dragged him down to the pit, he heard the words of Jesus. In what language, he didn't know, but they reached out to him like a beacon of light in the dark.

"Not my will, Abba, but yours be done."

Longinus's vision cleared. The moon poured light on the garden, and stars flamed like torches in the sky. The breeze rustled the leaves over his head and cooled his wet cheeks. He pulled in a deep, rasping breath. His legs shook as he struggled to his feet and leaned against the rough bark of the olive tree.

What had happened? What kind of evil had passed by him? An evil he couldn't fight with a sword, but that this man had vanquished with his words. *Not my will, Abba, but yours be done.*

Jesus was standing now, his back to Longinus.

It was time to warn him, speak to the man he'd wondered about for so many months. Longinus started forward, his legs still quaking, but a blaze of torchlight stopped him midstride.

Voices rang out, and a dozen torches flickered through the trees, arcing out to surround the man in the clearing. The flames glittered on the gold embroidery of the temple guard uniforms. Behind the temple guards, a troop of Pharisees and priests labored up the hill. Even Caiaphas trudged up the path with a handful of slaves and scribes.

Longinus moved out of the trees. If they ran now, they could get away. These men weren't trained to give chase. They could lose them in the dark, find a place to hide. A new sound stopped him—one he knew like his own voice. Commands shouted in Latin, marching feet, and the clank of armor and shields.

A column of fully armed legionaries pushed into the garden behind the priests. Silvanus rode in front, his vitis raised and his sword at the ready.

It was too late to run. They'd never escape the legionaries. Longinus had missed his chance to warn Jesus. And now what could he do—unarmed and outnumbered? He pressed his back against the tree, his heart hammering in his chest. If they found him here, he'd have some explaining to do to Pilate.

Three of what looked like Jesus' disciples struggled in the grasp of six legionaries overseen by Cornelius, but Longinus couldn't even help Jesus' friends. Without his sword, his vitis and insignia, he was naked, as helpless as a baby, more pathetic than the unarmed temple guards.

Slipping through the shadows of the trees, he made his way closer to Jesus and finally was able to clearly see the man he'd looked for all these months. Jesus stood tall in the moonlight, his long white tunic unbelted and streaked with dirt. His head was uncovered, and his hair clung damply to his face.

Longinus leaned forward. He'd spent most of his life around men of power—centurions, generals, he'd even glimpsed Caesar once. But this man radiated another kind of power—the latent power of an oncoming thunderstorm or the dormant force of the sea. He had the power to overcome death with mere words. Why wasn't he using it?

A Jew with a short, trimmed beard and fine cloak led the legionaries and guards. His eyes shifted from Jesus to the faces of the captured disciples. One of the younger disciples struggled against Cornelius's grip. "Judas!"

So that was Judas, the betrayer. Cornelius slammed the hilt of his sword against the young disciple's head, and he fell to his knees with a grunt. Longinus clenched his hands into fists but didn't move.

Judas approached Jesus like a snake sliding through the garden. Jesus didn't move, not even as Judas bent close and kissed him—the kiss of peace, just as Stephen had given Longinus that last day. But this kiss was one of betrayal.

The captain of the temple guards stepped forward. He was older than Longinus and soft around the middle. A muscle twitched in his cheek, and he licked his lips. "Are you Jesus the Nazarene?"

The clouds shifted, and the moonlight brightened over the hillside. Jesus lifted his head and seemed to grow taller. "I am." His voice echoed over the silent garden like the call of the temple trumpets.

Several temple guards turned away with shouts. They fell to their knees like they'd been struck by lightning. Silvanus's horse shied. The centurion muttered a curse and brought him back to his place.

I am. What did those words mean? Was it something that only the Jews understood?

Jesus moved toward the captain. The guards shifted as if to protect their leader, but Jesus said only, "I ask you, who are you looking for?"

"Jesus of Nazareth. Are you the man?" The captain's voice wavered on the last word.

"I told you that I am. So if you are looking for me, let these people go."

Longinus glanced at the bound men. Jesus, like the best of generals, negotiated for the safety of his men first. His father used to say to him, it takes great strength to fight your enemies but even greater strength not to fight. Whatever enemy Jesus had faced in the garden just moments ago was infinitely stronger than these men, and Jesus had vanquished it with mere words. But this time, he was choosing not to fight.

"Let them go," the captain said to Silvanus, his voice cracking.

Silvanus sneered but nodded to Cornelius. As the legionary

untied their hands, one of the older Jews lunged for Cornelius's sword and scraped it out of its scabbard. He lurched toward Caiaphas.

The young disciple shouted, "No, Peter!"

The first row of legionaries pulled their swords and rushed forward.

Peter stumbled, holding the sword with both hands like a club. Caiaphas backed away, pulling his servant in front of his body like a shield. Peter brought the sword down, missing the high priest but glancing off the servant.

The man screamed and clamped a hand over the side of his head. Blood spurted through his fingers.

Longinus looked for a weapon—a stick, a rock, anything. He had to get Jesus away before this turned into a bloodbath. There was nothing but leaves and twigs around him. What could he do? Fight his own men with sticks and stones?

A rustle and flash of green caught his eye. A slight figure scuttled through the trees toward the clearing. There was no mistaking Nissa's long wild hair and compact form. What was she doing here? Following him? She moved through the gaps between the trees to his right and toward the open clearing. She was going to get herself killed, rushing into the battle breaking out in the clearing.

Longinus lurched to Nissa and grabbed her around the waist. He dragged her back into the cover of trees.

She struggled against him. "Let me go! I have to see him."

He pulled her close, wrapping one hand around her waist and clamping the other over her mouth. "Silence," he hissed in her ear.

He expected more of a struggle, but Nissa stopped abruptly, her gaze riveted on the men in the clearing.

The scene was a silent tableau, as though carved in stone.

Legionaries surrounded Peter, swords drawn but motionless. Peter, the sword dangling in his hand, stared at the high priest's servant lying prostrate on the ground. Jesus knelt over the servant. His hand cupped the man's ear, but the blood had stopped flowing and the man no longer cried out in pain.

The servant scrambled to his feet, never taking his eyes from Jesus. He backed away, then turned and fled from the garden.

Jesus turned to the disciple with the sword. "Put away your sword, Peter. Shouldn't I drink the cup the Father gave me?"

Peter dropped the sword and sprinted toward the trees. The other two disciples followed, crashing through the bushes and into the dark forest.

Three legionaries moved to follow the men. "Let them go," Silvanus commanded. "Our orders are to make sure this man gets to the Sanhedrin." Longinus's arms tightened around Nissa. Jesus had healed the servant, had stopped a battle that surely would have ended in death for his disciples. But still these men couldn't see that he was no threat to them. Were they blind or just stupid?

Two legionaries wrenched Jesus' hands behind his back and wrapped a rope around them. Jesus didn't flinch as they knotted it tight. They shoved Jesus in front of the temple guard. The guards backed away, glancing nervously at each other.

"Take him!" Caiaphas's face was pale beneath his swaying phylacteries. The guards surrounded Jesus and pushed him down the hill, toward the city.

Silvanus pulled himself up onto his horse and signaled to his men. The cohort pivoted and marched down the mountain and into the valley.

Nissa squirmed against Longinus.

He dropped his hands and stepped away. "What are you doing here?"

Moonlight glinted off cheeks streaked with dirt and disheveled hair. She wiped her hand across her mouth.

"I was supposed to warn him. But . . ." She bit her lip.

He rubbed his hand over his tunic, erasing the imprint of her lips on his palm. They had both been too late. A twist of anger pulled at his gut. She had delivered Dismas to death. She was no better than Judas.

She moved out of the shadows. "I have to follow them."

"Follow them?" What did she want with Jesus? "Why?" As soon as the words left his mouth, he regretted them. *I don't care what she does.*

"He has power over the Sanhedrin . . . they won't be able to do anything to him. He'll walk away from them."

"And then what?"

"Then he can help Dismas. He has to."

"Help Dismas?" Was she crazy? Dismas was a dead man. And why would Jesus help a thief? Longinus shook his head. "Go home, Nissa. You've done enough harm today."

"I won't abandon him." Her mouth hardened into that stubborn line he knew so well. She'd lied to him and betrayed her friend. Now she wanted to undo it all.

She looked up at him, her ink-black eyes reflecting the moonlight. "Longinus. I'm sorry—"

Sorry? *As if that makes up for what she's done.* "Don't speak to me."

She moved closer. "Please, forgive—"

He closed his hands over her arms. "Forgive you?" She'd lied to him, made a fool of him. She was a thief and a murderer. He'd never forgive her. He pushed her away. "Some things can't be forgiven."

She stumbled backward with a choked cry, then ran after the receding torchlight, leaving him alone in the cool darkness of the garden.

Let her go. She means nothing to you now.

Longinus leaned against a tree and rubbed his aching head. The garden was quiet now. No evil or despair permeated the air, no evidence that an innocent man had been betrayed by a friend. Jesus' friends had run, deserted him, but Longinus wouldn't. Not after what he'd encountered here with the man he hadn't even met.

He needed his sword, his armor, his insignia of office. He had some influence with Pilate now. He would insist that Pilate stop the Sanhedrin before they went too far. One innocent man had already been condemned tonight. He wouldn't let these conniving Jews do the same to Jesus.

Chapter 29

NISSA PUSHED HER way through Pharisees and priests in the courtyard of Caiaphas's palace. It wouldn't be long now. How Jesus would defeat the Sanhedrin this time, she didn't know. But he would. And then she would beg for him to do the same for Dismas.

A knot of people pressed together near the gate to the inner courtyard. She sidled through but found a guard barring the way with a gold-tipped staff. "This is not your concern," he said to a group of men who looked like pilgrims from Galilee, blocking them from entry. Another group, dressed in linen with gold rings and embroidered cloaks, passed by him without challenge.

Nissa slipped to the side and slunk around the edge of the courtyard. She'd need to find another way in. A fig tree stretched up and over the wall. She clambered up the spindly branches and eased over the warm bricks. Lowering herself as far as she could, she let go of the branch and fell with a thud on the hard ground.

She scuttled close to the shadow of the wall, behind a trickling marble fountain. On the other side of the inner courtyard, a fire blazed in a brazier. At least ten men stood around it warming their hands. Some were temple guards; others looked like Pharisees. Behind the fire stood the door to the palace and another guard.

"He's in there now?" a man asked, his face lit by the light of the fire.

A temple guard nodded. "They are listening to witnesses. He claims God is his father. He calls him Abba." The guard laughed. "Proof enough he is crazy. Abba!"

A servant girl hurried by with more wood. Nissa pulled closer to the wall.

A Pharisee held his hands over the flames. "He's a fraud, I say."

The girl stacked more wood on the fire. Sparks swirled upward, lighting the faces of the men in the circle. She pointed a dirty finger at one of them. "Aren't you one of that man's disciples?"

The man froze. "I am not."

But he was. Nissa had seen him in the garden. He was the one who had attacked the high priest's slave and run away. Now he was denying he even knew Jesus.

The temple guard left the fire. "You are. I've seen you with him."

The man shook his head and stepped back, looking behind him toward the gate like he was going to run. "I tell you, I am not."

"You are."

His voice rose. "I don't know what you are talking about."

The guard from the door moved closer, joining in the accusations.

Nissa inched forward. This was her chance. She clung to the shadows, then darted through the door and into the palace.

The sounds of the courtyard faded. The marble entrance hall, bigger than her own house, was empty. Torches blazing in sconces dispelled the gloom. Richly covered chairs and burnished urns lined one wall, while a series of unlit doorways gaped like open mouths along the other.

Raised voices rang from a double arch at the end of the hall. Nissa made herself as small as she could and crept along the wall toward the voices.

She leaned around the doorway and took a quick glance into

the bright room. It was filled with men. Men in priestly robes, Pharisees, even some Sadducees. All had their backs to her. All but one.

Jesus faced the body of men. His tunic was ripped and dirty, like he'd been thrown to the ground. His hands were still tied. As she watched, a temple guard stepped forward and struck him across the face.

She jerked back. What was happening? When would he prevail over them, outwit them like he had at the temple?

A scuffle of sandals and a shout of protest sent her scurrying into a dark doorway before a temple guard dragged a man from the room and threw him into the hall.

He stumbled and righted himself, running back toward the arch. "I must see Annas and Caiaphas!" Nissa peeked around the door to get a better look. This man had been in the garden, too. He was the one who had led the guards and kissed Jesus just before they'd arrested him. The one named Judas.

The guard stopped him with one huge hand. With the other, he landed a blow in the man's belly, doubling him over.

"Please," he coughed out. "Please, I didn't mean to—You must let him go."

His words twisted in Nissa's gut. Hadn't those same words pounded through her head in the carcer as Dismas and Longinus made their grim agreement?

A priest appeared in the doorway. "Judas, you have your money. Now let us do the rest."

"No!" Judas fell to his knees, his hands clutching at the man's embroidered tunic. "He is an innocent man."

"That is no longer your affair. Deal with your guilt as you must." The priest signaled to the guard, who dragged Judas from the room by one arm.

"Please, listen to me." He struggled wildly, but the guard threw him out into the night.

Nissa's pulse fluttered, and her mouth went dry. She knew what it was to betray an innocent friend.

The shuffle of many feet and shouted orders sent Nissa farther back in the shadows. A flank of temple guards appeared, Jesus bound between them. A pack of priests and Pharisees followed like wild dogs.

"Bring him to Pilate." Caiaphas spat the words out as if they had a bitter taste. "The charge is blasphemy, and the sentence is death."

In moments they were gone, leaving the great marble hall echoing. Despair swept through her. Her shaking legs could hold her no longer. She slid down the cold stone wall into a puddle on the floor.

Blasphemy. Death. Where was the man who had turned the Sanhedrin from the adulterous woman? Where was the power he had shown in the temple, and when he'd cured Cedron and all the others?

Jesus hadn't outwitted the Sanhedrin this time. He had been abandoned by the God he called on. Even his own followers had abandoned him. He'd been betrayed and condemned, just like Dismas.

Jesus couldn't save Dismas. He couldn't even save himself.

LONGINUS PACED THE length of the marble anteroom as the sun lightened the eastern sky. He shoved his helmet under his arm and rubbed his gritty eyes. His breastplate was polished and gleaming, his vitis and sword at his side. It would be soon now. Pilate was usually up early, if he slept at all, and Longinus would be the first to talk to him about Jesus, before the Jews and Silvanus got to him.

The steward appeared as silently as a shadow. "He'll see you."

Longinus strode forward, resisting the urge to wipe his damp hands down his tunic. He'd reported to the governor of Judea many times. But never to beg for his mercy on a man bound and waiting in the carcer.

He stepped through an arched doorway into a wide chamber.

Marble columns soared to the vaulted ceiling. Long, velvet panels draped the walls, muffling the ring of his sandals. Wide openings along the eastern wall framed the expanse of the agora and, beyond it, the upper marketplace.

Pilate sat in a cushioned chair at the far end. Silvanus stood next to him, his face twisted in a smile. Longinus's stride faltered. *How did that ugly dog reach Pilate first? Probably bribed the steward.*

Pilate inclined his head to Longinus. He was a big man, powerful despite his age. He had a long face with deep-set, hooded eyes. His short, gray hair receded from a furrowed forehead. "Centurion, I hear you are to be congratulated." Like all those of the upper echelons of Roman society, Pilate spoke Greek. Except when he'd had too much wine; then he switched into Latin like the rest of the men.

Longinus eyed Silvanus.

"You've captured the temple murderers. Your father would be proud."

Longinus jerked his head in assent as guilt twisted through his gut. He'd won his sword and his passage to Gaul, not that it mattered now. Dismas—bloody, broken, and innocent—would die today. He couldn't help Dismas, but he could help Jesus.

Pilate rubbed a hand down his face. "That should get the Sanhedrin off my back. And a crucifixion will subdue the troublemakers."

Longinus ran his tongue over his dry mouth. "Legate, the Jews arrested a man last night named Jesus. I—"

Pilate held up his hand. A muscle under his eye twitched as he sent a sidelong look toward Silvanus. "Silvanus also tells me you had Scipio's murderer."

Longinus blinked. How could he answer? The truth would brand him a traitor, but he wouldn't lie. "Silvanus shouldn't believe everything he hears from spies and gossips."

Pilate's brow furrowed, and he glanced at the scowling Silvanus.

Silvanus pointed a finger at Longinus. "He's a friend of the

Jews. His father might have been a great centurion, but his loyalty is—"

"That's enough." Pilate's voice hardened like obsidian. "I've heard all I need from you, Silvanus. Go now. Get the men from the carcer, and bring them to the stone bench."

Silvanus glowered but obeyed. As he strode past Longinus, he shot him a look of pure venom.

Pilate rose from the chair and walked to the arched openings facing the agora. He folded his arms over his chest and gazed at the approaching dawn.

As the sound of Silvanus's steps faded, Longinus stared at Pilate's back. The best he could hope for was dishonorable discharge. If Pilate believed Silvanus, he could be flogged, even executed.

Pilate's shoulders rose and fell with a deep breath. "You've been here most of the winter, centurion. Tell me. Is this man—the Galilean—is he a threat to Rome?"

Longinus blinked at the abrupt change in subject. But this was his chance to speak for Jesus. "Only to the temple authorities, the high priests, the Pharisees."

Pilate's back was still to him. "The ones in power."

"But the people, the masses here for the feast, they love him."

Pilate turned to him, his toga swirling. "Love him enough to follow him against six thousand armed legionaries?"

Longinus shook his head. "He doesn't call for revolt." He dismissed Stephen's cryptic farewell. *Be ready. The revolution is coming.* The Samaritan didn't make sense most of the time.

Pilate's expression became skeptical, and his eye twitched again. "One more uprising in this barbarian outpost and Caesar will have my head."

"But Jesus is—"

"I know. Innocent. Peaceful. A healer. I've heard all about him. From you, a few Jews, my own wife." Pilate's shoulders bowed like he had the weight of the empire upon them. "Sometimes the innocent have to pay the price for the guilty."

A chill ran down Longinus's back. *Like Dismas.* But Jesus wouldn't, not while he was alive to stop it. "It doesn't have to be that way. You can stop this."

Pilate looked at him, his hooded eyes unreadable. He settled into his chair, arranging the folds of his toga around his lap. "You mean the Passover amnesty?"

"Yes." The governor had the option to release one prisoner, decided by the people, at Passover. A gesture of mercy from Rome.

Pilate finished smoothing his toga. "You're sure this Jew isn't a threat?"

"I'm sure."

Pilate pursed his lips and fixed his gaze on Longinus. "We have Barabbas. If I give them the choice, you say these people will choose Jesus?"

A choice between Barabbas, who had killed a family of Jews, and Jesus, who'd healed the sick and lame? Longinus's shoulders relaxed, and his heart slowed. "Yes." Of course they would choose Jesus.

"Go now." Pilate waved a hand. "Take three hundred men. If you can't keep those crowds of Jews under control, we'll have more than three dead today. And I don't want to be in this city any longer than necessary."

Longinus turned and marched toward the door. He'd make sure the Jews behaved and Jesus was set free.

"And Longinus?" Pilate's voice rang out across the marble and velvet.

Longinus stopped.

"Did you release Scipio's murderer?"

Longinus slowly faced his legate. The truth or a lie? He swallowed. "The man was defending himself."

Pilate pressed his lips together. "I owed your father a debt. Consider it paid."

Longinus's throat closed, and he jerked his head in a nod. *No more chances.*

"You will be loyal to Rome and Caesar, as your father and Scipio were."

Longinus raised his chin. "I understand." The words stuck in his throat.

Pilate returned his gaze to the window, and Longinus retreated. He'd been warned. Any hint of his allegiance shifting and he would see no mercy. His gut tightened. Was he still loyal to Caesar, a man who called himself a god? Or had his allegiance shifted to the Jewish healer, the man he had yet to meet but who vanquished death with mere words? *Not my will, Abba, but yours be done.*

Chapter 30

LONGINUS DIRECTED HIS men to surround the agora as the morning sun warmed the stone walls and lightened the sky to an iron gray.

"Petras, the south side. Any troublemakers, get them out. No blood; keep your swords sheathed." Any sign of unrest, and Pilate wouldn't hesitate to make an example of all his prisoners.

Longinus circled the agora on Ferox. The wide courtyard that fronted the palace was half filled with Jews. A band of priests and scribes hurried through the arched entryway and pushed their way close to the stone bench. Clusters of Pharisees bunched near the front, their heads bent together, their eyes shifting over the crowd, while troops of shabbily dressed shepherds lingered in the back.

Longinus craned his neck to see to the back of the crowd. These weren't the people who had welcomed Jesus less than a week ago. Where were the pilgrims who had come with him from Bethany? The fishermen and farmers of Galilee who called him the Messiah? Did none of them know their messiah had been taken in the night?

A cold fear crept up his back. The Sanhedrin had planned well. Priests, Pharisees, and Sadducees, rich men whom Jesus had angered—they were all here. And by the look of the ragged men gathering near the back, they had called in some poor rabble to do their dirty work. But the rest, where were they?

This is trouble. His gut churned as he pushed through the crowd, listening to snatches of conversation.

"Death penalty."

"—calls himself a king."

"No friend of Caesar."

Then, from a group of Pharisees close to the front, the most chilling words of all: "Give us Barabbas."

Longinus jerked Ferox to a halt. *These infernal Jews are two steps ahead of me.* They already knew Pilate would offer them Jesus in the Passover amnesty and were spreading the word to call for Barabbas instead. Longinus scanned the crowd. Was there no one who would speak for Jesus? He needed to gather supporters for Jesus, enough to counter the demands of the Sanhedrin's crowd.

Pilate appeared at the top of the palace steps and settled himself on the stone bench. "Bring forward the thieves."

Not yet. I need time.

Marcellus approached Pilate with Gestas and Dismas. The murmurs of the crowd waned.

There was no time. A few minutes to condemn the thieves, then he'd bring out Jesus and Barabbas and offer the amnesty. The crowds, instead of accepting Jesus, would call for Barabbas, and Pilate would be cornered.

Caesar or Jesus? Longinus had to choose, and fast. He slid off Ferox and signaled to Petras. "Get on. Keep the crowds under control."

Longinus pushed his way through the crowd, using his vitis to clear a path. He wouldn't allow this innocent man to be crucified. His heart pounded as though he were going into battle against a horde of armed barbarians. He slipped into the carcer and down the stairs. He wouldn't have difficulty overpowering one guard. Two would be harder. And then where would he take Jesus? Anywhere out of Jerusalem. He had friends in Bethany; perhaps they would help.

He reached the bottom stair as two legionaries and Silvanus

dragged Barabbas out of his cell. Silvanus slammed his vitis on the back of Barabbas's neck. The man went down with a crash. Silvanus looked at Longinus with a scowl. "What are you doing here?"

Longinus's mouth went dry. *I can't fight all three of them.* "I've come for the Jew."

Silvanus narrowed his eyes. "Pilate told me to get him."

Longinus nodded to Barabbas, already stirring. "You have your hands full."

Silvanus jerked his head at his men. "Get him to Pilate."

The legionaries dragged the groggy prisoner up the stairs.

Longinus tensed. Just him against Silvanus.

Silvanus turned on him, his hand going to his sword. "You might be Pilate's favorite, but you're a Jew lover, eh? I had a talk with the little thief just now."

Longinus clenched his teeth. How much had Gestas told him?

"Seems you let another Jew go. A girl. Now I know who she is and where to find her."

Nissa. Longinus tightened his hands into fists. Silvanus would find her, and he would be brutal. Longinus charged at the head centurion.

Silvanus moved like lightning. His vitis crashed into the side of Longinus's head. Longinus raised his arm to deflect another blow, but Silvanus cracked his armored forearm across Longinus's cheek. Pain arced through his head as the walls tilted. Longinus reached out to stop his fall, his ears ringing. His arms were caught in an iron grip. A brutal shove sent him lurching into the cell Barabbas had left. He pushed himself up in time to see the door slam behind him. "Silvanus!" He pounded on the door.

Silvanus's voice seeped through the thick walls. "See if your friends will help you now." The muffled rattle of the lock ramming home and Silvanus's satisfied laugh followed.

A second door creaked open, followed by Silvanus's voice,

harsh and demanding, "Get out here, Jew." The clump of Silvanus's tread sounded on the stairs, followed by silence.

Longinus crossed the tiny room and jumped to wrap his hands around the bars on the window. He pulled himself up just long enough to catch a glimpse outside. The practice square was empty. All the men were on the other side of the palace, keeping the peace.

He slid down and slumped against the wall. *I've failed him.* The Pharisees and the rabble they controlled would choose Barabbas for the amnesty, and Pilate would have no choice but to crucify Jesus. *This is my fault.* He had suggested the amnesty to Pilate. He had put Jesus right into the Sanhedrin's hands. And now there was nothing he could do to make it right.

LONGINUS CROSSED THE width of the cell for the hundredth time. His throat ached from calling out for someone to set him free. Light filtered through the high barred window, and the air became warm and musty. What was happening? Perhaps Jesus had convinced Pilate he wasn't a threat. Perhaps someone had come forward—the disciples or even Joseph, the Pharisee—to speak for him.

Finally he heard the march of feet outside the window. He hoisted himself up to catch a glimpse of the practice yard. A forest of sandaled feet and armored shins moved past.

"Marcellus! Petras!" His voice was dulled by the thick earth walls, unheard in the outside din.

From what he could see, the entire cohort was assembled. Longinus's stomach twisted. That could only mean one thing.

Silvanus's voice echoed against the stone walls. "Tie him to the post."

Longinus banged his sword against the iron bars. He crossed to the doors and pounded, desperation flooding through him. "Let me out."

No answer.

Silvanus's guttural cry sounded as he let the whip fly.

Longinus heard the snap of leather and bone on flesh.

Jesus did not cry out, even as the whip hit again and again.

Longinus closed his fist and slammed it into the oak door hard enough to send a jolt from his knuckles to his elbow.

He sank to his knees. The words in the garden came back to him.

Abba, take this cup from me.

Words spoken by the man now enduring the most agonizing torture. Longinus shivered as he remembered the oppressive evil in the garden. Had Jesus known what was to happen? Had he asked to be spared? The sound of the whip went on. Every legionary knew to submit to the will of a higher power—their centurion, their general, Caesar. Even to the point of death. From the moment his betrayer had kissed him, Jesus had accepted this fate. *Not my will, Abba, but yours be done.*

Jesus had prayed in the garden, asking for this cup to pass him by. Longinus closed his eyes. Would this god of Israel hear the prayer of a pagan, a legionary who had killed more people than he could count? If their god struck him down here in the carcer, at least he had tried.

Pater. He swallowed hard. Jesus had used the Hebrew word. *Abba.* Yes. *Abba. I beg you. If this man is from you, help him. Save him.*

The slap of the whip continued. Silvanus's bellow sounded like a battle cry.

Nothing. What had he expected? A voice from the heavens?

The slap of the whip stopped. An eerie silence fell outside the window. Longinus crossed the room and pulled himself up again. Silvanus barked a dismissal to the cohort.

The men filed out, leaving Silvanus standing over a blood-soaked body.

Was Jesus even alive? Longinus's arms ached, but he gripped the bars tighter and pulled himself closer to the window.

Silvanus cut the bloody rope around Jesus's hands. Jesus

crumpled to the ground, his chest heaving, his body shaking like an earthquake. His mouth fell open, as if to cry out, but no sound emerged. Silvanus kicked him in the ribs. "Get him to Pilate."

Longinus slid back to the ground. Bile rose in his throat, and his eyes burned. He brushed his palms over his burning eyes. Back to Pilate? Then he hadn't been sentenced yet.

Longinus squeezed his eyes shut. *Abba. Help me. Help him.* The priests of the temple would scoff at his attempt at prayer, but it was all he could manage.

A muffled roar echoed from the agora. "Give us Barabbas! Crucify him! Crucify him!"

The black despair from the garden seeped into Longinus's soul like icy water.

It's too late. Give up.

He pushed himself to his knees, resisting the dark hopelessness. As long as he had breath in his body, he would pray and hope that this god of the Jews could hear him. *Abba. Help me . . . help him . . . have mercy on us . . . have mercy . . .*

THE CLATTER OF sandals on the stone stairs outside roused Longinus. He jumped up as the lock rattled and the door swung open.

Marcellus rushed in.

Longinus grabbed his sword from the floor and darted out the door. "What happened?"

Marcellus shook his head and swallowed, his face white. "Silvanus . . . it was like he was trying to kill him." He leaned against the door like his knees were weak and motioned up the stairs. "Go."

Longinus took the stairs two at a time. He followed the sounds of shouts and jeers to the corner of the practice square. What he saw there made his stomach heave and his feet turn to stone.

Jesus sat on a stone bench. At least ten legionaries surrounded him, jeering and laughing. Blood streaked his face and clotted in his hair and beard. A crown of reeds circled his forehead, and what looked like long thorns stuck out at angles and pierced deep into his skin. A red cloak was draped over one shoulder, but the other . . .

Longinus stumbled to a halt.

The other shoulder was nothing but ribbons of flesh, barely clinging to the bone beneath.

Silvanus knelt before him, his helmet off, a cup of wine in his hand. "Hail, King of the Jews." He raised the cup and drank, then spit a stream of the liquid into Jesus's face. Jesus flinched. His breath came in tortured gasps as he struggled to remain upright.

Fierce anger darkened Longinus's vision. He grabbed Silvanus from behind, pulling his shoulder around. Silvanus's face still held a cruel smile as Longinus smashed his fist into it with a satisfying crack.

Blood spurted from Silvanus's nose. The cup dropped, and he pulled his arm back, his huge fist lifting like a battering ram. Before his blow landed, Longinus delivered a powerful jab to Silvanus's slack jaw, knocking him to the ground. His head hit the stone-paved ground with a crack. He groaned and lay still.

Longinus faced the surrounding legionaries. His breath rasped in his throat as he pulled his sword and pointed it to each in turn. "Back off."

The clatter of footsteps sounded behind him. He glanced over his shoulder. Marcellus skidded to a halt behind him. He stood, shoulder to shoulder with Longinus, his sword in his hand. "You heard him. Get back."

The legionaries stepped back, their faces uncertain.

Longinus looked at the bloody man on the bench. These legionaries would obey him, but only for a short time. They wouldn't let him walk out of Jerusalem with their prisoner—not without a fight.

His legs trembled as he approached Jesus, afraid to even look at the face of the man he'd longed to meet but, instead, had condemned to this torture. The man he had watched in the garden.

The man who, even stripped and bleeding, had a dignity beyond that of Caesar.

Longinus fell to his knees in front of Jesus. He bowed his head, his heart swelling with a feeling he had never known—reverence, devotion . . . loyalty. More loyalty than he'd felt for any general, even Caesar.

Now that he was free, he'd save this man or die trying.

We'll move quickly. I won't have to kill my men, just slow them down. He'd find a safe place, someplace close until he could get this broken man out of the city. He tensed, ready to make his move, but a burden weighed on his shoulders like a heavy yoke, pressing down on him. He looked up, into the face of the man before him.

Jesus gazed on him, and the burden increased. A burden of knowledge, a heavy knowledge of a task so great, so terrible, it took his breath away.

He squeezed his eyes shut. Not that. *No. Do not ask this of me.*

A tingling heat burned through him, filling his chest. The weight on his shoulders increased until he was sure he'd be crushed beneath it.

I can't.

His ears rang with the voice from the garden. Jesus' prayer, a prayer that seemed to echo over centuries and empires. *Not my will, Abba, but yours be done.*

Longinus opened his eyes and pulled in a shallow breath. *Of course, it must be me.* He, the only Roman who believed in Jesus, must be the one to pound the nails, to crucify him.

Jesus looked at him still, his eyes full of understanding. No fear of death, no panic. Just peace. Jesus was ready to die.

The peace Longinus longed for was right in front of him but beyond his grasp, and death—what he feared the most—was all he had to offer this innocent man.

Chapter 31

NISSA'S BODY ACHED from the soles of her feet to her pounding head. Her hair was damp with the moisture of the night air, but her eyes were as dry as the streets of Jerusalem. How many times had she walked through the city? Searching for what? For whom?

Not for Cedron—she couldn't face him.

Not for Longinus—he would never forgive her.

The streets were cold and empty, the houses barred and shut. There was no shelter from the cold that wrapped itself around her heart.

She couldn't undo what she had done. She could never make it right. She was more alone than she had ever been. Her God had abandoned Jesus, who healed in his name, just as he had abandoned her as a child.

As she dragged her numb legs up the Stepped Street, the trumpets rang out from the temple walls. She turned to the east, where the sky was lightening. Dawn already? Despair tightened around her chest like an iron band. Today Dismas would die.

She pushed her feet to move more quickly. Her breath quickened as she passed the temple, where the great doors were already opening to admit the earliest pilgrims for the preparation day. Today, at the ninth hour, the lambs would be sacrificed; the river flowing under the temple would darken with their blood. At dusk, when the trumpets blew, Passover would begin.

She wound through the streets of the upper city. The towns-people were stirring. A servant pulled a sleepy donkey; a woman passed by with a water jar on her head. Shouts sounded around the next corner, where the upper market fronted Herod's palace. Was she too late? Had they already sent him to Golgotha with his cross? She quickened her pace.

She rounded the corner to see well-dressed Pharisees, priests, and what looked like shepherds in the agora. She ducked under the arm of a linen-clad Jew and veered around a knot of rough-looking Galileans.

When she reached the entrance to the palace, her heart cramped like a closed fist in her chest. Three crosses leaned against the arch. Two men stood before them. Gestas, stripped to the waist, hurled curses at the crowd. Dismas stood silently, his gaze fixed on the ground, his naked back bearing the stripes of the whip.

But the sight of the third man choked her with despair.

He slumped on a bench, a crown—what looked like a crown—pushed onto his head with thorns as long as her little finger piercing his brow. His tunic was dark with blood and dirt.

And before him, kneeling as though in homage, was Lon-ginus.

Longinus's body was bent in sorrow, his face etched with grief. The urge to comfort him—to smooth her hands down his face—filled her. She jerked forward, then stopped herself. *He doesn't want my comfort.*

Two soldiers shoved Gestas to his cross. They tipped it, lean-ing the crux on his shoulder. Another ordered Jesus to his. Jesus stood, his body trembling, and stumbled forward.

Dismas darted to Jesus, catching him before he fell. Jesus leaned on the tall Greek, turning his blood-soaked face toward him. For a moment, neither man moved. Then Jesus spoke, just a few words, too low for Nissa's ears, but they changed Dismas's bearing as though he'd been given a treasure. His back straight-ened, his shoulders rose. For a moment, he looked younger, freer.

Two soldiers jerked Dismas away and leaned a cross on his back. Even as he doubled over with its weight, his gaze remained on Jesus.

Nissa started at the sound of Longinus's deep voice. He had mounted Ferox and was snapping orders to his men. She pulled back into the shadows.

Longinus moved close to Jesus. He growled a command to the soldiers, and they lowered the cross onto Jesus' back. Jesus bowed under its weight, blood dripping from his brow onto the stone paving.

When Longinus raised his vitis, Marcellus and the cohort flanked the crosses. Longinus barked out a string of commands in Latin.

Nissa understood just one word: "Golgotha."

The procession moved toward the Jaffa Gate at a slow and excruciating pace. Nissa wormed through the crowd. She darted through the line of soldiers and drew close to Dismas. His shuffling feet stopped, but he didn't raise his head to look at her. A soldier advanced, his hand raised as if to strike.

She cringed. *I'm not leaving his side.*

Before the soldier could land a blow, Marcellus shoved him aside. He nodded at Nissa and motioned toward Dismas. "Be quick about it."

Nissa's breath stuck in her throat. She raised a hand to Dismas's face, pushing the matted hair away from his brow.

His dark eyes closed. "Mouse," he gasped. "This is no place for you."

"I won't leave you, not this time." Her voice cracked. "You are innocent."

He shook his head. "Mouse." He stopped for breath and turned his face to where Gestas labored in front of him. "I'm no better than him."

"No." She put her hands on his trembling shoulders. *How could he say that?*

"Mouse." A flash of anger strengthened his voice. "There

is much I regret in my life. Stealing, whoring. My wife and my little girl." His voice cracked. "But this"—he pushed up under the burden—"this might be the only good thing I've done." He looked back to where Jesus struggled with his cross.

She swallowed hard. *How could dying on a cross be a good thing?* What had Jesus said to him in that moment before he took his cross?

Nissa clutched at his robe and buried her face in his shoulder, breathing in the faint whiff of peppermint and cloves that lingered among the scents of dirt and blood. *Not for me, Dismas. I'm not worth it.*

Marcellus prodded Dismas. The soldier's face was grim, but he didn't shout or curse like the ones who surrounded Gestas.

Dismas clenched his jaw and bore up under his burden. "Go, Mouse. Let my death be honorable, even if my life was not." His legs trembled as he dragged the cross forward.

Nissa fell into step beside him. *I won't go, not this time.*

The streets were lined with men and women, baskets in their hands or lambs in their arms, readying for the Passover. Some jeered at the men dragging crosses. A few older boys followed along beside the two thieves, scooping up stones and throwing them. Dismas ducked his head, but not before one caught him just below his eye.

Rage rose in Nissa. She stamped up to the boy and pushed him hard in the chest. He dropped his stone and stepped back, his mouth agape. Another pulled his arm back to throw, and she ran at him, knocking the stone from his hands. She darted back to Dismas, shielding him with her body. "Leave him alone, you dogs!"

A woman shouted an insult. Nissa glared at her until she dropped her gaze and turned away. A group of old men spit at Gestas and moved to do the same to Dismas. She lifted her cloak, shielding him while she kicked dust at the old men.

Women who looked like pilgrims from Galilee gathered under the Jaffa Gate, wailing and sobbing. Not for Dismas, surely. Nissa looked over her shoulder. Jesus had fallen.

Longinus was off his horse, standing over the bloody man. A soldier let his whip fall on Jesus's back. Longinus advanced on the soldier, his face like a thundercloud, his vitis raised in silent threat. The soldier shied back into the ranks.

Dismas groaned and swayed under the weight of his cross. His legs shook like saplings in the wind. Nissa reached out, but she was too late. He fell forward, the heavy beam smashed into the stone street, his body pinned beneath it.

Nissa pulled at the beam, her nails digging into the damp, slippery wood. Dismas keened like a dying animal. Sweat and blood trickled over his closed eyes.

Nissa pulled off her mantle and bunched the soft wool in her hand. She wiped his brow and his eyes. She fit her shoulder under the beam and strained to lift it. *My God, you may have abandoned him, but I will not.* The weight tore at her shoulder, wood biting into her skin, her legs shaking with the burden.

Dismas lurched to standing and wedged his shoulder under the cross. He took most of the weight, and they moved together, dragging the cross with them. Dismas's rasping breath matched the slow cadence of their feet. The scrape of wood against stone mingled with the wails of the women.

The crowds thinned as they moved away from the city. The morning light brightened the hills of silver olive groves, but Nissa saw only the white rocks of Golgotha rising up before them.

The weight of the cross doubled as they mounted the hill. Spasms of pain shot through her neck and back. A whip slashed at Dismas; she flinched, but he didn't falter. A few steps more and they were at the top of the rocky outcropping.

Dismas stopped, his head bowed, his chest heaving with great breaths.

The weight of the cross lifted from her back, and she collapsed into the dirt, her body shaking. Golgotha. This was where Dismas would die. But she would not let him die alone.

Three soldiers grappled Gestas to the ground as he cursed the crowd, the gods, even the sky, but his voice held the terror of someone who knew he was about to die. Three others stretched Dismas on his cross.

Nissa threw herself next to him and held his face in her hands as a soldier bound each arm to the crossbeam. Another pushed the point of a long iron nail against his palm. Nissa pressed her cheek against Dismas's rough face. His jaw tightened beneath hers as the hammer rose. At the clash of iron, his body seized upward, arching as a groan of agony broke from deep within his chest. Nissa's stomach writhed, and her heart seemed to rip asunder as they hammered the second nail and moved to tie Dismas legs to the bottom of the beam. Dismas jerked as another nail pierced his feet, and a low moan shook his body.

Rough hands wrenched Nissa away and flung her onto the rocks. She squeezed her eyes shut. Blackness swam around her, and nausea rose in her throat. There would be no mercy. Not for Dismas, and not for her.

The exultant voice howled. *Look what you've done.*

The voice was right. It had always been right. This was her fault. She was worthless, useless. It would be better if she had never been born.

She opened her eyes to see the soldiers raising the cross. Dismas's head swung wildly, and blood streamed from his mouth where he had bitten through his lower lip. A hollow thud echoed over the hilltop as the bottom of the cross found its niche in the rock.

Nissa crawled to the foot of the cross, her mouth as dry as a potsherd, her bones as soft as wax. She inched up on her knees, reaching to touch Dismas's foot, pierced by a black nail and dark with blood.

She leaned her head against the damp wood that smelled of blood and sap. *My God, my God, why have you abandoned me?* She closed her eyes, and blackness descended upon her.

Chapter 32

Longinus suffered every tortured step Jesus took as they approached the ascent to Golgotha. He swept the crowds back with his vitis but couldn't stop their insults or the rocks and debris they flung at the man who staggered, barely alive, under the cross.

Numb, he watched men gather at the top of the hill. Golgotha. The place of the skull. His gut twisted. Here he would order the death of this man, pound the nails, raise the cross. And these men, these pious Jews, were rushing for the front row.

Where were all those who should be here—Jesus' disciples and friends? Had the cowards all abandoned the one they called the Messiah?

He wouldn't abandon this man—the one he would crucify today with his own hand—whether he was a man or the son of the one God, as Stephen had claimed.

He would do what Jesus had so clearly willed him to do. His Father's will. As soon as Jesus was dead, probably before, Silvanus would run to Pilate and accuse Longinus of treason. It didn't matter. His friends were now his enemies, and his enemies—the Jews, the followers of Jesus—they hated him, too. He was more alone than he had ever been.

Wood scraped against the dirt and rock. Jesus's breath rasped in and out of his chest in tortured gasps. He swayed and fell, the heavy wood beam falling across his shoulders and pushing his face into the dirt. Two legionaries closed in on him, kicking and shouting. He didn't move.

Longinus smacked his vitis against a legionary's helmet. "Help him up." The legionary obeyed, setting Jesus on his feet and moving ahead to push the crowd back from the path that wound up the rocky hill.

Longinus's muscles tensed as Jesus dragged the cross one step forward. He was weakening. He'd left so much blood at the flogging pillar, he should be dead already. It would be more merciful for him to die here, at the bottom of the hill. Anything was more merciful than what awaited him on Golgotha.

He must die on the cross. Longinus knew it in the same way he knew that he must be the one to get him there.

He jumped down from Ferox and moved to a knot of bystanders—a man and a few women and children. All had the ebony skin of the southern provinces, Cyrene by the look of them. The women wept and covered their faces, pulling children into the folds of their garments. The man had wide shoulders, thick arms, and eyes full of pity.

"You there."

The man jumped and looked behind his shoulder.

Longinus pointed his stick. "Help him."

"Me?" The man shook his head. "I don't even know him."

"Carry the cross for him, to the top of the hill."

The man backed up, a terrified look on his face.

Longinus took a long, slow look at the women and children. He'd never hurt them, but this man didn't know that. He raised his stick toward them. "Now."

The man jerked forward and hurried to catch up with Jesus. He ducked under the cross and wrapped his thick arms around the beam. When he lifted it from Jesus' shoulders, Jesus crumpled to the ground again.

He didn't move. The Cyrenian looked at Longinus, a question on his face. Longinus's mouth went dry. He slid his hands under Jesus's arms and lifted him from the dirt. For a moment,

Jesus' weight was in his arms. His muscles were hard and sinewy, and he smelled of blood and sweat. He was like any other man Longinus had crucified . . . until he lifted his head to meet Longinus's eyes. There, in that gaze, Longinus glimpsed the peace that he sought—the peace Stephen had found—like water flowing from a never-ending source.

Jesus could stop this. Longinus could see his power even now, feel it under his hands. Yet Jesus refused to wield it. Why would a god—*the* God—want his own son to die like this, on a Roman cross? What had Pilate said? *Sometimes the innocent have to pay the price for the guilty.* Just as Dismas was doing for Nissa. So who was Jesus saving from death? Whose punishment was he taking on his shoulders?

Longinus leaned Jesus against the Cyrenian. They stepped together, the big man shortening his long steps to accommodate Jesus' shuffling gate. Longinus pulled himself back onto Ferox and urged the horse up the hill. Dismas's cross was already raised. He trembled on it, a low groan coming from him. Gestas cursed at the world. The thieves hadn't lost as much blood as Jesus; they would last a long time. Perhaps even days.

He hardened his heart at the sight of Nissa, huddled at Dismas's feet. Her anguish was well deserved. If he could, he'd shorten the thief's agony on the cross. That was all he could do for Dismas.

Jesus fell to his knees at the top of the hill. The Cyrenian dropped the cross between the two thieves, his breath heaving. He glanced warily at Longinus.

Longinus waved him away. "Go now. Back to your family."

But the man retreated to the edges of the crowd, his eyes on Jesus, the fear in his face replaced with grief.

Longinus eyed the dismal hilltop where the Romans crucified murderers and thieves, insurrectionists and rebels. Jesus wasn't a rebel, not like the others. This man was something else. A prophet? Perhaps. He had spoken to God in the garden. A priest and healer? Yes. Longinus had seen his miraculous power.

But more than that, even as he knelt beside the wood of the cross with a crown of thorns on his head, he had the air of a king.

Two legionaries halted in front of Longinus, waiting for orders.

This was the last chance. Longinus couldn't stop what was about to happen, but Jesus could. He bent over the kneeling man. Jesus raised his face to look into Longinus's eyes.

Longinus heard the echo of the words in the garden. *Not my will, Abba, but yours be done.*

Longinus nodded to his men. They pulled Jesus to his feet and yanked his tunic over his head. His wounds reopened, and bright blood flowed over his back and chest. Clothed only in his linen undergarment, he shivered in the cold wind gusting over the hilltop.

Longinus swallowed, his mouth tasting like dust and just as dry.

The wails of the women grew louder.

A legionary hefted the mallet and chose a nail the length of his hand and as thick as his finger. The other two threw Jesus onto the cross. The sun dimmed, like a shadow had fallen across the heavens.

A searing pain ripped through Longinus's temple. He must be the one. He, the only Roman who knew this man wasn't a criminal but something more than any of them could understand. He pushed the legionary aside and jerked the mallet from his hand.

Jesus didn't struggle. The two legionaries stretched one arm along the crossbeam. Jesus opened his hand to receive the nail. Longinus knelt beside the cross. He fit the point of the nail into the palm of the man who had healed the blind, raised a man from the tomb. *Forgive me.* He lifted the mallet and let it fall.

Iron rang on iron. Jesus cried out. His back arched, and blood spurted onto the dark wood and the white stone. Twice more, Longinus lifted the mallet. Twice more Jesus cried out until the nail head lay flush against his palm.

Longinus fought the sickness that threatened. He scrambled to the other side of the cross, where his men held Jesus' other hand. Three rings of the mallet, and the other hand was nailed.

Longinus closed his eyes and pulled in a breath. The tang of blood pervaded the air. Groans from the thieves and the mocking voices of the crowd pressed down on him. The legionaries moved to the bottom of the cross, pulling Jesus' legs straight and positioning his feet over the block of wood that would hold the nail. They looked up to Longinus.

Longinus's chest squeezed tight, too tight to pull in a breath. He backed away from the cross. *No. I can't do it.*

Jesus' head lolled to one side. He opened his eyes and fixed them on Longinus.

Longinus wrenched off his helmet, dropped it on the ground, and swiped a hand across his wet eyes. He kneeled and laid his hand on the feet that had walked the roads of Galilee and the streets of Jerusalem.

The legionary pushed down hard on Jesus' feet, flattening the arches against the wooden block, stretching the tendons of his ankles until Jesus let out a low moan.

Longinus positioned the point of the nail. He raised the mallet, and it fell. The nail pierced the soft flesh, and blood poured from it, over his hands. Another strong, square blow sent the nail through bone and into the wood. It was done.

Jesus lay on the cross, his muscles standing out in tension, the tendons of his neck tight and defined. The shadows deepened, as though night were falling in the middle of the day.

Longinus dropped the mallet, his heart straining against his chest. He bent double, coughing and spitting bile from his empty stomach. He wiped his face with his blood-covered hands. He had feared for Jesus in the garden last night. He had felt the presence of death, and now he knew why. He was the instrument of that death. Surely the god of the Jews would strike him down. *I hope he does.*

His men looped rope around the cross and raised it between the thieves.

Men and women gathered. Some shouted insults and threw stones; others watched silently. In front, in the shadow of the cross, stood a group of women and the young disciple who had been in the garden.

Longinus longed to go to them, to beg their forgiveness. *I am their enemy.*

Nissa lay crumpled at the foot of Dismas's cross. The blood of innocent men was on both their hands, a crime that could never be forgiven.

Footsteps shuffled, and donkeys' hooves struck stone. A group of Jews—Pharisees, priests, the ones who had gathered in the front during the trial—approached the cross. One pointed to the sign affixed above Jesus' head. "It should say, 'This man claimed to be King of the Jews.'"

Another spit at the foot of the cross. "Let him come down now, and we will believe in him."

Anger surged through Longinus. Hadn't they done enough? Must they now mock him during his agony? He struggled to his feet, clutching his vitis. He'd make them regret their harsh words. At least he could do that for the man on the cross.

He approached them with his vitis raised, but Jesus strained forward, pushing his feet against the block of wood and taking a deep breath. His voice rang out. "Abba, forgive them." He battled for another breath. "They know not what they do."

The Jews gasped. "How dare he!"

Longinus froze. *How could he?* Forgive the men who had falsely accused him, betrayed him, given Pilate no choice but to execute him? A new thought cut through his disbelief, and the vitis dropped from his slack fingers. *Abba, forgive them.* Did he . . . Could he mean all of them? Even the man who had brought him to Golgotha and pounded the nails into his hands and feet?

He turned his gaze to the bleeding man on the cross. No.

Forgiveness should bring peace. The peace he'd seen in Stephen. He had a knot of guilt in his gut. He held out his hands, covered in the blood of an innocent man. No, Jesus didn't mean him. He wasn't a Jew, one of the Chosen People. He wasn't even a good man, like Stephen or the thief who had given his life for Nissa. He was a Roman centurion. A killer. There would be no forgiveness—and no peace—for him.

Chapter 33

NISSA OPENED HER eyes, the sky and land still spinning around her. Her head rested on the wood of the cross; her arms were wrapped around the base. The sky was the color of soot, as though night were falling.

From the center cross, words scraped through the air. "Abba, forgive them. They know not what they do."

Forgive them? Just as he had forgiven the woman that day so long ago. How could he?

She raised her face to Dismas. He was struggling to get his breath, his eyes on Jesus. "Listen to him, Nissa. Have you ever heard such words?"

Longinus stood beside Jesus' cross, his blood-covered hands outstretched. His helmet lay on the ground, and a smear of blood covered his face. His mouth was pulled tight as if to keep it from trembling.

She sank down into the dirt. There was no forgiveness here in this place of pain and despair. Only regret for what couldn't change.

Two women—she'd seem them last night, the mother of Jesus and the beautiful one—and a young man inched closer to Jesus. Longinus moved away from Jesus—reluctantly, it seemed. The women rushed forward and threw themselves at the foot of the cross. Just like Nissa, they huddled there, but their tears flowed freely, while hers were locked deep inside her.

A man spit at the base of the cross. "He saved others. Why can't he save himself?"

Gestas, on the other side of Jesus with no mourners at his feet, struggled to take a breath, then croaked, "Yes, save yourself and us, King of the Jews."

Dismas jerked up with a groan of agony, raising himself enough to take a rasping breath. "Gestas, don't you fear God?"

Nissa's heart cramped in her chest.

Dismas gulped in another breath. "We . . . we deserve our punishment." He pulled himself higher on the cross and looked toward Jesus. "But this man is no criminal."

Dismas's voice dropped to almost a whisper. "Jesus." He bowed his head as Jesus turned to look at him. "I am a sinful man." Dismas pushed his feet against the block of wood, his legs trembling with effort. "But I beg you, remember me when you come into your kingdom."

Nissa looked at Jesus—covered in blood, pinned to a cross, almost dead. *What can Dismas see that I do not?*

Jesus answered like a king. "Amen, I say to you," he croaked, as though the words tore at his throat. "This day, you will be with me in Paradise."

The scribes scoffed, and the legionaries laughed. Gestas threw another curse before groaning and slumping down. But Dismas looked at Nissa, his eyes cleared for a moment of the agony that had clouded them. "Did you hear him? Today, Nissa, I will be in Paradise."

A lump in her throat choked off Nissa's breath. She rested her cheek on the damp wood. If only she could believe it. She'd thought yesterday that this man could save Dismas, but he couldn't save anyone.

A Pharisee spit in the direction of the cross. "The world is rid of two fools today. One who says he is the son of God, and one who believes him!"

I wish I could believe it. If Dismas went to Paradise today, the Lord was, indeed, merciful.

You know better, the voice whispered from a lightless place that threatened to swallow her.

Jesus raised his head. His words rang out over the windswept hillside and echoed the despair in Nissa's heart. "My God . . . my God . . . why have you abandoned me?"

LONGINUS STOOD BESIDE the cross and looked up at the sky. The sun was hidden, as though a storm approached, but no smell of rain or cool wind freshened the air. Instead, a hot, fetid wind blew, and the smell of death surrounded him—blood, fear, and the heavy sweetness of incense from the temple.

A group of legionaries played dice and drank wine. The others stood guard, their faces stoic, but Longinus knew they were hoping the men would die quickly so they could get back to their tents and have their dinner. He'd been in their position plenty of times.

He, too, hoped for quick death. Jesus' tortured breaths were like a knife cutting into his soul. He could do nothing for this man but stand beside him. Was he the son of God, as Stephen had claimed? *I don't know who he is.* But he'd seen him defeat the specter of death in the garden. And Longinus knew this cross, this suffering and death—for some reason known only to Jesus—was willingly borne. And it was done at the will of the god of Israel, the Abba that Jesus had prayed to in the garden.

He would stay until the end, until Jesus took his final breath. Then Silvanus would come, and Pilate would have no mercy.

A legionary, one of Silvanus's lackeys, labored up the hill, his cloak blowing wildly in the wind. The man stopped in front of Longinus. "You are to report to Pilate immediately."

Silvanus hadn't wasted any time. Longinus's hands itched to strike out at the centurion's messenger. "After he's dead."

"Immediately."

Longinus let out a long breath. Whatever they did to him, it couldn't be worse than what Jesus was suffering. A Roman citizen couldn't be crucified, but there were many ways to die.

"You've done your duty. Go back and tell Pilate I'll be there when I get there." He returned to his position beside the cross. Everyone—except these women and a disciple hardly more than a boy—had left Jesus. He wouldn't.

Jesus hung limply, his head bowed, his breath quick and shallow. He opened his eyes as Longinus approached, looking at him alone. Longinus dropped his gaze to his bloody hands. Did Jesus despise him? Hate him for pounding the nails, for inflicting this torture? *If I could do something to ease his suffering, I would.*

"I thirst." The words left Jesus' lips like a sigh.

Longinus jerked to attention. He ran to the legionaries, grabbed a hyssop branch, and speared it through a sponge floating in a jar of sour wine.

He carried the dripping sponge to Jesus and raised it to his cracked and bleeding lips.

Jesus put his mouth to the sponge and swallowed. Jesus' eyes met his for a moment. The peace he saw in them stretched to eternity. Longinus pulled the sponge away, his heart pounding. How could this man—dying on a cross—have such peace?

Jesus pushed his feet hard on the block at the base of the cross and took a short breath. His gaze went to the younger woman and the lone disciple. Finally, he looked at the older woman.

His mouth formed words, hardly more than whispers. "It is finished."

The shofar blew from the temple mount, signaling the sacrifice of the lambs for Passover was complete. Jesus' head fell to the side. His straining legs and arms relaxed, and his body sank low on the cross. As the last echo of the horn faded, Longinus bowed his head and closed his eyes. It was over. Death had triumphed, victorious even over this man who had worked miracles.

A deep tremble shot through his legs. He opened his eyes.

The ground shook. The wind howled like a pack of wild dogs. Men and women shouted and grabbed one another to steady themselves.

Where was Nissa? There, still wrapped around the base of Dismas's cross.

The legionaries standing in formation broke ranks but didn't run. Marcellus stumbled toward Longinus. "What is it?"

Longinus shook his head. The wrath of God? Or the wrath of the underworld?

The trembling intensified, and the sky continued to darken into a night without stars or moon. What was next? Hail? Lightning bolts? His men called out to their gods and looked at the sky. He needed to get them out of here.

One of the scribes approached through the gloom. His face was white and his chest heaved, but he motioned to the crosses and raised his voice over the wind. "They can't stay up there. It's Passover."

Longinus's hands tightened into fists. *The wrath of God descends, and these scrupulous cowards worry about Passover?* He pushed the scribe aside and nodded to Marcellus. "Get the mallet. Break their legs." At least he'd be able to shorten Dismas's suffering.

Marcellus picked up the iron mallet and slammed it into Gestas's shin. Gestas screamed. The next blow broke his other leg. Gestas's body slumped, unable to support him. His screams turned to gasps for air as Marcellus moved on to Dismas.

The earth shuddered and groaned. Stones tumbled from the side of the hill down into the ravine below. The hot wind increased, spinning coils of dust over the hill.

Nissa threw her body against Dismas's cross. She pressed her cheek against his feet, her hands covering his lower legs. If Marcellus swung the mallet, surely he'd hit her.

Longinus looked up at the Greek, dying for Nissa's crime. Jesus forgave the men who had sentenced him to death. His heart hardened. *But I can't forgive Nissa.* She didn't deserve forgiveness any more than he did. He staggered toward Dismas's cross as another tremor shook the earth. He'd make sure Marcellus could do his job.

The scribe intercepted him. "Wait. What about him?" He jutted his chin toward Jesus.

Jesus? Longinus stepped between the scribe and the center cross. "He's already dead."

"I have to make sure." He glanced around, his eyes wild with fear. "Now. Break his legs, too."

Longinus raised his voice over the screaming wind. "He's dead, I tell you. Now go back to your precious temple."

The scribe didn't back down. "If you don't do it, I'll find someone who will." His voice cracked. "I want to know the man is dead. And I want it done now."

Longinus's vision narrowed. What more did these infernal people need? Hadn't this man's body been abused enough today? Hadn't these women before them witnessed enough? But the scribe's face was set in stubborn lines.

Longinus stomped to a sentry and tore his spear from his hand. "You want to see that he's dead?" The wind wailed over the hilltop. His stomach twisted in a knot as he approached Jesus' left side, raising the spear.

The women and the young disciple drew back, their eyes wide.

Using all his strength, Longinus thrust the lance into Jesus' bloody side, piercing through his ribcage to where he knew the heart of Jesus lay still and unbeating. He yanked the spear out again. *That should show this fool that Jesus has nothing left to give.*

Blood poured from the wound and splashed over Longinus's hands and arms like a lamb sacrificed on the temple altar. For a moment his hands were covered in red. Then, from the same pierced side, came water—clear and clean—water that washed away the blood, cleansing him like a rushing stream.

Longinus dropped the spear. A burst of energy shot through

him, like he'd been struck by lightning. Hot and cold. A pain so profound and searing it slammed him to his knees. He clutched at his chest, unable to breathe. His vision failed, and a roaring filled his ears.

I'm dying.

Suddenly, a silence came over him, a calm stillness, like in a deep forest. A profound peace suffused him. A peace so immense, his heart was surely too tiny to hold it, his mind too puny to grasp even a corner of its meaning.

I'm not dying. No, for the first time he was truly alive. His vision cleared, and he held out his hands. They were clean. Like he'd just washed in the Pool of Siloam. He looked up at Jesus, his heart swelling like it would burst from his chest. *Even dead, he could give me this peace.* He raised his voice, speaking to the howling wind, the rumbling clouds, the quaking earth. "Yes, this man was the son of God."

Peace filled him, but chaos still reigned on the hillside. The scribe was already halfway down the hill. Marcellus stood next to Dismas's cross, the mallet hanging limply in his hand, his eyes wide as he looked from Jesus to Longinus. Nissa stared at him. Dismas groaned and drew a tortured breath.

Longinus looked up at the man next to Jesus, meeting the innocent thief's eyes. They were full of pain but also peace. Peace that he knew had come from Jesus, just like he'd seen in Stephen. Peace that was within him now.

Forgive them. They know not what they do.

Longinus stood, his mind clear and his body free from the heavy weight he had brought to Golgotha. He pointed to Dismas. "Marcellus. Help him."

Marcellus stepped forward, gripping the mallet again.

Longinus went to Nissa. He pulled her away from the cross and wrapped his arms around her. Her arms flailed; her fists struck at him. He pulled her closer, restraining her against his armored chest. He bent and whispered in her ear, "It's better this way, Nissa."

Dismas pushed himself up to gather a last breath. "Mouse," he gasped.

Longinus loosened his hold, and Nissa strained toward the man on the cross.

"You are worth dying for." He nodded to Marcellus and closed his eyes.

Marcellus raised the mallet and took aim.

Longinus pulled Nissa tight against him, covering her ears with his hands. He buried his face in her hair, wishing he could shut out the sound of breaking bones and Dismas's scream.

He waited until Dismas's tortured breaths ceased. Nissa shook in his arms. If only he could give her the peace Jesus had given him. If only it could seep from him into her and lighten her sorrow. He looked at Jesus, limp and bloody on his cross, like any of the hundreds of criminals he'd executed. And Dismas, just another Greek pickpocket.

But they were so much more than that.

Dismas had died for Nissa. And Jesus had died to give him—a Roman, a pagan—the peace he longed for. How he knew he couldn't say, but he knew it like he knew the wind blew and the ground quaked beneath him.

And he could share it with Nissa. But first, he must forgive her.

"Nissa." His throat closed tight. How could he tell her? Here, where the skies threatened to fall upon them and the earth to split open. He tipped her chin up, meeting her red-rimmed, frightened eyes. *Show her.*

He bent his head and set his lips on the soft curve of Nissa's cheek. A kiss of peace. A kiss that—he could only hope—would tell her what he couldn't say. *I forgive you. Forgive me.*

For a breath of time, they stood motionless. The wind, the tremors of the earth, the darkness—all faded as he willed her the peace he'd been given. *Shalom.* He lifted his head. Her eyes were wide, her lips parted, but no words came from her.

A shout sounded over the wind. A cohort of legionaries

crested the hill, led by Silvanus. When he saw Longinus, he shouted to his men, and they surged forward.

Silvanus's words came back to him. *I had a talk with the little thief.* Longinus gritted his teeth. He needed to get Nissa to safety, to tell her that Gestas had given her away. He looked behind him. The other side of the hill was a sheer cliff. Marcellus stood to his right, but he couldn't ask him to take on this fight.

He dipped his head and whispered to Nissa, "Get out of here. Now. Leave Jerusalem." He pushed her behind him and faced Silvanus.

Twenty men advanced with Silvanus, their swords raised. "Longinus. On Pilate's command, I arrest you for treason against Rome," Silvanus bellowed.

Longinus willed himself not to turn to see if Nissa had followed his order. *Go, Nissa. Before Silvanus realizes who you are.*

Marcellus came to his side, his hand going to his sword.

"Don't." He put his hand on Marcellus's shoulder and growled into his ear, "Just make sure she gets out of the city."

"But—" Marcellus shook his head, his eyes still on Silvanus.

Longinus pulled himself up. He was still a centurion—at least for a few more moments—and he had given an order. "Leave me."

Marcellus nodded and stepped back.

Another earthquake shook the ground. Silvanus and his men staggered. They looked at the sky, then to their commanding officer.

Silvanus motioned with his vitis. "If he fights you, kill him."

Longinus moved forward, pulling his sword. The men advanced. He could kill a few of them, maybe even Silvanus. But he couldn't fight the whole cohort, and he didn't want to. The weight of his father's sword was no longer welcome in his hand. It seemed foreign, like an object from another lifetime.

He dropped the sword on the still-quaking ground and raised his hands. His killing days were done. He'd face Pilate on charges of treason. He would be flogged, perhaps even executed. It didn't matter. It was finished.

The legionaries surrounded him. One struck a blow that bent him double. Another wrenched his hands behind his back. The peace instilled by the blood and water glowed inside him. It was so absurd, he almost laughed as the ropes tightened around his wrists. He knew now where his loyalty lay. It was with this man—the son of God—dead, on the cross behind him.

Finally, he was fully alive. And now he was not afraid to die.

Chapter 34

NISSA DRAGGED HER aching body through the streets of the upper city, keeping the two soldiers in sight. They pushed a hand-cart, carrying Dismas and Gestas away like offal.

She felt no hunger, although she hadn't eaten in days. No thirst, even as the hot wind dried her throat with every breath. Her mind spun with the words and images of Golgotha.

Dismas was dead. *You are worth dying for.*

Jesus was dead. *My God, why have you abandoned me?*

Longinus, bound and hauled away by his own men. She put a hand to her cheek. That kiss, what did it mean? A tiny hope, like a bubble of water in a dry well, rose inside her. The kiss had felt like forgiveness, but how could he forgive her? Why would he?

Before she could even speak, Marcellus had pushed her away from the crosses, warning her to leave Jerusalem: "They know where you live. Get out before they come for you." What did it mean? What would they do to Longinus? Her stomach coiled in knots. *It's my fault.*

She stumbled at the Jaffa Gate and fell to her knees. People pushed past her, hurrying to get to their Passover meal. If she could just stop here for a while, just make sense of what had happened. But she couldn't rest; she had to follow the men who had Dismas. She wouldn't let the wild dogs tear his body to shreds and scatter his bones. She would do this last thing for him. After that, she didn't care what happened to her. It didn't matter.

She dragged herself to her feet and followed the rumbling handcart to the western wall, out the Dung Gate, and into Gehenna. Of course, they would take them here, to a place already defiled.

Ten paces outside the Dung Gate, Nissa pulled her mantle over her face. It did nothing to block the stench. Fires smoldered among the rubble. Piles of rotting carcasses buzzed with flies and crawled with maggots. Shards of broken pottery cracked under her feet like dry bones.

The soldiers stopped next to a brushy scree. She stumbled into a copse of trees, their shadows deepening as the day grew dimmer. She could hide here, give the soldiers time to finish, then go to Dismas.

A movement deep in the murky shade of the trees made her catch her breath. It was a man. Who was out here, on Passover, hiding? She ducked sideways. A crow cawed and flapped away, its cry loud enough to wake the dead. The man didn't move or turn. Something was wrong.

Her eyes adjusted to the gloom, and a scream froze in her throat.

It was a man, but he dangled from a rope, his feet hovering a handbreadth above the ground. His eyes bulged over a slack mouth, but even in death she recognized him. Judas.

She covered her mouth and turned away. Her empty stomach heaved, and a wave of dizziness washed over her. His voice filled her mind. The desperation. The despair. *Deal with your guilt as you must,* the priest had told him. And he had, in the only way he could.

The hot wind gusted, rustling the dry leaves and sending Judas's body spinning. *He did what he had to do.* The bleak voice coiled through her mind, familiar and intimate, the only companion that she hadn't lost. *You are worthless, just like your father always said. God has abandoned you. You are just like Judas.*

She stumbled out of the trees. The soldiers clattered back toward the Dung Gate with their empty cart. Gestas and Dismas lay in a heap at the foot of a sloping hillock. She threw herself down beside Dismas's lifeless body.

Was the voice right? Had it been right all along?

Dusk crept over the hills, and the shofar blew, signaling the beginning of the Passover feast. She knew what had made Judas put the rope around his neck. Anything would be better than living with what he had done. Even death had to be better. Was he at peace now? Had he atoned for his sin?

A bark and howl of wild dogs sounded not far from her.

Her body weakened, and her throat was as dry as the wasteland surrounding her. *It doesn't matter if I die out here.* She'd lost everyone. She'd disgraced Cedron, Dismas was dead, Longinus arrested. Marcellus had said not to go back to her home, and that could mean only one thing. Gestas had betrayed her before he died. They would find her, and soon.

But what would happen to Longinus? Marcellus's face had been grim as he'd pushed her down the hill of Golgotha. *Do you know what Pilate does to traitors?*

The names beat in her head like a drum. Cedron, Dismas, Longinus. Her sins had betrayed them all. She'd be better off dead, just like Judas. But not until she'd done what she came to do.

Dismas lay facedown. She laid a hand on his shoulder. It was cold but not yet stiff. She pushed, rolling him over, then pulled and tugged until he looked like he was sleeping, his hands crossed over his bare chest.

Nissa forced herself to look at Gestas. She couldn't leave him like that, crumpled in a heap. He was a murderer and a thief, but so was she. She grabbed a fistful of his tunic and pulled him to lie next to Dismas. She stood, panting, her head spinning. Two thieves: one good, one bad.

She began the slow process of covering Dismas's body with rocks. First over his blood-covered legs, then his chest and shoulders. She gripped the last stone, looking long at his peace-filled face before it was hidden forever from this world. She remembered his quick smile and his whisper of a laugh. His love of women—all women. How he'd saved her from Longinus so long ago. *You aren't worth dying for, Mouse.*

She squeezed her eyes shut. But he had died for her. With his last breath, he had renounced his own bitter conviction and all that the dark voice had told her: *You are worth dying for.*

And to Jesus he'd said, *Remember me when you come into your kingdom.* What made Dismas—a thief hanging on a cross—say such outrageous words to a man hanging next to him? Dismas had known something that she did not, and he'd taken the secret to this shameful grave.

Longinus, too, had treated Jesus like a king. *This man was the son of God.* A Roman—a pagan—believed Jesus was the son of God. Longinus, who had risked everything, been arrested and taken away by his own people for her sake. But not before he had given her a kiss of peace. Maybe even forgiveness.

Were they right to believe Jesus was more than a man? Were those words—*Abba, forgive them*—meant for her as well?

Look what you've done. You are just like Judas. You don't deserve forgiveness. The voice was strident now. *Jesus was just another false prophet. Now he's dead, just like the rest.*

Who should she believe? Dismas and Longinus? Or the voice that had brought her into this pit of despair and hopelessness?

The hot wind whipped over her, dry and smelling of death. Dust coated her throat, and her eyes burned with grit. A small whisper spoke like a rustle of dry leaves: *Trust in his mercy.*

What if she once again called on the Lord and he didn't answer? Dismas had courage, even on the cross. Longinus had risked everything. Did she have enough courage to turn back to the Lord? Fear clawed her chest. *What if he turns his face from me again?* Would she end up like Judas, dead by the hand of despair?

Thunder rumbled in the distance, like an approaching army.

She wet her cracked lips, tasting blood and dust. Even if she could pray, what words would express her sorrow? A song of the Tehillim, words she'd cried out as a child, came back to her like a long-forgotten melody. One small prayer—one crack in the dam she'd built around her heart—whispered from her dry throat. *"Forsake me not, O Lord. My God, be not far from me."*

The wind blew harder and colder, snatching the plea from her mouth. Lightning flickered over the city walls. But a trickle of strength flowed through her, like water on parched earth. Her voice grew stronger. *"Come quickly to help me, my Lord and my salvation."*

She stood, raising her face to the sky. Her throat loosened and her prayer flowed forth like a rushing stream. *"Have mercy on me, God, in your goodness."*

Tears welled in her eyes, and for the first time since she was a child, she let them fall. Years of unshed tears flowed from her eyes like a libation. A song of supplication fell from her lips and soothed her heart like balm. *"Wash away all my guilt; from my sin cleanse me."*

A drop of water fell on her forehead; another mingled with the tears on her cheek. Her heart lifted as a third drop fell on her parched lips. *"Wash away all my guilt; from my sin cleanse me."*

She lifted her face to the sky. *"Wash me, O my God, make me whiter than snow."* Thunder rumbled, the sky opened, and the rain came down.

NISSA WOKE TO the golden light of morning. Her eyes were filled with grit, and her tongue clung to the roof of her mouth. Her body was sore. She felt every bone and joint, but her heart felt as light as the wisps of clouds above her, as clean as the raindrops sparkling on the branches of the cedar trees.

In the deep of the night, as she had poured out her sins to the Lord, the rain had soaked her, poured over her, washed away blood and dirt. When the rain stopped, a warm wind scented with mint and cloves wrapped around her, like a father's loving arms around his child. She had slept curled against the trunk of the cedar.

The dark voice was silent now. She searched for it, but it was gone. Nissa was free. Free of fear and despair. Free of the lies.

She gathered more stones and buried Gestas. With each stone, she prayed for him. *Lord, have mercy.* She bowed her head over the two stone cairns. It wasn't a proper burial for a Jew or a Greek, but it was all she could do. She touched the top stone on Dismas's cairn. *Good-bye, my friend.*

The Lord had never abandoned her. She had abandoned him. All those years, she had turned her back on him. Refused to trust him. As her sins had increased, the dark voice had grown strong, poisoning her mind and blinding her to God's mercy.

Now, her eyes had been opened. Dismas's death would not be in vain. He had set her free. And now that she was free, she had the courage to do what was right.

Chapter 35

NISSA PUSHED THROUGH the gate and into the empty court-yard. "Cedron?"

Firewood lay scattered; shards of a water jar littered the ground. Her cedar chest lay in pieces near the fire, its meager contents crushed under the imprints of hobnailed sandals. She hurried to the door of the house. Sleeping mats trampled and no sign of Cedron.

She had to find Longinus and had hoped that Cedron would be able to help, but the Romans had been here first. Had the Zealots risen up against the soldiers? Was Cedron in trouble, or were they looking for her? As she dashed back into the street, turning toward the synagogue where Cedron and the Zealots met, she barreled into a wide chest covered in linen.

"Nissa. Where are you going so fast on the Passover?" Gilad's hands closed over her bare arms. He glanced into the courtyard. "And who did that? One of your customers?"

Nissa wrenched her arms from his grip. *I don't have time for this.* "I need to find Cedron."

Gilad smoothed his hand over his beard. "Pay me the rent, or I'll find Cedron for you." His hand lashed out and caught her wrist, squeezing hard enough to make her gasp. "You are looking rather pretty today, Nissa. Perhaps you'd like to pay me in trade?"

Nissa's blood heated. She had no time for his snide insinua-tions. "I'm warning you, Gilad. Let me go."

He captured her other wrist, and his grip tightened. "Or what? Your centurion isn't here today." He smirked. "And I don't think he'd mind sharing."

How could she ever have dreamed of him as a husband? Longinus was ten times the man Gilad was. Nissa jerked her hands up, then down, breaking his grip on one wrist just as Longinus had taught her. With the other hand, she pulled him forward, then thrust her palm up, slamming it into his nose. Gilad bent double, his hands over his face and blood spurting over his fine tunic.

Satisfaction surged through her as she sprinted down the street toward the synagogue. Longinus would have been impressed. She reached the synagogue and burst through the doors. Inside, men jumped, some of them grabbing swords or pulling their daggers. When they saw Nissa, they relaxed.

"Where is Cedron?" she panted.

"Nissa, where have you been?" Cedron moved out of the dim recesses of the synagogue. His head was uncovered, and his tunic wrinkled and stained with sweat. "Nissa, do you know? The earth quaked, the curtain over the Holy of Holies tore in two, the sky—"

"I know, I know." She grabbed his hands and pulled him into the light. "Why are you here? Are you hurt? Did you fight?"

His shoulders slumped, and he motioned toward the men huddled in the back of the synagogue. "No. We hid here. The Pharisees are searching the city for anyone who believes in Jesus."

Nissa peered through the murky light. Some men wore makeshift armor; all had swords and daggers.

Cedron sank down on a bench. "We were ready for a revolution. Judas said it was coming. Then he—"

"Judas?" Her stomach twisted at the memory of the man hanging from the rope. "You were waiting for Judas?"

A young man with a wispy beard stood. "We were ready to fight with Jesus."

Cedron put his head in his hands. "I've been wrong about

everything. I was so sure there would be a revolution, so sure that Jesus was the one."

Nissa sat down beside him. She wrapped her arms around his waist and laid her cheek on his chest. Cedron had been wrong about the revolution. But he had been right about so much else. Trust in the Lord, he had said. Now she would. "Cedron, I have to find Longinus."

He pulled back and looked at her face. "Why, Nissa? I thought—"

"I heard about the centurion Longinus," the youth broke in.

Nissa turned to him. "Heard what?"

"One of the other centurions brought him in yesterday. He's charged with treason."

Nissa's pulse sped up. "What did they do to him?"

The young man shook his head. "I don't know."

It was already midday. What if she was too late? She jumped up and moved toward the door, but Cedron stopped her with a hand on her arm. "Nissa, what are you doing? We need to get out of Jerusalem, together."

She looked at Cedron. She wouldn't leave Longinus, not now. She reached up and ran a hand over his eyes, the eyes that Jesus had opened. "I have to help him."

"A Roman?"

A man who believes in Jesus, too. "A man. A good man."

"Nissa, how can you—"

"He helped us. Remember?" She looked into his shadowed eyes. "He saved me, even when he knew who I was. And he believes in Jesus, too."

Cedron's brow furrowed. "Jesus wasn't our messiah. Nissa, he's dead. Everything we thought is wrong."

She lifted his hand and kissed it. "I'm not sure that you were." She wasn't sure of anything anymore. Except about what to do next. "I'm going to find him."

Cedron swallowed hard and straightened his back. "If you must go, I'll go with you."

"No." This was her risk to take for the man who had risked all for her. "I don't want you taken by the Pharisees. Don't worry. *I have trusted in thy mercy; my heart shall rejoice in thy salvation.*" She gave him a last squeeze and hurried out of the synagogue.

She skirted the Hippodrome and climbed the sloping streets toward the temple. The sun was already high in the sky. Passover songs of praise and thanksgiving carried over the breeze—no doubt especially loud and joyful because of the life-giving rain that had finally come. Would Pilate already have condemned Longinus? Was she too late?

Scores of soldiers lined the roads and stood guard at the street corners. At least a hundred stood sentry at the temple gates. She zigzagged through the crowds, just a dutiful Jewish woman hurrying home on the Passover. If the soldiers noticed her at all, that's what they'd see—just what she wanted them to see.

As she reached the agora outside of Herod's palace, her pulse quickened. Two sentries stood at the arched entrance to the barracks. She sidled close to the opening and peeked in. The camp was teeming with soldiers. Outside the squat building where she had been brought as Mouse, a line of sentries stood guard.

Relief eased her pounding heart. Surely they wouldn't have that many guards if Longinus had already been executed. He was there, and she had to see him. After that, she didn't know what she could do. She slipped into a crack beside the gate where she could watch and listen. *My Lord, do not forsake me now. Be my help.*

After what seemed like hours, the horns blew, announcing the end of Passover. Long shadows stretched over the streets and empty marketplace outside the barracks. The soldiers on duty at the gate were joined by two replacements. Nissa strained to hear them and make out the unfamiliar Greek words.

"Is he dead yet?" one of the sentries asked.

His replacement shook his head. "Not yet. But it won't be long."

The other replacement spoke fast, and Nissa could only make out the words "Silvanus" and "Pilate."

The sentry gave up his place and turned toward the barracks. ". . . dead by morning, either way." The first two marched away, and the new sentries took their places.

Nissa pushed herself into the narrow recess of her hiding place. She had to get to him soon, before Silvanus killed him. *The Lord is my strength and my shield; my heart trusts in him and I am helped. . . Please, O God, show me what to do.*

Across the marketplace, from the direction of the palace, came a familiar Roman face. Marcellus, the soldier who had taken her from the cell, who had warned her to leave Jerusalem after Longinus was arrested. *Thank you, Lord.* Surely he would help.

She darted out of her hiding place and met him halfway across the agora. "Please, I beg you. Help me get to Longinus."

He grabbed her by the arm and dragged her into the shadows of the wall. "What are you doing here? I told you to leave the city."

She straightened, looking him in the eye. "I'm not leaving him. I have to help him."

"Not leaving—" He looked behind her at the entrance to the camp. "He's in the carcer because of you, woman. He might be dead already. What more do you think you can do for him?"

She leaned against the cold wall. He was right. What could she do after all she'd done wrong? *Get him out. Save him.* "I know you can get me to him. I'll do the rest."

Marcellus snorted. "Escape?" He looked at the line of sentries. "Impossible. His best chance is to see Pilate. I've been trying to get to him since yesterday, but he won't see anyone. He's been at the shrine since the earthquake, making sacrifices to Mars." He rubbed his hand over his face. "And Silvanus almost killed Longinus already. I don't know how much longer I can keep him from finishing the job."

Escape might be impossible, but she had to try. "Just get me in." She clutched his armor-clad arm. "Please."

He blew out a long breath. "Be at the gate at the changing of the guard. When the horn blows. I'll get you in, but I can't guarantee anything else."

Nissa's heart lightened. *That's all I need for now.*

"Watch for my signal, and be quick."

She nodded.

Marcellus brushed past her but turned back. "And Nissa?" His mouth turned down, and his eyes were sad. "Don't expect much help. He's in bad shape."

LONGINUS LAY IN the corner of the cell, clutching his ribs as pain cut off his breath. At least a few were broken. His head throbbed from a lump the size of a fig, and one eye was swollen shut. His mouth tasted of blood, and he could feel a space in the back where he'd lost a tooth when Silvanus had worked him over.

He opened his good eye. The sun filtered through the window. How long had he been here? He remembered the long night after Jesus had died, Silvanus coming at him with his fists and vitis until he knew nothing but pain. Then Marcellus. He'd stopped Silvanus, assured Longinus that Nissa had left the city, and brought water. When he'd left, he'd locked the carcer door. Not so that Longinus couldn't get out but so that Silvanus couldn't get in.

The pain came in waves, ebbing and flowing for what seemed like a lifetime. He drifted into darkness. Suddenly, he saw himself in battle, men and boys falling around him. He reached for his sword, but it wasn't there. They called out to him for help, but he was powerless. The battle faded, and he was alone in a vast green forest, the breath of dawn breaking through the trees and peace filling him. There was Nissa, coming to him. Mist swirled, and she disappeared from his sight.

He opened his eyes to the damp cell, moonlight filtering

through the high window. Why was he still here? When would Silvanus come to finish the job or to bring him to Pilate? Or would he just be left here to die? If he went to Pilate, at least his sentence would be swift. Longinus had no defense. He had released Nissa, just as he'd freed Stephen and would have freed Jesus if Silvanus hadn't stopped him. He was a traitor to Rome, and he knew his fate.

He bowed his head. *Your will, Abba, not mine.*

Jesus had washed him clean. Finally he understood the peace he'd seen in Stephen, who had spent months in this cell. Longinus no longer feared death, but he did fear for Nissa. *Please, Abba, keep her safe.*

The lock on the door rattled, and Longinus tensed. This was it. The end—either from Silvanus or Pilate. The door opened, and a torch blazed, blinding him. A wave of nausea swept over him as hands pulled him up and propped him against the damp wall. But it wasn't Silvanus's ugly face or even Marcellus he saw as his sight returned. *I'm dreaming again, and I don't want to wake up.*

Nissa ran a soft hand down his battered face. He flinched. *For a dream, that hurts.*

"Longinus, can you hear me?" Her voice cracked with a soft sob. "Can you walk?"

He reached for her, but she seemed far away. In the torchlight, tears shone on her cheeks. *Now I know I'm dreaming.* His Nissa didn't cry. Not even when Dismas died.

She put her face close to his, and her warm breath brushed his ear. "I'm going to get you out of here. You need to help me." She set the torch on the floor, slipped her hands under his arms, and tugged.

Hot shards of pain ripped through his ribs. He groaned. "Don't do that." He pulled her closer until her head rested under his chin and buried his hands in her soft hair. *Might as well enjoy the dream before it disappears.*

"We have to go, before Silvanus comes back." She pulled at him again.

This time the pain was very real. He smelled the damp mustiness of the cell and the burning tallow of the torch. *No. This can't be.* "Nissa. Get out." The words scraped his throat.

"Get up. Come on, Marcellus is—"

He pushed her away, crawling up the wall until he half leaned, half stood, to look down on her. She was real, she was here, and she was in great danger. "I told you"—the room swam around him—"to get out of Jerusalem."

She glared up at him. "I don't follow orders very well, or had you forgotten?" She propped her shoulder under one of his arms and bore up, taking his weight. "Now, come quickly. We don't have much—"

The cell door slammed open.

Silvanus stepped in, his eyes gleaming in the torchlight. "What have we here, eh? Two for the price of one?" He advanced on them. "The gods have smiled on me today."

Longinus pushed Nissa away just before Silvanus kicked him in the gut. He crashed to the floor, the room spinning around him.

Silvanus's meaty hands closed around Nissa's loose hair. He threw her to the ground in front of Longinus. "I was looking forward to killing you. Now I'll let you live to see me kill your little thief." He kicked the door shut. "But I won't kill her just yet."

Nissa scuttled as far away from Silvanus as she could, into the farthest corner of the cell. Longinus pushed himself up and staggered into the middle of the room, blocking her from Silvanus. He had to stop him; he knew what Silvanus would do to her. "Don't touch her."

Silvanus let out a low laugh. "Who will stop me, Jew lover? You?"

Longinus lunged for the sword—his sword—that hung at Silvanus's side. Silvanus dodged him and swept out an arm, knocking Longinus to his knees. A curtain of pain dimmed his vision. Shouts sounded, and when his sight cleared, he saw Marcellus, his sword drawn, standing over a prone Silvanus.

"You take orders from me, legionary," Silvanus barked, pushing himself onto his knees.

Marcellus circled around Silvanus until he stood in front of Longinus and Nissa. "You are the primus pilus, but I'm the optio ad carcerem."

Silvanus's jaw snapped shut, and his eyes narrowed.

"This is my domain, centurion. Even Pilate will tell you that."

"So you'll let these two go?" Silvanus stood, and his hand went to his dagger. "I'll have you executed for treason within a day."

Marcellus glanced over his shoulder to Longinus, his face indecisive.

"No." Longinus stood up straighter. "He'll take me to Pilate. I'll take my punishment. But this girl goes free."

Nissa darted to his side. "I'm going with you."

Before he could open his mouth, she had turned to Marcellus. "You know what happened. I'm the Mouse. He only let me go because . . ." She pressed her lips together and glanced up at Longinus. "Take us both to Pilate, together."

Marcellus looked from Nissa to Longinus, his brow furrowed. "Yes. They'll go to Pilate when he returns from making his sacrifices."

"No, not her," Longinus ground out, turning on Marcellus.

"It's the only way." Marcellus moved close to him. "She won't be safe anywhere," he hissed. "Not from him or his men." He jerked his head toward Silvanus.

Longinus slumped against Marcellus. He was right. Her chances with Pilate were miniscule, but with Silvanus, they were nonexistent.

Silvanus grunted. "Go ahead. Take them to Pilate." He stalked from the cell and called back over his shoulder, "And when he's done with them, I'll get them both to myself."

Hours later, three legionaries pulled Longinus from his cell and pushed him up the stairs.

"Where is Nissa?" Ribbons of pain shot through his ribs as he stumbled through the empty camp and toward the blazing torches that lit the entrance to the palace. Bolts of pain streaked through his head, and each torch doubled into two fuzzy globes of light.

"I'm here." Nissa waited at the entrance of the palace with Marcellus.

Longinus stepped close to see her in the dim moonlight. She seemed unhurt. "Are you . . . ? Did they . . . ?"

"I guarded her myself," Marcellus answered.

He turned to his legionary. "Take her away. She shouldn't be here; you know that." He heard the note of pleading in his voice but didn't care.

"It's too late, Longinus. Silvanus is already with him. Perhaps, because of your father . . ."

Longinus shook his head. He'd used up Pilate's debt to his father. Still, he'd plead for Nissa. *I'm ready to die. But please, Abba, let Nissa go free.*

The legionaries pushed him up the stairs and through the anteroom outside Pilate's chamber.

Pilate sat on the cushioned chair, one elbow on his knee, his balding head resting in his cupped hand. Silvanus stood beside him, his armor and eyes glittering in the torchlight that did little to lighten the massive room. Through the framed openings on the eastern wall, the sky was faintly less black. Dawn was coming.

Longinus drew himself up. *The last dawn I will see.*

Silvanus stepped forward. "Here is the traitor."

Pilate raised his head and looked at Longinus silently. Blue shadows drooped below his eyes, and the wrinkles on his brow and cheeks had deepened into furrows. Longinus knew Pilate worried about the god of the Jews. He worried about revolution. And now he'd order the execution of his best friend's son.

Pilate nodded to Silvanus. "What charges do you bring against this man?"

Silvanus looked pleased with himself. Too pleased. "Treason." He paused. "And impiety."

Pilate paled. "Impiety?"

Silvanus's voice rose. "He follows the god of these people. He hasn't made sacrifice to Mars for months, and when we crucified the Jew, he called him the son of a god, the god of Israel. My men heard him."

Longinus clenched his teeth. So he was not only a traitor to Caesar but also to all the gods that Pilate feared. Silvanus had planned well.

"Longinus." Pilate stared intently at him, his hands gripping the arms of the chair. "Is this true?"

Impiety—there was no worse crime in Pilate's eyes. But Longinus wouldn't lie, not now. He straightened his back and squared his shoulders. "Yes."

Pilate stood, his eye twitching convulsively. He stumbled to a window and leaned on its ledge. "Your father was a good friend to me, loyal to Caesar and to our gods."

Longinus didn't flinch. *My father was willing to die for Caesar. I'm willing to die for my king.*

Pilate spun toward Silvanus, his toga swirling around his shoulders. "What about the girl?"

Silvanus grabbed Nissa and pulled her from Marcellus, throwing her at Pilate's feet.

"You are the Mouse?" Pilate barked.

"I am." She answered in Greek. She crawled closer to Pilate. "I beg you. Have mercy. Please, release him." Her Greek was stumbling, but Pilate understood her. He stared at her bent head.

A jolt of pride ran through Longinus. Nissa was, indeed, a brave woman. But of course they wouldn't release him. If he didn't find a way to free Nissa, they would both die. Longinus stepped toward Pilate, dropping to his knees. Arrows of pain shot through his battered body. "In my father's memory, I ask for this. If you were ever a friend to him, let her go free, I beg you."

Pilate turned on him. "You shame your father's memory. A Roman begging for the life of a Jewess. I won't shame him further by granting it." He waved a dismissive hand at them. "Silvanus, the girl goes to the Sanhedrin. Let them do with her what they will. As for Longinus"—his lips turned down and jaw hardened—"his punishment is death."

NISSA CLOSED HER eyes as a wave of fear passed through her. She would be given to the Sanhedrin, and Longinus would die.

Silvanus's hand closed on her tunic, and he jerked her up and into his hard chest.

Longinus lunged for Silvanus, but the guards pulled him back.

She moved her lips in prayer. *The Lord is my strength and my shield; my heart trusts in him and I am helped.* He was with her, as he always had been.

She met Longinus's gaze. Even with his face bloody and broken, she could see that he was no longer her enemy. *He forgives me.* His forgiveness and these few moments together would be enough to face what was coming.

Suddenly, a shout and clatter of sandaled feet rang out from the palace entrance. A soldier—another centurion—sprinted through the archway and skidded to a stop before Pilate. His face was as white as a marble column, and his breath came in gasps.

Pilate jumped to his feet and barked questions in rapid Greek. Nissa couldn't follow him.

The soldier shook his head and stuttered. Nissa understood one thing: the man was terrified. He swallowed and clamped his mouth shut, like he was afraid to say more. His wide eyes went to Longinus.

Longinus spoke. "Cornelius, slow down. The tomb? Jesus's tomb?"

The younger centurion's chest rose and fell. "Yes, we rolled a stone across it; it took three of us to move it." His words were slower, more controlled.

Silvanus grunted and dragged Nissa more tightly against him. She struggled to draw a breath.

Cornelius's voice rose. "We were there. No one came. I didn't fall asleep, I swear to the gods. The stone, it cracked down the middle. The earth shook and a light . . ." He licked his lips and looked at Pilate. "A light. It was . . . beautiful."

"And then what?" Longinus glanced at Nissa, his brows lowered. She could almost read his thoughts. *What happened at the tomb? What more could they do to Jesus?*

"The light . . . left." Cornelius's voice broke. "There was wind. And sound. Everyone ran. I stayed—I couldn't move, I didn't want to. Then the wind was gone, and I saw . . ." He drew a shaking breath.

No one spoke. Silvanus's hold on Nissa loosened. Nissa glanced up to see him watching Pilate with a scowl on his face. Pilate's chest rose and fell as though he had run across the city. His eye twitched wildly. "What did you see?" he demanded.

Cornelius shook his head and blinked, like he still couldn't believe it. "I went to the mouth of the tomb and looked inside . . ."

Nissa's chest expanded; heat rushed through her limbs like fire.

Cornelius glanced up at Pilate, swallowed hard, and whispered, "It was empty."

Chapter 36

Empty? How could it be empty? Longinus twisted away from his guards and grabbed Cornelius by his shoulders. "Did they steal the body?"

Cornelius shook his head violently. "We were there the whole time."

Pilate stood. "Then how is it empty?" His voice rose in panic.

Longinus looked into Cornelius's terrified eyes. "Did you go in? What did you see?"

"I looked in." He glanced sideways at Pilate. "The burial cloths, that's all I saw. Nothing else."

Guards pulled Longinus away, and he didn't fight them. An empty tomb. Earthquake and light. What could it mean? Jesus was dead. He'd seen him take his last breath. And his disciples? They were too cowardly to steal a body, even if they could break through stone.

Pilate collapsed in his chair. "The earth quaked?"

Cornelius nodded, his eyes wild. "Wind and lightning. Just like when he was crucified." He turned to Silvanus, his voice rising. "The stone cracked like it was . . . like it was made of clay." Then, to Longinus, "The light . . . everyone ran—" He lunged forward, grabbing a fistful of Pilate's tunic. "I didn't fall asleep, I swear it."

Pilate jerked back, pulling the cloth from the soldier's grasp. He barked an order at the guard: "Get him out of here."

The guard dragged Cornelius from the room.

Pilate's lips trembled, and his face shone with sweat. He raised a shaking hand to his eyes and took a deep breath. "This god—this god of the Jews—is angry. I've prayed and offered sacrifice, but it is not enough." He looked to the door, to the windows, as if a spirit would come and take him away.

Silvanus snorted. "You don't believe in this Jew? That he was the son of a god?"

"I don't know what to believe," Pilate snapped, rounding on Silvanus. "You are as guilty as I. Your flogging killed him as surely as the cross." He pointed a shaking hand at Silvanus. "Get out of my sight."

The legionaries wrenched Longinus toward the door, and Silvanus jerked his head to his men. "Get him to the carcer. I'll give this woman to the Jews."

Longinus strained toward Nissa. *Please, Abba, save her.*

"No!" Pilate's roar stopped Silvanus midstride. "Wait."

Longinus held his breath.

Pilate approached him. "You believed in this dead man, this son of a god?"

Son of God. Longinus took a deep breath. If these were his last words, so be it. "I believe in the man that you ordered crucified. Jesus of Nazareth. I believe he is the son of God. If that sentences me to death, then I gladly die for him." As he said the words that Stephen had once uttered to him, the immense peace he'd felt at the foot of the cross rushed over him again.

Pilate paced away, then back to him. "Do you know where the body is? Some trick of the Jews?"

Longinus shook his head. "I do not." His own words to Stephen came back to him. *He has power over life and death, and he has a reason to be here that no one understands.* There was a reason he'd died there on the hilltop of Golgotha for all to see. A reason he had forgiven those who had killed him. And there was a reason for the empty tomb. Longinus just didn't know what it was.

Pilate rubbed at his eye. "This god of the Jews—will he punish me? Should I fear him?"

Longinus considered his legate. Pilate feared the gods, any gods. But would Jesus or his father seek revenge on Pilate? *He comes to bring mercy,* Stephen had said. *And all he wants in return is everything.* Longinus chose his words carefully. "No." How could he explain in a way that his Roman legate could understand? "I believe he came to bring mercy."

Silvanus snorted. "Mercy is weakness. And the Jew is dead."

Pilate stared at Longinus like he'd spoken another language. "Mercy?" His gaze went from Longinus to Nissa. He paced to the window, rubbed the top of his head, and let out a long breath. "Then I, too, will show my mercy, as an offering to this god of the Jews."

Longinus held his breath as hope welled in him. *Mercy on him or on them both?*

Silvanus clenched a fist around Longinus's tunic. "He's a traitor to Caesar!"

Pilate raised his hand over Longinus. "You are discharged from service. Your pension is forfeit. Don't show your face in Rome or ever let me see you again." He spoke to the guards. "Release him."

The legionaries looked at Silvanus, then back to Pilate. Their hold on him loosened; then they stepped away. Longinus stumbled to Nissa, but Silvanus pulled her away. "What about her?" he asked Pilate.

Please, God of the Jews. Abba. Free Nissa.

Pilate stared at Nissa, his eye twitching frantically. "Mercy on her as well." He turned to the window and bellowed, "All of you, out of my sight!"

Nissa looked at Longinus, a question in her face.

He'd explain later. Right now, they needed to get away from Pilate before he changed his mind. He grabbed her hand and turned, right into Silvanus.

Silvanus's face was red, and a shower of spittle accompanied his words. "Hope that you and I never meet again, Jew lover. If we do, I'll make sure you pay for your treason." He jerked away, thundered orders to his legionaries, and stomped from the room.

When Silvanus had disappeared, Longinus pulled Nissa toward the arch. His head throbbed and his ribs felt like they were on fire, but he urged her on, across the palace courtyard and into the empty agora. When they reached the upper market, he stopped and slumped against a marble column. They were free, both of them. *Thank you, Abba.*

He had no home, no silver, no land. His body was broken, he'd lost his father's sword, and he'd never get to Gaul or anywhere else. He was stuck in this backward province, with this fierce woman and her sharp tongue, with these fanatical Jews and their talk of the one God.

And he had never felt such joy.

He looked down on Nissa's bent head. They were both free. And he knew exactly what to do next.

NISSA RAN BESIDE Longinus, her hand in his. Out of the palace, across the courtyard with its fountains and groves of blossoming fig trees, and into the deserted agora as the rising sun defeated the shadows of the city wall.

What had happened in the palace? They were at the brink of death, and somehow, the most powerful Roman in Judea had shown them mercy. Longinus was alive, and they were both free. And all because of the empty tomb.

However it had happened, she knew whom to thank. *Give thanks to the Lord, for he is good. His mercy endures forever.* And if he had shown mercy to her, then surely Dismas was in Paradise. Her spirit soared like a bird released from its cage.

Longinus stopped and leaned against a column. One hand still clutched hers, the other pressed against his ribs. Fresh blood darkened the hair at his temple. The memory of his kiss of peace made her drop her gaze to his freckled feet. Could he still want her after all she'd done?

He squeezed her hand.

She raised her eyes to his knees, then to his chest. She took a breath and looked into his battered face. "You're hurt." Should she offer to take care of him? He had no home, no family. He'd lost everything for her sake.

He shook his head. His mouth curved into a smile, and his dimple flashed. "I'll live, pretty Nissa."

Pretty Nissa. Did he mean it? A smile pulled at her own mouth. *Idiot Roman.*

Longinus dipped his head and set his lips on hers. They were warm and rough and tasted of salt. He bent lower, wrapping his arm around her waist and crushing her against his chest. She pulled back and looked into his face.

His eyes, the color of the sky above, showed only joy. His arms, wrapped tight around her, held the solace that she longed for. He'd sacrificed everything—his position, his pride, even his own body. And he offered it all to her. *I don't deserve it.* But she would take it and spend her life giving everything back to him.

She fit herself into the curve of his warm body and stretched up on her toes to meet his lips with her own. Like stepping from the cold shadows into the sun, warmth flooded through her. This was not a kiss of peace. This was a kiss of hope and longing. This was a promise of what was to come.

The clatter of hooves on stone broke them apart. Nissa leaned on Longinus, her legs weak and trembling.

Marcellus rode to them on the horse that she'd seen for the first time here in the market, the day she'd met Longinus—he a Roman centurion and she a thief. Now they stood together, both of them changed forever and bound by what they'd seen—suffering and death, miracles and mercy. Love and forgiveness.

Marcellus slid from the horse and approached Longinus. "What will you do now?"

Longinus looked down to Nissa, his amber brows raised.

She nodded at his unspoken question. There was only one thing to do, and they would do it together.

Longinus pushed away from the wall. "We must go to the tomb."

Marcellus frowned. "You'll never make it with your—"

Longinus grunted and put a hand over his ribs. "I've been worse off. Don't worry about me."

Marcellus sighed and offered the horse's reins. "Take Ferox. It's just past Golgotha, over the hill."

"Silvanus will have your hide if he finds out," Longinus said.

Marcellus pushed the reins into Longinus's hands. "Let me worry about Silvanus."

Longinus bent and held out his hand to Nissa. She fit her foot into his palm and jumped, pulling herself up on the horse and scooting forward in the saddle.

Longinus leaned on Marcellus, his hand braced on the younger legionary's shoulder. "Thank you, my friend."

Marcellus grunted and boosted Longinus into the saddle.

Longinus flinched as he settled behind her, his breathing shallow.

Marcellus looked up at her. "Take care of him."

"I will." She would take care of the idiot Roman. She'd wrap his ribs and treat his wounds. They'd need a place to stay and food. Somehow, they'd find it. There would be time—plenty of time—to make plans. After they saw the tomb.

Longinus's arm curved around her waist. With a nudge to the horse, they started toward the city wall. Longinus urged him into a gallop and tightened his hold on Nissa. They thundered past groggy slaves carting water and an early-morning cart lumbering out the Jaffa Gate.

Outside the city, the horse lengthened its stride. A shiver chilled her as they passed by Golgotha. She didn't understand what had happened there. But whatever had happened at the foot of the cross—and at the tomb—had changed her forever.

She was no longer abandoned, no longer alone. Dismas had died for her, and somehow, Jesus had set them all free.

The empty tomb—whatever they found, whatever it meant—wasn't the end. It was just the beginning.

LONGINUS SPURRED FEROX up the last hill and pulled him to a halt at the top. The sun had risen on the eastern horizon, its rays glowing gold at the edge of the world and tipping the clouds with pink. A garden lay in the valley below. Green grass sparkling with dew surrounded it like an emerald sea. A soft breeze, scented with mint and a hint of cloves, swept up the hill and eddied around them.

A few men gathered at the mouth of a cave near the edge of the garden. Longinus recognized two—the young disciple from Gethsemane and the older one who had taken the sword to Caiaphas. Nearby, the women who had been at the cross knelt beside a massive stone, as big as an altar, split down the middle as though hit by lightning.

His eyes swept over the land before him. What was this? People hurried from every direction—groups of two and three—as though late to a feast.

From the north, Galileans in traveling clothes rushed, their voices raised in wonder. A group of women with children in their arms followed. From the western gate of the city came Cyrenians—the man who had carried the cross and his family. And behind them, two men: a tall form he recognized though he couldn't see his scar, Stephen, with Joseph the Pharisee beside him.

Nissa sat up straighter and pointed. "It's Cedron and the Zealots."

Yes, there were the would-be rebels and Cedron coming from the Dung Gate. Longinus caught his breath as sun glinted off armor. "Look. Marcellus. And . . . is that Cornelius?" *This God is full of surprises.*

They came from every direction. Drops forming trickles, trickles joining into streams, streams converging into rivers. All flowing toward the empty tomb.

"What does it mean?" Nissa breathed.

What could it mean? All of them: men and women, Jew and Gentile, rich and poor. Pharisees, Zealots, Samaritans, and pagans. A paltry number—not even half a cohort—but what did numbers matter when your king was the son of God? Longinus pulled Nissa closer and spurred Ferox down the hill to join the conflux. *It can only mean one thing.*

The revolution had begun.

Acknowledgments

A BOOK IS NEVER the accomplishment of just one person. Without the encouragement, prayers, and skills of family, friends, and colleagues, I doubt any story would make the journey from idea to final production, and *The Thief* was no exception.

Thank you, Bruce, my husband of almost twenty-five years. They say that opposites attract; then they drive each other crazy. I prefer to see you as my other half. Thank you for sharing your life with me.

To Rachel, Andy, Joey, and Anna, I'm grateful for every day I get to be your mom. Thank you for your never-ending optimism and encouragement.

Thanks to my family, especially Mom and Dad—examples of real love and enduring faith. To my sister Rachel, for your ridiculous confidence in me and excellent brainstorming in the earliest stages of *The Thief*. And to my sisters Jennifer and Rebecca and my brother, Steve: thanks for your enthusiastic support. Love you all.

Thank you, Laura Sobiech and Anne Brown. Through joy and laughter, heartbreak and tears, you both have shown an amazing strength and holiness that inspires me. It is an honor to call you friends.

Every writer needs critiquers she can trust. I'm blessed with those who are both gentle and brutally honest: Regina Jennings, Cathi-Lyn Dyck, Wendy Tarbox, and Cheryl Boom. Thank you, my skilled and outspoken friends. You make it possible for me to hit "send" with confidence.

Chris Park, it's a privilege to have an agent like you. Thanks for being my advocate and holding my hand when I need it. To the team at Howard Books, especially Jessica Wong, thank you for your skill and wisdom, and Bruce Gore, for your beautiful cover designs.

As always, the Holy Spirit was with me every moment, bringing people into my life at just the right time to inspire, guide, and lift me up. May I always hear and heed the whisperings of the Spirit.

A Howard Reading Group Guide

The Thief

Stephanie Landsem

Introduction

The second book in The Living Water Series, *The Thief*, tells the story of two unlikely friends—a Roman centurion and a poor Jewish girl living in first-century Jerusalem during the height of Jesus' ministry. Longinus, the Roman centurion, feels aimless in the wake of his friend's tragic death, while Nissa is overwhelmed by guilt about her secret life as a thief. Together they witness Jesus restore sight to Nissa's blind brother, and increasingly find themselves drawn toward this healer and prophet. Could Jesus be the answer to their prayers?

Questions and Topics for Discussion

1. "You aren't worth dying for, Mouse. Nobody is" (p. 12). Discuss this first introduction to Mouse and Dismas, the two best thieves in Jerusalem. How would you characterize them? How does this statement foreshadow later events in the story? Do you think it's possible to be both a "good" and "bad" person? Use examples from the story and your own life to support your answer.

2. On page 26, a possible theme of the novel emerges when Nissa concludes, "She was a failure at everything—everything but stealing." How does failure haunt both Nissa and Longinus? What have they each "failed" to do? Do you think failure is a motivation for the choices they make?

3. Consider the main characters' relationships with their parents. In what ways are they typical relationships? In what ways are they atypical?

4. Cedron's faith in God is unshakable. On page 43, he prays, "The Lord is my strength and my shield . . . my heart trusts in him and I am helped." Why does Nissa not share her brother's faith? What makes her believe God has abandoned her?

5. Revisit the scene where Jesus cures Cedron of his blindness, beginning on page 58 and running through page 62. Is this scene similar to the story found in the Bible? How does the event act as a catalyst for the rest of the happenings in the novel—both good and bad?

6. In the beginning of the story, Nissa is in a somewhat unique position in her family as the sole breadwinner. Consider the ways in which Nissa defies expectations as a woman living in first-century Jerusalem. Would you call her a rebel? Why or why not?

7. At what moment do you think Longinus and Nissa fall in love? What is ironic about their love story?

8. Discuss the character of Longinus. Do you like him? In what ways does his character change throughout the story?

9. What symbolism can you glean from Nissa's alternate persona, "Mouse"? How is she a "mouse" in her life as a thief? As Nissa?

10. "She climbed the steps up to the shimmering water. She wouldn't bathe today. No amount of water, no matter how pristine, would wash away her guilt. No almsgiving would atone for her sin" (p. 175). Talk about Nissa's role in the murder of the priest. Do you think that Nissa is guilty? Why or why not?

11. On his way to the garden of Gethsemane, Longinus's "feet seemed to fly along the stones" (p. 248). For the first time since his friend's death, Longinus has light feet and an unburdened heart. What reasons can you give for Longinus's new outlook on life?

12. In what way(s) is Nissa's situation with Dismas similar to Judas's situation with Jesus? Draw similarities between the two situations—who is Nissa most like, Jesus or Judas?

13. On page 262, Pilate says, "Sometimes the innocent have to pay the price for the guilty." Explain how this is true in several instances in *The Thief*.

14. What is "the revolution" referred to at the end of the story? Do you think that Longinus and Nissa live happily ever after?

Enhance Your Book Club

1. *The Thief* explores a moment in history that is still very much a part of our collective unconscious—the execution of Jesus and his subsequent resurrection. Have a movie night with your book club and watch *The Passion of the Christ* (2004). Is the Jesus depicted in the movie similar to the Jesus depicted in *The Thief*? Can you find similarities between the novel and the movie?

2. On page 159, Longinus wonders to himself what he would "give to find the peace [Stephen] had?" In many ways, Stephen represents a turning point for Longinus—a man he had wanted to find and put to death, but then decides to forgive and release. What did Longinus ultimately give to find the peace Stephen has? Share with your group what this sort of peace would look like for you. How would it manifest in your life? What would you give—or have you given—to have such peace?

3. Revisit the scene on page 187 when Nissa goes to the Pool of Siloam and struggles to decide if she should accept Longinus's marriage proposal. Plan a trip with your book club to a local pool, lake, or beach. Ask each member to share a time when they had to make a tough decision. How did you decide what to do? In retrospect, did you make the right decision? Did Nissa?

A Conversation with Stephanie Landsem

1. *Your Living Water Series involves serious and intense research on first-century life. Describe the process that went into the making of this novel. What was the most challenging part of your research project?*

I like to think of research for a new book like the beginning of an archeological dig. I start by mapping out where I need to dig—where I need a little information and where I need to go deeper—then I delve in. Sometimes, I find exactly what I'm expecting, and that's great. But on the best days, I unearth entirely unexpected bits of information that can flesh out a character, bring the setting to life, or even change the course of the story. I love when that happens! The most challenging part of research is knowing when to stop—when to put away the research books and start writing the story that has taken shape in my head.

2. *The Thief is a fiction story based on historical events. In your estimation, how much of this story is true? How much is made-up? What is the line between fiction and fact, and is it important to you in the writing process?*

Each book in The Living Water Series is based on an actual encounter with Jesus as recorded in the Gospel of John: the woman at the well, the man born blind, and the raising of Lazarus. I stay true to these accounts, but from them I can branch out into conjecture and imagination. I don't want to rewrite the Bible, and I know that's not what my readers want either. What I want to do is imagine the settings, the culture, and the historical era so well that when my readers go back to the pages of the Bible, it is with fresh eyes and a new understanding.

3. *Who is your favorite character in the story and why?*

I love Nissa. She's rough around the edges, quick-tempered, and speaks her mind even if it gets her in trouble. But she's also lonely and hurt. Underneath her tough exterior, she wants what we all want: security and love—and she's looking for it in all the wrong places. I like to think that if I lived in her time, I would have been the friend she so desperately needed.

4. *How did you come to be a writer?*

I've always loved to read. As a child, I probably got in trouble more often for late-night reading than for just about anything else. Reading is a way to live many lives, to visit other times, places, and even new worlds. You know you've read a good book when, after the last page, you feel like you've been changed in some way. I wanted to do that, too. I wasn't at all sure I could, but with lots of prayer, hard work, and tons of encouragement from my family and friends, I hope that I'm becoming the writer I've always wanted to be.

5. *Do you consider Nissa somewhat of a renegade, especially for her era?*

I think Nissa didn't want to be different. She wished she could be like other women. She knew that stealing—not to mention pretending to be a boy—was wrong, but because of her own failings and her family life, she felt she had no choice. I think many women, especially young women under the influence of our culture, can find themselves backed into a corner much like Nissa, with seemingly nowhere to go and no one to turn to. And unfortunately, I think many of them feel as abandoned by God as she did.

6. *The story weaves between Nissa's and Longinus's points of view. Ultimately, whose story is this?*

Both Nissa and Longinus witness a miracle and try to make sense of what they see: Nissa as an insider—a Jewish woman—trapped by her own laws and culture, and Longinus as an outsider looking in and not understanding what he sees. I think the reader ultimately gets to decide which character they identify with the most.

7. *According to your bio, you've explored ancient ruins and historic buildings across the world. Is there a particular place you've visited that inspired the setting for* The Thief?

I wish I could say Jerusalem inspired the setting, but I have yet to visit the Holy Land, although it is on the top of my wish list. When I picture the settings in *The Thief*, I often think of the narrow streets and cramped marketplaces of Tangier, Morocco—one of my most memorable travel experiences. The streets teemed with people and animals, and the markets overflowed with shouting merchants, colorful rugs, and every kind of food. Even though it was crowded, chaotic, and a little frightening, I loved it.

8. *Share with us your literary influences? Where do you go for inspiration?*

Like many Christian writers, I love Tolkien, C. S. Lewis, and George MacDonald. I often go back to their books to be inspired by their skill, wisdom, and imagination. When I read just for fun (which isn't often enough), I'm all over the place: historical fiction, mysteries, thrillers, and sometimes YA and middle-grade fiction, so that I can talk books with my kids. Any good book, regardless of genre, that keeps me turning pages and leaves me satisfied at the end is an inspiration.

9. *What would you name as the major theme(s) of this story? What do you hope readers will remember about your novel?*

Many Christians, myself included, have heard the story of Jesus' crucifixion so many times, we can hardly grasp its meaning. I hoped that by showing a parallel story—Dismas as the innocent man giving up his life for a sinful woman—we could envision Jesus' sacrifice for us with new eyes and better understand its profound impact in a more personal way.

10. *Can you share some news about your next novel in The Living Water Series—The Tomb?*

The third book in the series tells of the ultimate miracle performed by Jesus not long before his crucifixion—the raising of Lazarus as witnessed by his sister, Martha. Everyone in Bethany admires Martha, the perfect Jewish woman. But Martha harbors a shameful secret, one that will shatter her spotless reputation in Bethany and destroy those she loves most. When her brother Lazarus falls ill, Martha must choose between the safety of the tomb she has built for herself and stepping out to receive 'the better part' offered to her by Jesus.

Turn the page for a peek at
Stephanie Landsem's novel:

THE *Well*

Available from Howard Books

Chapter 1

DREAD COILED LIKE an asp in Mara's belly as the watery light of dawn seeped through the chinks in the roof of the clay house.

Only a short span of dirt floor stretched between her mother's corner of their one-room house to where Mara and her little brother lay pressed against its farthest wall. Mara's worn cloak, pulled over their heads like a shield, had failed to block out the carnal whispers that had drifted through the confines of the dark room during the long night. Shame and fear had twined with tormented dreams until she prayed for dawn.

Now, as the murky beams of weak light puddled on the floor, Mara raised her head and strained to see through the gloom. *Is Alexandros still here?*

Relief trickled through her stiff limbs. Her mother slept alone in the corner. When had Alexandros left? And where did he go? How could Mama be so foolish? *Please, Lord, let no one find out about him.*

Mara's bare arms, prickly with cold, were wrapped around Asher's small warm body.

She slipped from under her cloak and eased herself away from her little brother. As she kissed his smooth cheek and tucked the tattered wool around his shoulders, he opened his sleep-clouded eyes.

"Shh, my sweet, go back to your dreams," she whispered, rubbing his back. Asher garbled a few words, wedged his thumb in his mouth, and closed his eyes again. Mara stroked his back until his mouth went slack and his breath buzzed in a steady rhythm.

Silently, she crept past her sleeping mother. Nava lay crumpled in the corner like a pile of dirty rags. She would not stir until mid-morning. Then she would act as if nothing had happened, as if she'd done nothing wrong.

Alexandros, a pagan from Sebaste, had visited her mother before. He didn't seem concerned about Nava's reputation. He ate their food, little as there was, complimenting Nava more boldly and laughing more loudly after each cup of wine.

Each time, they had been lucky. No one in Sychar seemed to know of his visits. Not yet. But the Sychar Samaritans did not abide sinners in their midst. When they found out—and they would find out—the strict townspeople would turn on them. They would surely stop providing the barley and oil that Mara's family needed so desperately. They could, according to the law, march down the hill and drive them out of Sychar. No one in Samaria would take in a disgraced woman, a crippled boy, and a daughter old enough to be married.

Starvation or exile. Which was worse?

Mara stepped outside into the damp chill of dawn. The birds, chattering more loudly as crimson light stained the eastern sky, seemed to be scolding her. They should be scolding her mother. *What are you doing to us, Mama?*

Tall cedars and even taller mountains surrounded the little house, throwing dark shadows over the doorway and onto the front courtyard carved out of the scrubby bushes. A jumble of chipped clay pots and jars sat along the wall next to piles of straw and kindling. A few paces away, a whisper of smoke rose from the black remains of the cooking fire.

The familiar rumble of hunger twisted Mara's stomach. Asher would be hungry too. The good people of Sychar gave them almost enough barley to live on. She knew exactly how much they had left: two meals' worth—if they were careful.

There would be no more if the town discovered Nava's shame. Mara bent toward the fire to add a handful of straw to the last glowing coal, but straightened with a breath of surprise as a looming form rustled out of the dark bushes.

"Good morning, Mara," Alexandros said, adjusting his short tunic.

She turned her head away, but not quickly enough to miss the smirk on Alexandros's lips.

"I'm thirsty, girl." He dangled a water skin in front of her averted face.

She glanced at him as she took it, careful not to touch his hand. His eyes were bleary and puffed—the result of the wine he had drunk last night—but his smirk of lingering satisfaction deepened. He didn't look ashamed of what he had done with her mother. But why should he be? A pagan from Sebaste need not submit to the strict laws of Sychar.

Mara ladled the last of their water into the skin as Alexandros leaned against the wall, watching her. He was a big man, solid and strong, with short brown hair and light eyes that she tried to avoid. His clothes were clean and well made, and gold rings flashed on his ears and fingers. She had heard whispers that some of the village women thought him handsome, but he reminded Mara of the wild dogs that prowled the hills, preying on lost lambs. She handed the water skin to him without a word and bent back to the fire.

He drained the water in several big gulps, then crouched down close beside her. "What do you have for food?" he asked.

Mara hunched her shoulders and inched away but didn't reach toward the cooking pot. If he ate their barley, she and Asher would go hungry today. She watched the tiny licks of flame devour the handful of straw. "Just some barley."

He grunted and waved his hand. "Don't bother. Barley's for animals." Alexandros heaved himself to his feet. "Time for me to go." He followed the worn path to the back of the house, where he had left his pack animal.

Mara fed a piece of kindling to the crackling fire. She couldn't let him leave without asking. She had to know. She stood, rubbed her damp hands down her dirty tunic, and followed Alexandros.

A rickety lean-to clung to the back of the house, and the garden stretched behind, tilled and planted. Alexandros unhobbled the huge, spotted donkey that had stripped the leaves from Mara's struggling fig tree while his master had defiled her mother. It bared its long, yellow teeth at her. Crossing her arms in front of her chest, she swallowed hard and blurted, "Are you going to Sychar? To the marketplace?"

If he showed up in Sychar, just over the hill to the east, at this time of morning, there would be questions. If they didn't know already, someone would surely discover where he had spent the night. She wouldn't be surprised if the bragging dog told them himself.

He stepped close enough for her to see his bloodshot eyes and the rough stubble on his jaw. She ducked her head and focused on his sandal-clad feet.

"Afraid that the pious Chosen Ones of God will disapprove of your mother's good fortune last night?" he asked.

Mara kept her gaze on his worn leather sandals, but her face burned like the rising sun. He knew what would happen if the strict villagers found out that her mother had entertained him overnight.

"What? Worried that the last of God's Chosen People won't give you and the boy any more barley if they find out that Nava shared her bed with a pagan?" He stepped even closer. She smelled his sour sweat and the stench of last night's wine on his breath.

Mara's legs weakened, and her heart pounded. Who would give charity to a woman who flouted the laws of Moses so shamelessly? Her mother had done more than lie with the pagan; she had put her family at his mercy. One word from him in the marketplace and . . . starvation or exile.

Alexandros ran a warm, moist hand over her hair and down her cheek. She squeezed her eyes shut. He cupped her chin and lifted her face. "Let me see those eyes of yours, girl." His hand tightened painfully on her jaw.

She opened her eyes. His face was close, his eyes narrow and rimmed with red.

A smile lifted his thin lips. "If you keep me happy, there won't be any reason for me to spill your secret, eh, girl?"

She wrenched her face away, fear drying her mouth. Alexandros laughed and jerked at his donkey, turning the big animal toward the path that ran west. "I'm low on merchandise. I'm heading to Sebaste this morning, then to Caesarea. Tell your mother I'll be back in a couple of weeks." He paused, and his gaze traveled from Mara's head to her dirty bare feet. He licked his pale lips. "I'll be looking forward to seeing you again." He started down the path, away from Sychar, but looked over his shoulder. "Don't worry, Mara. This will be our little secret . . . for now."

Mara's heart slowed its frantic pounding only when Alexandros and his donkey disappeared around a twist in the path.

She rubbed her face where the imprint of his fingers still burned, then picked up the empty water jar. A trip to the well, where women traded gossip like men traded grain in the marketplace, would surely tell her if anyone in the village already knew of her mother's shame. She threw a striped cloth over her long, tangled hair and started up the steep path.

Mara crested the ridge above her house and descended into a wide valley, her lips moving over her morning prayers. She prayed first for Asher and then for her mother as Gerizim, the mountain of blessings, rose on one side and Ebal, the mountain of curses, swelled on the other. She thanked the God of Abraham for the recent rains that had watered their garden and then asked for her grain jar somehow to be filled. She begged that her mother's secret shame would remain known only to her.

Lord, send the Taheb to your people. The ancient appeal eased her mind like a soothing balm. Someday the Taheb, the Restorer, would come.

She passed the outskirts of Sychar, just a cluster of clay houses and a marketplace. A few women stood in the shadowy doorways. She knew them all by name, had known them all her life. Some turned their backs to her as she passed. A few shook their heads, their mouths pinched in disapproval. If they found out what Nava had done last night—if just one had seen Alexandros this morning—their outrage would descend like a plague of locusts.

Just past the village, the path met a wider, deeply rutted road. It came from Jerusalem and stretched north through Galilee, all the way to far-off Damascus. Her pace slowed as she walked past wide swaths of green barley and groves of silver-green olive trees. Around a sharp curve lay Jacob's well, the only source of water in Sychar. She dragged her feet around the bend, forcing her head up and straightening her shoulders. She had done nothing wrong.

Jacob's well, a hole in the ground ringed by a low wall of rock, was surrounded by half the women of Sychar. Facing the brood of women was never easy, but the covey of young mothers stung the most. They crowded together like a flock of sparrows, chirping and twittering, shutting her out. Mara had once been their friend, but none of them had spoken to her in years. Some were no older than her fifteen years but already married and proudly showing swollen bellies or babes in their arms.

The older women huddled in bunches, murmuring in low voices that stopped abruptly as Mara approached. Several heads jerked up. They looked at her with narrowed eyes and down-turned mouths. Mara's hands grew damp and slippery on the smooth clay jar, and her legs trembled. She stumbled, almost dropping the heavy jar. *They must know. What will they do to us now?*

Mara lowered the jar from her head and pressed it to her chest. A burning heat crept up her neck, but she refused to look down—that would be a sure sign of guilt. In the quiet, the bees droned in the lavender bushes and birds chirped their morning song.

She straightened her shoulders and met Tirzah's stare, then Adah's. The undeclared queens of the village, the two women made it their business to pass judgment on the less fortunate of Sychar. Usually, that meant Nava.

Adah's bulbous eyes flicked from Mara's wild, tangled hair to her dirty feet. Her head swiveled on her long neck, and she bent her tall, bony frame to whisper into Tirzah's ear. Adah was married to Shimon, a prosperous merchant in Sychar. She was his second wife, a fact that Mara could never forget.

Tirzah smirked and whispered back to Adah. Tirzah was married to Zevulun, the richest man in the village. She seemed to have more flesh than mere bones could support. Her face blended into her neck in cascading folds of skin, and her fine linen dress stretched over the wide expanse of her midsection.

At last, Adah and Tirzah turned back to the cluster of women. Mara let out the breath she had been holding. *Something is going on, but it isn't about Mama.* This time.

Mara hugged her jar and stepped in line for the well. The women's voices were somber, their faces grim. If they had been talking about Nava, she would hear the outraged gasps and titters that signaled scandal. No, this seemed to be another sort of bad news.

When the older women had filled their jars, Mara crouched close to the low rock wall. She lowered a dried gourd down the well, and a cool breeze stirred from its depths. From that first draw, she took a long drink, forcing the water down her tight throat. Then she sent the gourd back down again and again, filling her jar to the top. It would be heavy, but she could make the water last two days.

"Good morning, Mara," said a soft voice behind her.

Mara turned and smiled at Leah. At least she was always kind. Leah's long, silver hair fell down her back in a thick, shining braid that caught the sunlight. Although stooped and frail, Leah still fetched her own water; she had no servant or daughter to do it for her.

"Let me help you with that, Leah." Mara reached for the old woman's water jug and set it on the edge of the rocky opening. She sent the gourd back down into the well.

"And how's your mother today?" Leah asked, her quick eyes darting toward the other women and back.

Mara replied carefully, "Sleeping when I left." She tipped her head toward the women. "What is it?"

Leah bit her lip. "They found Dara this morning, dead, on the east side of Mount Ebal."

Mara dropped the rope, and the full gourd splashed back down into the well. "Dead? What happened?"

"She must have been gathering wood and fallen down a ravine. Jobab always said she was clumsy." Leah took the rope from Mara's still hands and began pulling.

Clumsy. She had heard Jobab—old enough to be Dara's grandfather—complaining in the marketplace about his young bride. Dara burned the stew and her hands as well. She broke her arm when she fell down a stony path.

A heavy ache filled her chest. Dara was her age and one of the few girls who still talked to her, although not since she'd married at the early age of thirteen. The girl had lived with Jobab on the far side of Mount Ebal and rarely came into the village. When she did, she rushed through her marketing, her head down and not a word for anyone. As though she was afraid.

Guilt brushed her spine like a cold hand. She should have made the climb to the shepherd's hut to find out why Dara had so many bruises and injuries.

Leah poured water into her jar with shaking hands. "She lost another baby last month. Jobab was so angry." Bright tears glittered on her wrinkled cheeks. "I should have told someone. I should have checked on her."

It wouldn't have mattered. A woman's word against a man's

never did. Dara was Jobab's second wife. The first had died not long after giving birth to a stillborn boy—fell and hit her head on a stone. Poor Jobab, the men would say, his wives died before they could give him an heir. Poor wives.

Mara brushed her hand over Leah's stooped shoulders. She lifted the heavy jar to her head and turned to the road. A flurry of motion caught her eye, then her path was blocked.

Mara stepped around the girl who had once been her best friend. "Good morning, Rivkah."

"Mara." Rivkah's smile stopped Mara mid-stride. Her eyes swept over Mara's tattered tunic, her uncombed hair. She ran a hand over her own dark braids, twisted into an elaborate design and pinned with brass ornaments. "I wanted you to be the first to know. Jebus and I are to be betrothed. The ceremony is today."

Mara sucked in her breath. She steadied the jar on her head. She and Rivkah had been childhood friends before Adah, Rivkah's mother, had married Shimon and turned her back on Nava. Like all little girls, Mara and Rivkah had spent their days talking about their betrothal ceremonies, dreaming of husbands and families. A husband meant security and protection and, most of all, children—the ultimate sign of God's favor. They had always assumed that Mara would be the first to marry, but Rivkah, more than a year younger, was betrothed first.

"You are blessed," Mara said. She heard the tremble in her voice. "Jebus will be a good husband."

"Yes, he will. He begged for the betrothal to be shortened. You know how men are." Rivkah smirked. "But it will be a full year. My father insisted."

Mara looked down at her bare feet and ragged tunic. *Yes, I do know how men are.* She stepped around Rivkah and hurried toward the road.

As Leah fell into step beside her, Mara slowed but didn't speak. She couldn't.

The path forked—one way went to the village, the other to

the valley. This was where they would part. Leah patted Mara's arm with her gnarled hand. "Your time will come, my dear."

Mara shook her head and swallowed hard. No, her time would not come. They all knew that. She nodded good-bye to the old woman.

The path blurred under Mara's feet, and the heavy water jar pressed down on her head. She should be mourning Dara—although she barely knew her—but she mourned for herself instead.

Rivkah was betrothed. And to one of the last unmarried men in Sychar. She couldn't even hope for a young, handsome husband like Jebus. Not anymore. Rivkah would be married in one year and probably with child soon after. *I'll still be struggling to feed Mama and Asher. No one will marry me.*

Today Rivkah's childhood dreams would come true. Her father and brothers would carry her in a litter to the house of her handsome groom. Her sisters and friends would scatter nuts and dance to the music of harps and tambourines. And Mara wasn't even invited.

I'd be content with any husband who treated me kindly and put food on the table. Anyone who provided clothes and a roof that didn't leak. Anyone who would take care of me and Asher.

No, there would be no betrothal for her. No man would make a marriage offer for Mara, daughter of Nava, the most disgraceful woman in Sychar.

"MAMA, YOU CAN'T let him come here again. You know that, don't you?"

Nava didn't answer. Mara knelt next to her mother's huddled body, hoping that she would listen to reason, but Nava just pulled her cloak closer around her shoulders and turned her face to the wall.

"Mama, if they find out . . . what will we do?" Mara's voice rose.

"What's the matter, Mara?" Asher piped up from the corner. "Mara, what is it?" He crawled to Mara and climbed into her arms. He was small for his age and too thin, but she had never seen a more beautiful child in all of Sychar. His almond-shaped eyes were deep green. Long, dark lashes brushed his high smooth cheeks. Asher snuggled up to her, and she pressed her cheek to his dark curls. She kissed the top of his head and breathed in his musty sweet scent.

Yes, Asher was a beautiful child. But he had been born lame. Not just lame—deformed. And in Sychar, deformity meant sin. Nava's sin.

He was in all other ways a perfect boy, but one leg, knotted and bent, hardly looked like a leg at all. The heel of his foot pointed sharply outward, like a misplaced elbow. The foot twisted so that the pink sole faced upward, and his deformed toes closed like a fist. But Asher's heart . . . his heart was as pure and sweet as the water from Jacob's well.

Mara pulled his thumb from his mouth. "Asher, no. You're almost eight."

Nava pushed herself up from her mat. "Let him be." She folded her legs and patted her lap. "Come sit on Mama's lap."

Mara pushed Asher into his mother's lap. "Stop treating him like a baby."

He snuggled up to his mother and stuck his thumb back in his mouth.

Nava didn't rebuke him. She pulled him closer and stroked his arm.

Even with dirty hair and a sleep-lined face, Nava was lovely. Her honey-toned skin was only slightly lined from thirty summers. Her teeth flashed white and straight behind dark, full lips. Long, black lashes and straight, black brows highlighted her perfect features. Even now, when other women showed signs of age, Nava's skin stretched smoothly over high cheeks, and her chin was a firm, straight line.

Mara dipped a worn wooden ladle into the water jug and

gave it to Nava. She had heard the same words her whole life: she was the image of her mother. Except for their eyes. While Nava's wide eyes were as green as Egyptian jade, Mara's were a startling mix of green shot with gold. No one had ever said they were beautiful.

Nava drank, then passed the ladle to Asher. "My poor baby boy. Why must God punish you for the sins of your mother?"

Blood rose in Mara's face. "Mama, you act as though you have no choice." Mara carried the heavy jar to the coolest corner of the house. "I didn't see you asking Alexandros to leave last night."

Even as Nava buried her face in Asher's skinny neck and wept, Mara didn't regret her words. Why couldn't she see the danger?

"Alexandros?" Asher said, looking from his sister to his mother. He puffed out his cheeks and lowered his brows, very much like the big pagan. "I don't like him."

"I don't either," Mara agreed. She gathered her damp cloak from the floor and shook it hard. If only she could shake some sense into her mother.

Asher squirmed in his mother's arms; she was still crying. Mara loosened Nava's grip on Asher and dragged him from her. "Mama is a little sad, Asher. Go outside and gather sticks. We'll make some breakfast." She sent him on his way with a forced smile and a little swat on his bottom. He crawled quickly through the door, dragging his lame leg behind him.

She crouched beside her weeping mother. "Mama, you can't let him come here again."

"It is for Asher. He needs a father."

I don't believe it. She isn't making any sense. "Asher has a father. Or did you forget about Shaul? You know, your husband?" She took a breath and tried to speak calmly. "Mama, Alexandros doesn't want to be Asher's father. He's not going to marry you."

Nava wiped tears from her cheeks. "At his age, Asher should

be learning a trade, not playing with toys. He needs a man to teach him."

"Yes. Shaul is the one who should teach him. If you would just . . ." If she would just get up in the morning and work hard all day. If she would just take care of her children. Then she could send word to Shaul—beg him to come back. They could be happy again.

But Mara couldn't say that. They never spoke of her mother's illness.

Nava lay down and turned her back on the room. She pulled her cloak over her head like a shroud, as though she intended to sleep forever.

Mara blew out her breath in frustration. Nava would not get up again today. Sleeping seemed to be her only refuge from the dark thoughts and sadness that bound her. *Lord, why do we have a mother who is not a mother at all? If she is the one who is sinful, why must Asher and I suffer?*

Mara left the gloom of the house and crouched by the cooking pot. The two looming mountains seemed to press down on her. Would she ever reap the blessings of following God's laws, or would she only see the curses that were sown by her disgraceful mother?

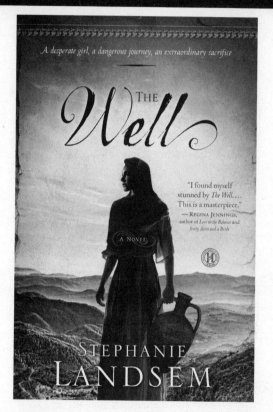